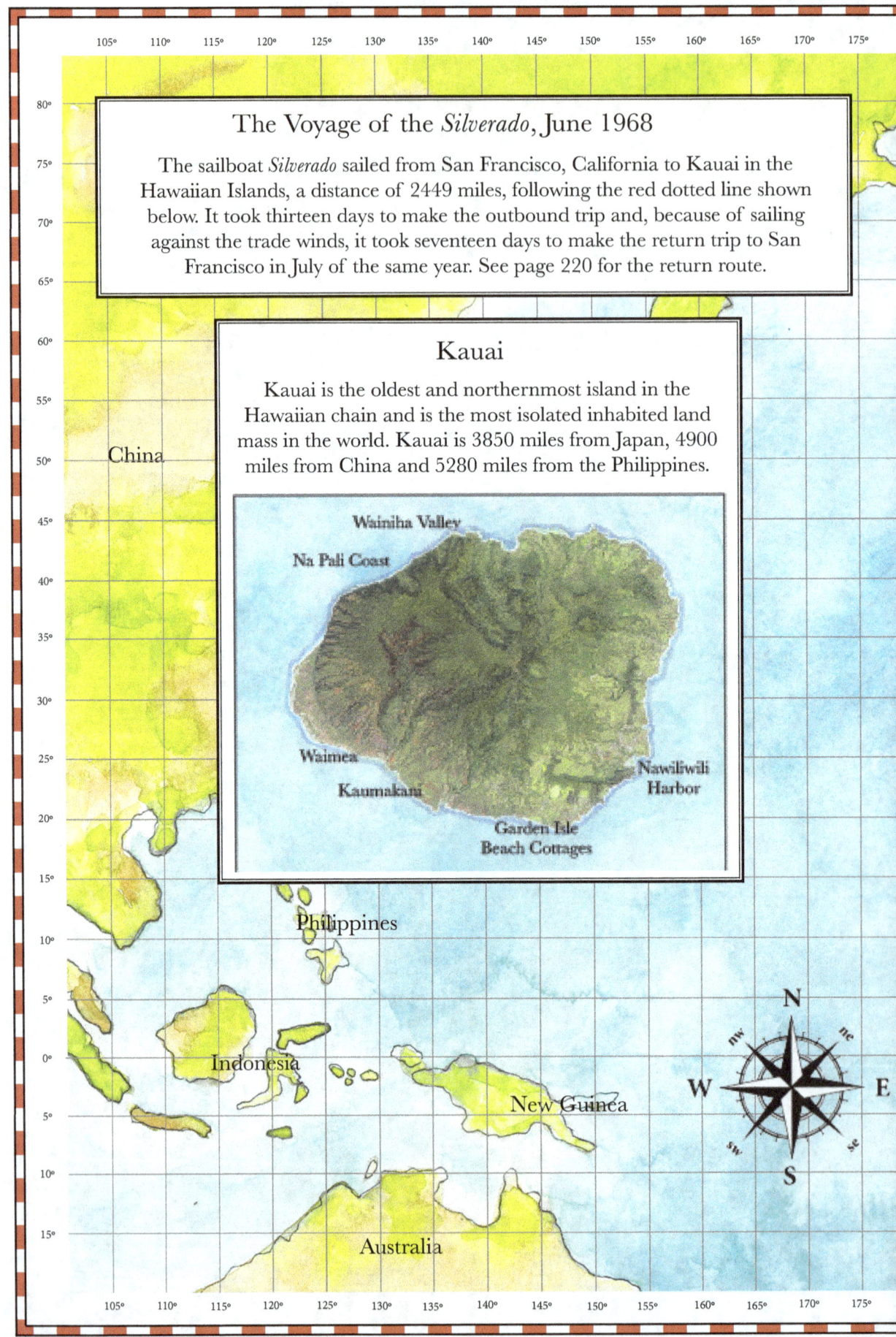

The Voyage of the *Silverado*, June 1968

The sailboat *Silverado* sailed from San Francisco, California to Kauai in the Hawaiian Islands, a distance of 2449 miles, following the red dotted line shown below. It took thirteen days to make the outbound trip and, because of sailing against the trade winds, it took seventeen days to make the return trip to San Francisco in July of the same year. See page 220 for the return route.

Kauai

Kauai is the oldest and northernmost island in the Hawaiian chain and is the most isolated inhabited land mass in the world. Kauai is 3850 miles from Japan, 4900 miles from China and 5280 miles from the Philippines.

Wainiha Valley

Na Pali Coast

Waimea

Kaumakani

Nawiliwili Harbor

Garden Isle
Beach Cottages

China

Philippines

Indonesia

New Guinea

Australia

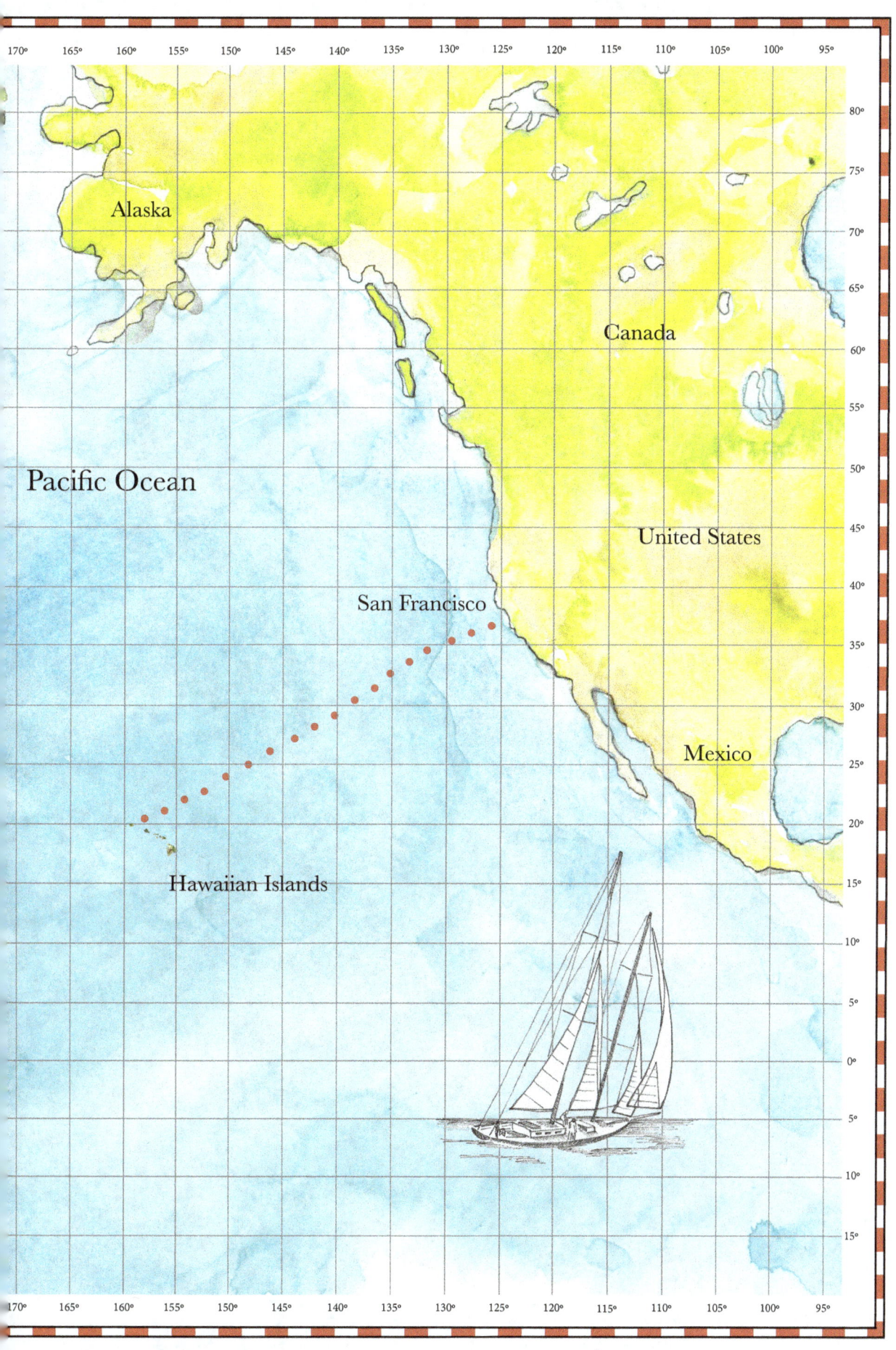

Voyage of the Silverado

Also by A. Cort Sinnes

The Silverado Trail

Voyage of the Silverado

Written and Illustrated by
A. Cort Sinnes

Printed in the United States of America

Alfred Cort Sinnes
P. O. Box 571
Napa, California 94559

This book was designed and produced by Hearth & Garden Productions

A. Cort Sinnes, Text, Design and Illustrations

Library of Congress Cataloging-in-Publication Data

Sinnes, A. Cort *Voyage of the Silverado,*
written and illustrated by A. Cort Sinnes

ISBN 978-0-692-91632-2

Cover: "*Off the Coast of Na Pali,*" by A. Cort Sinnes

For (the one and only) JP

To be in your orbit was as good as it gets. What a surprise to pull back the curtain and discover the magic was real – magic with the beat and flavor of genius, transforming the mundane into the miraculous. Thank you for sharing so completely. And, yes, I vow to remember, whatever the question, the answer is *yellow*.

Preface

Many of the places and events in this book are real: Napa Valley, California is one of the most important wine-producing regions in the world (and some say one of the most beautiful small valleys to be found anywhere). There really is a school, in the California coastal town of Pebble Beach, named after the great Scottish writer Robert Louis Stevenson. Stevenson himself spent part of the summer of 1880 on the slopes of Mount St. Helena, living in an abandoned mining camp named Silverado. And Gustave Niebaum, a Finnish sea captain did, indeed, found a famous winery in the heart of the Napa Valley in 1879. The theft that starts Nick Sinclair on his search actually happened the year I started writing this book. As to the thieves – well, they too are well documented – although not everyone will care to believe the "facts" that come to light in this book. As for me, I believe it all.

A.C. S.
Napa 2018

Table of Contents

Prologue

August 2012
Grandpa Nick's house
Rutherford, California

If you haven't read the first book in the The Silverado Journals, *The Silverado Trail*, let me bring you up to date. My name is Joaquin, I'm 14 years old and I live in the Napa Valley. Yes, that Napa Valley. My grandfather lives in a big, old Victorian house surrounded by big old oak trees and vineyards. My mom, dad, and I live down the lane from Grandpa, but it's all part of the same property that includes the winery, Eagle's Nook, which my grandpa inherited from his grandmother. My grandfather, Nick, is an artist and a writer. He's got a cool studio and workshop in an old barn next to his house. I like to hang out there. He lets me use his tools and make stuff. He's always around to show me the right way to do things. He says I can use anything I want as long as I'm careful and put things back where I found them. He's a stickler about that. At the end of the first book, I had just finished reading a journal that my grandfather wrote, like almost 45 years ago. He called it *An Account of the Fantastic Events of the Summer of 1967*. Something about

Grandpa's house in Rutherford.

the word "fantastic" bothered me. I knew it meant like really cool, but I was pretty sure it had another meaning and that maybe my grandfather was trying to tip me off to something by using it. I looked up "fantastic" and sure enough, it also meant "fanciful, remote from reality" – in fact, it's Middle English origins meant "existing only in the imagination." Well, going with that definition, the story he told in the journal definitely qualified as "fantastic." It was about as remote from reality as you could get – at least any reality I know. Here are the high points of the first journal. See what you think:

The story takes place in 1967 and starts on the first day of summer vacation. My grandfather was 14 years old, like I am now, and just home from boarding school. Home was his so-called aunt and uncle's pony farm here in St. Helena. His mom, dad, and brother were all killed in a car accident when he was little. His Grandma Hattie was his guardian, but she thought he'd be happier living with Walter and Ma-D, the owners of the Twin Oaks Pony Farm. On the first night my grandfather arrived, Walter's prized Shetland pony disappeared. Or more to the point, was stolen.

Let me back up for a minute and explain something. The real beginning to this story happened in 1879 when Captain Gustave Niebaum, my great-great-great grand- father (legally, not by blood; he adopted my great-great grandmother) discovered stowaways aboard his ship who just happened to be gnomes, one of which was the gnome king, King Gob. I know it's a stretch, but that's what Captain Niebaum wrote in his ship's log. Unfortunately, when they made a stop in Kauai, five of the gnomes (tired of the long voyage and even more tired of being seasick) jumped ship

The first journal Grandpa wrote.

and disappeared. My third-great grandfather and the gnome King made a deal: if the remaining gnomes would dig the caves for his new winery in the Napa Valley, called Eagle's Nook, he would grant them their freedom, which is how they wound up living on (or more accurately, in) Mt. St. Helena. Can you believe it? I couldn't.

The first journal describes how my grandfather eventually got his Uncle Wal- ter's pony back. Pretty straightforward, right? Well, according to my grandfather, it was those gnomes I just told you about who stole the horse. When a seafaring rel- ative you've never met writes about discovering a band of gnomes aboard his ship more than 130 years ago, that's one thing. But when it's your grandfather who's telling you the story and he's standing right in front of you, that's where it starts to get a little weird, at least for me. I mean, when was the last time you saw a gnome?

By the end of the first story, Grandma Hattie and the king of the gnomes, King Gob, got all buddy-buddy, and the gnome king's son, Prince G, had become friends with my grandfather and his best friend Chuy, who were all about the same age. King Gob and Grandma Hattie agreed to have my grandfather, along with Chuy and Prince G, go to Kauai the following summer to bring Dagywn, the gnome sorcerer, back from wherever he was hiding on Kauai. Are you following all this? Dagywn was one of the five gnomes who jumped ship back in 1879 and the one tribe member King Gob wanted back, big time. Did I tell you the gnomes live like practically forever? Or that my grandfather, Chuy, and Prince G were sailing to Kauai on Grandma Hattie's 78-foot sailboat? What did the dictionary say about the word *fantastic*? "Far from reality." I'll say.

All of this wouldn't mean that much to me except something strange happened a few days ago. I was over at my friend Darren's place. He was all excited because the night before someone had stolen a barrel of his dad's wine (they own a winery) and that someone had left a leather pouch filled with a bunch of gold nuggets on the floor where the barrel used to be. When I told Grandpa Nick about it, he got all funny-acting and took me up to the attic and handed me the first journal and told me to read it. In that journal, he says when that prize Shetland pony was stolen back in 1967, he found a leather pouch filled with a bunch of gold nuggets in the horse's water trough – basically the same thing that had just happened at my friend Darren's place. After reading that, everything started looking a little different to me. I mean, could my grandfather's journal be telling the truth? I'd be the first to admit that my grandfather is a bit on the eccentric side (like he always wears two different colored socks, takes his own tin of anchovies to the pizza place we go to, and he turns around three times if a black cat crosses his path – that one really cracks me up) so it's possible that his story is just something he made up. But that doesn't explain how a leather pouch filled with gold nuggets I saw last Thursday at Darren's place showed up in a journal he wrote 45 years ago. Now *that's* strange – very strange. After I'd read the first journal, Grandpa Nick asked me if I wanted to read the second one (there are three in total) and I said "sure." If I'm being honest, part of me wanted the story to be real and I wanted to see what happened next. The logical me figured there was a practical explanation of why these pouches of gold were showing up so many years apart. I figured that one way or another, after I'd finished the second journal, I'd be closer to whatever the truth might be – and I really didn't think it had anything to do with gnomes, you know?

One more thing: There's a bad guy in grandpa's story by the name of Nigel Stayne. Nigel was a Scottish photo-journalist who had been hired by Lord Higgenbotham, one of the world's richest publishers of newspapers and magazines. Nigel referred to himself as "the badger," a reference, I guess, to his ability to successfully go after a story, no matter how difficult. Lord Higgenbotham lived in England and had a distant relative who had sailed with Captain Niebaum on the voyage when the gnomes were discovered as stowaways. Lord Higgenbotham had grown up hearing stories about those gnomes from his uncle. He heard them so often, he just

xvi

assumed the stories were true and that the gnomes were for real. The people he shared the story with weren't buying it and thought he was crazy. Higgenbotham's point in hiring Nigel was to have him take photographs of the gnomes for his publications, killing two birds with one stone: proving that he wasn't crazy and selling a few gazillion newspapers and magazines in the process. Nigel traveled to the Napa Valley and figured out that my grandfather and he were on the same mission: my grandfather to find the gnomes and get the horse back and for Nigel, to photograph the gnomes and, hopefully, put his hands on some of their gold. To say that Nigel and my grandfather were enemies is to put it mildly. At the end

Oh yeah, I forgot to mention that there are homing pigeons in this story and they are very cool. Wait 'til you hear about them.

of the first adventure, Nigel got thrown in jail for being in the country illegally and had to be bailed out by Lord Higgenbotham. Neither Lord Higgenbotham nor Nigel Stayne were happy campers and both, for their own reasons, wanted revenge on my grandfather for ruining their plans. I had no idea what to expect in the second journal but, like I said, my grandfather's right in front of me, alive and kicking, so I guess he survived whatever he claims happened in the second journal. Here goes. See you on the last page.

I had grandpa do this painting so you could see what the attic looks like.
Hard to believe how much stuff is up there and how he knew just where
to look for the journals — on the shelves to the left of the brick chimney.

Chapter I

Another Voyage into the Past

August 12, 2012
Grandpa Nick's house
Rutherford, California

Grandpa Nick and I were back up in the attic. He was opening the same small locker he had opened when he gave me the first journal last week. The first one had only taken me a few days (and nights) to read. We were up in the attic to get the second journal.

"What else is in there?" I asked, pointing to the open locker.

"Stuff. Old stuff."

"Can I see?"

"You've really got to get the difference between 'can' and 'may' down. 'Can' means can you physically do something; 'may' means do you have permission to do something. It's 'may,' not 'can.'"

"Okay, I get it. You don't have to be such a grouch."

"All right, all right. Here, let's take this down to the kitchen. Probably shouldn't keep it up here anyway," he said.

We lugged the locker back down three flights of stairs, and put it on the big table in the kitchen. I sat down next to him as opened the locker and started to go through the stuff inside.

"Here, take a look at that," Grandpa said, handing me a small plain cardboard box.

"What is it?"

"Open it up. See for yourself."

Inside the box was a lumpy, paper-wrapped parcel and a small red velvet box. I took the paper off the parcel and immediately recognized what I had seen the other day at Darren's house: a leather pouch filled with something heavy. I looked at Grandpa and he nodded. I undid the drawstring and looked inside.

"Go ahead, pour it on the table."

I did as he said and there in front of me was a pile of gold nuggets.

"Holy cats!"

"Yeah, pretty amazing, huh?"

"Is this the gold from your story? From the gnomes who stole the horse?"

"No. Once Walter got the gold back from the sheriff, he had it converted to cash. This pile is from Captain Niebaum. Remember the story? I'm sure he kept it for sentimental reasons; he certainly didn't need the cash."

"It's just like what I saw at Darren's house the other day."

"I don't think the gnomes change the way they do things unless they have to."

Okay – on the Scale of Weirdness, this was definitely a 10, I thought to myself. "Is that what I think it is?" I asked, pointing to the red velvet box.

"Probably. Take a look."

Sure enough, wedged inside the box was the sapphire and rhodium amulet and it was really beautiful: all dark sparkle and mysterious. I was finding it hard to believe that this was what I just read about in Grandpa's first journal: the amulet he accidentally lost when he fell off the rock wall on Mt. St. Helena, spying on the gnomes – the one King Gob had given Captain Niebaum as a sign of friendship between him and the tribe of gnomes. Like I said, part of me wanted the story to be real and now, with the gold nuggets and the amulet in front of me, it started to feel that way, not just some fantastic, made-up fairy tale. I was a little stunned.

"Well, do you want to read it or not?"

Startled out of my thoughts I said "What?"

"The second journal."

"Oh, yeah."

"Are you sure you can handle it? You're act-ing a little freaked-out."

"I'm not freaked out." But in truth I was. I wondered what was in the second journal and how much more weirdness I was in for.

I took the journal into the sunroom, which was on the east side of grandpa's house. I liked the

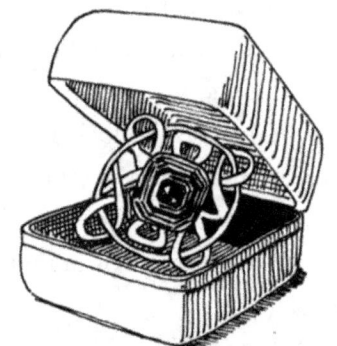

The sapphire and rhodium amulet.

sunroom. It was filled with overgrown plants and a lot of light. There was a big cage with love birds who made funny "squeak-tweet" noises as they jumped from perch to perch, and the gentle sound of water splashing from a small fountain that

I could hear but not see. Best of all, it had a couple of comfortable chairs out there, ones where you could put your feet up while you read. I made myself comfortable in one of them and opened the second journal. On the first page there was a pen-and-ink drawing of a sailboat and the words *The Voyage of the Silverado, An Account of the Remarkable Events of the Summer of 1968*.

Interesting, I thought to myself. *He's changed from 'fantastic' to 'remarkable.'* I wondered if that was important but then decided I was over-thinking the whole thing. Better to just start reading it and figure out whether any of it was true or not later. At least there wasn't a drawing of a finger pointing at me, warning me to "Stay Out," like there was in the first journal.

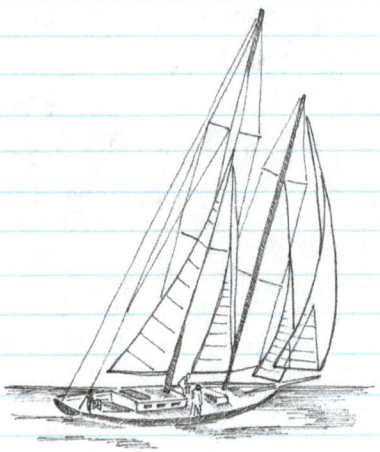

The Voyage of the Silverado

An Account of the Remarkable Events of the Summer of 1968

Chapter II

Party Interrupted

December 23, 1967
Grandma Hattie's house
San Francisco, California

"Sinclair residence, Doyle speaking."

"Hi Doyle, it's Mr.... it's Tim Becker, Nick's English teacher."

"Oh yes, Mr. Becker, how are you?"

"I'm fine, thank you. I was wondering if Nick was available; it's rather important."

"Yes, I'm sure he's here somewhere. If you'll hold the line, I'll find him for you."

"Thanks, Doyle."

Doyle, Grandma Hattie's houseman, put the telephone down on the kitchen counter and went looking for me. The huge house (more properly called a "mansion," I suppose) was absolutely crawling with the people that made San Francisco interesting. The occasion was Grandma Hattie's Christmas party and anything that could be hung with lights, shiny ornaments, or evergreen swags and red ribbons, was. The house was practically vibrating with all the people, layer upon layer of sound — laughter, Christmas music, plates and glasses clinking and clanking and the din of seemingly endless conversation. Doyle found me in the library talking (practically yelling, actually) with Cyril Magnin, who everyone simply called "Mr. San Francisco."

"Mr. Magnin, Nick, sorry to disturb you, but you have a call, Nick. It's Mr. Becker. He says it's important."

I excused myself from Mr. Magnin and quickly walked to the kitchen. I couldn't imagine why Mr. Becker would be calling me, especially during Christmas vacation and so late at night.

"Hello. Mr. Becker, it's me, Nick."

"I'm glad I got you, Nick. Sounds like I'm interrupting a party so I'll get right to the point. You need to know that someone was in your dorm room tonight and they got away with something."

"What?!"

"Like I said. One of the campus security guards noticed a light in your room and decided to take a look. By the time he got to the second floor, some guy dressed in black was just coming out of your room carrying a book. When he saw the security guard he ran down the hall and disappeared."

"Aw shi..."

"Yeah, I know. Are you thinking what I'm thinking?"

"Probably. The only thing I have that anyone could possibly be interested in is my journal from last summer, and the only person who'd be interested in it is Nigel Stayne."

"That's what I figured. So you think it was him?"

"No, I doubt it was actually him. After getting deported back to Scotland last summer, he's still too hot to risk coming into the country. He must have hired someone to steal it for him."

"I'm glad we had a copy made. I'll have another one made for you."

"Thanks. It ticks me off that Nigel has the original. Darn it."

"Yeah, actually this *is* pretty bad. It means Nigel is going to know about our plans for next summer."

"Man, I didn't see this coming," I said. "Guess I should have kept the original with me. I never thought he'd steal it, but I don't know why not. He's such a low life."

"Don't beat yourself up, Nick. We'll deal with it."

"Thanks, but this really changes things."

"I think you're probably right, but right now we can't do much about it. Go back to your party. We'll talk after Christmas."

"Okay. Thanks for calling... I guess. Oh, and Merry Christmas."

"Merry Christmas to you, too."

I hung up the phone and shook my head.

This was not good.

.   .   .

A couple of days after Christmas, I received a postcard from Scotland with a photograph of the town of Kelso on the Tweed River on the front. On the other side the hand-written message read:

Nice job on the journal, although I feel I've been portrayed rather badly. I'm not such a bad sort, as you would have found out if we'd teamed up. Things could have gone rather better for us both. Ah, well, there's always next summer (by the way, thanks for all the details). See you in Kauai. Yours faithful-

ly, Nigel

"What a shmuck!" I thought when I'd finished reading it.

I'd been looking forward to this summer's voyage to Kauai, even though I had no idea how we were going to go about finding Dagywn once we got there. Now I was going to have to let everyone know that we were going to be like a baseball team stepping onto the field with two strikes already against us. *Not the best way to start an adventure,* I thought to myself, *not by a long shot.*

. . .

Dear Reader: Please note that, like in my first journal, I've had to make up some of the information in the story, simply because I wasn't present when it happened. That said, I'm fairly certain that what I'm about to write is accurate, if not in the details, it's accurate in the spirit of what I think actually happened.

. . .

Sometime in late November, 1967
Nigel Stayne's cottage
Kelso, Scotland

To this day, Nigel had no idea what made him do it, but it had certainly changed everything. When he was staying in St. Helena last year there were several times when the local weekly newspaper, *The St. Helena Star,* had been useful in his investigation. He distinctly remembered the day he walked into the offices of the *The Star* on Main Street and requested a subscription to be sent to his home in Scotland. The clerk who took his order said that if there were a prize for being the subscription that was sent the farthest away, he'd win it. In an uncharacteristically good mood Nigel said that just being able to read it on a regular basis would be prize enough. In actuality there was no real reason for him to want to read it. But then, shortly after returning home, he discovered how important his decision had been.

The newspaper only covered local news and, truthfully, there simply wasn't that much news that took place in the small town of St. Helena from one week to the next. The editors filled the space with an amusing column called "The Police Blotter" which recorded all the police doings for the week and a "gossip" column called "Aunt Helena." Sometime in early November, Nigel noticed an Aunt Helena column that practically jumped off the page. It read:

Aunt Helena heard from Hattie Sinclair, of Eagle's Nook winery, that her grandson, Nick Sinclair, has settled in to his junior year at Robert Louis Stevenson School in Pebble Beach. Not only is he on the Honor Roll but also a member of the school's championship sailing team. Go Nick! Your old friends in St. Helena are cheering you on.

That one short paragraph told Nigel where Nick went to school and gave him the idea of arranging to have Nick's room broken into. He wasn't sure of what he'd find there, or if he'd find anything useful, but it was worth a try. Any information was better than none. Nigel convinced Higgenbotham to pay a local petty criminal in Pebble Beach for the break-in. When Nigel found out it was Nick's journal the thief had gotten away with, he couldn't believe his good fortune. Talk about a treasure trove of information!

Ever since he had Nick's journal in his hands, he had been trying to come up with a plan to get what he wanted: to have Nick lead him to the gnomes so he could photograph them and help himself to some of that gnome gold. Not to mention make good on his contract with Lord Higgenbotham and get paid for the words and pictures he would take. After the disgrace he had suffered attempting the same endeavor last summer, it would be sweet to finally succeed and never have to deal with that crazy, megalomaniac publisher again.

After a couple of weeks of brainstorming, Nigel felt he had settled on the perfect plan. "Brilliant, brilliant, brilliant! I'm bloody brilliant," Nigel said as he paced around his low-ceilinged cottage. His two Jack Russell terriers just sat there, heads cocked, watching him walk and rant.

What Nigel's newest plan lacked in finesse it made up in brute force. His original plan was to simply meet Nick when he arrived in Kauai and follow him, just like he had done in California. But then he had another idea: why deal with that punk kid at all? Why not just go back to California and deal with the gnomes directly without any interference from Nick, someone he decided he disliked intensely? Nigel knew from last summer exactly where the gnomes lived, what their daily routines were and, unlike the last time he started out, he knew that the gnomes were, in fact, real. And the fact that Nick was going to be a couple of thousand miles across the Pacific Ocean where he couldn't interfere was icing on the cake. "Excellent!" Nigel had said to himself.

Nigel started out thinking he would put together a small band of "special operatives" to help him carry out his mission. Ex-military guys. But the more he thought about it, the less he liked the idea. Were more guys a benefit, or were they a liability? Nigel thought about one of the many things his father had taught him, including one of his favorite sayings: "he travels fastest who travels alone." Nigel didn't need any help finding his way around Mt. St. Helena and more guys meant more chances to be spotted by those watchful gnomes. No, it was better to go it alone, Nigel thought to himself. He'd follow his father's advice.

Once he had decided to go to Mt. St. Helena instead of Kauai, and to go it alone instead of taking a band of mercenaries with him, Nigel needed to come up with a step-by-step plan of action. He wasn't simply going to go up to their cave and walk in, was he? Or was he? No, no, he thought to himself, they'd capture him before he got anywhere near the opening to the cave. That wasn't going to work. He instinctively knew that whatever it was that he came up with, the plan going to have to be bold and quick. He knew the longer he hung around on that mountain, the more likely it was that he would get caught.

And then from out of the blue, this morning it came to him. Big, bold, fast and yes, beautiful, he thought to himself. It would take considerable footwork, but with his brain power and Higgenbotham's money, it could be done.

"Time to make a list," Nigel said out loud. Since he had been arrested and deported for being in the country illegally the last time he was California, the first thing on his list was:

1. Come up with a new name for myself. *Something I've always wanted to do,* he thought as he wrote. It followed that to go with the new name, he'd need new a new passport, driver's license and credit cards, so number two was:

2. Get Higgenbotham to get me a new identity and everything that went with it.

And then:

3. Get a U.S.G.S. (United States Geological Survey) map of Mt. St. Helena.

4. Identify the parcel of land behind the gnomes' cave.

5. Get Higgenbotham to purchase the parcel.

6. Find a local heavy equipment operator in St. Helena who had a D-9 bulldozer.

Just writing the word "bulldozer" gave him a sense of power. "Those little buggers won't know what's hit 'em," Nigel said to himself. "I am so blinking brilliant!"

Too bad he didn't remember another saying his father had taught him: "pride goeth before a fall." And the fall, when it came, would turn out to be colossal.

Grandma Hattie's house in the Pacific Heights neighborhood in
San Francisco — what JP called "a pile of bricks."

Chapter III

The Team Gathers

June 7, 1968
Last day of school
Robert Louis Stevenson School
Pebble Beach, California

I've been thinking about this day since last September and each time I do, my stomach falls like an elevator or I get those jittery butterfly feelings you get when you're excited — or scared — about something. The two problems that especially make my stomach fall through the floor are, one, that my nemesis, that rat bag Nigel, is probably going to be waiting on the beach when we arrive in Kauai in a few weeks and second, how in the heck, exactly, do you go about finding a wizard gnome who has lived on a tropical island for nearly 100 years? I have no idea how to deal with either situation.

Apart from my own problems, as far as I know, things are going according to plan. At least I think they are. Mr. Becker, my English teacher and sailing instructor, is a take-charge kind of guy and he's the one in charge, thank goodness. He's got lists and lists of lists he's been working on since last September. Tomorrow morning we (that's me, him, and his fiancée, Tova Evans) are going to leave school at 7 and drive the five hours or so up to St. Helena to pick up Chuy and G, and then to go Grandma Hattie's house in San Francisco. Right now I'm packing and trying to keep my brain from going in a million different directions at once.

The plan is to spend the next week at Grandma Hattie's and set sail for Kauai on Saturday, June 15th. Mr. Becker says it's going to be a busy week outfitting the *Bluebird* — that's the name of grandma's sailboat. In addition to assembling everything we'll need, we also need to assemble people: Chuy and G, Mr. Becker's friend, JP, who's going to be our cook, and the other deckhands, making a total of nine on board. JP's going to fly into San Francisco from Kansas City the day after tomorrow and will take a cab to Grandma Hattie's. Chuy and G presented more of a challenge because, seeing as how he's a gnome, G would attract too much attention on any form of public transportation. So at one of our weekly meetings we've been holding since September, Mr. Becker and I decided that it made more sense to pick G and Chuy up first in St. Helena and then go to Grand-ma Hattie's. It's all starting to feel a little complicated and real.

The next morning, after a lousy night's sleep, Mr. Becker, Miss Evans and I met in the parking lot behind the dorms. It was just getting light and in addition to the typical Pebble Beach overcast sky, there were wisps of ground fog drifting around campus. Except for the sea gulls overhead, the whole scene was very quiet which, for no real reason, made us all talk quietly, as if we were planning a heist or something. It was the first time I'd met Miss Evans and she immediately told me to call her "Tova," saying if I didn't, she'd call me "Mr. Sinclair." I liked her right off. She teaches nursing at the Monterey Peninsula College and Mr. Becker told me that she had grown up in Pebble Beach and had even more experience sailing than he did. Back in October, I made a copy of my journal for Mr. Becker and he asked if it was okay if Tova read it. I said "sure." I'm glad she knew about G and what she was getting herself into before she said yes to the trip.

Mr. Becker just bought a new Volkswagen Westphalia camper van; it's very cool and has plenty of room for all our gear. Once we got loaded up, I sat in the back seat and we headed north up the coast and then onto Highway 101 which would took us to the Bay Area. The back seat was a fair distance away from the

Mr. Becker's brand new 1968 Volkswagen Westfalia camper van.

front seats so it made it hard to hear anything that was being said up there. Mr. Becker, Tova and I tried to carry on a conversation, but settled on a comfortable silence as we cut across the flat farmlands of California's Central Valley. It didn't take long for me to nod off (probably because I slept so little last night), but I jerked awake when I heard the van stop and the front doors slam shut. "Where are we?" I asked groggily when Mr. Becker opened the sliding door from the outside.

"Calistoga. Time for something to eat. We've got time."

"Cafe Sarafornia? Cool. How'd you know about it?"

"I saw the sign as I was driving by. I remembered it from your journal. It's where Walter went to get you guys hamburgers after you found Quicksilver, right?"

"Yeah. Good memory. A hamburger sounds good. I'm starved."

We sat in a booth and all ordered cheeseburgers. It felt good to be with Mr. Becker and Tova. Even though he was my teacher, it felt more like we were all friends. I wonder if they are as excited as I am about this soon-to-be adventure. It kind of felt like it.

After we finished our breakfast, or lunch, or whatever it was, we got back in the van and headed up Mt. St. Helena. In our last communication via the "pigeon post," G and I agreed that we'd meet at the turnout at Robert Louis Stevenson State Park on top of Mt. St. Helena at 11 o'clock. Oh jeez, I haven't told you about our "pigeon post" have I? Last summer was filled with a lot of crazy, amazing things, but one of the best was the discovery of homing pigeons. Somewhere in the back of my brain, I've always known they existed, but didn't know that much about them. I don't know who said "necessity is the mother of invention," but that's how it happened. After everything had more or less settled down last summer, G and I wanted a way to communicate like every day, especially when we

One of my
homing pigeons.

started planning this trip to Kauai. Gnomes being gnomes didn't provide us with many opportunities — I mean, it's not like they have telephones, electricity, or anything, so we had to go further back in time when none of that mattered, which is how I came up with the homing pigeon idea. Granted, you have to build a place for them to live, and to feed them and all that, but all things considered, they're pretty easy to take care of. The first cage I made was a simple one, but

Uncle Walter got a little carried away building the dovecote.

then Uncle Walter went all nuts and built this big house for them called a dovecote. Ma-D made fun of him and wanted to know if he was going to move into it, it was that big and that nice. After it was done and painted, I thought it looked great and the pigeons seemed to love it.

They're called homing pigeons because, let's say I give you one of my pigeons and you give me one of yours. If I take your pigeon to my house and let it go, it's going to fly back to your location just like the one of mine I gave you of mine is going to fly back to my place when you let it go. And they're fast. Very fast. There's these special little copper capsules that attach to the pigeon's leg that open up and you can put a tiny message in there for the other person to read. The whole thing is way cool. Instead of the U.S. Postal Service, G and I had our own private 'pigeon post."

So, anyway, that's how G knew what time we were going to pick him up and everything — because I had called Doyle a couple of days ago and asked him to go over to the pony farm and send a message to G. We arrived at the turnout on Mt. St. Helena about ten minutes early and parked the van. About a minute later there was knocking on the sliding door of the van. I opened it and there was G, grinning from ear to ear, with some kind of a rustic backpack on his back. Apparently he had arrived early too. Having read my journal back at school, Mr. Becker and Tova knew what to expect, but there was no denying the look of surprise on their faces when they saw G for the first time. G took off his rucksack and threw it in the van and then scrambled inside, waving and say "hi" to everyone at the same time. After introductions and handshakes, Mr. Becker said we had a schedule to keep and we took off down the mountain to pick up Chuy at his house. Mr. Becker and Tova both played it cool and didn't make any kind of fuss over G being like three feet tall and all.

Once we arrived at Mee Lane on the valley floor, Mr. Becker dropped me off at Walter and Ma-D's so I could basically say hi and goodbye at the same time. Mr. Becker drove further down the lane to pick up Chuy. Walter, Ma-D and I had a quick catch-up. Even though they knew about the trip to Kauai they seemed a little confused about why I was going. If I told them the truth, they would have been a lot more confused. Thank goodness Henry, Walter's hired hand, wandered in the house to say hi and I didn't have to make something up. I ran outside to give Snoops a good scratch on the head and a quick look inside the bunkhouse that I had adopted as my "room." Everything looked the same, including my lucky straw cowboy hat hanging on the coat rack. I almost left it behind but then decided I was going to need all the luck I could get and took it with me. If it blew off somewhere on the Pacific Ocean, so be it. I heard the van coming back down the lane, so I went back inside the big house and said my goodbyes to Walter and Ma-D and I told them I'd see them later in the summer, and, yes, I would send postcards to let them know I was okay.

It was great to see both Chuy and G on the back seat of the van. They squished over and made room for me. We were all excited. No denying it; this was real now.

We turned south on Highway 29 and headed to Grandma Hattie's in San Francisco. Chuy, G and I talked the whole trip which took just over an hour. The last fifteen minutes or so I had to give Mr. Becker directions to Grandma Hat-

The conservatory at Grandma Hattie's house in San Francisco.

tie's and then suddenly we were parked outside of her place and everyone went silent. Let's just say Grandma's house is a little imposing.

"That's your grandmother's house?" Tova asked incredulously.

"Yes. And, yes, I know, it's... what can I say? It's Grandma's. Come on, let's go."

We each got our duffel bags, satchels, and backpacks and clumsily climbed up the front steps. Chuy and I instinctively walked as close as we could on either side of G, shielding him from nosy neighbors. I opened the huge front door and yelled out "Grandma, we're here."

Grandma came down the massive staircase and paused about halfway down.

"Oh my," she said, raising both hands into the air. "And to think, I thought the Summer of Love was last year."

Admittedly, we were a rag-tag group. Mr. Becker had let his hair grow almost to his shoulders, Tova was wearing a long, brightly-colored, tie-dyed skirt (and she had a single small daisy behind her ear which I thought looked great), Chuy was wearing a Ringo t-shirt and then there was G, wearing his usual assortment of coats, sweaters, leggings, and a long scarf wrapped several times around his neck.

Grandma called for Doyle, and told him to take everyone to their rooms, saying breezily that "we'll get reacquainted after you're all settled in." As everyone was headed upstairs Grandma called up from the foyer "cocktails at 6 in the conservatory. Ta-ta."

.   .   .

Everyone assembled in the leafy, plant-filled conservatory at 6. Grandma Hattie was at her gracious best, trying to make everyone comfortable, but there was no denying that the house itself, to say nothing of Grandma, were kind of intimidating and everyone seemed nervous. Grandma Hattie had talked several times to Mr. Becker on the telephone regarding the outfitting of the *Bluebird*, but had never met him in person. She was quick to corner him and pepper him with questions.

"So good to finally meet you in person, Tim."

"Likewise, Mrs. Sinclair."

"Oh, please, call me Hattie. Have you had a chance to get down to the *Bluebird*?"

"Not yet. That's first on the agenda for tomorrow morning. I'm anxious to see the progress. Have all the improvements been made?"

"So I'm told. We'll see tomorrow."

"Are you still planning to depart on the 14th?"

"If all goes according to plan."

"How long before you reach Kauai?"

"It's 2,225 nautical miles. Again, if all goes well, probably two weeks."

"And then it's off into parts unknown?"

"Presumably. But you should know, I'm pretty much leaving that part of the trip up to your grandson and G, and Chuy, of course. It's their quest, so to speak. I'm in charge of getting them there safely and back home again."

"And see to it that you do, Tim," Grandma said sternly. "Speaking of which, when do you think that will be?"

"Well, there's no way of knowing how long this 'quest' will take, but for us — Nick and me — to make it to school on time, we have to be back in San Francisco no later than the second of September."

From somewhere below came the sound of a discreet cough. Grandma Hattie looked down and saw G smiling back at her.

"Oh! G. I didn't see you there."

"Sorry to interrupt, ma'am, but I was wondering if I could have a word with you?"

"Of course."

"I'll leave you two alone," Mr. Becker said.

"No, no. This probably concerns you too, Tim. Please stay."

"What is it, G?" Grandma asked.

"My father was adamant that I address this with you right away. He didn't want there to be any misunderstanding."

"Yes."

"Well, he reminded me about his agreement with you that he should fund this venture and he gave me this," G said, holding a large leather satchel which appeared to be quite heavy.

"I think I know what's in there," Grandma Hattie said.

"Yes, and to be honest, I'll be happy to be rid of it. It's very heavy."

"I can see that. What, exactly, would you have me do with it?"

"As you know — how can I say this — my father does things the way we've always done them. He has no idea that you Uplanders don't make payments in gold. I was wondering if you could have this exchanged for the paper money you use?"

"Well, I can't say that I've ever been asked to do such a thing, but I'm sure my banker will be able to help."

"It would be much appreciated," G said, struggling to hold the satchel up to Grandma. She made to grab it but realized how heavy it was and looked to Mr. Becker for help. He took it from G and said "what would you like *me* to do with it?"

"Let's put it in the safe in the library. Would that be all right with you, G?"

"Sure. I'm just glad to be rid of it."

"I'll go to the bank tomorrow. I don't see why there should be any problem converting it to cash."

"I'm glad you brought this up, G," said Mr. Becker. "I'm going to have to pay for the improvements to the *Bluebird* sooner rather than later. I have a feeling the workers would have been surprised to receive payment in gold nuggets. It would have been like we were back in the days of the gold rush in 1849."

"That's even before my time," Grandma Hattie said. "Now, who's hungry?" she said to no one in particular. "I've had Katia set up a smörgåsbord in the kitchen. We're going informal tonight. I figured you youngsters would prefer it that way. Besides, I think it would please Capt. Niebaum to have a little of his Finnish heritage represented on this momentous occasion. Let's face it, if it weren't for him and the stowaways, none of us would be here right now. Last one to the pickled herring is a rotten egg."

With the stroke of a paintbrush, Grandma Hattie had
the Bluebird *turned into* the Silverado.

Chapter IV

Be Prepared

June 8, 1968
Grandma Hattie's house
San Francisco, California

Everything went fine last night, except when Katia, Grandma Hattie's German cousin who worked as her cook, caught sight of G. She nearly dropped the tray she was carrying and got this stricken look on her face. I saw her cross herself when she turned around.

Everyone (except Grandma, who never got up early) was back in the kitchen by 8:30 the next morning, having coffee, toast, boiled eggs and bacon. Mr. Becker suggested that Chuy and I go with him down to the St. Francis Yacht Club to check out the *Bluebird*. I looked around and saw G talking with Tova on the other side of the kitchen. "What about G?" I asked Mr. Becker.

"What about him?"

"What's he going to do?" I asked.

"I'm not sure. I thought he wanted to stay out of the public eye," he said.

"He never said that exactly. In fact, I don't think anyone did."

"Maybe I assumed it. He could cause quite a... a commotion."

"I might be wrong," I said, "but I think if we treat him normally, other people will too." This thought didn't just occur to me in Grandma's kitchen; I'd been thinking about it all school year. I may have come to the wrong conclusion, but I thought it was worth a try for everyone's sake.

"It's your call, Nick," Mr. Becker said.

"I say he goes with us," I said looking at Chuy, who nodded in agreement. "After all, he's the one paying for all this."

"Okay. But we're leaving in ten minutes."

. . .

Mr. Becker, Tova, Chuy, G and I went to the yacht club in Mr. Becker's van. From Grandma's house it was just a ten-minute drive down the hill to the marina district. We parked right in front of where the *Bluebird* was berthed. We walked up the gangplank and were greeted by the guy in charge of the job;

The St. Francis Yacht
Club flag of San Francisco.

there were three other guys working below decks. To a one, they all gave G a quick double-take but that was it. No one gave him a third look. I was glad, at least so far, to be proven right — that if we treated him normally, other people would.

While Mr. Becker went over stuff with the supervisor guy, Chuy, G and I explored the sailboat. There was a lot to explore, all of it slightly foreign and more than a little daunting. Even though I had done a fair amount of sailing at school, it was always on much smaller sailboats and I had the feeling it would be easy to make a mistake on the *Bluebird*. The *Bluebird* had three private cabins and ten berths, which were basically beds built in to the side walls of the sailboat (called bulkheads), with drawers underneath the beds. There were three small bathrooms which, for some reason, were called "heads," and three showers. Everything below decks was either made of wood or wood-paneled, including the "galley," which is what the kitchen was called. And all of the wood was finished with a shiny varnish.

Mr. Becker caught up with us and asked if I'd mind going back to Grandma Hattie's to meet JP, Mr. Becker's friend, the one who was going to be our cook for the trip. He was due to arrive in a half hour or so. It was a short walk back to Grandma's, so I took off as Mr. Becker gave Chuy and G some mimeographed sheets of paper with diagrams and terms on them. I heard him tell them that even though he and the crew he hired would be doing the actual sailing, it was a good idea for both of them to know what things were called on the sailboat, just in case they were called on to lend a hand. As I headed down the gangplank I could see they had serious looks on their faces.

The hike back to Grandma's was all uphill. The limp I'd had all my life, the result of a foot injury in the crash that killed my family, rarely bothered me much. But the long, uphill slog left me huffing and sweating by the time I pushed the big front door open. I heard voices coming from the kitchen so I headed there and found JP already there, sitting on a stool, trying to have a conversation with Katia. Even though I hadn't been introduced to JP yet, I could tell it wasn't going well. And even though he didn't know me from a can of paint, JP jumped off the stool when he saw me and walked over, hand outstretched, and said "John Puscheck. That's ketchup spelled backwards, kind of. Everybody calls me JP. How do you like me so far?"

I laughed as I shook hands with him and said "Nick. Nick Sinclair. I don't know what that is spelled backwards."

"It's Rialcnis."

"How'd you do that?"

"Naturally. I'm dyslexic."

"Dys-what-sic?"

"Dyslexic. Basically it means that I see words backwards. But that doesn't mean I'm backwards, although there might be people who disagree with that.

What it looks like belowdecks on the Silverado — all shiny, varnished wood, dark and cozy.

What can I say except, boy am I glad to see you!" JP said, rolling his eyes and motioning with his head in the direction of Katia who, thankfully, had her back to us.

"Let's get out of Katia's way. Follow me. Why don't you bring your stuff?"

We walked to the conservatory. JP put down his satchel and a big package he was carrying and looked around.

"Wow. Quite the place. Who owns this pile of bricks?"

"My grandmother."

"And who's Katia?"

"Actually, she's my grandmother's cousin, from Germany. She cooks and does other stuff for my grandmother."

"Don't tell her, but I don't think she's going to win any 'Miss Congeniality' contests anytime soon. I was trying to ask her if there was a barbecue around. She looked at me like I was from another planet. I brought this brisket from Kansas City," he said, patting the large parcel wrapped in pink butcher paper. "13 pounds of prime Missouri beef. Thought maybe I could do some ceremonial cooking."

"Ceremonial cooking?"

"Yeah, you know: cooking something for the sake of cooking and figuring out what to do with it later."

"I guess I didn't know. You need a barbecue?"

"Yeah, is there one around?"

"I think there's one in the garage. Let's take a look."

We went outside and walked around to the side of the house where the garage was. The garage doors were open and Doyle was there, polishing the limousine. I introduced JP to Doyle.

"Nice ride," JP said, motioning to the limousine.

"Not exactly a high performance vehicle, but it's smooth. The power of velour," Doyle said.

JP laughed. "I like that — 'the power of velour.' I'll have to remember that. Nick said there might be a barbecue somewhere."

"Now there's a question I don't get very often. As a matter of fact, there is a barbecue. I'll show you."

Doyle led JP to the back of the garage where they found the barbecue and pulled it out into the driveway. It wasn't long before Doyle had JP set up at the workbench, which was now a make-do kitchen counter. "Here's the key," JP said, holding up an old mayonnaise jar filled with a dark red powder. "My very own dry rub. Thirteen herbs and spices: award-winning, time-honored and super-secret," he said as he shook the jar over the huge piece of beef, patting it in place with his hand. I had no idea what a "dry rub" was, but it looked like JP knew what he was doing.

"Now if I could just find a beer, we could get this show on the road," JP said.

"I believe there's some in the basement refrigerator," Doyle said. "Mrs. Sinclair likes to keep some on hand for when we have Dungeness crab."

"Well let's take a look, Doyle. My bottom lip is twitching."

It wasn't long before the barbecue was smoking away in the driveway and people driving by were slowing down to stare. JP would smile, wave his tongs and lift his beer to them. Let's just say that life in Pacific Heights was mostly lived behind closed doors. Life in the streets, or more accurately, in the driveway — was definitely a novelty. Grandma Hattie arrived by taxi about an hour into JP's production. She came around the corner of the sidewalk with a horrified expression on her face.

"Oh my god. Is it on fire?"

"What?" JP asked.

"Is the house on fire?"

"No, ma'am. I'm smoking a brisket. I'm JP, by the way," he said, holding out his hand to grandma.

"Pleased, I'm sure," she said, shaking his hand somewhat warily. "Have you got another one of those?" she said, pointing to John's beer.

"Of course," he said

"I'm not much of a beer drinker, but I do enjoy the cold part right off the top, especially when we have crab."

"So I hear," JP said. "I think you're going to like it with brisket, too."

Grandma had Doyle find her a stool and she sat there in the driveway with her beer, watching the smoke billow out of the barbecue, talking with JP like they had known each other forever.

"A half hour ago I was exchanging a bag full of gold for cash at my bank and now I'm at a barbecue in my own driveway. Things are getting interesting around here."

"Exchanging gold for cash? Should I ask?"

"It's a long story. I told my banker I'd taken up prospecting, but I don't think he believed me. Such a lack of imagination. If I'd told him the truth — that a gnome had given me the gold, he would have gone around the room backwards."

. . .

Mr. Becker, Tova, Chuy, and G got back to grandma's house late in the afternoon. It wasn't long before JP had enlisted the help of Mr. Becker and sent him off to the grocery store with a list of what he needed. Around 6 o'clock the whole group moved from the driveway and followed JP into the kitchen where he put the brisket in the oven for its second stage of cooking. About the time he was shredding a mountain of cabbage for coleslaw, Katia couldn't take any more and clomped off up the stairs and slammed shut the door to her room. Doyle and I rolled our eyes and shook our heads. Grandma was deep in discussion with G and Tova; it was my impression that they were talking about G's cash and whether or not it was a good idea to put Tova in charge of it until G was more comfortable with using it. There was no mistaking that a distinct party atmosphere had taken hold, only to be increased when JP instructed no one in particular to "get on the horn and invite some good eaters over," to which Grandma responded by getting on the phone and inviting a couple of her neighbors for an impromptu dinner. "Haven't talked to them since the Christmas party," she said as she put the phone down.

Some of the neighbors had houseguests or kids, and brought them along too. There was quite a crowd in the kitchen when JP took center stage and said "Now here's how you do it. You take a slice of Wonder Bread, which doubles as a napkin in the Midwest, and fold it gently in half so it forms a triangle. First in is a couple of slices of brisket, then a few dill pickle chips, topped with just enough coleslaw and a squirt of barbecue sauce over the whole thing. That's it: Your basic Kansas City fold-over brisket sandwich. Eatin' doesn't get much better."

Everyone dove in with considerable enthusiasm, seemingly hungry not just for JP's food, but for the fun that seemed to follow him like cans on a wedding car. Not surprisingly, Katia never reappeared in the kitchen that night. Probably because there was too much laughter for her taste.

. . .

The week went by in a blur with folks coming and going from Grandma Hattie's house at all hours, everyone on their own schedule and with their own lists of what they needed to get done. On Thursday the sailing crew Mr. Becker had hired — Jon, Mike and Chad — showed up, but stayed on the sailboat instead of

Grandma's house. JP kept us all fueled, one night with fish and chips, the next with what he called "State Fair Food," including homemade corndogs on sticks, and one night Grandma Hattie insisted on Dungeness crab, so she could introduce JP to the delicacy in return for him having introduced her to the Kansas City fold-over sandwich.

On the Friday before we were to depart, Grandma Hattie summoned me into the library, asking me to close the sliding doors behind me. I wondered what was up.

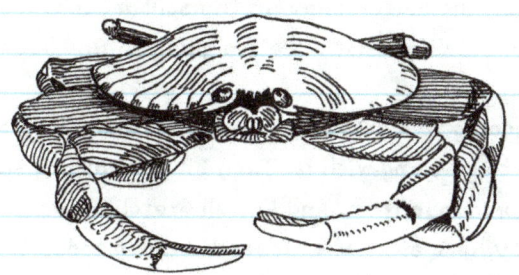

A San Francisco specialty:
Dungeness crab.

"I've been thinking about a couple of things, Nick. They might be delicate and then again, they might not. I thought I'd run them past you to see what you think."

"Sure, Grandma."

"Well, first, that nasty man Mr. Stayne said he was going to meet you in Kauai, didn't he?"

"Yes. And I have no idea of how I'm going to handle him."

"No, I don't suppose you do. Too many variables, I think. But I was thinking more about what he was after. He wants to photograph a gnome, right? To give to Lord Higgenbotham?"

"He as much as told me himself that's what he's after."

"And do I assume correctly that you don't intend to keep G under wraps while he's in Kauai?"

"No. I was thinking of taking a different approach. A more normal one."

"But if Nigel is indeed waiting for you in Kauai and you show up with G in tow, what's to stop him from just photographing him then and there and jumping back on a plane to England?"

I was silent for a minute. I thought I had thought my plan through, but I hadn't thought about what Grandma had just said. And of course she was right.

"I hadn't thought about that. What are you thinking?"

"Well, I'm thinking that you're going to have to take measures to make sure that Mr. Stayne doesn't get what he wants."

"Like how?"

"Here's where it might get a little sticky. I think we need to convince G to undergo what we ladies call a 'makeover.'"

"What do you mean?"

"What I mean is that I think he is going to have to ditch his 'layered look' in favor of clothes that are a little less 'foreign' looking. And he's going to have to get a haircut — a normal young man's haircut. If it's done right, he'll look like a regular boy and we'll have robbed Mr. Stayne of his opportunity to get his photograph. What do you think?"

"I think you're right. I can't keep him hidden away on the sailboat the whole time. And I don't want to. I'm guessing that if we are going to find Dagywn, it's going to be because of G."

"Okay then, here's what we're going to do. You'll go and tell G what the plan is and convince him it's important to go along with it. Then I'll go shopping and bring some clothes home for him to choose from. And I'll call Gretchen, my hairdresser, and ask her to come by here after she closes her shop today to give G a haircut. I don't want him to have to sit in a chair at her salon with a bunch of gossipy old women. Go find G and tell him what we're going to do. And be firm."

I did as I was told and am pleased to report that G understood the importance of grandma's plan and offered little resistance other than saying "this ought to be interesting." Grandma returned a couple of hours later with Doyle trailing behind her with a load of bags and boxes, saying that "the clerk at Saks was most helpful and said we can return anything you don't like, but I must say it would have been more fun if you were a girl." I decided to leave the decision process to G and Grandma. It wasn't long before Gretchen showed up and I took her to the library where Grandma and G were waiting. G had already changed into some of his new clothes, a white polo shirt, jeans and a pair of Keds — and I have to admit, he looked remarkably different, at least from the neck down. The fact that he still had very long hair, done in dozens of small braids, all pulled up into a bun on top of his head gave him a decidedly exotic look. I guess Grandma hadn't said anything about G being a gnome, because when Gretchen first saw him she let out a gasp. I've got to say she regained her composure quickly, walked over to him and said "now what did you have in mind, young man?"

"Normal," Grandma said, butting in. "Just a normal boy's haircut, and not one of those mop-top, rock-and-roll cuts."

"Well, let's start by undoing the bun and the braids and see what we've got to work with," Gretchen said.

Clearly G wasn't going to have much say in the matter. The whole process took more than an hour (untying those little braids wasn't easy), but after Gretchen was done, G had, in fact, been transformed. I couldn't quite tell what G thought when Gretchen handed him a mirror to look at the results. It must have been something of a shock but all he said when he saw himself was "that should work. Thank you." I was convinced that he could pass for "normal," whatever that meant. Grandma seemed pleased with herself and said to Gretchen "Mission accomplished! Now, Gretchen, let's you and I have a martini."

And now it's the 15th. All the commotion of the last week has ended and we're having a picnic brunch on board the *Bluebird*. As hard as it is to believe, today is the day we depart. It's a very big deal. Grandma Hattie had brought basket after basket of food in the trunk of the limousine, which Doyle carried aboard.

While Doyle laid out the baskets on top of the main cabin, Grandma pulled me aside and handed me a piece of paper.

"What's this?" I asked.

"You know it's going to take two weeks to get to Kauai and at least that long getting back, so I got to thinking that once you get there, it's probably best to stay somewhere on terra firma. I remember when your grandfather and I used to take long trips on the *Bluebird*. The quarters can start to be a bit confining and, how should I say this, 'fragrant.' I had my travel agent look into it and she gave me the name of a place she stayed on Kauai last year. She said it was most charming."

"The Garden Isle Beach Cottages?" I said, reading what was written on the piece of paper.

"She's made reservations for three cottages, one for you, Chuy and G, one for Tim and Tova, and one for JP. I assume the crew would prefer to stay on the boat. Oh, and she said it was quite near Nawiliwili Harbor, where you'll be docking. The address is there on the piece of paper. And don't forget, G has instructions from his father to pay for all expenses. Make sure he does."

"Thanks Grandma," I said, a little taken aback that she was paying so much attention to the details of our trip. She turned away from me and addressed the group.

"Excuse me, but has anyone bothered to look at the stern?" Grandma Hattie asked, motioning with half a croissant to the rear of the boat. Naturally all of us moved to the stern and looked over the side. A small canvas sheet covered the stern, held in place with a couple of ropes. Everyone turned and looked at Grandma Hattie.

"What's going on Grandma?" I asked.

"Doyle bring me the champagne. We're going to have a rechristening ceremony. I know tradition has it that one is supposed to smash a bottle of champagne on the stern, but first of all, this is good champagne and I intend to have some of it, and second, considering the woodwork has just been refinished, I don't intend on damaging one square inch of this beauty. So, if Doyle will open the champagne and Nick, you take off the tarp, let's take a look, shall we?"

I removed the tarp and saw where *Bluebird* had once been, *Silverado* was now written in metallic gold letters across the stern. I have no idea how she pulled it off without anyone noticing, but she had. Very typical for Grandma. She gently poured a little of the champagne over the stern, pronouncing "I now rechristen this boat *Silverado*." Everyone clapped and cheered while Doyle distributed paper cups and filled them with champagne.

Even though Grandma and I weren't very touchy-feely, I went over and gave her a hug.

"Now don't go getting all emotional, Nick. I just did what I thought was the right thing to do. The *Bluebird* has a new life now. It seemed only fitting that she have a new name. Do you approve?"

"Most definitely."

"Good. Then Doyle and I are going let you and the crew get to it. Now, don't forget, once you arrive in Kauai, I want you to call me every Sunday and report in. And don't forget the time difference between California and Hawaii. You'll be two hours behind us, so if you call around one o'clock your time in Hawaii it should be fine. No, make that 2 o'clock your time. I've been known to need an extra cup of coffee on Sunday mornings. All right, now off on your adventure. Safe travels. And good luck finding what's-his-name, that wizard fellow."

With that and a backwards wave as she walked down the gangplank, she was off. Within the hour we'd cast off too, sails rigged, headed due west, through the Golden Gate and beyond... to what?

I had absolutely no idea.

If you ever get the chance to sail under the Golden Gate Bridge, be sure and do it.

Chapter V

Blue Water Sailing and Late Night Discussions

June 15, 1968
At sea, San Francisco en route to Kauai

It's kind of hard for me to explain what it felt like to be aboard the *Silverado*, sailing under the Golden Gate Bridge, out from the bay (which is basically like a big lake), into the open ocean with the horizon stretching, left, right and center, as far as the eye could see, unimaginably big. For one thing, there was a physical sensation: the waves on the bay are short and choppy and make for a bumpy, up-and-down ride. Once you're outside the Golden Gate the waves change into big, rhythmic rollers, pushing the sailboat forward on strong, slow swells. You can't help but sense their power, which at least to me, felt awesome and more than a little frightening. Ever since I'd first seen her, the *Silverado* looked big to me; now it felt small.

In addition to the physical sensations, I had this sense of pure exhilaration and excitement. To be honest, I felt like jumping up and down and yelling because, well, just because... and I wasn't thinking about getting to Kauai, or looking for Dagywn, or anything else. The excitement I felt was for right then and there. Looking back on it, I think what I was feeling was joy.

Whatever I was feeling, I wouldn't be telling the truth if I didn't mention that it was combined with sheer terror. No kidding. Almost immediately it sunk into my brain that once you're out there, miles from shore with nothing but ocean in every direction, clear to the horizon, you can't jump overboard and swim to shore — swim home to your safe and steady bed. Nope. The boat becomes your whole world. It's your transportation, your source of food, your place to sleep, what provides your safety and last but hardly least, the place where you interact with the other people, your crewmates, for friendship and support. I didn't like admitting it, but I was pretty much overwhelmed by it all. It made me a little weak in the knees, which, for the record, is not a good thing aboard a boat bobbing about in the ocean. I actually had to go below deck and just sit on my bunk for a while and let everything catch up with me.

A little later, after we had passed the Farallon Islands and were so far out to sea we couldn't see the coast any more, Mr. Becker checked in on me, Chuy and G to see how we were doing. He explained to us that we were now "blue

The Farallon Islands, a few miles outside the Golden Gate.

water sailing." By the looks on our faces, he could tell we had no idea what he was talking about so he explained that once the vessel you were sailing on was beyond the continental shelf, it was considered blue water sailing. There were more blank looks because none of us knew what the "continental shelf" was, either. He told us that any continent, like say North America, doesn't end where the coastline meets the ocean. There's an area of land under the water that's an extension of the continent which can extend for miles under the ocean's surface. Basically what he was trying to tell us was that we weren't doing some fair weather day sailing in coastal waters. No, we were a long way out to sea, which was a completely different kind of sailing, way more difficult, and, potentially, more dangerous than any sailing I had done at school. He also told us that for most of the outbound trip we would be doing what's called "downwind sailing," which is basically sailing the same direction that the wind is blowing. He got out a chart that showed our route from San Francisco to Kauai. I thought I knew my geography, but I was surprised how far the Hawaiian Islands were from California. I mean, they were practically in the middle of the Pacific Ocean, the biggest ocean on the face of the planet. And I hadn't realized how far south they were. For some reason I thought we'd head out straight west from the Golden Gate and in a couple of weeks reach Kauai. But no. They were so far south that if they could be considered off the coast of anywhere, it would be Mexico. He said that we'd be sailing in the same direction of what's called the "trade winds," winds that blow more or less constantly in the same direction. In our case, the trade winds were called northeasterly, which completely confused me until Mr. Becker explained that the direction of the winds were the direction from which the winds were coming, not the direction they were going. So the trade winds we were dealing with may have come from the northeast, but they were headed to the southwest, which was the direction we needed to sail to reach Kauai. Everything Mr. Becker had just explained left me with the feeling that how I imagined this trip and what it was actually going to be like were two very different things. I certainly hadn't planned on being scared, but I definitely was. And my guess was that Chuy and G were too.

Scared or not, along about the third day into the trip Chuy, G and I had basically settled into a routine, as had Mr. Becker and Tova. Every day they were the first ones up and on deck at 6 in the morning doing, if you can believe it, calisthenics in their swim suits. The first morning I found them doing their exercises they asked me to join in, but I felt a little awkward so I declined. Tova said I'd better be careful or I'd become *"eine Schwächling."*

"Wie sagt man das, Tim, *ein bleistift hals?"* she asked Mr. Hayes.

"Literally?" he asked her.

"Ja."

"A 'pencil neck'," he said laughing. "But I don't think Nick needs to worry about becoming a pencil neck, Tova."

"Well, at least he should have a bowl of our muesli. It will put some meat on his bones and keep him regular."

Again, I respectfully declined. I was looking forward to JP's breakfast instead of the bowl of twigs and nuts I saw them eating yesterday. And I was regular enough, thank you very much. To each, his own, right?

Since Chuy, G and I didn't have specific duties sailing the sailboat, we were pretty much free to do what we wanted. The one specific job we did have was cleaning up after each meal, but that didn't take very long. I don't know about Chuy and G, but I was surprised that I had so much free time, something I wasn't used to. It didn't take long to discover we all had brought books. We decided to just keep them together on one of the built-in shelves and treat it as an impromptu "lending library." I mention this because G spent most of his time reading and luckily had plenty of books to choose from. A couple of days before we left, I went to the bookstore near grandma's house and bought a guidebook to Kauai. Having never been to any of the Hawaiian Islands, I figured it might prepare us a little. One morning I pulled the guidebook off the shelf. Right in the beginning it had what the authors called "Kauai Fun Facts: Things to Know About Kauai." Here's what I read to the guys:

• Kauai is the northernmost island in the Hawaiian chain and is the most isolated inhabited land mass in the world. Kauai is 2390 miles from California, 3850 miles from Japan, 4900 miles from China and 5280 miles from the Philippines.

• Kauai's Mt. Waialeale is the wettest spot on earth, averaging 450 inches of rain per year producing eight major, majestic waterfalls, including the Waimea Canyon's Waipoo Falls, which fall 800 feet.

• Kauai's weather is described as "nearly perfect," ranging from 75 to 85 Fahrenheit, with not much change season to season or from day to night. Rain showers usually fall in the evening and early morning, mostly over the mountain ranges.

• Seventy percent of the island is inaccessible by foot.

• Kauai's unofficial "Birds of Paradise" are the island's wild chickens.

• Kauai is the home of the legendary Menehune. In ancient stories these were small people who performed amazing feats of engineering and construction.

• And perhaps the most interesting and unusual fact is Kauai's building code dictates that "no building shall be taller than a coconut palm tree," thus the four-story limit on vertical construction. Because of the limit, there are no high-rises in Kauai and there never will be.

After I read the facts out loud, Chuy said "so it sounds like it's a small island with great weather, a lot of beaches and waterfalls, and you can only explore 30 percent of it on foot, which means that if someone wanted to hide out — like our man Dagywn — he'd have a big advantage."

"That, and it's so far away from any other place on the planet, it almost sounds like you can't get there from here or anywhere else," G said. "It's interesting, though, that the Menehune got a mention — almost like the authors were saying they were real."

"That's funny coming from you, G," Chuy said. "You're real, aren't you?"

"Yeah, but the only time we get mentioned is usually in kid's books, not guidebooks to someplace real," G said.

"Look at it this way, G," I said, "if you, your dad and the rest of guys got to Kauai on Captain Niebaum's sailing ship almost a hundred years ago, we'll get there too. And call me crazy if you want, but I'm guessing that the Menehune are definitely for real."

All in all, I'd say I got a pretty lukewarm reaction to my "fun facts." I put the guidebook back on the shelf where it stayed for the rest of the trip.

Chuy spent some time on his own learning to tie knots and some of the time with Jon, Mike, and Chad, the deck hands, trying to pick up on the basics of sailing without getting in their way. I found myself spending a lot of time in the galley helping JP. Not that I knew anything about cooking, mind you. Between Ma-D, the cooks at school and Katia, there wasn't much opportunity to hang out in the kitchen, let alone help with the preparation of a meal. Which got me to thinking about the similarities between dictators and cooks, but JP disproved my theory. He seemed to enjoy company in the galley and I picked up some basic things like peeling potatoes and how to handle a knife without cutting my fingers off.

Breakfast was at 7, lunch at noon and dinner at 6:30. After cleaning up after our first dinner at sea, Chuy, G and I found ourselves above deck, in front of the main cabin. There were a couple of hatches there that we could lean up against and watch the sun set. It became our after-dinner hangout. I think it was Chuy who first asked G about what it was like living on Mt. St. Helena in a cave. What followed was a days-long description of gnome life. He started by telling us that being a prince didn't mean that much, because being the gnome king didn't mean that much either. In fact, being the gnome king was kind of an inside joke, which surprised me and Chuy. The tribe of gnomes that G belonged to was set up as a collective, with everyone contributing to the good of the tribe. All their wealth was considered to be owned by the tribe as a group and any one of them could have access to it after petitioning the Exchequer (the gnome officially in charge of their wealth) and then having the tribe vote on it. The idea of someone owning something didn't make much sense to them. Sure, people had their own clothes and maybe some tools and furniture, but those were considered the basic essentials of living. Everyone in the tribe had some part in procuring food, or preparing it, to keep its members well-fed.

But even though the tribe was self-sufficient and detached from the out-side world, the gnomes understood there were times when it was important to have someone they could put forward as their leader, someone who supposedly represented them.

"Not to put too fine a point on it, it helps if the person the tribe elects as "king" is not overly smart," G said. "On the rare occasion when it's necessary to talk with someone outside our tribe, the "king" acts as our representative and repeats memorized answers deliberately designed to confuse whoever asked the question. The role of king has always been our first line of defense against anyone who wants to pry into our world, especially Uplanders."

"Who tells him what to say?" I asked.

"There's a Council of Elders. They begin teaching a new king when he's very young."

"Since your dad is the king and you're the prince, are you going to be the next king?" Chuy asked.

"No, the term prince is just meant as a further diversion, in case I'm ever needed to back him up. When my father gets too old to be king, the tribe will elect another one."

"And you won't be 'prince' anymore?" Chuy asked.

"No. My title changes to 'the   °honorable'. It's just a way of acknowledging that I served the tribe, but it's not used much."

Chuy, who had a way of asking direct questions, asked G why the gnomes were so short.

"Because we are," G. replied. "It's that simple, but I have to admit that lately I've been interested in what you'd call the scientific reasons why we are the way we are. Our tribe doesn't have a written language. Everything we know is from the stories each older generation tells the younger generation. Because we don't have books, there's nothing I can, as you'd say, 'look up,' to explain it. I decided to see if you Uplanders had any theories about it, but it's very difficult for me to find what I'm looking for, considering it involves hiding out in libraries overnight. Anyway, to answer the question, it's pretty straightforward. This guy from Transylvania named Baron Franz Nopsca, discovered back in 1914 that creatures that lived in small isolated communities, like caves or islands, became smaller is size over time. And because they breed only amongst themselves, they stay small. Just a few years ago, some scientist published a paper where he used the term 'island dwarfing effect', which seems to have caught on but, for whatever reason, nobody has ever applied it to us, probably because they don't believe we exist, except in fairy tales. Sorry, Chuy, I've probably told you more than you want to know."

"No, no, I'm interested. Can you explain how you do your magic?"

"No, not really. It's like being small, it just is. I can tell you it has to do with vibrations and being in tune with them. Everything you see, living or not, has its own unique vibration. It's amazing what you can do if you're tuned in and recognize the difference between one vibration and another. If you're adept at reading vibrations, like we are, the vibrations can be manipulated, which looks like magic to you. For us, it's just being connected with our surroundings. We're part of everything and everything is part of us. Just like your hands or your feet are a part of your body and you have control over them. It's that simple. It only looks like magic to you because you've forgotten what your ancient ancestors knew."

"Doesn't sound simple to me," Chuy said.

"And the things that you take for granted, like electric lights and automobiles and transistor radios, don't seem simple to me," G said, and they both laughed.

"Okay, okay," Chuy said, "I get it."

I think all of us went to bed a little blown away that night, even G. I don't think he ever expected to have a conversation like that with anyone, especially a couple of Uplanders.

. . .

The Åland Islands, between Sweden and Finland.

One night JP came out after dinner and joined us. We played dominoes right on the deck and G continued telling us about gnome life. JP was the only one who hadn't read my journal, so G explained to him about how Dagywn the wizard, along with the other four gnomes, had jumped ship in Kauai back in 1879 and how badly his father, King Gob, wanted them all back, especially Dagywn.

"Good luck with that." JP said, looking at me.

"Yeah, I know." I said, shaking my head.

"So why were they even stowing away in the first place?" JP asked. "Our tribe has been living in the Aland Islands for eons, but then the local Up-landers went and built a church close by where were living. I don't know if you know it or not, but the one thing gnomes can't stand is the sound of church bells, so my father gathered a group together to look for another place to live."

"Aland Islands?" JP asked.

"Yeah. They're in the Gulf of Bothnia, in between what you call Sweden and Finland."

"Never heard of 'em," JP said.

"Yeah, that's why we liked them so much. Hardly anyone knows about them."

"What's the deal with the bells?"

"Oh, it's a big deal with us. For a long time, gnomes and Uplanders lived to-gether pretty well. We rarely crossed paths and when we did, we kept it cordial on both sides. Then some of the powers that be in one church and another de-cided that the gnomes were part of the devil's world, which is about as untrue as anything can be. Gnomes don't even believe in the devil. But anyway, ever since then, things between the Uplanders and the gnomes haven't been good. And the bells just symbolize everything bad that's been said and done to the gnomes. Bad juju."

G went on to explain that on the Aland Islands, the men gnomes and the women gnomes lived in separate spaces and that there was a third area where they came together when they wanted to for parties, dances, and the like, to which JP muttered, "hear hear." G also explained that the women gnomes, called gnomides, were basically in charge of everything important but they made it look like the men were in charge, just to keep them happy."

"Well, that's nice of them." JP said. "I'm starting to think you gnomes have got it all figured out. Where do I sign up?"

"With your temperament, I think you'd probably fit in with the tribe, JP, but your size would be a problem."

"I'm just as god made me."

"Aren't we all?" said G.

"What are you talking about?" JP said indignantly, patting his considerable stomach. "I've been working on the perfect pear shape for years now."

"It's not your girth that would be a problem, it's your height," G said.

"No one's ever complained about it before."

"Well, when's the last time you hung out with a bunch of gnomes?"

"You've got me there," JP said. "I didn't know y'all were such an exclusive group."

"I wouldn't say 'exclusive,' more like private. We've spent the last few hundred years trying to protect our privacy because every time we stick our heads out, they get clobbered. The Uplanders, not all, but most, hated us without knowing anything about us and actively hunted us down. Our privacy became a matter of life and death. I've got to tell you, there were plenty of old-timers in our tribe who were completely against my coming on this trip with you guys. If it weren't for Nick and his grandma's friendship with my father, I wouldn't be here. Do you see what I'm saying?"

"I do," Chuy said. "Even though my family has lived in the valley longer than most of the gringo families, most of them still look at me like I'm an outsider. Sometimes it's just easier to stick with your own kind."

"I'm sure what you're both saying is true," JP said, "but there's something to be said for people who are willing to take risks and reach out across the divide. Look, none of us would even be here right now if it weren't for the open-mindedness of Nick, his grandmother, your father, G, and you, too Chuy," JP said. "We wouldn't be on this adventure right now if everyone just stayed in his or her own corner, refusing to experience something different."

Everyone was quiet for a bit. Then G said "there's truth in what you said, JP, but I also spoke the truth. But I get what you're saying. Here's to risk-takers! Here's to all of us!" A small, spontaneous cheer went up, signaling that we'd reached the end of the conversation. JP started to pick up the dominoes off the deck, saying it was time for him to "seek the horizontal."

"Speaking of sleep, have you gotten used to sleeping at night?" I asked G.

"Kind of. It still feels weird to me, but I'm getting the hang of it. Sometimes I wake up in the middle of the night and think that I should be up and doing something."

It was a beautiful night and no one was making any moves to leave the deck. Jon and Chad were trimming the sails like they did every night. Since we weren't in a hurry to get to Kauai, Mr. Becker had instructed them to fly minimal sails at night, just enough to keep the boat going in the right direction, but not so much that it would be necessary to make quick adjustments if the wind shifted. With minimal sails, only one crew member had to stay up to sail the boat, while the other two got to sleep through the night.

We were just about ready to go below decks when all of a sudden we saw a small slice of light on the horizon, like the tip of a fingernail, and realized that it was the full moon rising. As it rose higher in the sky it made a path of light on the water, sparkling and shifting in shape, from the horizon to where we were sitting. It was mesmerizing, so much so that Chuy and I talked about sleeping on the deck. G thought it was a bad idea, saying it would be too easy for him to roll overboard in the middle of the night. Then JP chimed in.

"You wanna' sleep out under a full moon?" he asked incredulously.

"Yeah, what's wrong with that?" Chuy and I asked, more or less in unison.

"I'll tell you what's wrong with that. You know that it's the push and pull of the moon's gravity that causes the tides to go from low to high and high to low, right?"

"Sure."

"Well, if it's that strong, what do you think it's going to do to your face if you sleep out here? You'll wake up in the morning and your features — your eyes, nose and mouth — will all be on one side of your face. Sometimes it even pulls your ear over."

"No way!" Chuy and I said, again in unison.

"Yep. Don't say I didn't warn you."

Chuy and I discussed it for a while and decided it was probably going to get too cold to sleep outside anyway and followed JP and G below decks. As soon as I got settled in my bunk, the image of my face with all my features on one side popped into my head. I turned the small light on above my bunk and decided to read for a while. From the aft of the sailboat I could make out the sound of JP laughing.

The full moon in the middle of the Pacific Ocean.

I was surprised when I looked at my watch and saw that it was 2 o'clock. No wonder I was so hungry. After I had finished Grandpa's first journal, I was just about
convinced that the gnomes were real; after getting started on this second one, my
old doubts came back. Everything I knew told me there was no way it could be a
true story. No way. What I needed was some proof, one way or the other. I went
to the bathroom and before getting something to eat, I went out into the yard.
There was something I had to check out. Like in the other journal, my grandfather had included small pen-and-ink drawings here and there in this one, too. In
the chapter where he talked about the homing pigeons he and G used to communicate, there was a drawing of what he called a "dovecote." It wasn't a word I was
familiar with, but I knew there was something like that at the back of Grandpa's
garden. I picked up the journal and took it with me. Sure enough, it was there at
the far end of the garden, almost completely hidden by a huge fig tree. The fig
branches arched all the way to the ground. I pushed them aside and compared
the drawing of the dovecote in the journal with the one right in front of me.
Taking into account the passing of 40-plus years, you could say they were exactly
the same. Even more interesting, there were doves or pigeons or whatever kind of
birds they were, flitting around inside. Even though it was barely visible through
the fig leaves, I had known it was there because I walked past it every week when
I mowed the lawn, but I guess I thought it was just some garden shed or something. I didn't know it was a home for pigeons, or whatever they were. There was
one more thing I wanted to check out, but I decided to make myself a sandwich
first. I went into the kitchen and made a bologna sandwich with mayonnaise and
lettuce. I grabbed some chips, a glass of milk and the journal and walked over to
Grandpa's studio in the barn next to the house.

Grandpa was working on a large painting. I asked him if it was okay to use
his computer. He said "of course" and I sat down in front of it with my lunch. It
wasn't a straightforward search so it took me awhile to find out what I wanted.

"Hmmmmm… "

"Find what you were looking for?" Grandpa asked.

"Basically that G was right with his 'island dwarfing effect' theory. Or at least it's possible he was right."

"It always made sense to me," Grandpa said, "although there wasn't much information on it at the time. There've been a couple of interesting finds in Indonesia – skeletons and the like – not that long ago."

"I saw that. Couldn't resist calling them hobbits, could they?"

"Apparently not. The heirs of J. R. R. Tolkien weren't exactly amused."

It always surprised me how much my grandfather knew. He didn't come off like a know-it-all, but when even really obscure subjects came up, he seemed to have some knowledge of them. I never saw him spend much time in front of the computer, so I have no idea of where he got his information. It's a little weird. One more Grandpa mystery.

"So if it's scientifically possible that a race of humans existed – or, according to you, still exist – that were only around three feet tall, I guess I can buy that, kind of," I said, "but what's with all the magical-mysto stuff you wrote about? How are they able to do that?"

"That I can't explain. All I know is they can. 'Ancient magic' is what G called it. Said us Uplanders had simply forgotten what we once knew because of all the new stuff we've chased after, one millennium after another. They've pretty much stayed the same since whenever. There's not much that's new in their lives. Doesn't really need to be."

"I've got to think about that."

"Best of luck. I've tried to figure it out for over forty years and haven't made any real progress."

"What about that dovecote in the backyard? Am I pronouncing it correctly?"

"That's how it's pronounced. What about it?"

"Is it the same one you drew in the journal?"

"Did I? Let me see."

I opened to the page where the illustration was.

"Well, I'll be. I'd forgotten about that. Yeah, that's the same one."

"How did it get from Twin Oaks Pony Farm to here?"

"I had it moved after Walter and Ma-D passed away. I always liked it, so I had it put in the garden here."

"Did you know there were still pigeons or doves still living in it?"

"Yes. Pigeons. Homing pigeons, to be exact. There's not much of the wire screening left, so they come and go as they please."

"Are they the same ones you used to communicate with G?"

"Descendants most likely. They only live for 15 years or so – less in the wild – which the ones in the dovecote kind of are."

"Could they still find their way to G?"

"Sure. But it only works if the sender is holding the receiver's pigeon. The sender releases the receiver's pigeon and it flies home. If the receiver wants to send a return message, he'd release one of the sender's pigeons and it would fly back here."

"Considering they're free to come and go, is it possible that they're flying back and forth all the time without carrying a message?"

"Kind of a long shot. More likely a *really* long shot, but I suppose it's possible. I'm not sure that that kind of specific homing information is transferred from one generation of pigeons to the next."

"How did you attach a message to the pigeon?"

"We wrote it on a small piece of very lightweight paper, rolled it up, put it in small copper vial and attached it to the pigeon's leg."

"Do you still have any of the vials?"

"Probably. I'd have to look for them. What's this about?"

"I don't know. I'm just interested. Do you think you could find them?"

"Oh, man. I'd have to think about it. Kind of like finding a needle in a haystack, you know? I'll try."

Summer was definitely winding down. In another week, I'd be back in school and all that it meant routine-wise. I decided it was okay to go back to reading the journal. My daily life would be different soon enough. One of the many odd things about my grandfather was that he had a hammock in his studio. He said he didn't think it was odd at all. According to him the hammock is one of the best inventions ever and the perfect place to take a nap. I wasn't so interested in a nap; I just wanted a quiet place to read. I more or less looked at the journal as my "job" until I finished it.

About an hour or so later, Grandpa was standing next to the hammock with his hand out, palm up, pointing in my direction.

"Found it. You're lucky I never seem to throw anything away."

On his palm was a small copper cylinder.

"Oh wow! Where'd you find it?"

"In my roll-top desk. With the rest of my letter-writing stuff."

What he produced next out of his pants pocket took me completely by surprise.

"And here. I'm not sure what you're up to, but if you're going to use the vial, you're going to need these," he said, handing me a packet of Zig-Zag rolling papers.

"Uh... why?" I stammered, trying to think what the heck he was suggesting.

"G and I found that they made the best writing paper to fit in the vial. Super-lightweight, too, which is important."

With that he went back to his painting.

"Grandpa, Grandpa, Grandpa," I thought to myself. "What next... ?"

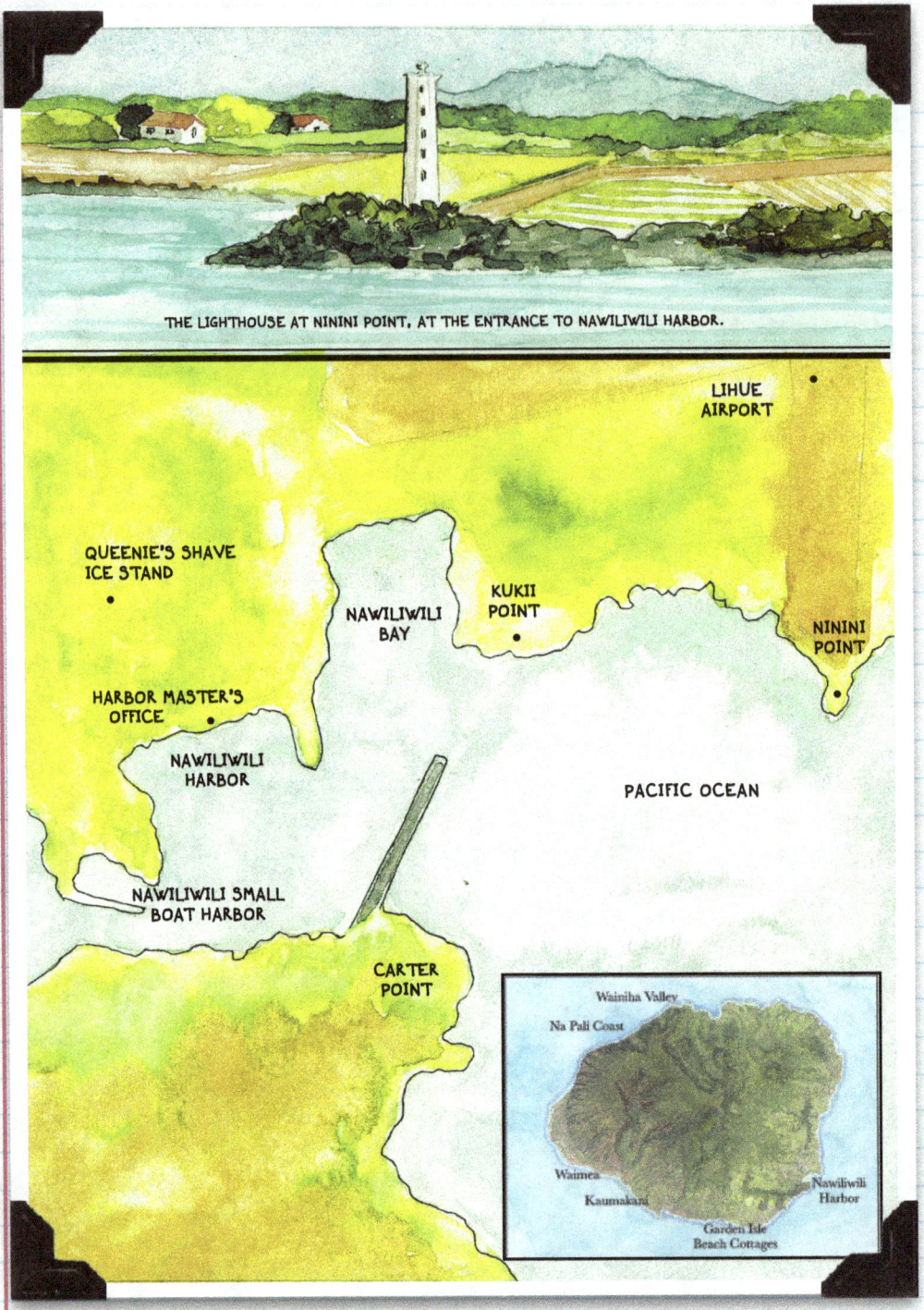

THE LIGHTHOUSE AT NININI POINT, AT THE ENTRANCE TO NAWILIWILI HARBOR.

LIHUE AIRPORT

QUEENIE'S SHAVE ICE STAND

NAWILIWILI BAY

KUKII POINT

NININI POINT

HARBOR MASTER'S OFFICE

NAWILIWILI HARBOR

PACIFIC OCEAN

NAWILIWILI SMALL BOAT HARBOR

CARTER POINT

Wainiha Valley

Na Pali Coast

Waimea

Kaumakani

Nawiliwili Harbor

Garden Isle Beach Cottages

The main harbor for Kauai, Nawiliwili, is on the southeast side of the island, next to the Lihue Airport.

Chapter VI

Nawiliwili and Beyond

June 26, 1968
Garden Isle Beach Cottages
Kauai, Hawaiian Islands

After thirteen days at sea, it was G who first spotted the sea gull on the bow of the *Silverado*, perched on the pulpit. Mr. Becker said that meant we were probably less than 30 miles from land. Everyone cheered and sure enough, a couple of hours later we were outside the Nawiliwili Harbor on the southeastern side of Kauai. Mr. Becker decided that it was probably best if we took the Zodiac ashore first and did a little investigating before bringing the *Silverado* all the way into the harbor. He wasn't even sure if it would fit in the area designated for small boats. Once we secured the Zodiac at the public dock, Mr. Becker and Tova went off to talk with the harbormaster and left me, Chuy and G to explore on our own. We made plans to meet them in two hours, back where we had tied up the Zodiac.

After almost two weeks of sailing, I can't tell you how weird it was to take those first steps on dry land — land that didn't move! My knees didn't seem to work quite right and I immediately started to laugh; so did G and Chuy. It felt great, but took some getting used to. We took off from the small boat harbor, walking up the hill, and started looking around. The first thing I noticed was that the air was different from anything I was used to. I mean, who notices air? But it felt like it was the same temperature as my skin and it was moist. It was like the air had substance which, I guess, it did with all those tiny particles of water. And it had a fragrance. Or a lot of them: part briny ocean smell, part flowery, part the way it smells back home right after it rains. The air itself made it feel like we were someplace much different from home — definitely someplace exotic. There were a lot of small businesses around the harbor: a place to rent kayaks, a couple of motels, several charter fishing companies, and right up ahead in front of us, a small corrugated tin shack with the sound of Aretha Franklin blaring out *"Think."* The shack had a sign on top that read "Queenie's Shave Ice."

"You want to try it?" I asked the guys.

"What is it?" asked Chuy.

We used the Zodiac to get back and forth from the sailboat to the public dock.

"Kind of like a snow cone, but different," I said.

"What's a snow cone?" asked G.

"Come on. You'll see," I said.

Little did any of us know what the seemingly simple decision to have a snow cone would set in motion. It changed everything.

There was a counter across the front of the shack and standing behind the counter was a skinny, white-haired woman, probably the same age as Grandma Hattie, wearing a tie-dyed muumuu. There was no wall under the counter so I could see she was standing on top of a plastic milk crate. Even with the milk crate, she didn't clear the top of the counter by all that much. As soon as she saw us stop on the sidewalk across from the shack, she started yelling "Step right up! Step right up! Don't be shy. Get the best shave ice in Kauai."

We all looked at each other and nodded, and walked over to the shack.

"Wottel' it be, boys?" she asked, leaning over the counter as best she could.

We looked at the hand-painted sign hanging on the front of the shack. Chuy and I decided on mango and G wanted pineapple. For an extra fifty cents you could get it topped with a scoop of vanilla ice cream, which sounded good to all of us. We placed our order and Queenie (at least I assumed she was Queenie) jumped off the milk crate and completely disappeared. While she was gone, Chuy elbowed me and said "check out the trophies," pointing to the back wall of the shack where there was shelf after shelf of silver and gold trophies of every imaginable size. A few minutes later, she reappeared and handed us the paper cones filled with shave ice and ice cream

"Thanks" Chuy said, taking his shave ice. "Nice trophies."

"Lifelong Kung-fu student," she said. "Number One in All-Island Competition ten years in a row. Maybe look old now, but still, don't mess with Queenie."

"I guess not," Chuy said, shaking his head.

"New in town?" she asked.

"Just arrived," I said.

"Where you from?"

"San Francisco."

"You the ones who came in on the *Silverado*?"

"How'd you know?" I asked incredulously.

"With these," she said, holding up a large pair of old, scuffed-up binoculars. "My late husband, rest his soul, was in the Hawaiian Territorial Home Guard during World War II. He taught me how to do surveillance. I keep my eye on anything that moves around here. I know everyone and everyone knows me."

"I'm Nick, by the way," I said, sticking out my hand, "Nick Sinclair. Now you know me too."

"I'm Kalani, but everyone calls me Queenie. That's because I'm related to the last Queen of Hawaii, Queen Liliuokalani. I'm her second cousin, four times removed. Who are your friends?"

"This is Jesus Martinez, but everyone knows him as Chuy, and this is G." I decided to leave off the "prince" part because it seemed like we were getting a little heavy on nicknames and royalty.

"Haole Menehune, eh? You know you're not the only one on this island," Queenie said, giving G the once over.

"What do you mean?" G asked.

"There're stories."

"Like what?"

"Like stories from long time ago. White Menehune showed up here from out of nowhere."

"Really?"

"Of course, really. Would I lie to you?"

"I have no idea. I don't even know you," G said, slightly perturbed.

I thought to myself that there was no way it was going to be this easy finding the gnomes and I was right. Just for the heck of it, though, I had to ask her, "You wouldn't happen to know where those white Menehune are, would you?"

"Who knows where any of the Menehune are? And besides, those white ones have been here so long they've probably turned brown by now," she said laughing. "Why are you so interested in the Menehune?"

"We're, ah, doing research on old Kauai for a school project."

"All the way from San Francisco aboard a fancy yacht to research old Kauai? What about that do you want me to believe?" she said chuckling. "Well, if that's your story and it's old Kauai you want to know about, you need to talk to my son."

"Why's that?" I asked.

"Because he's president of the Kauai Historical Society. Runs the museum in the library building in Lihue. No one on this island knows more about old Kauai than he does. Except me maybe. His name is Dr. Okole."

"Where's the museum?"

"You could throw a rock from here and practically hit it," she said, pointing north.

"Is it close enough to walk?"

"Not with that limp of yours. And Shorty over there, he's not exactly dressed for the tropics, is he?" she said, motioning with her head in G's direction, rolling her eyes at the same time. "He'd keel over from heat prostitution before he ever got there."

"You don't miss much, do you?" I said, "But I think it's 'heat prostration.'"

"I told you, I'm trained in surveillance. Not English pronunciation."

"Can I call for a cab somewhere?"

"You can't, but I can," she said, putting her fingers in her mouth and issuing one of the loudest whistles I've ever heard. She nodded her head in the direction of a huge banyan tree across the street. Sure enough, a few seconds later, a young man climbed out of the tree, ran across the road, and was standing next to us.

"This is my son-in-law, Kaliko, but everyone calls him Kal," Queenie said. "He drives a taxi."

"Nice to meet you, Kal," I said, shaking his hand, starting to feel a little left out in the nickname department. "Do you think you could drive me and my friends to the Historical Society?"

"Sure thing, boss."

I walked over to where Chuy and G were standing, working on their shave ices. I explained to them what was up and that we should at least take a quick look to see if the Historical Society had anything that might be of use to us. Besides, it would make good use of the short time we had before we were to meet up with Mr. Becker and Tova. They agreed. As we were walking toward Kal, G pulled on my sleeve and held me back. "Did she just call me 'Shorty'?" G asked.

"As a matter of fact, she did."

"What about her? That's kind of the pot calling the kettle black, isn't it? She's not that much taller than I am. At least I don't have to stand on a milk crate to make myself seen."

"Jeez, G. Let's not get into this right now. Don't forget about that black

Queenie's Shave Ice stand was a small shack next to the road that led from the harbor to downtown Lihue.

belt she has."

"Okay, okay," he said as we slid into the back seat of Kal's taxi. Just as we were about to take off, Queenie appeared from out of nowhere, sticking her head through the back window saying "If you see my granddaughter there, remind her she's supposed to take over the stand at 3, will you? She'd forget her head if it wasn't attached."

"Okay, I guess," I said as we pulled off and onto Rice Street. It only took about ten minutes to get there. "Is this it?" I asked Kal.

"Yeah, boss. Just go inside. They'll show you where the Historical Society is."

"Thanks," I said as G paid the fare, counting the money out carefully.

We walked inside and were greeted by a rush of cool air and a receptionist seated at a desk directly in front of us. I asked for Dr. Okole and she said "Room 3-G. Down to your left."

We walked down the hall and found Room 3-G which had "Kauai Historical Society" painted on its frosted glass window. I knocked on the door and a female voice said "Come in."

We walked inside what looked like a large classroom. The walls were lined with wooden file boxes and flat files and metal bookcases everywhere. The room had a cluttered look to it, like whoever was in charge was trying to fit too much stuff into a too-small space.

"Hi," I said to a rather remarkable-looking teenage girl. She was about my height, had long brown and blond dreads past her shoulders and was wearing a Jimi Hendrix t-shirt with what looked like a ten-foot-long knitted scarf around her neck in every color and pattern imaginable. She was very tan and had startling green eyes.

"Ah, we're looking for Dr. Okole."

"That's my dad. He just stepped out down the hall. He'll be back in a flash. Can I help you?"

"Well, I'm Nick and these are my friends Chuy and G."

"Far out," she said, looking at G. "Nice to meet you. I'm Mad. Don't take that the wrong way. I'm not mad but I am Mad. It's short for Madison." Now I was definitely feeling left out for not having a nickname. But what was the point of having a name, if everyone was just going to call you something else? Nothing came out of either G's or Chuy's mouth; they just stood there, wide-eyed, looking at Mad until she broke the awkward silence.

"What can I help you with? I give my dad a hand around here."

"Ah, yeah. We just arrived from the States. We're here to do some re-search on Old Kauai for a school project. Actually we met your grandmother and she told us to come here. Oh, and before I forget, she asked me to remind you that you're supposed to relieve her at 3."

"You met my tutu? Isn't she a trip?"

"I'll say," I heard G say under his breath.

"'Old Kauai' is kind of a broad subject. Is there something specific you were looking for?" she said, looking directly at G.

"Menehune, actually," I said.

"Why doesn't that surprise me?" she said, still looking at G. "Well, you've come to the right place. We have a whole section devoted to the 'legendary little people of Kauai'."

Just then Mad's dad walked through the door and she introduced us all around and told him what we were looking for.

"You'll have to excuse the confusion, but the Historical Society is under-going a reorganization. The library was kind enough to loan us this room while we look for a permanent home for our collection, which, by the way, goes back to 1914. But Mad's right, we have quite a bit on the Menehune. I'll show you where it is. We followed Dr. Okole, heading to the back of the room. I let Chuy and G go first through the narrow aisles between the shelves of books and Mad and I brought up the rear. Just as we were passing a large, messy desk with Dr. Okole's name plate on the front of it, G stopped suddenly and stared at something on the doctor's desk.

"What is it, G?" I said, coming up beside him.

"Um, I'm not sure. I'll tell you later."

We caught up with Chuy and Dr. Okole without saying anything more. "Here it is," said Dr. Okole, motioning to two long bookshelves along the back wall of the room. "It's arranged in alphabetical order by the author's name. It's not how it should be done — it should be arranged by subject matter — but we're getting there. That's what Mad's helping with. Making things easier to find. Speaking of which, can I help you find something specific?"

"Ah, I'm not sure," I said, "and we're a little short on time today. But it's good to know all this... this... information is here. Can we come back another time and look through it?"

"Of course. That's what we're here for. Come back any time. We're open from 10 to 4, Monday through Friday. Where are you off to now?"

"Back to the harbor."

"Don't you have to relieve Tutu, Mad?"

"Yeah."

"Then why don't you give these guys a lift? You've got time."

"Sure. Thanks, Dad."

We all thanked Dr. Okole and followed Mad out the back of the library to the parking lot. The sudden blast of heat and humidity took my breath away.

"Arggh!" Mad said, as she unwound the long scarf from around her neck. "I hate air conditioning! I practically freeze to death in that place. Here we are."

Where we were was in front of a white Volkswagen bug convertible with the top down.

"Cool," Chuy said. "Shotgun."

G looked at me, not understanding.

"It means he wants to ride in the front passenger seat," I explained.

"Okay, I get it. I guess," G said as we slid into the back seat.

"How long have you had your license?" Chuy asked Mad.

"Just got it. But don't worry. I've been driving since my feet could reach the pedals. Put your seat belt on. The harbor, right?"

We took off from the parking lot and made our way down to the harbor. Mad was right: She was a good driver. I don't even know how to drive a stick shift yet. We all got out of the car and thanked her.

"Where you guys staying?"

"At the Garden Isle Beach Cottages."

"Oh, yeah. That's a cool spot."

Chuy walked over to me and whispered in my ear "can we invite her to

Mad's dad had a cool Volkswagen "bug" convertible that she got to drive.

dinner?"

"Sure," I said. "I don't see why not. JP is always looking for good eaters. Hey Mad, you want to come to dinner tonight?"

"I can do that," she said, putting the bug into reverse. "What time?"

"Ish-ish," that's what our friend who does the cooking says," I said.

"Groovy. Ish-ish it is, then. On the dot," she said smiling. "See you then."

We waved her off, with Chuy looking very pleased with himself.

We got to the harbormaster's office just as Mr. Becker and Tova were walking out the front door.

"How'd it go?" I asked.

"Good. We're all registered and legit now. How'd it go for you guys?"

"Most excellent," Chuy said.

"We got a lot done in a couple of hours. What now?" I asked.

"Let's get back on board and get our stuff. Then we should check in at the Garden Isle, don't you think?"

"Sounds like a plan," I said.

. . .

We had to make a few trips back and forth in the Zodiac to get all our stuff onto the dock. On the last one, Chad waved goodbye and headed back to the *Silverado*, leaving all of us standing on the dock.

"Now what?" Mr. Becker asked.

"Now we get a cab. I'll be right back." Considering I couldn't whistle like Queenie, I walked up the hill and over to the big banyan tree. I called up and, sure enough, Kal answered and scrambled down the tree.

"Can you give me and my friends a ride to the Garden Isle Beach Cottages? Everyone's down at the harbor with their gear."

"Sure thing."

"If you don't mind me asking, Kal, how come you sit in that tree?"

"Because it's the only place around here where I can sit down in the shade, other than next to Queenie's shack."

"So why don't you sit over there?"

"Queenie says I'm so ugly I'd scare off customers."

"Got it," I said, thinking that Mad was right: Queenie was a trip.

We got in the taxi and drove down to the harbor and loaded everyone up. There was so much luggage that Kal had to use a bungee cord to keep the trunk closed. Mr. Becker and Tova seemed impressed that I knew how to find a taxi, not to mention where to find the taxi driver.

Both Grandma Hattie and Mad were right: 1) the Garden Isle Beach Cottages were close to the harbor and 2) like Mad said, it was a very cool place. It had been built in the 1940s, after World War II. It was a series of individual, one-story white cottages with dark brown shingled roofs, set in a lush, dense garden that opened up on the south side to a wide, flat beach and a big, placid horseshoe bay, like a giant "U." It was beautiful. Our three cottages were next to each other all in a row. Chuy, G and I took the first one, JP was in the middle, and Mr. Becker and Tova took the last one on the right. Each cottage had a covered front porch that overlooked the bay and the Pacific beyond. Inside, the rooms were cool and dark, paneled in knotty pine, just like my room back at Ma-D's and Walter's. I felt right at home as soon as I walked in. There were no televisions in the rooms and no telephones. Each cottage had a bedroom, living room, bathroom, and a small efficiency kitchen. There were also couches to sleep on in the living room.

Chuy and G took dibs on the twin beds in the bedroom which left me to sleep on one of the daybeds in the living room, which was fine by me. Eventually I learned that a daybed, or a couch for sleeping, was called a *punee* in Hawaiian, pronounced "poo-nay." I walked out on the front porch. The view of the ocean was something else; no doubt about it, we were in paradise. I looked to my right and saw JP standing on his front porch.

"Whaddaya' think?" I shouted.

"Pinch me. Is this for real?"

"I know. Great, huh?"

"I don't think I'm in Kansas City any more. I'm about to take off for the grocery store. Any requests?"

"None that I can think of. No, wait a minute. Can you get us some Nescafe?"

"Crunchy coffee?" John replied with mock horror. "I didn't know anyone drank that stuff."

"When you make it with milk instead of water, it's really good. Chuy taught me."

"Whatever you say."

"Oh, I almost forgot. We invited someone for dinner tonight. Is that okay?"

"Of course. Is she cute?"

I laughed. "Better ask Chuy that."

"I get it. See you in awhile. Dinner is at . . ."

"Ish-ish, I know."

•   •   •

I went back inside the cottage and was starting to unpack the few clothes I brought when I realized that with all the activity I'd forgotten two things: First, I hadn't thought about Nigel Stayne once. Like I said before, I half expected him to be standing on the dock when we arrived, but he was nowhere to be seen, thank goodness. It was a relief not to have thought about him for a day, but even so, I couldn't help but wonder what he was up to. The second thing I forgot was to call Grandma Hattie. I remembered seeing a pay phone on a wooden post in the garden next to the Garden Isle office, so I walked over there and placed a collect call to her. Doyle answered the phone and said that Grandma was out playing bridge. He wanted to know how the trip across the Pacific had been and what Kauai was like. I did my best to give him the headlines and then told him to tell Grandma that I'd call her next Sunday, like she'd asked, and then we rang off, as Doyle liked to say. As I walked back to the cottage, I felt like San Francisco was a million miles away and a part of someone else's life.

•   •   •

We all met at JP's cottage around 6:30, including Mad, who fit right in like she'd known everyone for years. Before serving dinner, JP asked whether or not she was a vegetarian. Mad said she wasn't.

"Whew. That's a relief," JP said, "I don't think I could have made myself shoot a plant."

Mad gave JP a double-take and then laughed. "You're funny," she said.

JP had made what he called a "picnic supper:" fried chicken, potato salad, sliced tomatoes and pickled green beans, not to mention brownies for dessert. So far there was one thing for certain: JP was a great cook.

He told us that the grocer told him that the chickens on Kauai were feral — wild, free to go wherever they wanted — descendants of the first chickens brought to the island by the Polynesians, some 800 years ago.

"I don't think Chuy or G remember, but I read them something on the trip here: 'fun facts about Kauai,'" I said. "Those chickens are Kauai's unofficial 'birds of paradise'."

"Well, whatever they are, they're skinny little things, but they pack a lot of punch, don't they?" We all agreed. "And you know what the girl checker said to me when I was paying for the groceries? 'I'm going to sock it to you for 36 dollars and 72 cents.' That was a first. She had a blond ponytail and was wearing cowgirl boots. I'm going back tomorrow. She can sock it to me for whatever she wants. Oh yeah, and I've got a question for you, Mad."

"What's that?"

"There was a notice on the bulletin board at the store for a fund-raiser for some guy running for city council. It said there was going to be live music and 'heavy pupus.' I'm almost afraid to ask. What are 'heavy pupus?'"

Mad laughed and said "I believe you on the Mainland would say 'substantial appetizers.'"

"I get it," JP said, "more than chips and dip and less than a pot roast."

"You've got it," Mad said.

During dinner we learned that Mad only ate standing up and, while she might not have been a vegetarian, she usually ate only white food. She was making an exception tonight because she said JP's food looked and smelled so good. To say she was unusual would be an understatement. JP tried to get her to take seconds, but she said she was "pau."

"Pow?" Chuy asked.

"Yeah. It's Hawaiian for 'done.' It's spelled p - a - u."

After dinner, Mr. Becker and Tova told us "youngsters" to go outside while they did the dishes and talked to JP. We went out onto the front porch where there were plenty of chairs. Even Mad sat down. The sky was just getting dark and the sound of the waves lapping on the shore was gentle and rhythmic. JP followed us out onto the porch, carrying an empty plastic water bottle with the top cut off. He walked down to the beach and put some sand in the bottom. Then he reached into his pocket and pulled out a candle and stuck it in the sand. He walked back to the porch and handed it to me and said, "Here, you might need this. My own version of a hurricane lamp."

"Cool," I said, putting it on the table between the chairs. "Will you light it?"

"Sure," JP said. "Just remember to blow it out when you leave," he said, going back inside.

"Is there anything you can't make?" Mad asked him.

Through the screen door he said "I can make just about anything except money," he said, laughing.

"No offense, but it doesn't look like you missed many meals lately," she said, smiling.

"No offense taken. As I told the boys, I've been working on the perfect pear-shape for some time now."

"You're a man of many talents, JP," she said.

"Mahalo," he said and went back into the cottage.

"Funny guy," Mad said.

"Great guy," I replied.

"So how long are you going to be here?" Mad asked.

Without even thinking, I blurted out "until we find what we're looking for."

"And what would that be?" Mad asked.

I looked at G and Chuy and they both indicated that I should tell Mad the story, which I did, or at least a shortened version of it.

"Far out," she said when I was finished. "I can tell you one thing."

"What's that?" G asked.

"You're not going to find what you're looking for at the Historical Society. You've already found the best thing there: that would be me. I know as much about this island as anyone. And if anyone can help you find that wizard guy, it's me."

"Will you help us?" asked Chuy, coming right to the point.

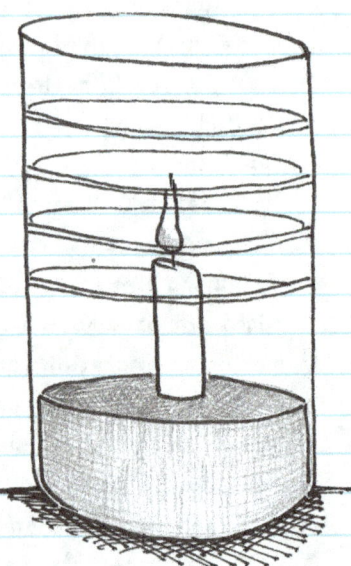

JP's homemade version of a hurricane lamp using a plastic water bottle and damp sand.

"Well, considering it's summer vacation, I've got the time. I help dad at the Historical Society and tutu at the stand, but not every day. Normally, I'd be in summer school by now, but I did so well in school last year, dad let me off the hook."

"How well?" I asked.

"How well what?" Mad said.

"How well did you do in school?"

"I got a 4.2."

Chuy whistled and then said "A 4.2? How'd you do that? A 4.0 is straight A's."

"Ever hear of extra credit?" she said, smiling at Chuy.

"What about your mom?" Chuy asked. "You haven't mentioned her."

"She and my dad got divorced a long time ago. She lives in San Diego now. I visit her every once in awhile. San Diego's okay but I like it here better. This is home. Guess it always will be."

"If I'm not being rude, where'd the green eyes come from?" Chuy asked.

"Yeah, wild, huh?" Mad said. "My mom has a 'Plantation Pedigree'. That's what they call a combination of Chinese, Portugese, Japanese and native Hawaiian around here. It was the ethnic make-up of most of the plantation workers back when. My mom's family were all plantation work-ers. To answer your question, I'm guessing my green eyes are from some Portugese ancestor."

"Sorry for interrupting but what's that?" I said, pointing to the spit of land on the right side of the horseshoe bay."

"What's what?" G asked.

"Just wait a minute, you'll see it." Sure enough it appeared again, a small white light that seemed to dance along the beach for a stretch and then disappear, only to reappear again.

"Somebody walking with a flashlight?" Chuy surmised.

"No, it's going too fast." I said.

"It's Pokee, he's riding his bicycle to check his set lines." Mad said.

"Who's Pokee and what's a 'set line'?" I asked.

"Pokee's, well, Pokee's a long story. But he lives out there on the point. And a set line is a fishing line with a lot of hooks on it, with floats attached to it to keep it on top of the water. It's kind of like a massive fishing pole without the pole, if you catch my drift. The line's attached to the shore so it doesn't float away. They're illegal, but nobody seems to bother Pokee much," Mad said.

"Wow. You really *do* know this island, don't you?" Chuy said.

"What can I say? It's a small island. Tutu says you can't fart..."

"... 'without someone else smelling it.' Yeah, we say that in our valley, too," I said.

"If you guys are done with the potty jokes," G said, "there's something else."

"What's that?" Mad asked.

"When we were at the Historical Society today I happened to see something on your father's desk."

"Like what?"

"A thin piece of wood, not that big, with markings carved into it."

"Oh, yeah, that. I think a teacher from Waimea Canyon Middle School brought it in. Kai Alana. That's his name."

"Did he say anything about it?"

"Just said a student brought it in for him to take a look at."

"Is there any way I could take a closer look at it?" G asked.

"Probably. Let me see what I can do."

"What do you think it is, G?" I asked.

"I'm not sure. I didn't see up close. Could be nothing."

"Or?"

"Or it could be our first clue."

After walking through what was basically a jungle, coming on Pokee's tidy house in a sunny clearing came as a surprise.

Chapter VII

Fright in the Night, Fright in the Light

June 27, 1968
Kauai, Hawaiian Islands

When I woke up, I was already sitting straight up in bed. My heart was beating like crazy. I was sweating and actually shaking. I've never been so scared in my life.

The room was dark except for some pale light coming through the sheer curtains on the garden side of the cottage. I looked at the electric clock on the table next to my bed: 3:02 a.m. I knew what had scared me so much, but I couldn't think about it yet. Should I lie back down? No, that felt too vulnerable. Should I get up and walk around? Not by myself. Definitely not. What if she was still out there somewhere? Instead, I just sat there and pulled the sheet tight around my chest and tried to stop shaking.

"Do you always sleep sitting up?" Chuy asked.

"Huh?" I said, trying to figure out where I was.

"Rise and shine. It's another day in paradise."

"What time is it?"

"7:30."

"Oh, man," I said, rubbing my face with both hands.

"Are you okay?"

"I'll tell you in a few."

I guess I'd fallen back asleep again, sitting up. It was all slowly coming back to me, whether I wanted it to or not. "Are you making coffee?"

"Yeah, want one?"

"Please. I need something." Without my trying or wanting to, images of last night's dream started popping up in my brain.

"Are you sure you're okay?" Chuy asked.

"Not really. I had this weird dream last night. Scared the crap out of me."

"Like what?"

"Like an unusually tall woman in a pale robe talking to me."

"That's it?"

"Not exactly. She didn't have a head."

"Whaaaaaat?"

"You heard me. She didn't have a head."

"Then how did she talk to you?"

"I have no idea. I don't even know what she said to me, but it seemed like a warning. Man, I am freaked out. I think I'll take a shower."

"Let's go swimming instead," Chuy said.

The thought of swimming in the ocean sounded like a good idea. It's times like these that I was glad to have a friend like Chuy, someone who knew more than I did about what might make things better. Little did either of us know what we were walking into, and I'm not talking about the ocean. We changed, grabbed our towels and coffees and walked the few steps from the cottage to the beach. There were a few early-risers here and there, sitting on towels, enjoying the early morning view. It was already warm and slightly humid. Like the first day we all arrived in Kauai, I was aware of the air again which, as strange as that was, felt comforting against my bare skin, almost like I was swimming through it. It was good to be outside in the sunlight.

Chuy and I put our towels on the beach and ran into the water. Fantastic. We both ran and slid into the water, bouncing up through the waves, laughing. Definitely better than a shower inside. By the time we got back to our towels, there was an older couple next to us, drinking coffee from a Thermos. We started talking to them and learned they had been coming to the Garden Isle for over twenty years.

"Where you from?" they asked.

"San Francisco."

"How about you?"

"Portland. Practically neighbors."

We all laughed. "Has this place changed much over the years?"

"Hardly at all. That's what we like about it," the woman said.

"Except for that monstrosity over there," he said, pointing left to a large, modern, multi-story hotel at the end of the point. "They started building it a couple of years ago. When they were excavating for the foundation they found some human bones and brought in some local Kauaiian natives. No question about it, the construction workers had uncovered an ancient burial ground, sacred to the native Kauaiians. The developers assured the locals that they'd put the burial ground back to the way it was and build the hotel on another part of the property. Believe it or not, right after that they brought in three big earthmovers and completely decimated the site during the night when no one was around to see what they were doing. There was a big stink about it, law-suits on both sides, but in the end the developers got what they wanted and the hotel was built. That's when it started."

"When what started?" I asked.

"These islands have mysterious ways. As beautiful as they are, a lot of strange things seem to go on here."

"Like what?" Chuy asked.

"Well, the developers sited the entrance of the hotel to take advantage of one of the largest banyan trees on the island. It became the focal point of the hotel, shading most of the huge front lawn, the sidewalk leading to the front doors and the big u-shaped driveway that led to the entrance. The tree was that big. And then, right after the hotel opened, thousands of mynah birds started roosting in the tree every evening and spent the night there, every night. The noise they made was deafening and the amount of shi . . . poop they produced was enormous and everywhere. Nothing the hotel staff did could scare the mynah birds off and it was just impossible to com-pletely clean the poop off every morning. The hotel had to close its doors a month after it opened. But not before something else started happening

The banyan tree in front of the new hotel was one of the largest on the island. Note the human figure to the left of the trunk to get an idea of how enormous it was.

that really put the nail in the coffin. There's talk now that the place is going be bulldozed and the point will return to the way it was. Like I said, this place has mysterious ways."

"What else started happening?" I asked.

"Talk started that the hotel was haunted. And the word spread fast."

"Haunted?"

"Yeah. Dozens of guests reported seeing a headless woman at the foot of their beds in the middle of the night, threatening them."

Some noise came out of my mouth, but I'm not sure what it was. Chuy took one look at me and said to the couple, "Good talking with you. I just realized we're late for an appointment. Hope to see you again," and grabbed me by the arm and led me back to the cottage. When we got there there was a note taped to the front door. Chuy sat me down on one of the chairs on the front porch.

"What the hell was that about, Nick? It had to be some kind of a coincidence. Right? Things like that just don't happen."

"Well, it just did. I think I'm going to throw up," I said.

"Please don't. Look, there's a note here from Mad. She's says she'll pick us up at 11."

Just then G walked out of the front screened door. "What's happening guys? Have you already been swimming?"

"Yeah, and a lot more," Chuy said.

"I think I'm going to take that shower," I said.

"Good idea," Chuy said, "are you sure you're okay?"

"What's wrong with Nick? What's going on?" G said, looking thoroughly confused.

While I was in the shower, Chuy explained to G what had happened, who didn't seem all that surprised or shocked.

"I always thought he was unusually tuned to vibrations, especially for an Uplander," I overheard him tell Chuy.

"So what are you saying?" I yelled from the bathroom.

"I'm not surprised that if someone you'd call 'supernatural' was trying to communicate a message to us, they'd use you to do it. Did you remember what she said?"

"I can't remember the specifics, but it felt like a warning."

"I've got a bad feeling about this... " G said, shaking his head.

Just as I was coming out of the bathroom and Mad was coming through the front door we both said "bad feeling about what?" at the same time.

Mad sat down in the living room and asked what was going on. Chuy explained what had happened and she was silent for a minute and then said "I think you had a visit from Madam Pele. People who she's visited sometimes describe her as not having a face or being headless."

"Madam Pele?" Chuy asked.

"Who's Madam Pele?" I asked.

"I forget, you're not from around here. Everyone on the islands knows who Madam Pele is. Legend has it that Madam Pele, who's the goddess of fire, lightning, wind and, most importantly, volcanoes, was the creator of the Hawaiian Islands. I probably shouldn't say this, but she's kind of a brat. She changes her mind a lot, throws tantrums, and generally does whatever she wants, no matter who it hurts. She has a bunch of brothers and sisters she's always fighting with, all of whom have supernatural powers, and she's very protective of the Menehune. She can start anything on fire just by looking at it and cause a volcano to erupt with the snap of her fingers. Oh, and she gets really ticked off if anyone takes anything — even a tiny rock — off the island. I'm not saying I believe in her or not, but I definitely wouldn't want to get on her bad side."

"What's with the headless bit?" I asked.

"I guess she doesn't want to be seen. Or maybe she just likes scaring people."

"Well, she's good for that." I said.

"How are you feeling?" Mad asked.

"All right, I guess. A little shaky."

"What do you say to getting out of here? There are a couple of things I wanted to show you."

"Sure, just let me get dressed." A few minutes later we were piling into Mad's bug. Chuy took the front passenger seat. Apparently he thought calling "shotgun" yesterday gave him permanent rights to sit there. I should mention that my idea about G seemed to be working: namely, that if we treated him normally, other people, like in public, would too. Of course the fact that he was dressed in normal clothes and had a... what had Grandma Hattie called it? "A normal young man's haircut" helped. To tell you the truth, when we were all out together, more people stared at Mad's dreads than at G. It made me feel a little better that at least something was working out.

"Where we going?" I asked.

"I thought I'd show you the Menehune Fish Pond. I don't know if it will do any good, but it's one of our major tourist attractions. Kauai is the oldest of all the Hawaiian Islands and we have a lot of legends, more than anyone else. And the Menehune Fish Pond is one of the most important ones."

About fifteen minutes later we arrived at a wide spot off the side of the Hulemalu Road that overlooked the ancient fish pond. To tell you the truth, it wasn't all that impressive: just a big pond surrounded by a bunch of green shrubs.

"So what makes it so special?" I asked Mad.

"For starters, it's about 1000 years old. It's not just any old pond. See on the left there? That's an opening that allows water from the stream to fill the pond. It used to have a slatted wooden gate there with openings in the slats that would allow small fish to enter the pond. The pond was rich with the food fish eat, so the fish quickly grew so large that they couldn't swim back through the slatted gate. So it became a small pond with a lot of big fish that were easy to catch. Ingenious, actually. The thing that makes it special is that it's completely lined with cut lava stones: 2,700 feet around the outside of the pond, five feet tall. And back then, the native Hawaiians who lived here didn't have the ability to cut stone. So, the question is who built it? Legend says it was the Menehune who built the whole thing in one night, by forming a line 25 miles long and passing the stones hand-to-hand, from the village of Makaweli to the pond here."

"Sounds like a tall tale to me," Chuy said.

"Not at all," G said. "It's completely do-able."

"In one night?" Chuy asked.

"No problem — if you're a gnome, or a Menehune, or whatever you want to call us. It's one of our specialties."

"Oh, jeez, this is all getting a little out there," Chuy said.

Sensing the tension, Mad abruptly said "who's hungry?"

Apparently we all were because we all answered yes.

"Climb in. Let's go," Mad said. A short ride later we were sitting on the covered porch of Bubba's Burgers, chowing down on "Double Bubba" burgers. Mad had a friend who worked there who made her a special "white bowl" - made up of steamed rice, sliced hard-boiled egg, and melted mozzarella cheese. I thought it was a little strange, but Mad said it was good.

"What about the yellow egg yolk?" I asked.

"I close my eyes when I eat it," she said.

When we were all finished, but still picking at the last of the French fries,

To all of our eyes, the crayon rubbing of the cartouche was pretty darn mysterious.

Chuy said, "I'm not trying to be critical, but Nick's brush with Madam Pele and our knowing about the legend of the fish pond isn't getting us any closer to finding Dagywn. I feel like we're spinning our wheels here. What about that thing G saw on your dad's desk, the thing he said might be a clue?"

"As it happens, I have it right here," Mad said, pulling a folded piece of paper out of her back pocket. "Well, not it, but a rubbing of it. I was just about to show G, as soon as he wipes the grease off his hands."

"A 'rubbing'?" Chuy asked.

"Yeah, we do it all the time at the Historical Society. All you need is a piece of paper and a flat crayon. You put the paper over what you want copied and just rub the flat side of the crayon over it and, poof, an instant copy. Comes in handy on gravestones."

"That's a cheery thought," Chuy said.

"Can I see it?" I asked.

"Sure," Mad said.

The image, in black crayon, was surrounded by a long and narrow rectangle with rounded corners, just about filling the standard piece of typing paper, from top to bottom. Inside the top part of the rectangle were stick symbols that reminded me of something I'd seen before but couldn't remember where. On the bottom half there was another, smaller rectangle, also with rounded corners, with more markings in it that looked nothing like letters, at least not like any I'd ever seen. None of it meant anything to me.

I handed it to G. Chuy stood up and looked over his shoulder.

"You know what it says?" Chuy asked.

"No, like I told you, we don't have a written language but the image below is what we call a cartouche: basically a signature made out of symbolic writing. I don't recognize it and as a member of our tribe, it's my duty to be able to recognize every other member of the tribe's cartouche and who it belongs to. It could belong to someone of another tribe," G said.

"Like the Menehunes?"

"Maybe. There can be as many differences as there are similarities between one gnome tribe and another. I suppose it's possible that they could use the same cartouche system as we do."

"Wait a minute, wait a minute," I said. "How old were you when Dagywn and the others jumped ship here in Kauai?"

"I'm not sure, but around 40 or 50," G said.

"And one of our years equal ten of yours, right?"

"Close enough."

"So, in our years, you were between 4 and 5 years old when it happened."

"Yeah, what are you getting at?"

"Would you even remember what Dagywn's and the others' cartouches looked like if you were that young?"

"No, not really. We aren't required to memorize everyone's until we're 100 years old. Ten years old by your way of counting."

"So that cartouche you're looking at could be Dagywn's or belong to one of the other guys who jumped ship, right?"

"You're right, it could be. Or it could be some random Menehune's."

"So we don't know what the writing says and we don't know who the cartouche belongs to. Is that where we're at?" Chuy asked.

"Looks like it," I said.

"Guys, guys, wait a minute. There may be someone who can help us," Mad said excitedly.

"Who?" we all said in unison.

"Remember last night when I said Pokee was a 'long story?' Well, part of his story is that he's an anthropological linguist. He studies different cultures' languages. Rumor has it that he's been working with the Menehune, but no one knows for sure because he's such a hermit. He practically never leaves his farm out there on the point and he's not very keen on having visitors. I went there once with dad when I was like seven years old. I remember him carrying me down the trail to Pokee's house because the whole place was booby-trapped to keep people out. But if anyone is going to know what that writing says, it's going to be him."

"Can we go see him?" I asked.

"That's what I'm trying to figure out. It's not that easy. He doesn't have a phone. I suppose I could write him a letter, but who knows how long that would take or if he'd even answer it. And I'm guessing he's still got the place booby-trapped, which I have no idea of how to deal with."

"What if we arrived by water?" I asked.

"What? Like swim there?"

"No. We've got a Zodiac we could use."

"Really?"

"Yeah, I just have to ask Mr. Becker, but I'm pretty sure he'll say yes."

"What are we waiting for?" G asked and we all piled into the bug and drove to the harbor. I had the harbormaster contact the *Silverado* via his ship-to-shore two-way radio and it didn't take long for Mike, one of the deckhands, to arrive at the dock in the Zodiac. We all got in and motored back to the *Silverado* where I talked with Mr. Becker, who was making some repairs to one of the winches. He gave his okay for me to use the Zodiac, telling me to be careful and to make sure everyone wore a life vest. We have a Zodiac at school and I've spent quite a bit of time with it so I felt comfortable operating it. I told him we'd be back in three hours or so.

Everyone got their life jackets on and we shoved off from the *Silverado* and headed west to Hanakappa Bay. I figured it was about 15 miles away and shouldn't take us much more than a half an hour. It was too choppy and windy for any of us to talk while we skirted along the coast, but just as we were arriving in Hanakappa Bay, Mad made a cutting motion across her neck for me to kill the engines, which I did.

"Can we go someplace calm so we can talk for a minute?"

I said sure and found a little protected cove and dropped anchor. I was surprised when it hit bottom so fast. The water was probably less than eight feet deep, bright turquoise and perfectly clear.

"What's up?" I asked.

"Before we go charging over there we should probably have some kind of a plan and I need to explain a few things," Mad said.

"Okay," I said. "Shoot."

"First off, once we get to Pokee's place, I think I should lead the group. I know it was a long time ago but I've been there before and there's a chance he'll remember me, or at least my dad."

We all agreed that was a good idea.

"And you should know a little something about Pokee. Like I said, he's pretty much a hermit and studies linguistics, but he's also kind of an electronics nut. I remember there being like twelve reel-to-reel tape recorders in his house and a shortwave radio and a bunch of other gear. But the big scoop is that his mother was a direct descendent of Madam Pele — sorry Nick — and his father a Menehune, or at least that's the gossip. Mixed race people are pretty much the norm all over Hawaii, but someone whose mother is related to a goddess and whose father's a Menehune, well, that's unusual."

"Wow. He's carrying quite the load," Chuy said. "No wonder he prefers to live alone."

"Okay. So that's it. Shall we go?" Mad asked.

Suddenly I wasn't nearly as excited about meeting Pokee as I had been, but I pulled up the anchor and started the engine anyway, and headed across the bay. Once we reached the spit of land on the far side of the horseshoe bay, I beached the Zodiac and Mad took the lead, yelling "Pokee" though cupped hands. Less than a minute later, sure enough, there he was standing in front of us, aiming a shotgun right at Mad. A short old bald guy wearing nothing but a pair of khaki shorts.

"Stop where you are or I'll shoot," Pokee said, not lowering the gun.

"Whoa, Pokee, it's me, Mad, Madison Okole, Dr. Okole's daughter. It was a long time ago, but we've met before, remember?"

"Of course I remember," Pokee said irritably, "what the hell you doing here now? I didn't invite you."

"No, no you didn't. But my friends here are in need of your services, so I decided to take a chance and just drop in."

"That was a stupid thing to do. I could have shot you." With that, he lowered the shotgun, which seemed like progress to me. Big progress.

"I know, but my friends are on a mission and it's kind of important."

"Well, don't just stand there. Follow me," he said.

We started off across the beach and Mad turned around and rolled her eyes at us. *Lord knows what we were getting ourselves into,* I thought to myself. I'll bet the others were thinking the same thing.

We followed Pokee up to the edge of what could only be called a jungle and maneuvered a very narrow path through the dense growth. After about five minutes of walking we came into a clearing with a small, low-slung house with a corrugated tin roof, surrounded by a tidy vegetable garden with mango and papaya trees here and there, hanging with ripe fruit. There was a small barn on the right with pigs in a pen and there were chickens everywhere, including a big rooster on the roof of the house, crowing. All things considered, it was a pretty idyllic scene.

Pokee led us around to the back of the house where a huge banyan tree shaded a stone patio, covered in bright green moss, that stepped down to a rushing creek. It was cool back there, made even cooler by the sound of the water running in the creek. It seemed like we were surrounded by every imaginable shade of green, glints of sunlight winking here and there through the tall canopy of foliage. Pokee leaned his shotgun next to the back door of the house, apparently having decided we weren't a threat, at least not one he had to shoot. He sat down in a wooden chair next to a small table, pulled a pipe out of his pocket and said "I'm afraid there's no place to sit. I don't have visitors," at which point Mad sat herself down on the stone patio in one smooth, effortless motion. The rest of us looked at each other and did the same thing, more or less. I felt like we were students sitting at the feet of the master which, I guess we kind of were. He filled his pipe with tobacco from a small leather pouch and then, to my amazement, snapped his fingers and produced a flame which he used to light his pipe. I looked around to see if anyone else had noticed, but it didn't look like they had. This was getting freaky.

"We won't take up much of your time, Pokee. I know how you like your privacy. But we were wondering if you could help us," Mad said.

"With what?"

Mad explained about the rubbing she had made from the piece of wood. Pokee asked how she came to take possession of the wooden carving, who found it, where it was found, how long ago and on and on. It was like he was a detective or something. Finally he asked to see it. Mad stood up and took the folded piece of paper from her pocket and handed it to him.

"Hmmmmmm... " was all he said. "And what would you like me to do with this?"

"Translate it," G said.

Pokee looked over the top of his glasses and said "And who are you?"

"G," he said.

"Oh, I'm sorry," Mad said, "I didn't introduce anyone. Well, you've met G now, and this is Chuy and Nick."

The introductions didn't seem to matter much to Pokee. Instead he looked straight at G and said "you're no Menehune."

"No sir, I'm not."

"Then who are you? Who are your people?"

"I'm from a tribe originally from Scandinavia: the Åland Islands. About a hundred years ago, an exploratory team, of which I was a member, left the Åland Islands to look for a better place to live. To make a long story short, the ship on which we were sailing made a stop here in Kauai and our wizard and four others jumped ship. We were not able to find them and so we sailed on to San Francisco from whence we continued to a spot on Mt. St. Helena in the Napa Valley. A few months ago, my father, King Gob, sent us on this mission to find our wizard and return with him, and hopefully the others as well, to the Napa Valley."

None of G's story seemed to surprise Pokee in the slightest. Or, if it did, he wasn't showing it.

"And you think this rubbing has something to do with your missing wizard?"

"Yes... or at least it's possible it does," G said.

"All right, let me make this brief. Since you're here, Mad has obviously explained I'm an anthropological linguist. Many years ago I became aware that the Menehune here on Kauai had a rudimentary written language, something I'm sure your friend G here knows most gnome tribes don't have. Most gnome groups are similar to other old Norse cultures, which were strictly oral. They told their stories by speaking them, sometimes in song — 'spoken down,' as we linguists say. What little writing they had was Runic, usually carved into wood, stone, or bone. Which is what makes the Menehune unusual. They took their Rune writing a step further than other tribes. Being part Menehune myself, I had some access to their so-called 'records,' and I've been working on translating them ever since. My work is limited, however, because once the Menehune found out I was related to Madam Pele — which I'm sure Mad has also told you — they didn't want to associate with me. They revere Madam Pele as much as any other intelligent person living on the island does, but she can be very unpredictable and dangerously destructive. They knew that anywhere I went there was always going to be the chance that she wouldn't be far behind, just to see what I was up to. So they stopped letting me visit them."

"Does that mean you can't translate the rubbing?" G asked.

"First, who said anything about the markings being Menehune?"

"Sorry, I guess I assumed," G said.

"Well, you're half right anyway. The top part is Menehune, which I may or may not be able to translate. I'll have to spend some time with it. Like I said, my work is seriously incomplete. The bottom half of the rubbing, that thing that looks like an ancient Egyptian cartouche, I have no idea what it means or says."

G stood up and walked over to Pokee. He turned his left wrist over and showed Pokee his tattoo. "Every member of our tribe has his or her unique cartouche. It's how we verify we are who we say we are in the rare circumstances when we have to prove ourselves. While we are required to be able to recognize every other member's cartouche, only the bearer of it knows what the writing actually represents."

"And I take it you don't recognize this cartouche?"

"No sir, I don't. But that could be because I was too young to take note of such things back before the wizard jumped ship."

"What's your wizard's name?"

"Dagywn."

"Does it have a meaning?"

"Roughly 'dawn,' or 'time of sunrise.'"

"All right. I have my work cut out for me. I'll let you know if I have any luck."

"Ah... how will you let us know? We're kind of on a deadline," Mad asked.

"I'll let your grandmother know."

"*My grandmother?*" Mad asked with disbelief. "You know her?"

"Of course. We've been friends forever."

"Why am I not surprised?" Mad said, mostly to herself. "If you don't mind me asking, how will you let tutu know?"

"I do mind you asking. Let's just say we have our ways," Pokee said and left it at that.

"Okay," Mad said testily, "let's just say that. But before we leave you alone, you said you visited them — the Menehunes. Can you tell us where?" Mad asked.

Pokee let out a big exasperated sigh. There was no doubt he was anxious to be rid of us. "If you're trying to find them, I don't think my experience will do you much good. Even though I'm half Menehune, they never completely trusted me. They actually blindfolded me, even during the part of the trip we were in an outrigger, but I don't think they took me to where they lived. It was just a meeting spot. They didn't trust me enough to take me where they actually lived. They probably thought Madam Pele would show up and 'accidentally' torch everything in sight. Once we got there, though, I'm sure we were in the Ho-nopu Valley. Do you know it?" he said, looking at Mad.

"Up on the Na Pali coast?" she asked. "You can only get there by water, right?"

"Yeah. You probably know it as 'the valley of the lost tribe.' Legend has it that it's where the last Menehune lived. I think they just thought I was dimwitted — that I'd naturally jump to the conclusion that if the Menehune had once lived there, then it was possible that they still lived there when I visited. But like I said, I don't think that's where they live, then or now. For what it's worth, while I was doing some research I stumbled across a reference to a census done for King Kaumuali' I, back in the early 1800s. The census takers registered 65 people self-identified as Menehune living in the Wainiha Valley. Granted, that's a long time ago, but who knows?"

"That's up north, isn't it?" Mad asked.

"Yes," said Pokee, "but you could be on a complete wild goose chase here, you know that, don't you? The Menehune have managed to stay hidden for a long time and you of all people, Mad, know there are thousands of places to hide on this island, places where no one would ever find you, no matter how hard they looked or for how long. And there's another thing. You all need to know that you're on dangerous ground here. The fact that you're here on this island with the intent to interfere with the lives of Menehune — even though the men you hope to find are technically not of our tribe — puts you at risk. In fact even coming here to see me puts you at risk."

"From whom? From what?" I asked.

"From Madam Pele. This is just the kind of intrigue she takes an interest in. And make no doubt about it, she's aware of virtually everything that goes on these islands. If you so much as take a pebble from this island, she'll put a curse on you until it's returned. She's very dangerous. Consider yourselves warned."

"For the second time," I said, under my breath.

The Na Pali coast was like something from another planet. One minute we were sailing past ordinary coastline and the next, there were surreal, bright green pinnacles, rising straight up out of the ocean.

Chapter VIII

Is Any Action Better Than None?

June 28 – 30, 1968
Multiple locations around the island
Kauai, Hawaiian Islands

I woke up way too early the next morning. The clock in the kitchen, which I could see from the daybed in the living room, said 5:10. I couldn't remember my dreams, most likely because I didn't want to, but I knew that's what probably woke me up — like I'd been working hard on something I couldn't figure out even though I had been asleep. It didn't seem right that I needed to clear my brain at 5 o'clock in the morning, but that's what it felt like. I snuck outside as quietly as I could and walked to the beach. Luckily, there was no one around and aside from a lot of different bird songs coming from every direction and the gentle lapping of waves on the shore, the scene was quiet and gray, both the water and the sky variations of the same non-color.

I walked barefoot along the waterline and tried to sort things out. For the first time in my life, I felt jumpy. I knew it had to do with my dream of Madam Pele and Pokee's warning yesterday. And, somewhere in the back of my mind was the question of Nigel Stayne. He was almost more ominous in his absence than if he were present. I felt like any minute now either one of them — Madam Pele or Nigel Stayne — might jump out from behind a rock or a tree trunk and come after me. Or maybe both of them at the same time. Now that would be something. No wonder I felt jumpy.

I read somewhere recently that worrying was a terrible use of one's imagination. And I've always seemed to know that worrying doesn't change anything, except it puts you in a lousy mood. So I knew better than to worry, but that's exactly what I was doing. The more I thought about it the more it felt like I had stepped into something way bigger than I originally thought it would be — whatever "it" was. Kauai, with all its mysteries, seemed very foreign and unknowable to me. If I had the same job to do back in St. Helena, I would feel on much firmer ground and know what to do next. That was the question: what to do next?

Without Pokee having to come right out and say it, I knew there was no rushing him translating the rubbing, so there was nothing I could do about that except wait. As far as Madam Pele went, the only thing I could do was try not to tick her off. Although according to Pokee just being on the island might be enough to get on her wrong side. And Nigel Stayne? Not a darn thing I could do about him either except wait for him to show up. It all added up to nothing except waiting. Not a very satisfying conclusion.

I walked back to the cottage and made myself of cup of coffee. Chuy and G were still asleep so I walked over to JP's. He was bustling around in the kitchen, seemingly using every bowl, pot and pan simultaneously.

"You're up early," he said. "Want a cup of coffee?"

"No, I've got my 'crunchy coffee.'"

"Oh, that's right. I don't know how you can drink that stuff," he said, looking up from what he was doing. "Jeez, you look like your cat just died. Are you okay?"

"I suppose."

"What's up?"

"Nothing. That's the problem. So far I've got a handful of nothing, but it feels like anything I might do is either going to cause trouble — for us or for somebody else, or both."

"Is it trouble you can handle?"

"You know, that's a good question. I'm thinking maybe not, and that's a feeling I'm not used to. I can handle stuff. But this is starting to feel different, like I'm playing way outside my league."

"That's how you improve your game, by playing against someone better than you."

"Yeah, or get squashed and humiliated, or worse."

"Well, you can always pack up and leave."

"No, that's not going to happen. We've already put too much into this to just give up."

"Then I suggest you follow my father's advice."

"Which is?"

"Do something, even if it's wrong."

I laughed. "Which it probably will be."

"What if it *is* wrong? At least it's one more thing you can cross off your list until you hit on the right one. Any action is better than none."

"I don't know, JP," I said, truthfully.

"Well, here's something I know: I'm making a good breakfast. Go get those slug-a-beds next door up and moving. And give Mad a call and see if she wants to come over. I think breakfast will be white enough for her."

A half an hour later we were all sitting around the dining table at JP's cottage, chowing down on cornmeal waffles and country sausage gravy, topped with a couple of poached eggs.

"That ought to lay down a base for whatever it is you're going to do today," JP said.

"I think I'm going to have to lie down," Chuy said. "I'm going to explode."

"And I think I'm going to have to expand my food choices to 'kind of' white. That was fab, JP," Mad said.

"So what are we going to do today?" I asked the group. They all just looked at each other and shrugged their shoulders.

"Yeah, I know," I said, "I'm feeling like we're in a major holding pattern here. We need to be doing something besides just waiting around for Pokee to come through. Speaking of Pokee, did anyone else notice how he lit his pipe yesterday?" I asked.

"No," they all said.

"He lit it by snapping his fingers. It was like there was a flame coming right out of his thumb and middle finger," I said.

"Wouldn't surprise me," Mad said, "considering he's related to Madam Pele."

"Well, what would we be doing if Pokee weren't working on the rubbing?" Chuy asked, changing the subject. Apparently no one else found Pokee's flaming fingers as strange as I did.

"Looking for the Menehune," G said.

"And where would we look?" I asked.

"If it were me, I'd start with caves," G said.

"What about the two valleys Pokee mentioned?" asked Chuy. "What were their names?"

"Honopu Valley and Wainiha Valley," Mad said. "Do all gnomes live in caves?" she asked G.

"I've never known a tribe that didn't," G said. "The two valleys seem like a long shot to me, unless there's something different about the Menehune I'm missing. How familiar are you with the caves around here, Mad?"

"First of all, are you talking about wet caves or dry caves?"

Everyone just looked at each other, probably not realizing that there was

Makauwahi Cave was basically like a big sunken garden that time had forgotten, but there were no Menehune to be found anywhere.

such a thing as a "wet cave." Mad explained to us that there were a lot of caves on Kauai right on the shore that were filled with water. After a short discussion, we all agreed there was no need to explore wet caves.

"Well then, as far as dry caves go, there's the Maniniholo and Makauwahi Cave. Do you think it's okay to take that off the wall?" Mad said, pointing to a map of Kauai thumbtacked to the wall in the living room.

"Sure," I said, "It's easy enough to put back."

I took the map off the wall and spread it out on the table. Mad pointed at the map, saying "Makauwahi is here, just a few miles away. Maniniholo is about halfway around the island, up here, but in the same direction as Makauwahi. It'll take us about an hour and a half to get there. You wanna' go?"

"Sure," we all said.

"Let me just check with my dad to see if he needs the car. I'll call from the pay phone."

It turned out Mad was free to use the car since her dad was going to a conference on the big island of Hawaii for the next few days. Since it was so close, we decided to go to Makauwahi first. If there was enough time, we'd go to Maniniholo next. And if neither of those caves turned up anything, we'd go to Honopu Valley. To be honest with you, it felt like we were just making busy work for ourselves while we waited for Pokee to translate the rubbing, but I kept my thoughts to myself. No sense in bumming out everyone else.

We drove east on Poipu Road for about ten minutes and then Mad pulled the car over to the side of the road and parked it. She explained that the rest of the road had such bad potholes that we'd never make it, especially with four people in the bug. Poipu Road petered out, but we kept walking until we reached the base of a small hill and found an opening in the rocks about four feet tall. All of us except G had to basically fold ourselves up to get through the opening. Once we were inside the cave opened up a bit and we could stand, but coming from the bright sunlight into the darkness made it impossible to see for a minute or so. When our eyes finally adjusted, we walked toward the light and came out into what could only be called a sunken garden. It kind of looked like a plant-and-tree-filled amphitheater, with high rock walls on all sides, ranging from maybe ten feet tall in some places to more than 20 feet tall in others. It had a level, grassy bottom, about half the size of a football field and, like I said, was filled with palm trees, flowering plants and a lot of birds. Mad said that where we stood now used to be the bottom of a river. Thousands of years ago, the river bottom simply fell into another cave below it and created the sink hole. We all agreed that it was a very cool spot but there was no sign of Menehune living there.

On the hike back to the car it went from being hot and humid to a downpour that lasted for just a couple of minutes and then went right back to hot and humid, this time with steam rising off of everything and mosquitoes everywhere. By the time we made it back to the car it was almost 2 o'clock. We were all still wet from the rain and in lousy moods.

Mad got behind the wheel and looked at her watch.

"It's going to take an hour and a half or so to get to Maniniholo and the same to get back. Depending on how long we spend there, we're talking over three hours. Whaddaya' say we head back to the Garden Isle and go for a swim instead?"

None of us needed much convincing. We spent the rest of the afternoon swimming and not talking about the Menehunes, except to decide that we'd take off after breakfast tomorrow and head up north to Maniniholo, which is what we did. And, as it turned out, it was a long way to go for a whole bunch of nothing. As soon as we got there we could tell it was going to be a bust. For one thing, the cave was practically right next to the road and part of a state park. There was no way the Menehune could hide out there. We decided to at least take a look at the inside of the cave and it was just about what you'd expect: big, dank, dark and stinky. No one said much on the trip back. Without asking, Mad drove straight to Bubba's Burgers, probably thinking we needed something to raise our spirits. After we finished eating, Mad said "Now what?"

We talked about it for some time and even though I don't think any of us thought it would come to anything, we decided that we should go to Honopu Valley, the so-called "valley of the lost tribe" that Pokee told us about. No doubt about it, we were all discouraged, but we agreed that it would be like we weren't doing our job if we didn't at least check it out.

I remembered that Mad had mentioned you could only get there by water and I wasn't sure how far I wanted to go in our Zodiac, so I said "Let's go back to the cottage and look at the map. I want to see how far away it is."

It turned out it was over thirty miles from the Nawiliwili Harbor to Honopu Valley, much further than I felt comfortable taking the Zodiac, especially if we encountered any rough water.

"Are there Zodiac charter companies around?" I asked Mad.

"Lots of them. That's how most of the tourists see the Na Pali coast."

I looked at the map again and saw that the coastal town of Waimea was about halfway to Honopu Valley. It seemed like it made sense to keep the trip on water as short as possible.

"How about in Waimea? Any charter companies there?"

"I don't know. Is there a telephone book around?"

"Right here," Chuy said, grabbing it from a table in the living room.

Mad looked through the phone book and said "Bingo. Captain Na Pali Adventures. Right on Kaumauli'I Highway. Shall we give him a call?"

"Sure, who's got a dime?" I asked.

G reached into his pocket and gave me a dime. A couple of minutes later I was on the pay phone, talking to Captain Na Pali himself. I made arrangements for an all-day charter and told him we only wanted to visit Honopu Valley. That was fine by him and we agreed to meet in Waimea at 9 o'clock the next morning.

The next morning, JP saw us off at a little after 8 o'clock, handing us a sack full of fried egg sandwiches and fresh oranges. "Gotta' keep your strength up," he said.

We piled into the bug and took off for the Kaumauli'I Highway. It wasn't hard to find Captain Na Pali's place. Just like Mad said, it was right off the road.

We parked and went in the office. The captain was there behind the counter. Somehow I was expecting some old salt with a gray beard, but the captain looked more like a college student. "Nice dreads," he said, looking at Mad. When we told him we wanted to go to Honopu he asked whether or not we were going to want to go ashore.

"Yes," I said.

"You know it's against the law for a boat to land on the beach, don't you?"

I turned around and looked at Mad, who simply shrugged her shoulders.

"Ah, no, we didn't."

"I can get you close to shore, but you're going to have to swim the rest of the way. Did you bring towels?"

"No."

"Well, I've got some extras I can throw in the Zo,' but it'll cost you five bucks extra."

We agreed, and when Captain Na Pali went to get the towels I went over to G. We'd been in the water together before, but it was always shallow and I couldn't remember if I'd ever actually seen him swim.

"You can swim, can't you?" I asked him.

"Like a fish," he said.

"Does that mean you swim under water?"

"Yep, but don't worry, I'll make it."

We walked down to the dock and piled in the Zodiac and headed northwest. After about half an hour we rounded Mana Point and started heading northeast and the landscape of the island changed completely. Where it had been fairly flat, now there were these monstrous pinnacles rising out of the ocean: skinny, tapered towers of red volcanic rock, partially covered in what looked like bright green moss. It was so fantastic, like magically leaving earth and finding yourself on another planet. When I looked it up later in my guidebook, I found out that some of the pinnacles on the Na Pali coast are more than 4,000 feet tall. No wonder they blew me away.

We continued along the coast, heading more east now, for another thirty minutes or so, and the landscape continued to get more surreal. Captain Na Pali slowed the engine and we drifted towards a small beach with a large rock formation jutting out into the ocean on the left side.

"This is it. You ready?"

"As ready as we'll ever be," I said.

"How long you gonna' be?" he asked.

"I'm not sure. An hour or two?"

"Can you be a little more definite? I'm going to have to go further up the coast where it's okay to beach this thing. I don't want to have to keep going back and forth until you guys show up."

"How about an hour and a half? That'll make it straight up noon."

"Okay, see you back here at noon," he said.

We'd all gotten used to wearing our swimsuits under our clothes, so we just stripped off our t-shirts and shorts, but because we'd probably be hiking on rocks, we decided to leave our sneakers on. We rolled over the side of the Zodiac and swam the short distance to the beach. G popped up last, sputtering as a wave basically pushed him on shore. We waved to Captain Na Pali as he roared off.

"Wow, look at that," Chuy said, walking up the beach.

The rock formation that jutted out into the water contained a long, wide arch that you could walk through to the other half of the beach. The middle of the arch was probably a hundred feet tall. It was truly monumental.

"Honopu means 'conch shell' in Hawaiian," Mad said. "Apparently the arch makes a conch shell-like sound when the winds are from the north."

"It sounds creepy," Chuy said.

I think we all felt it: a little weirded-out at being so isolated and, well, alone. But there was something else, too. The beach and the small valley above it, surrounded by those unreal pinnacles, had a presence. The pinnacles looked like giants shrouded in moss, standing at attention, protecting something. To be honest, it felt like we were intruding, just by being there.

As if reading my mind, Mad said "It's considered a sacred place, this valley. The cliffs surrounding the valley are said to be the burial site for ancient local chiefs. The old ones believed that once a chief died, his bones held supernatural powers, and if a stranger found them, the supernatural powers could be used against the tribe. After a chief died, a warrior from his tribe would take the chief's bones and hide them in the cliffs. I suppose it was an honor to be chosen to do it, but to protect the members of the tribe, the warrior who hid the bones had to be killed afterwards to make sure the location of the bones remained a secret."

"Oh, jeez," Chuy said.

As beautiful as it was, the place was getting creepier by the minute. I looked closely at a V-shaped opening in the rocks at the back of the beach. It looked like it was the only place you could climb up to the valley behind it, and it didn't look any too easy.

"And people used to live here, in the valley?" I asked Mad.

A huge stone arch divides the beach at Honopu in half and makes strange moaning noises when the wind is from the north.

"Yeah. There are remains of ancient temples up there. Not to mention bones and skulls."

"Great," I said, thinking we had an hour and a half before Capt. Na Pali came back. "Should we at least try to get up there?"

"Yeah, I guess," said Chuy, half-heartedly.

"Sure," G said.

"I'm in," said Mad.

With that we walked over to the opening in the rocks and started inching our way up the almost vertical rock walls, maybe twenty feet straight up. Climbing bothered my gimpy foot but it wasn't so bad that I couldn't ignore it. It was very slow going, but eventually we made our way to the top. We looked up the valley; it looked like someone had rolled a bunch of boulders down the hill. As relatively small as it was, there wasn't going to be anything easy about exploring this valley. Speaking of small, it was G who, because of his size, made his way through the boulders without much effort. He was way out in front of the rest of us, frequently disappearing completely from view. We had been scrambling over and around the rocks for about a half hour and none of us had come across anything of interest. But, I had to admit, if anyone asked us what we were looking for I, for one, wouldn't be able to say. It wasn't as if we were going to bump into a Menehune sitting on a rock, just waiting for a meet-and-greet. It was getting hot and the mosquitoes had decided to attack. At least they were attacking me. I was just thinking that we ought to start getting back to the beach when G started yelling "Up here." We followed his voice and found him kneeling down looking at a small recess between a couple of rocks.

He turned to us and said "That's what I think it is, isn't it?"

We all took turns looking at it.

Mad just gasped and put her hand over her mouth.

Chuy said, "That's it. I'm outta' here."

I looked down into the darkness and saw the unmistakable form of a human skull looking back at me. I felt my stomach turn and looked at G and said "I think we'd better get outta' here."

I doubt whether any of us remembered much of the hike down the rock-strewn valley, except that it was a lot faster going down than up. Once we were all on the beach, we decided that we wouldn't tell anyone about what we found until we had talked to Mad's dad about what to do. He'd know. We were all relieved to hear the sound of the Zodiac coming east. Without even talking about it, we were all wading in the water before Captain Na Pali was even close. I think it's safe to say we were all more than ready to leave the Honopu Valley. And not come back.

.   .   .

Back at the cottages, we were all pretty low. I ran into Mr. Becker walking to the office.

"Hey, Nick. How's it going?"

"To be honest, not great."

"No leads at all?" he asked.

"Not really. One maybe, but we don't know yet."

"What are you going to do next?"

"That's just it. We don't know. I kinda' thought that having G along would be like having some kind of superpower we could use to find the Menehune, but I guess it doesn't work that way. No gnome radar. No nothing."

Mr. Becker laughed and told me to hang in there and added "We've still got plenty of time," which, for some reason, actually made me feel worse.

I looked at my watch and realized I was supposed to have called Grandma Hattie a half an hour ago. I hustled over to the pay phone and made a collect

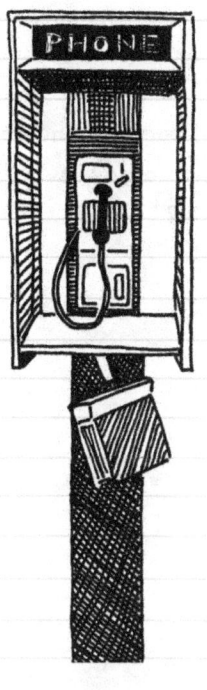

The pay phone at the Garden Isle Beach Cottages was in the middle of their tropical garden; none of the cottages had telephones or televsions.

call. The operator put the call through and Doyle answered.

"I have a collect call from Nick Sinclair in Kau-ai. Do you accept the charges?" she asked. Doyle said yes and told me to "hold the phone" while he got Grandma. I always thought that was an odd thing to say: I mean, what else was I supposed to do except "hold the phone?" Because I was so far away, in the middle of the Pacific Ocean, grandma decided that it was necessary to shout her end of the conversation, which made the conversation a little difficult. I was relieved that she didn't ask if we'd made any progress in finding Dagywn. She just wanted to know that I was okay. Which I was, I guess. For some reason I found myself talking very loud. Strange. We made small, LOUD talk for a couple of minutes and then I told her that I'd call her next week, hopefully with some good news on our search. I hung up the phone, my ears ringing.

.   .   .

Without talking about it, our not-so-merry band of explorers found ourselves on the front porch of the cottage. Three days in a row of no progress. I knew it was going to be hard when King Gob first talked about what he wanted me to do, but not this hard. I was at a complete loss so I just asked the obvious out loud.

"Anyone have an idea of what to do next?"

"I do," said Mad. "Let's go to Queenie's and get a shave ice. While we're there we can see whether or not Pokee's called." *At least it was something to do,* I thought to myself. She drove us over and there was a line of people in front of the shack. We worked our way to the counter and placed our order. Mad asked "Tutu, have you heard from Pokee?"

"Oh, yeah."

"Oh yeah?"

"Yeah."

"When?"

"Maybe it was yesterday."

"TUTU! Why didn't you tell me?"

"Can't you see I'm busy? Crazy busy. Maybe you should come and help me instead of running all over the island with these new friends of yours."

Mad ignored the jab and asked "What did Pokee say, Tutu?"

"He said he figured it out, whatever that means."

Mad turned to us and said "Let's go!"

. . .

I spent the next couple of hours reading in the hammock. I read so much that the words on the page were starting to get blurry. I needed to do something besides being a slug, so I went up to our house and put on my gym shorts and running shoes. My folks were still gone to some conference in San Francisco, something to do with the winery. It felt odd to be in our house by myself and for it to be so quiet. I ran my regular run, through the vineyards and on some back roads up against the foothills hardly anyone knows about. The vineyards were just starting to turn brilliant colors, from golden yellow to bright red, and the foothills were a dusky, almost misty-looking pale blue. It felt good to be outside after being inside all day. I'm on the cross-country team at school; it wouldn't be long before I'd be running with my teammates again, but on the sidewalks through town, not like this at all.

I like running. Especially when I reach that point where there's a steady, strong rhythm to the sound of my feet hitting the ground. Kind of like a train on a flat stretch of tracks. It's then that I can stop thinking about running and just allow my mind to wander. I got to thinking about the characters in Grandpa's journal. They seemed real enough. I wondered if Grandpa had stayed in touch with them. If so, I wondered if I could contact them and find out their version of what happened – or, more to the point, even *if* it happened. That didn't feel quite right – too much like I didn't believe what my grandfather had written and wanted to go behind his back to prove him wrong. I'd have to think more about that. One thing I did know is that I wanted to try sending a message to whoever was at the other end of where the pigeons flew every day. That was going to take some research on the computer. I had no idea how to even get close to a pigeon, let alone how to attach that vial thing to one of their legs.

When I made it back home, I took a shower and changed my clothes and walked down to Grandpa's. I walked in the kitchen just as he was taking a pan of lasagna out of the oven. Doyle was making a salad in a big wooden bowl.

"You're just in time. Where you been?"

"Out on a run. Needed the exercise after reading all day."

"Yeah. I noticed a lump in the hammock. Every once in awhile, it moved. I thought you were sleeping. Where are you?"

"Standing in front of you."

Doyle tried, unsuccessfully, to stifle a laugh.

"That I can see. I mean in the journal."

"Mad has introduced you to Pokee. I guess he's figured out what the rubbing says but he hasn't told you guys yet. It's quite a tall tale, Grandpa."

"What do you mean?"

"Pele? *Really?*"

"Yeah, *really*. Now there's someone I wish I hadn't met."

"You mean you actually met her?"

"Oh, that's right. You haven't gotten there yet. I won't spoil the story."

"You've got to be kidding me. You met Madam Pele?"

"Yeah. And it wasn't pretty."

"And you had a dream where a headless woman talked to you and the next day some strangers told you that a headless woman was scaring off guests from a hotel built on sacred ground? I don't know, Grandpa. I think you're pulling one over on me."

"Ye of little faith… "

"Yeah, well… where were you, Doyle?"

"In San Francisco. With your great-great-grandmother."

"So you can't confirm any of this?" Truthfully, when it came to this story, I trusted Doyle way more than my grandfather.

"Not that part of the story. Like I said, I wasn't there."

We had dinner in the kitchen – lasagna, salad, and garlic bread – one of my favorite meals. I gotta admit, Grandpa Nick was a good cook. I inhaled seconds of everything.

"So are you still in touch with Mad?" I asked, barely believing that Mad even existed.

"Infrequently. But every once in awhile. She's got a big-deal job."

"Like what?

"She's way up there in the World Bank. She's also ranked number two of flamenco guitar players in the world. She may be the smartest person I've ever met."

"Really?" I said. And then, thinking to myself, *Flamenco player – could he really just have made that up? Talk about random …"* I continued, "From the way you described her… "

"Yeah. Remember she was 16 at the time. But there was a lot going on under all those dreads."

Either he has a good imagination or he's not making this stuff up, I thought to myself.

"What about JP?"

"He was a great guy. *Sui generis.* Do you know what that means?"

"No."

"It's Latin for 'in a class by itself.' He had a talent for life. And art. And cooking. He was a master of having a good time and making sure other people did, too. We became really good friends."

"Was?"

"Yeah. He died way too young. He was the one who introduced me to the Kansas City Art Institute and why I eventually went there. He lived in Kansas City. His answering machine used to say that you'd reached 'the Foundation Foundation, where your support supports support.' He was one funny guy," Grandpa said laughing and shaking his head at the same time.

"What about... ?" and I caught myself. *Why hadn't I thought about him before? He lived just down the road.*

"What about what?" grandpa asked.

"Nothing. I've just got a lot questions. I'll do the dishes," I said, wanting to change the subject.

"In that case, I'm going to watch TV. I'm hooked on that *Walking Dead* show. Doyle, you in?"

"I don't think so. Last time I watched I had nightmares."

"*Walking Dead?* Really?" I asked.

"Yeah. You got a problem with that?"

"No, no. Not at all." Like I said, when it comes to my grandfather, it's one unexpected thing after another.

After I finished the dishes, I decided to go out and have a talk with the pigeons. Let them know we were about to become new best friends. I was definitely going to have to do some research on them. But first I had to sort through what I knew about Uncle Chuy. I knew he and my grandfather were best friends when they were kids and I know that Grandpa Nick married Chuy's sister, Anna, my grandmother, and that Grandpa Nick and Grandma Anna had divorced a long time ago – before I was even born. And I vaguely knew that there were some bad feelings there, all around. But Uncle Chuy was just that, my uncle, or more exactly, my great uncle. He was a blood relative. And he was there in Kauai that summer with my grandfather. I needed to talk to him.

It would be easy to just ride my bicycle to his house on Mee Lane. Easy. Right. Then why was my gut telling me that it was going to be easier to tie a letter to a pigeon's leg than it was going to be talking to Uncle Chuy?

*Lincoln Avenue is the main drag in the small town of Calistoga,
at the very northern end of the Napa Valley.*

Chapter IX

Vitae Obscura

July 1, 1968
Napa County Fairgrounds RV Park
Calistoga, California

It had been a little over three months since Nigel had come up with his change of plans, namely to forget about Nick in Kauai and, instead, confront the gnomes directly on Mt. St. Helena. Even though his plan was fairly simple, there had been dozens, if not hundreds of details to attend to. Luckily he had Lord Higgenbotham's assistant, Phillipa, to help make the plan come together. He also felt lucky that he only had to meet Lord Higgenbotham in person once and that was just before Nigel had left London for California. At their meeting in Higgenbotham's office, his lordship was busy writing something at his desk. When Nigel sat down across from him, Higgenbotham never even looked up from his desk, simply saying "Don't screw up this time, Badger. Be off." Nigel had no intention of screwing up. Failure was not an option.

And so Nigel found himself back in the Napa Valley with a new name, Gordan Fergusson, a new passport and a new plan. And no Nick to deal with. As he pulled onto the main drag of Calistoga, he was feeling pleased with himself. He liked being on familiar ground and Calistoga, after last summer, was now familiar to him. In fact, it reminded him of his hometown, Kelso, in Scotland. They were both the same size, each with a population of around 5,000 people, both had water running through them: Kelso had the beautiful River Tweed and Calistoga had the headwaters of the Napa River, not much more than a creek, but running water nonetheless. And both towns were quaint, seemingly frozen in an earlier time, popular with visitors.

Nigel would have preferred to have stayed at the Bothe State Park like last year, but he couldn't take the chance that the same park ranger would still be at the front gate and recognize him, this year with a different name and a fake passport. He just couldn't take the risk of being found out, as there was no way he was going to wind up in jail again, like he had last year. Instead, he had Phillipa arrange for an Airstream trailer to be parked at the Napa County Fairgrounds RV Park, which was just on the outskirts of Calistoga.

*The Napa Valley R.V. Park in Calistoga, where Nigel
had to stay, to avoid being recognized.*

When he got there, he was disappointed to see that the so-called "park"
was little more than a big, flat parking lot, with a few big RVs and trucks parked
here and there, a half dozen people sitting in folding camp chairs, and just
a few trees on the very perimeter of the site. Pretty dispiriting, actually.
Nothing like the ancient redwood forest he camped in last year at Bothe. And
no rock fire pits he had enjoyed so much. *Oh, well,* he thought to himself, *I'm
here on a mission and it has nothing to do with enjoying myself. I'll do that
later, after I've got what I came for.* He had no problem finding the Airstream
trailer Phillipa had arranged to be there and tried to ease his disappointment
with the thought that, with a little luck, he'd only be there for a few days. That
was the plan: In and out and return home with the goods as quickly as possible.
He had a good feeling about this. He was going to succeed.

He parked his rented Wagoneer next to the Airstream and found the key ti
the trailer where Phillipa had said it would be, on top of the right tire. Before
letting himself in, he looked around the RV park; luckily there wasn't anyone
even close to him; the fewer people he had to interact with, the better. Inside

the trailer Nigel found everything he had asked Phillipa to supply, minus the gun. Nigel didn't want to take that chance again. It had caused a lot of trouble last year and, honestly, he didn't think he'd need one this time. He'd given every detail of his plan a lot of thought.

Tomorrow morning he was scheduled to meet the Caterpillar operator up on Mt. St. Helena at 7 o'clock. Together they would drive to the five-acre piece of property Nigel had Lord Higgenbotham buy near the summit and work out the details of the operation. Right now, Nigel was hungry. It was a beautiful evening and, given how close the RV park was to town, he decided to walk and find a restaurant. When he returned a couple of hours later after a good meal and a glass of wine, he was ready for bed. As soon as his head hit the pillow he was asleep, and slept like a man without a worry in his life. Too bad he didn't know about the curse.

Last year, when Nigel followed Nick to the gnomes' cave and subsequently got caught, King Gob and his men figured they hadn't seen the last of him. Considering Nigel didn't get what he wanted — namely the photographs of the gnomes to give to Lord Higgenbotham to publish around the world — it was a safe bet he'd be back to try again. Before the sheriff came and took Nigel away, King Gob had one of his men cast a seldom-used curse on Nigel known to the gnomes as *Vitae Obscura*. As curses go, it's a fairly mild one and, if it's not renewed, it only lasts for a couple of years — hardly a wink of an eye given the way gnomes kept time. The curse works by tinkering with a person's unique vibration, just enough so they're a little bit "off," and prone to making bad decisions, but mild enough so the victim doesn't know anything is wrong. If you've ever said to yourself "what was I thinking?" after you've done something ridiculous or really stupid, it's possible you've been cursed with *Vitae Obscura*. In Nigel's case, if a curse can be said to work like a charm, this one certainly did.

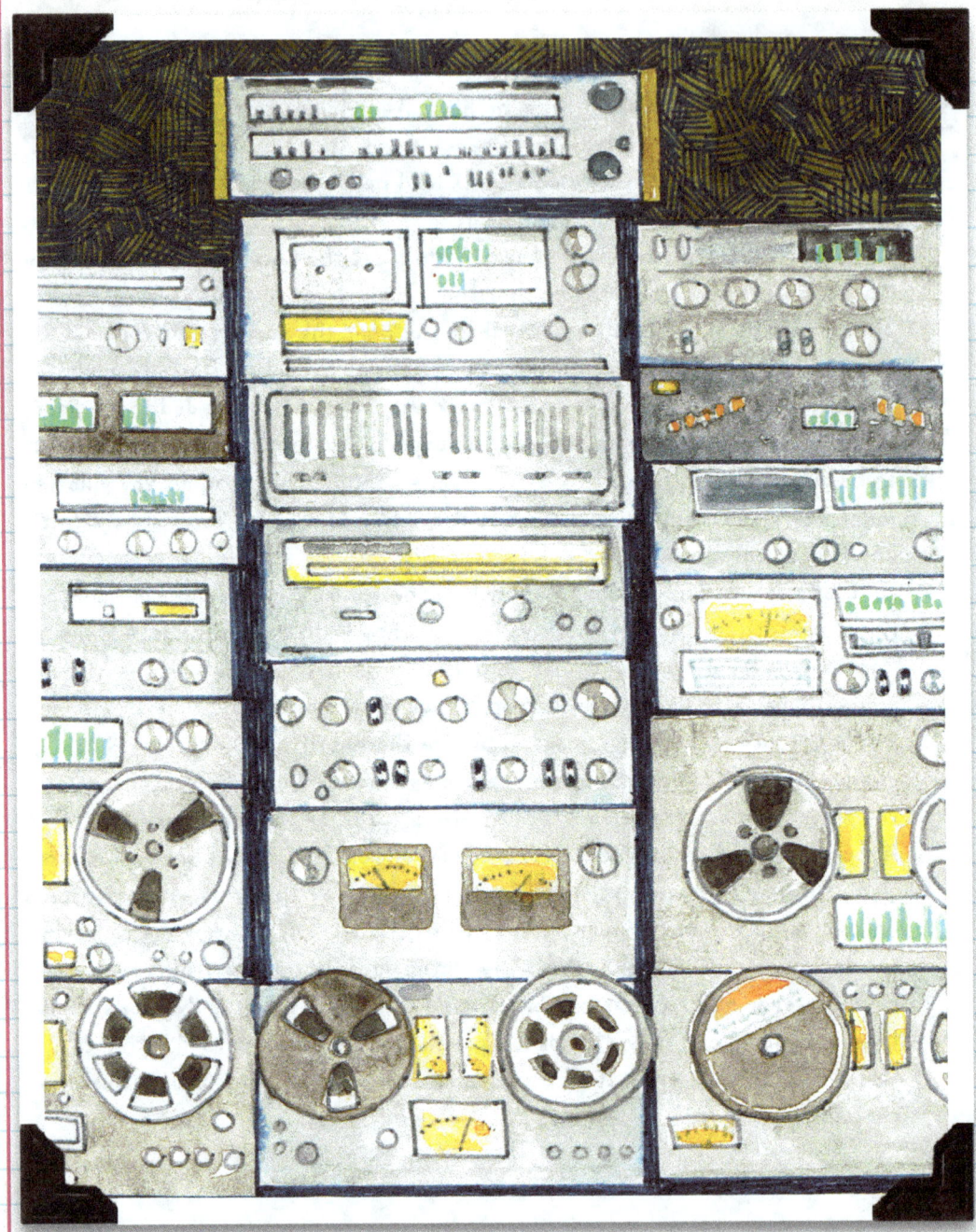

It was safe to say that Pokee's interest in all things electronic bordered on the obsessive.

Chapter X

Now What?

June 30, 1968
Pokee's house
Kauai, Hawaiian Islands

"Shoot!" Mad said.

"What?" we all said at the same time as we were getting into her car.

"I forgot. We can't just drive to Pokee's. I forgot to ask him the last time we were there if he still had the entrance to his place booby-trapped. Double fudge!"

"Double fudge?" Chuy asked.

"Whatever," Mad said.

"We could take the Zodiac," I said.

"Getting it from the yacht is kind of a hassle, but yeah, we could. Wait a minute. The Garden Isle has a little aluminum boat with an outboard motor. I bet they'd let us use it. I mean, we're just going to the end of the bay."

"Worth a try," I said.

When we got back to the Garden Isle Beach Cottages, I was elected to ask the owners if we could borrow the boat. After I assured them I knew how to handle it, and considering they'd be able to see the boat the whole time we were gone — Pokee's house was that close — they said yes. It was beached at the far end of their garden, but they said with four of us, we'd be able to easily carry it into the water — it wasn't that heavy. In just a few minutes we were motoring across the horseshoe bay, up to Pokee's house. Mad reminded me not to run over Pokee's set lines. We'd be in big trouble if we screwed up his means of catching fish. I steered well clear of the floats and in a few minutes we were on the beach in front of his property. We pulled the boat up on the sand and walked the path through his jungle to the house. We found him on his hands and knees, working in his vegetable garden.

"I was expecting you sooner," Pokee said, looking up from the weeds he was pulling.

"Yeah, well Queenie kind of forgot to tell me you called."

"Withholding information: Part of her role as a surveillance operative, no

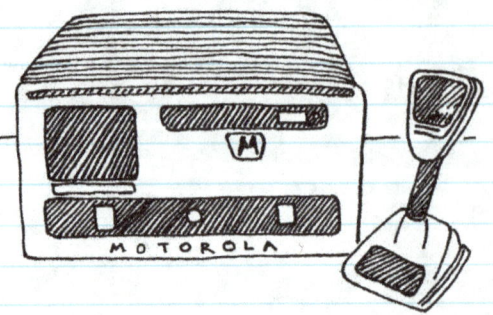

Mad correctly guessed it was a two-way radio Pokee used to communicate with Queenie, although she had never seen one at the shave ice stand.

doubt."

What can I say? She's a strange one, even if she is my tutu."

"Well, the coconut doesn't fall far from the palm, you know," Pokee said, looking straight at Mad.

"Thanks, Pokee, I'll remember that." Mad said sarcastically. "Can we talk about the rubbing?"

"Of course, of course. That's why you're here, isn't it?" he said, straightening himself up. "Come on in the house."

The rest of us followed Pokee and Mad into Pokee's house. The dark, low-ceilinged front room was cluttered with a dizzying array of electronic equipment. Reel-to-reel tape recorders, turntables and two-way radios were stacked on top of each other on one wall and the rest of the walls were covered with floor-to-ceiling bookcases, jammed with books every which way, just the way Mad had described it when she was here as a child. It was easy to see why she remembered it all these years later. It was definitely memorable. All the furniture in the room: end tables, chairs, even the couch, were covered with stacks of books. At one end of the room was a round dining table with an amber-colored glass lamp hanging low over the middle of it. The round table was the only piece of furniture in the room that wasn't covered with books. The rubbing was the only thing on it. Somehow I wasn't surprised to see a large, very brightly-colored parrot sitting on a stand next to the table. "Hello, who's this? Hello, who's this?" it asked repeatedly. Apparently it wasn't used to Pokee having guests. Pokee looked over the top of his glasses and said "Quiet, Polly!"

"*Polly? Really?*" Mad said in disbelief.

"What's wrong with 'Polly'?" Pokee asked.

"I don't know. I guess I expected something a little more original. Does she want a cracker?" Mad said mockingly.

"I wish you hadn't said that." Pokee said, just as Polly started squawking "Polly wants a cracker. Polly wants a cracker," repeatedly. "Will you excuse me?" Pokee asked as he picked up the parrot stand and took it and Polly into another room and closed the door. Even with the door closed we could hear the muffled sound of the parrot asking for a cracker, over and over again.

"Now, do you want to know what the rubbing said or not?" Pokee said, clearly peeved. "This is why I don't have people come to my house," he said, under his breath.

I was the first to say "Yes, please."

"It says 'Get me out of here.'" Pokee said, holding up the rubbing and looking at us. "By the looks on your faces, I'm guessing that's not what you were expecting."

"Not exactly," I said. "I'm not even sure what it means."

"Well, that's pretty obvious, isn't it?" Pokee said testily.

"As a statement, it is," I said, "but given the circumstances, I'm not sure I get it."

"Circumstances?" Pokee asked.

"Were you able to decipher the cartouche?" G asked, sensing where I was going with my question.

"You said your wizard's name meant 'sunrise' or 'dawn,' right?" Pokee asked G.

"Yes."

"Well, as far as the Menehune writing goes, I'm certain I'm right about that. The markings inside the cartouche are runes: an alphabet of sorts used by ancient northern European and Scandinavian people. I'm no expert on runic writing, but I'd say with 80 percent certainty that the cartouche belongs to your wizard."

"Holy smoke," I said.

"Now what?" G asked no one in particular.

"I have absolutely no idea," I replied.

We all thanked Pokee repeatedly and started to leave. We could still hear Polly asking for a cracker in the other room. "This is going to go on for days," Pokee said, motioning with his head to the room where Polly was, "even after I give her a cracker — or twelve. Drives me nuts."

"I'm very sorry," Mad said.

If we were never invited back to Pokee's house, it was probably because of Polly's inability to keep her beak shut.

"Not as sorry as I am," Pokee replied.

Just as we were about to go through the front door, Mad turned and pointed to something on the wall of electronic equipment. "Is that what you use to communicate with Tutu?"

"The two-way radio? Yes. Didn't you know?"

"No. You know how she is. Loves her secrets."

"Perhaps I shouldn't have told you," Pokee said.

"No, no. It's all right. Your secret is safe with me," Mad said and winked at him.

"All right. Then be off with you. I've got to deal with Polly. And if you have any more questions, ask your father, Mad. He knows as much about these things as I do."

"Are you asking us not to come back?" Mad asked.

"As politely as I can," Pokee said with an unconvincing smile.

Even though we hadn't thought about it yet, that's exactly what we ended up doing: talking to Dr. Okole. And Pokee was right: Mad's dad did know as much as Pokee.

That's Jack and Jenny, the miniature donkeys we got for King Gob last summer, along with the cart which should have held two people, but was just big enough to hold Gob on his own.

Chapter XI

The Earth Moves

July 2, 1968
Mt. St. Helena
Napa Valley, California

As planned, Nigel met the Caterpillar operator, Chet, on top of Mt. St. Helena at 7 o'clock the next morning. Nigel told Chet to follow him up a road, which wasn't much more than a dirt fire trail, for about fifteen minutes. Nigel unlocked a metal gate and they drove onto the property Nigel had had Lord Higgenbotham purchase. Most of it was relatively flat and covered with weeds, with huge pine trees here and there. They got out of their vehicles and walked over to a clearing. Chet was confused as to what Nigel wanted him to do.

"So this is the place where you want me to start digging?"

"Yes. Over there, right at the base of that rise."

"How big and how deep?"

"I have no idea."

"What am I digging?"

"I'm sorry. I don't understand the question."

"Well, normally I know what I'm digging before I start. Like a pond, or a swimming pool, or a ditch next to a road."

"They're all holes, aren't they?"

"Sure, but they're all different. Do you have a set of plans?"

"Plans?"

"Yeah, plans?"

"No. No plans."

"So, Fergie, you just want me to start digging... over there?"

Nigel bristled at being called "Fergie." He hadn't counted on his new last name being shortened into something that a pet heifer might be called. "Yes. I don't see what the problem is."

"How do I know when I'm done."

"I'll let you know."

"So you're going to be here the whole time I'm digging?"

"Yes."

"Okay then. But just so you know, it's $200 an hour for me and the Cat."

"That won't be a problem. When can you start?"

"As soon as I get the Cat in place. It's just down the road. I'd say an hour or so."

"Then get busy, Chet. It's important that I'm done and out of here as quickly as possible."

. . .

The gnomes were all asleep by the time the Caterpillar operator started digging and they were known for being sound sleepers — all except for Wycoff, who was plagued by insomnia. He was the first to sense that something was wrong. Like all gnomes, Wycoff was acutely aware of the vibration of rocks around him and of the mountain itself. But he was sensing something else: it was not the normal constant vibration he was used to, but an uneven series of high notes and low notes and occasional rumbles. He pulled himself out of bed and walked outside the cave. He wasn't used to being outdoors while it was light out and he felt a little unsure of himself. He cocked his head to one side and strained to hear the sounds he'd heard inside the cave: some clanking, like metal on metal or maybe metal on stone. He followed the sound further up the mountain, scrambled to the top of a huge boulder and peered down the other side. Sure enough, about a hundred feet below, a tractor was digging into the base of the incline. Wycoff scanned the surrounding forest, shielding his eyes from the light, and almost immediately spied an Uplander, leaning against the trunk of a huge pine tree. The Uplander looked familiar to Wycoff. But who was he? "Of course," Wycoff said under his breath, "We thought you'd be back."

Wycoff set off on as fast as he could back down the moutainside. He had to inform the king immediately, even though it was against almost every rule of the tribe to wake the king when he was sleeping. The only exception was if the welfare of the tribe was threatened; Wycoff thought about it for a moment and decided that a mechanical monster chewing away at their mountain certainly qualified. Even so, standing in front of the door to the king's private chambers, Wycoff shuddered. Gathering his courage and knowing how hard of hearing the king was, he didn't even bother to knock, but just let himself into the anteroom of the bedroom. Wycoff had never had to awaken the king before and he didn't really have a plan. He imagined the worst as he pushed open the door and was greatly relieved, not to mention surprised, to see the king standing in front of him, wearing a long red nightshirt and matching cap.

"What are you doing here, Wycoff? It's the middle of the day, isn't it?"

"Ah, yes, Your Highness, it is. I could ask you the same thing: what are you doing up at such an hour?"

"Something's wrong. I don't know what it is, but I feel it in my bones."

"You're quite right, King Gob, something is very wrong and I think you need to see it with your own eyes as quickly as possible."

"What are you saying, Wycoff?"

"I'm saying you need to come with me right now, Your Highness. I'm going to go hitch Jenny to the cart. While I'm gone, why don't you put on a coat or something. We're going into the forest. I'll be back for you in a few minutes."

"Is all of this really necessary, Wycoff?"

"Well, I suppose you could go in your pajamas, if you wanted to, Your Highness."

"No, no, no. I mean this trip into the forest."

"Yes, Your Highness. It is of the most important importance. I'll be back shortly."

Wycoff ran down to the corral where the two miniature donkeys were kept and hitched the female, Jenny, to the wooden cart. He ran back up the stairs and got the king down the stairs, holding on to him all the way. It took some doing, but he managed to get the king seated in the cart and they took off through the forest at a steady pace, Wycoff running next to the cart. They went around the south side of the mountain and slowed when they had a view of the back side. The king couldn't believe his eyes and started to yell, "Stop that, stop that right now, you idiot!"

"Your Highness," Wycoff said directly in the king's ear, "I don't think we should let them know we're here. Do you recognize who that is leaning against the tree?"

"I can't say for sure at this distance, but he looks like that viper from last year. The one we put in the hole."

"That's him all right. Nigel Stayne. Remember? Nick warned us that he'd probably be back and now there he is — with that mechanical monster eating into our mountain."

"Tell me, Wycoff, do I surmise correctly that if they dig much further, they'll breach an opening in the side of our dwelling?"

"In my estimation, yes, Your Highness."

"And am I correct in stating the first thing they'll uncover is our storehouse, the one where we keep the gold and quicksilver?"

"That's correct, my king, since the storehouse is at the very farthest reach of the caves, that's what they'll uncover first, digging from the direction they are now."

"Then they must be stopped!" the king hissed. "Rouse all the men immediately. We'll storm the mechanical beast and defeat it."

"No, your Highness. If you will, please listen to me. Let cooler heads prevail. The mechanical beast is much too large and strong for our men to overtake. I have a plan that I think will work. Will you hear me out?"

"As much as I hate the word 'no,' you may be right, Wycoff. I'll listen to your plan on the way back. The first thing we must do is organize the men and move our valuables on the double. I cannot countenance that rat touching so much as one nugget of our gold. Onward! Now!"

Wycoff explained his plan to the king on their way back to the cave, huffing and puffing all the while, but managing to make himself understood. He had to repeat it twice, louder the second time, but when he was done the king laughed out loud.

"Oh, that's rich, Wycoff. Good thinking! There'll be extra rations of grog when we're done. Let them eat dirt, those miserable cretins!"

You can't fault us for not trying — we drove forever on the
unmarked roads on either side of Highway 50 and never
found a thing except a Dead End sign. Pretty sad.

Chapter XII

Dead End

June 30, 1968
All over Highway 50
Kauai, Hawaiian Islands

We didn't exactly speed, but we didn't waste any time getting to the Historical Society office. I know we took Dr. Okole by surprise as we kind of tumbled into his office, all of us trying to get through the door at the same time.

"Greetings," he said, suppressing a laugh.

We all said "hi" while Mad went over and gave her dad a kiss and said "Welcome home."

Somewhat bewildered, Dr. Okole said "To what do I owe the pleasure?"

"We have questions," Mad said.

"Like what?" he said.

"Like where'd that come from," Mad said, pointing to the carved piece of wood on his desk.

"You remember — you were here — Kai Alana brought it in. The teacher from Waimea Canyon Middle School. He thought I might be able to tell him something about it."

"Did he say where he found it?"

"May I ask what all this is about?" Dr. Okole asked.

"I made a rubbing of it for G because he thought he recognized something on it."

"And?"

"And we took the rubbing to Pokee. He translated it for us."

"Pokee? Really?"

"Uh huh."

"Hmmm. That's interesting. And what does it say, this rubbing?"

"'Get me out of here'."

Dr. Okole laughed and then asked "What about the glyphs?"

"G, do you want to answer that?" Mad said, turning to G.

"It's the symbol for one of the members of my tribe."

"Tribe?"

"Gnome tribe."

Dr. Okole pushed his glasses up and pinched the bridge of his nose. "Do you guys want to sit down? I think we need to talk."

We pulled some chairs over to Dr. Okole's desk and sat down. "Now, can you tell me a little more of the story? I'm in the dark here," he said.

"Do you want me to explain?" I said, looking at G. He nodded in agreement. I gave Dr. Okole a shortened version of why we were on Kauai and who we were looking for, namely Dagywn.

"And is this Dagywn's 'signature'?" he asked, pointing to the carved cartouche.

"Pokee is eighty percent certain it is," Mad said.

"Eighty percent? Those are pretty good odds," he said. "By the way, how did you get to Pokee's house?"

"We just kind of showed up by water," Mad said.

"I see," Dr. Okole said, shaking his head. "And what do you want from me?"

"Did Mr. Alana say anything about it?"

"Not much, other than a student gave it to him."

"Did he say anything more?" Mad asked.

"Hold on. I took some notes," he said, shuffling papers around on his desk. "Here it is. The student's name is Lani Kahale. She's a seventh grader. She said she found the carving at the bus stop on Highway 50 at Kaumakani."

"The bus stop?" Mad asked.

"Yeah, she said it was nailed to a telephone post right next to the bus stop. She stands there nearly every day and was fairly certain it hadn't been there the day before. She took it to Mr. Alana because it was so strange, but also familiar. He brought it to me thinking I might be able to decipher it."

"Lani said it looked 'familiar'. Like how?" Mad asked.

"The school's mascot is something they call a 'minihune,' their term for a young Menehune. Because of that, they teach the legends surrounding the Menehune as part of their curriculum. Lani said that, for some reason, the carving reminded her of the

Waimea Canyon Middle School's mascot — a "minihune."

Menehune. Maybe she'd seen something
similar in a book or something."

Mad turned to me and said "Are you
thinking what I'm thinking?"

"Probably," I said.

"Dad, can I borrow the car for a little
longer? We need to go and take a look at
that bus stop."

"Okay, but be careful. And be back here
by six to pick me up. We're having dinner
with Queenie tonight."

"Oh jeez. Okay. I'll be here at six. Oh,
and Dad?"

"Yes?"

*It was really weird coming
across a human skull when we
exploring Honopu Valley.
I don't think Dr. Okole was
amused by our find.*

"We found a human skull this morning. In Honopu Valley."

"A skull? In Honopu Valley? Mad, what in the world have you been doing?"
Dr. Okole said, his voice agitated.

"Looking for a gnome wizard."

"You're making me a little crazy" he said. "How'd you get to Honopu Valley?"

"We chartered a Zodiac from Captain Na Pali."

"Who paid for it?"

"Mr. Got Rocks over there," she said, pointing to G, who gave Dr. Okole a
brief wave.

"I don't know, Mad, this is all a little much for me. Just make sure you're
back by 6. And you need to show me on a map where you found the skull."

"I will. At Tutu's tonight."

And with that we were off again. West on Highway 50 to Kaumakani, which
Mad said was below Waimea, where we just were this morning. This morning?
Really? That trip on Captain Na Pali's zodiac felt like a week ago. It didn't take
long to get to the bus stop next to the small, pinkish-orange post office.

"Well, this is completely unremarkable," Mad said, looking at the small
metal sign that had a picture of a bus on it and the word "STOP" below it. "But
there's the telephone pole," she said, "so at least that's for real."

There was an unnamed road that intersected Highway 50 on both the left
and the right side.

"Shall we try going left first?" Mad asked.

"Sure," I said.

We traveled down a barely-paved road with a lot of potholes and reached a cluster of similar-looking houses with corrugated tin roofs and lots of overgrown tropical plants, right next to a narrow beach and the ocean beyond. We crisscrossed the few streets that made up the neighborhood and didn't see anything out of the ordinary.

We then went back up the road we came in on, crossed the highway and started up the narrow, red dirt road on the other side. It extended for as far as we could see, with flat fields on either side. Mad explained that the fields used to be planted with thousands of pineapple plants before they stopped growing pineapples on Kauai. A little further up the road, on the right hand side, Mad pointed out another cluster of houses she said used to be plantation housing, built by the plantation owners for the workers, now long gone. The road began to rise, with more twists and turns, and nothing but green rolling hills on both sides. We kept going for twenty minutes or so, the same scene repeated after every turn, until the road simply ended with a big sign that read "Dead End."

"Well, I guess that just about says it all," I said.

"And I thought we were onto something, what with Pokee's translation and knowing where the carving was found. What a bummer," Mad said.

"Maybe we're onto something and we just don't know it," Chuy said.

"What's that supposed to mean?" G asked.

"I don't know. Just something positive, you know?"

"I'm not feeling it, Chuy," I said. "Come on. Let's go, Mad. Your dad said not to be late."

. . .

Mad dropped us off at the Garden Isle, saying she'd see us tomorrow even though we didn't have anything planned or any leads to look into, which worried me. I didn't say it out loud to anyone, but I was beginning to think we were going to return home empty-handed. There was the sound of jazzy music and good smells coming from JP's cottage so we stopped in. JP was hustling around in the kitchen wearing an apron and Mr. Becker and Tova were in the living room, dancing and laughing. I felt like we were interrupting a party, but JP, Tova and Mr. Becker insisted we stay.

"Where's that Mad girl?" JP asked.

"She's having dinner with her dad and grandmother," Chuy said.

"Just as well. There's no way I could disguise this as white food," JP said.

"What is it?" I asked.

"I found a barbecue grill up by the office, so you're in for a treat. Kansas City-style ribs, macaroni and cheese and coleslaw. It's gonna be goo-ood. How'd you guys make out today?"

"Not so good," I said.

I explained how we were all stoked to have Pokee's translation of the carving and Dr. Okole's information on where it had been found, but we still came to a dead end — literally.

"Listen, Nick," Mr. Becker said, "I told your grandmother my job was to get you guys to Kauai safely and back home again and that I was going to leave your search to you. But I can't help offering you some advice, if you want it."

"Sure, we'll take it. Right now we've got a whole bunch of nothing."

"Well, whenever I'm in a similar situation, I take a time out," Mr. Becker said.

"A time out?" G asked.

"Well, it's possible to think too hard about something, so hard that you don't let other ideas and options into your head. If it were me, I'd schedule a day off — like tomorrow — and have some fun. And most of all, don't let yourself think about your problem. If you free your mind up for just a little while, you might be surprised what pops up, all on its own."

"I don't mean to be rude, Mr. Becker, but having fun is the last thing I'm thinking about right now," I said.

"Come on, Nick, take a surfing lesson or something. Tova and I did today and it was great. There's a surf school just over on Poipu Beach.

"Surfing lessons, yes!" Chuy said. "You in, G?"

"Sure. Why not? Probably won't have that opportunity again for awhile."

"Nick, you in too?" Mr. Becker asked.

"I guess so."

"I'll take that as a yes."

As it turned out, Mr. Becker was right about both things. The surfing lessons were fun and not thinking about our problem for a day changed everything, but in ways no one, not even Mr. Becker, could have imagined.

The big horseshoe bay in front of the Garden Isle Beach Cottages.
Pokee's house was practically at the tip of the point pictured above.

Chapter XIII

Do You See What I See?

July 1, 1968
Poipu Beach
Kauai, Hawaiian Islands

Mad dropped by the next morning wanting to know what the plan was. She was a little surprised when I told her "surfing lessons," but said she was up for it. She had already dropped her dad off at the Historical Society and had the car for the day. Our lesson wasn't until 3 o'clock so we spent the morning playing cards at the round table in our cottage. Mad taught us to play four-handed solitaire, which was just like regular solitaire, but you got to play on everyone else's piles in the middle of the table. The person with the most cards played on the piles won the game. It was fun, but I have to admit that it felt strange not to be doing something to try and find Dagywn. Every time I thought about it, I tried not to think about it, like Mr. Becker said. It wasn't easy.

When we first got to the Garden Isle, JP told us that he'd make breakfast and dinner for us, but we were on our own for lunch, though there would always be stuff for sandwiches in the refrigerator. Around 12:30 we traipsed over to JP's cottage, made sandwiches and took them out to his front porch to eat. After that we did what most people do when they come to Kauai: went swimming and hung out on the beach until it was time to go to surf school.

We got our towels and stuff and Mad drove us to Poipu Beach, which was only a few miles away. When we got to the surf school, a young guy named Dan introduced himself as our instructor and shook hands with all of us. When he got to G, he said "Cool. It's good to get started early," which was kind of funny considering G was over 150 years old, at least according to gnome years. Mad told him not to include her in the lesson because she'd been surfing since she was four years old.

We were all pretty good but G was the star, which may have had something to do with his low center of gravity or maybe because he was tuned in to the vibrations of the waves and the surfboard or some gnome thing like that. One time when I was upright on the board for more than a few seconds I caught sight of Mad off to my left, hot-dogging it, repeatedly kicking out over the top

*The Poipu Surf School wasn't much more than a
clearing in the palms, right next to the beach.*

of the wave and then back to curl, looking for all the world like a pro. I wondered if there was anything she couldn't do.

   After our lesson we were all a little too keyed up to just go back to the
Garden Isle, so we decided to hang out on the beach and watch the next group
of students. There were four of them — probably tourist kids in their early
teens — and one kid who didn't look much older than five. *Kind of young to
be taking a surf lesson on his own,* I thought to myself. Feeling protective, I
kept my eye on him. Like G, he was a natural, picking up the teacher's instructions quickly. The more I watched him the more I realized I had been wrong; his
moves were way too confident and skilled for a 5-year-old.

   I elbowed G and said "Do you see what I see? Check out the small guy."

   "Yeah. He's good."

"I'm getting something else," I said.

"Like what?"

"Dude! Look closely."

"For crying out loud..." G said under his breath.

"We need to talk to him."

"Yeah, we do."

Mad noticed us huddled and turned away from Chuy, who was shamelessly flirting with her, and asked "What's up?"

"Take a look at that kid on the yellow surfboard. What do you see?"

"A kid on a yellow surfboard who's too good for his age."

"Look closely. Remind you of anyone?"

"What are you looking at?" Chuy asked.

"The kid on the yellow surfboard," Mad said. "Watch him. That is so far out!"

"Yeah, I can see he's good but 'far out'?" Chuy said.

"Look closer, Chuy," Mad said and then turning to me, "Are we going to talk to him?"

"Absolutely. I think we should have G go down and meet him when he gets out of the water."

"I guess I'm not getting this," Chuy said, "What's the big deal?"

"The big deal is, we may have just found the missing link. Watch," I said.

G walked down to the edge of the surf and was there when the "kid" got out of the water. They were about thirty feet from us so we couldn't hear what they were saying but when we saw them slap their hands together, we guessed it had to be something good. We were so focused on the two of them, I guess we didn't notice what was going on around them. Even if we had seen what happened, I don't know that we could have done anything about it, or even if we should have. But someone took a picture of the two of them, one of them holding a small surfboard, standing face-to-face with animated expressions on their faces. Admittedly it was a cute photo, especially if you thought they were a couple of 5-year-old kids. Turns out the photographer was a tourist who sold the picture to *The Garden Island*, Kauai's daily newspaper. And whoever put the photograph in the newspaper also thought they were a couple of kids, because the caption that ran with the photo said "Never too young." What happened after that, no one could have predicted. But more on that later. Right now, G and his new friend were walking towards us.

"Guys, this is Leo. Leo, this is Mad, Nick and Chuy." Seeing them side-by-side, you'd think they were brothers. I wasn't sure where to start, but Leo seemed completely at ease, so I just started with the big question first.

"You're a Menehune, right?"

"That's right."

"Wow. That's cool," I said, my heart beating so hard I was pretty sure other people could hear it. "Are there other Menehune around?"

"Sure, there's a group of us. Been around for a long time."

"Where do you live?"

"In the hills above Kaumakani."

"Really? Weren't we just there yesterday?" I asked Mad.

Mad just shook her head up and down with a look of disbelief on her face. Chuy's mouth was stuck in the open position.

"To tell you the truth, Leo, we've been looking all over for you — and your tribe. But I gotta' say I didn't think we'd find you here — surfing."

"Yeah, we know."

"Know what?"

"We know that you've been looking for us."

"How'd you know that?"

"Well, it's not every day that a gnome from another tribe comes to Kauai. Word gets around pretty fast."

"So why didn't you get in touch with us? We were beginning to think we'd never find you."

"We did."

"What do you mean?"

"That's why Dagywn put the carving on the telephone post. So you could find us."

"Dagywn?!"

"Yeah, Dagywn. That's who you're looking for, isn't it? Him and his mates?"

"Yeah, yeah. That's who we're looking for, but . . . oh, man, my mind is blown!"

"He always told us that it would happen one day. He's my father."

"Let me get this straight: Dagywn's your father?" I couldn't believe what I'd just heard.

"Yeah."

"Listen, Leo, is there any way we could come for a visit?"

"Sure."

"Like right now?"

"No. Right now's not a good time. By the time I get home the meeting will probably have already started."

"Meeting?"

"Yeah, it's the monthly meeting of our Cooperative. It's kinda' important."

"Cooperative?"

"It's what we call our group."

Thoroughly confused, I juat said, "Okay. How about tomorrow? Tomorrow morning?"

"Sure."

"So how do we find you?"

"You know the unmarked road that cuts across Highway 50, right by the bus stop at Kaumakani?"

"Like I said, we were just there yesterday."

"Well, we're just about a mile up that road on the right hand side. You can see it from the road."

"What? Your cave?"

Leo laughed. "No, no cave. It's a group of houses. They're the only thing out there besides the old pineapple fields."

"Houses?"

"Yeah, you'll see. I've got to get going. So I'll see you tomorrow? Around 10?"

In a daze, I simply said "yes" and told him it was good to meet him. I'm not sure he knew how good it was but he said "likewise," and took off on his bicycle and disappeared around the corner of the surf school office.

I looked at G, Mad and Chuy and said "am I dreaming?"

"If you're dreaming, we're all dreaming, and I've never heard of a group dream before," Chuy said.

The only thing I could think was *Mr. Becker, you're a genius.* And I told him so when we got back to the Garden Isle. Considering this was exactly what we had come a very long way to do, everyone was in a celebratory mood that night. Chuy found the local "top 40" station on the radio and we had a impromptu dance party. After so much worrying it was good just to have fun. Something told me there was still a lot we had to do but, for today, I was following Mr. Becker's advice to forget about it. Tomorrow would come soon enough.

. . .

August 12, 2012
Grandpa Nick's house
Rutherford, California

I looked at my watch. It was still early so I decided to call Uncle Chuy to see
if we could meet. I started heading back to Grandpa's house but stopped and
thought for a minute. Somehow it seemed better if I called Uncle Chuy from my
house, even though it made me feel like I was being sneaky, but that's what I did.
Uncle Chuy was surprised to hear from me, but said it was fine if I came over.
We agreed to meet at his house at 1:30 on Tuesday, a couple of days away. My
parents were still gone so I grabbed some clothes and went back to Grandpa's.
He was still watching TV in the den off the kitchen. I poked my head in and said
good night just as some zombie dude appeared on the television, blood dripping
from his teeth.

"Jeez, grandpa, really? I can see why Doyle wouldn't watch this."

"You don't know what you're missing."

"I think I do. See you tomorrow."

I spend enough time at Grandpa's that there's a bedroom I call my own, up
on the third floor in what used to be the servants' quarters. It was small, but I
liked the cozy feel of it. It had one tall window which looked east across the valley.
It also had a padded window seat that was a great place to read, especially with
the window open. I stretched out on the bed and thought about what I was going
to ask Uncle Chuy on Tuesday, still feeling a little like a spy or traitor to Grandpa
or something. I had decided to think about something else when the idea popped
into my head that if I could send a message to Prince G, maybe, somehow, some
way, he would send a message back and it would prove, more or less conclusive-
ly, that he was real. Using a homing pigeon to send a message seemed like the
ultimate in spycraft to me and I didn't want Grandpa to know what I was doing
– at least not yet. All I was trying to do was figure out if his story was real. It was
Grandpa's story, but he had given the journals to me to read. It was my duty to
figure out whether I was being duped or not. By talking to Uncle Chuy, I was
just being responsible, not some stooge who believed everything he read. At least
that's what I told myself.

The next morning, I got up early and did some computer research on homing pigeons. I know some people that say Wikipedia is not all that great, but when

I need to find out about something I don't know anything about, I start there. Sure enough, there was an entry on homing pigeons and it was pretty interesting. There was one part that caught my eye. Here's what it said: "Historically, pigeons carried messages only one way, to their home. They had to be transported manually before another flight. However, by placing their food at one location and their home at another location, pigeons have been trained to fly back and forth up to twice a day reliably, covering round-trip flights of up to 160 km (100 mi)." I looked it up and according to MapQuest, it was a little over 20 miles from Grandpa's house to Mt. St. Helena, so the pigeons could definitely fly that distance. Now I needed to know if Grandpa was feeding them, something I'd never seen him do. I wished there was some easy way of following the pigeons when they left the dovecote to see where they went, but there just wasn't. I came to the same conclusion as I did last night: a message back from Prince G would not only prove that the pigeons flew from here to where the gnomes supposedly lived on Mt. St. Helena, it would prove that G actually existed. Now I'd just have to figure out how to do the whole 'attaching-a-message-to-a-pigeon' thing. I did some more research and found out there was a Sonoma County Racing Pigeon Club, basically just west and over the mountain from where I was sitting. That was promising, I guess. And YouTube had one black-and-white short video from World War II showing a soldier attaching a rolled-up message to the leg of a pigeon and letting it fly off. It was blurry and there was no sound, so there was no real explanation of how to do it. Just when I was trying to figure out where to look next, grandpa walked into the studio carrying a mug of coffee.

"Top of the morning," he said.

"Morning."

"What are you doing up so early?"

Without even thinking about how top secret my project was, I just blurted out, "Homing pigeons. I'm trying to find out about homing pigeons."

"Why the sudden interest in them? They've been in the yard a long time."

"Yeah, well, I'm trying to figure out how I just walked past them all this time. But I didn't know they were homing pigeons until I read about them in your journal. Heck, I didn't even know what a homing pigeon was until yesterday."

"Well, they've been around for thousands of years."

"I just read that on the computer. Ancient Greece and all that."

"Fascinating creatures, actually."

I asked grandpa to draw a picture of my room on the third floor so you'd know what it looked like.

"Do you feed them?

"What?"

"Do you feed the pigeons?"

"Not any more. Not in a long time. I stopped when I left the doors of their coop open and basically set them free."

"Do you think it's possible that... ?" I stopped myself mid-sentence. I almost forgot I didn't want Grandpa to know I was going to try and get a message to Prince G.

"Do I think what's possible?"

"Do you think they could be trained to carry messages back and forth again?"

"With a little effort, sure. Who were you thinking of sending messages to?"

"Darren," I said, thinking fast.

"Darren?"

"Yeah."

"Don't you already text him messages on your phone?"

"Yeah, but sending him one using a pigeon would be a whole lot cooler."

"Well, I'll grant you that. Imagine if everyone gave up their cell phones and started using homing pigeons instead. That would certainly change things."

"Will you help me? I've looked on the computer and there's nothing that's like step-by-step, you know?"

"That doesn't surprise me. I can't imagine that keeping homing pigeons is all that popular any more. Give me some time and I'll look in the library. I may still have the book I used to get started back in the day. I'm not in the habit of throwing books away."

"Really? Could I look for it?"

"Sure. But I can't tell you where it might be. My books aren't all that well-organized."

"If it's there, I'll find it. What's the title?"

"Now you're pushing it. I have absolutely no idea. Probably something like *Practical Pigeon Keeping*.

As it turns out that wasn't the title, but it wasn't all that hard to find. And that's not all I found.

The front door to Grandma Hattie's summer house in Rutherford.

Chapter XIV

Counter-Attack

July 2, 1968
Mt. St. Helena
Napa Valley, California

Nigel was sitting on the ground, his back against a tree trunk, wishing he had brought a book with him. It had been a very long day. Except for a lunch break, Chet had been clawing through the earth all day. The way Nigel figured it, Chet should have broken through to the cave by now. Nigel wondered if his calculations were correct or not. He hated being uncertain about anything. Granted, deciding on the location to start digging involved some speculation on his part, but surely he couldn't have been very far off. After all, he knew the location of the entrance to the gnomes' cave and he knew approximately how deep the main cave was because he had been "escorted" through it on his way to being lowered into his hole-in-the-ground holding cell after being captured last year. Earlier, at home in Scotland, he had carefully charted these locations on the United States Geographical Survey maps he had ordered sent to him. He couldn't have made a mistake. In the middle of his worrying he was surprised to hear Chet turn the Caterpillar's engine off.

"What's the problem?" Nigel asked.

"No problem. It's quittin' time," Chet said.

"Quitting time?! It's only 4 o'clock," Nigel said, looking at his watch.

"Yeah, and that's quittin' time. Read your contract."

"No, no, no, no. It's not quitting time. I'll pay you extra. I'll pay you double. There's hours of daylight left."

"No matter. Overtime has to be approved before the contract is signed. You did read the contract, didn't you?"

"Of course I did," Nigel lied.

"Well, I guess you missed that part. See ya' tomorrow," Chet said, walking off.

"Wait, wait," Nigel called, but Chet just kept walking back to his truck.

"I can't bloody believe this," Nigel said to himself. If it would have done any good, he would have gone over to the hole and continued digging with his hands. "This is not good," Nigel said out loud to himself. The simple fact was that there was nothing to do but go back down the mountain to his trailer and wait until tomorrow morning, which is exactly what he did. But by the time he got to the RV Park, he felt like he was going to jump out of his skin. Having that hulking machine just sit there overnight, along with a half-dug hole, made him incredibly uncomfortable. In his heart, he knew there was no way the gnomes weren't going to notice it. And then what? He didn't even want to think about it.

· · ·

It was rare that the king had such urgent work to attend to. He found it energized him and made him feel "kingly." The first order of business was to summon Wycoff and inform him of his decision to move the gold, quicksilver and their other riches to a new location. As Chancellor of the Exchequer, Wycoff was the obvious choice for the job. The second thing he needed to do immediately was to dispatch Whitbeck to fetch the sheriff. Last year, when the sheriff arrested Nigel, he had given his business card to the king and told him not to hesitate to call in the event that Nigel showed up again — however unlikely considering it was the sheriff's intent to have Nigel deported.

"Unlikely, maybe," the king said to himself, "but I saw for myself that the rat is back. Now where did I put the sheriff's card?" he mumbled to himself. "Ah, yes. In the inside band of my crown — I'm a clever one, aren't I?" he said, chuckling to himself. "And the crown... the crown. Where is my crown?" He only wore it on special occasions and had a recollection of putting it somewhere it would be safe and out of the way. But where? "Yes, yes, yes, of course. Hmmmmm... Whitbeck!" he bellowed. A few seconds later, Whitbeck appeared in the king's bedchamber.

"Your Highness?"

"Whitbeck, I'm in need of your services. Will you get what is under the bed? I'm afraid I'm not as agile as I once was."

"Certainly, Your Highness," Whitbeck said, thinking the king's lack of agility might have something to do with his astounding girth. He tried to imagine the king on his hands and knees but quickly banished the thought before he started to laugh. Whitbeck pulled up the covers and peered under the bed. "Your crown?"

"Of course. What else is down there?"

"Dust balls as big as rats, Your Highness."

"Forget about those. Get me the crown."

Whitbeck had to flatten himself and slither halfway under the bed to reach it. Standing up and brushing himself off, he ceremoniously handed the crown to the king with both hands, bowing slightly.

Luckily, the sheriff had given King Gob his business card the year before.

"Your Highness."

"Yes, yes, Whitbeck. You're a little heavy with the 'Your Highnesses' today. 'Sir' will be sufficient."

"Yes, Your sir... ah, sir."

Instead of putting the crown on as Whitbeck expected, the king reached inside the crown, pulled out a small paper card and handed it to Whitbeck.

"You are being charged with a most important task, Whitbeck. Most important."

"Anything you command, sir."

"Last year when the sheriff arrested Nigel, he gave me his card and told me if I ever needed his services again, to call him. He said his information was on this card."

"His information, sir? What does it say?"

"How should I know? That's what you're here for."

"Sir, if you'll excuse me, I can't read either. I have no idea what's on this card."

"Hmmmmmm... the proverbial fly in the ointment. What to do, what to do?"

"We could have someone translate it for us, sir."

"Yes, good idea, Whitbeck. Take the card to Nick. He'll translate it for us."

"Sir, Nick is in Kauai, in search of Dagywn, remember?"

"Of course I do. A simple slip of memory. Let me think," he said, rubbing his chin. "Aha! What about Hattie? You could take the card to Hattie and she'll translate it."

"I'll do it, sir. I know the way. After it's translated, then what would you have me do, Sir?"

"Get to the sheriff as soon as you can and tell him we need him here on the mountain at first light tomorrow. Now off with you and don't dilly-dally. I'm counting on you, Whitbeck. This is of utmost importance."

With that, Whitbeck was gone and the king was off on his next task. He walked down the long corridor to the exchequer, where Wycoff had an office. The king couldn't remember the last time he visited Wycoff at his office, but he remembered where it was. As caught off guard as Wycoff was to see the king, he quickly grasped the gravity of the situation and said he would summon the men immediately and get to the business of moving everything within the walls of the exchequer to another location.

"And one more thing, Wycoff."

"Yes, Your Highness?"

"Quickly! This needs to be done as quickly as you can!"

"Yes, Your Highness," Wycoff said, running out of the office.

The king's next stop was to see Boogs and Boodle, the Bumm brothers, who ran the carpentry shop and sawmill. He found them at work in their own cave off the central corridor. They were even more surprised than Wycoff at the king's impromptu visit. Once again, the king explained the situation and what was going to be needed. He even drew a picture of what he had planned, which the Bumm brothers understood immediately. The king explained that they would have to work as fast as they had ever worked because later, along with the rest of the men, they would be needed for a special assignment which he would explain to all of them when the time came.

.   .   .

Whitbeck used his one special power — the ability to appear and disappear at will, and to travel great distance in the process — to take himself to Hattie's house in the valley below Mt. St. Helena. He remembered her house well from the year before, when he and the king, Prince G, and Wycoff met with Hattie and Nick. It was a night that was hard to forget, he thought to himself as he crossed the porch to the front door. He knocked and a young man answered.

"Ah, is Hattie in?"

"No, I'm sorry, she's not at the moment. May I help you?"

"It's Whitbeck. Perhaps you remember me from last year when I was here for … ah, the meeting."

"Of course I remember Whitbeck. It's an evening that would be hard to forget. It's good to see you again. Please come in."

Doyle closed the front door and they stood in the elegant, tall-ceilinged

foyer, where it was cool and pleasantly dim. Whitbeck, being completely un-
used to bright daylight, found the shadows comforting.

"Thank you, Doyle. That's it, isn't it, Doyle?" Whitbeck said, with a slight
bow.

"You have a good memory, if I do say so."

"Thank you."

"May I be of assistance in Hattie's absence?"

Whitbeck hesitated for a moment and then said "Well, I don't see why not.
You see, we're — that would be the king and I — we're in need of some translation. Last year we had need of your sheriff's assistance and he gave the king
his card in case we ever needed him again. I'm afraid that day has come and we
are in rather urgent need of his services."

"I'm sorry to hear that," Doyle said. "May I see the card?" Looking at it,
he asked, "What would you like to know?"

"The sheriff said the card contained his 'information.' I assume that means
that it contains where I can find him."

"Yes, it does. His offices are at 825 Brown Street in Napa."

"I'm afraid I don't completely understand. What does '825 Brown Street'
signify?"

"Well, every street has a name so you can tell one from another and every
house or other building has its own number so you can find it on the street."

"I feel a little like I'm asking too much of you, but this difficulty we find
ourselves in is of such urgency that I'm prepared to take risks. I think I
understand what you're saying about street names and house numbers, but...
how do I say this? You see, the king sent me on this mission because my one
unique power is the ability to travel from one place to another in an instant.
But in order to do so, I have to be physically familiar with both Point A and
Point B, if you catch my drift. And I'm sorry to say, I've never been to... what
was it? '825 Brown Street?'"

"I'm catching your drift, Whitbeck. And don't worry about asking too much.
I'm at your service. What if we just called him?"

"Called him. From here?"

"Yes."

"Would he hear us? Wouldn't it be better if we stood on the porch?"

"No, no. We'll use the telephone to call him."

"'Telephone?' Now you've got me. Can you explain?"

"The easiest way to put it is, you've got your magic and we've got ours.

A telephone is an electronic device that allows us to talk to another person across great distances, just like you and I are talking right now. Everyone who has a telephone has a unique number. When you dial that number on your own telephone, the other person's telephone rings and they pick up the receiver and then you can talk to one another."

"I get it," Whitbeck said, "it's not that dissimilar to my powers: you have to know the other person's number in order to make the connection, right?"

"Exactly."

"Do we know the sheriff's number?"

"Yes, it's here on his card."

"And do you have a telephone?"

"We do indeed. Shall we give him a call?"

"Oh, yes. Yes indeed."

"Follow me," Doyle said, leading Whitbeck into the kitchen and then to the wall phone that was in the pantry. "Do you want me to dial the sheriff's number?" he asked Whitbeck.

"If you would be so kind."

Doyle dialed and was connected to the sheriff's secretary. He asked to speak to the sheriff directly and after a brief hold, had him on the line.

"Sheriff Lyman, this is Kevin Doyle calling from Hattie Sinclair's. I have someone with me who'd like to speak with you. It's Whitbeck, who I believe you met during the incident on Mt. St. Helena last summer."

"Of course. He's there with you now?" Sheriff Lyman asked with some surprise in his voice.

"Yes, let me put him on," Doyle said, handing Whitbeck the receiver. Instead of putting it to his ear, Whitbeck held it out in front of his face and just started talking at it.

"No! Hold on sheriff. Like this, Whitbeck," Doyle said, putting the receiver on Whitbeck's ear.

"Hello, hello?"

"Yes, this is Sheriff Lyman. Is this Whitbeck?"

"Yes sir, it is. You'll have to excuse the confusion. I've never employed a telephone before."

"No problem, Whitbeck. What can I do for you?"

"I've been sent by King Gob. He asked me to tell you that Nigel Stayne is back and we are in need of your assistance. His Highness asked if you could meet us at the entrance to our cave at first light tomorrow."

"Tell the king I'll be there, Whitbeck. Will you and the others be all right until then?"

"Yes, I believe we have the situation in hand. But tomorrow the situation could be different. So I can assure the king that you'll be there?"

"Yes, of course. Be careful until then, Whitbeck. I'll see you tomorrow."

"Thank you, sheriff. Goodbye," Whitbeck said, and handed the receiver to Doyle.

"Mission accomplished?" Doyle asked Whitbeck.

"Thanks to you, Doyle. You have my appreciation. Now, on to other missions. If you'll excuse me."

"Of course."

And with that, Whitbeck more or less evaporated before Doyle's eyes.

.   .   .

By the time Whitbeck got back to Mt. St. Helena, the gold and other precious items had been moved and the Bumm brothers had produced a sizeable stack of lumber, milled to the king's specifications. The king had assembled all the men in the meeting hall and was about to address them when Whitbeck appeared.

"Ah, Whitbeck, you're back. I trust you were successful in your endeavor."

"Yes, Your... Sir."

"And the sheriff has agreed to be here first thing tomorrow morning?"

"Yes, Sir. He said he'll meet us at the entrance to the cave at first light."

"Excellent, excellent, Whitbeck. I knew I could count on you. Now you're just in time to hear my most exceptional plan for stopping this heinous transgression in its tracks."

His plan? Whitbeck thought to himself. *It wasn't that long ago that it was my plan, but why am I surprised?* he mused, shaking his head as he listened to the king explain the scheme exactly as Whitbeck had explained it to the king not two hours earlier. The king was wrapping up his speech with a string of platitudes like "one for all and all for one" and "speed is of the essence," when Whitbeck blurted out "Your Highness!"

Shocked at being interrupted, the king stared directly at Whitbeck and practically shouted, "What is it now, Whitbeck? Can't you see I'm busy?"

Whitbeck was about to claim the plan as his own, but decided on a less disruptive tack. He calmly walked over to the king and whispered something in his ear.

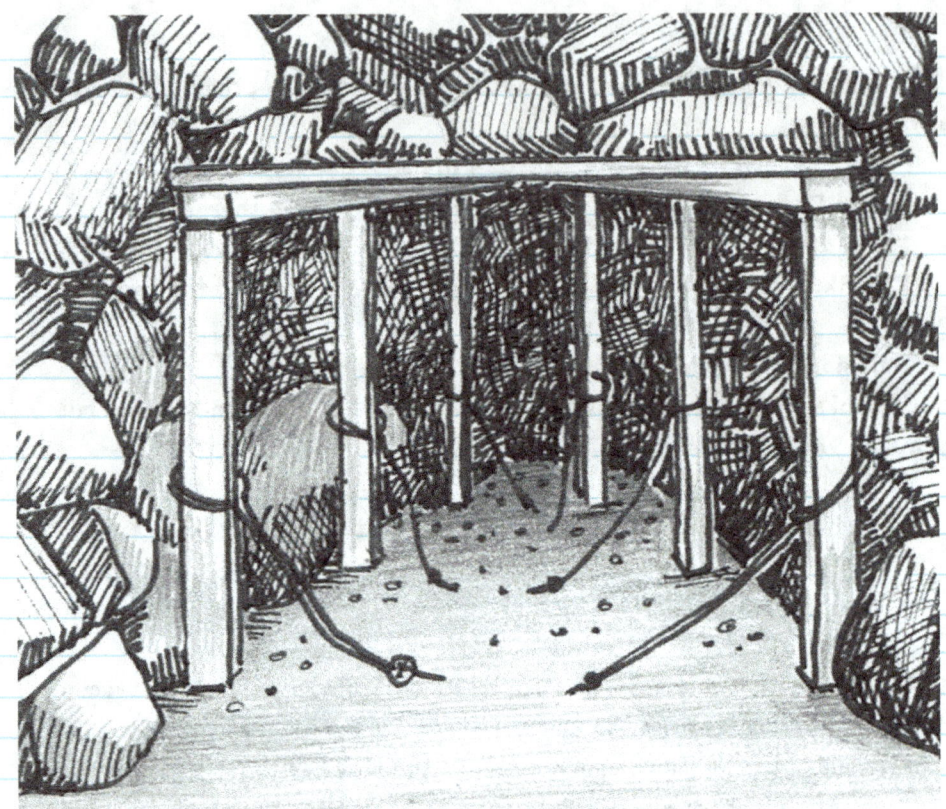

*King Gob explained the trap set in the cave, designed
to stop a Caterpilar tractor in its tracks.*

"Ah, of course. Right, right. I was just getting to that."

The king had forgotten to mention the key to the whole plan, without which it would all come to nothing.

"And men, do not forget to bring stout ropes, as many as you can put your hands on. With these ropes we shall be victorious and bring the mechanical beast to its knees. Now scurry! Many hands make for light work!"

The Menehune had definitely settled into the old plantation tract.
The place looked well taken care of, with multiple
community garden plots filled with fruits and vegetables.

Chapter XV

As the World Turns

July 2, 1968
Back on Highway 50
Kauai, Hawaiian Islands

I'd been watching the clock since 5 a.m. Now it was a little after 6. I figured I wasn't going to be able to fall asleep again so I might as well get up. It was one of those nights when my brain was racing so fast that it felt like I hadn't slept at all. Somewhere in the mess of all those thoughts and images, Nigel was lurking. It wasn't surprising that I had dreamt about him, but something seemed off. I made a cup of coffee and went out to sit on the front porch. The sun was just beginning to color the world and the air was pleasantly warm and humid. A million tropical birds seemed to be singing at once. I had no sooner sat down when G walked out on the porch.

"Morning," I said.

"You're up early," G commented.

"I could say the same about you."

"Weird dreams."

"Not surprising. We've got a big day ahead of us."

"No, the dreams weren't about Dagywn or any of that. They were about Nigel."

"That's weird."

"Why?"

"I dreamt about him too."

"Hmmmm. I wonder if it means anything," G said.

"It means we're both wondering where the heck he is," I said.

"In my dream, he was back on Mt. St. Helena."

"You know, that's not as weird as it sounds. He could very well be there. I mean, why not? He could just waltz right up there with no interference from you or me."

"I think you're right. He's not stupid. I'll bet you he *is* there."

"Should we warn your dad to be on the look-out?"

"Like how?"

I thought about it for a minute and realized there was virtually no way of getting information to the king: no telephone, no mail delivery or a way of getting him a telegram, not even a homing pigeon, and even if we could get word to him, it wouldn't matter because he wouldn't be able to read it anyway.

"Wow," I said. "I know how important privacy is to you all, but there's a real downside to being so isolated when someone needs to tell you something."

"It's never been a problem, really. We've just never found it necessary to communicate with the outside world."

"It's frustrating though. I feel like we ought to be able to do *something*."

"With half of the world's largest ocean between us and them? I don't think so. I think my dad and the rest of the guys are on their own on this one. Remember, we don't know if Nigel is there or not. If he's not, no problem. If he is, the tribe is resourceful. We'll just have to trust that they'll figure things out. We've been around for a long time and faced plenty of dangers – and we're still here. There's nothing either of us can do about the situation right now, so I we should probably stop thinking about it. If worrying changed anything, then we should be worrying, but it doesn't. So no worrying, Nick. Okay?"

"Okay, okay. I'm familiar with your theory on worrying."

"We've got a while before Mad shows up. What now?"

"I think I'm going to go back to bed. I feel like I didn't sleep a wink last night."

"Good idea. I think I'll do the same. It'll be like old times."

"What do you mean?"

"Sleeping when it's light outside. Good thing I've had a lot of practice."

.   .   .

The four of us were in Mad's car, heading down Highway 50 to the exact spot we were the day before yesterday. It still blew my mind that we had been on the right track and didn't even know it. What was it Chuy had said when we hit the Dead End sign? That maybe we were onto something and just didn't know it? He was certainly right about the "not knowing it" part.

Mad turned right off the unmarked road, towards the houses she had said were built for the plantation workers back in the day. We bumped slowly along the red dirt road through flat, empty fields on both sides, fields that used to be filled with rows and rows of pineapple plants. We finally reached the first grouping of houses set amongst a cluster of big, umbrella-like trees and flowering shrubs. It seemed like a small tropical oasis set down in the middle of a huge, barren landscape. I definitely had butterflies in my stomach. When Mad turned the engine off I was aware of how quiet it was. We all got out of the car and just stood there, looking around. No sign of life. Just some brightly-painted cottages with rusted corrugated tin roofs and, peaking through the foliage, a few chickens pecked the dirt. From out of nowhere there was a very loud, mechanical-sounding VROOOOM, which made us jump. We were all a little on edge.

"What does that sound like to you, Chuy?"

"A lawnmower."

"That's what I thought. Let's check it out."

It was such a familiar sound — a reminder of normal, day-to-day life back home — that I immediately felt grounded and not so jumpy. I mean, how weird could things be if someone was using a lawnmower, right?

We followed the sound and soon spied a short fellow, shirtless, wearing a pair of Madras shorts and flip-flops, mowing a small lawn in front of a very yellow cottage. I waited until he turned around and then waved at him. The lawnmower sputtered to a stop and I said, "Excuse me sir, but could you tell me where we could find Leo?"

"It's about time you showed up. What took you so long?"

"Is that you, Dagywn?" G said, walking over to him.

"Of course it is, G, who'd you expect? Don Ho?"

They hugged each other and then Dagywn held G at arm's length and looked him over. "Well, I wish I could say you've grown in the past, what, 90 years? At least you've gotten older. What were you the last time I saw you? Fifty years old?"

"Yeah, about that," G said. "You don't look anything like I remember you."

"Well, what can I say? There have been changes. Lots of changes. Aren't you going to introduce me to your friends? At least I assume they're your friends."

"Sorry. Yes, they're my friends. This is Mad, Nick, and Chuy. Guys, this is Dagywn."

We shook hands all around and then Dagywn showed us to a wooden table with benches on both sides, set out in the shade of a big koa tree next to his house. To say this wasn't exactly what I was expecting would be a massive understatement.

"How about something to drink?" Dagywn said. "I'll be right back."

He came back in a couple of minutes carrying a tray loaded with a pitcher of iced tea, glasses and a plate of cookies. We all helped ourselves and settled around the table and waited for someone to say something. Dagywn broke the silence with "So, what brings you to these parts?"

"Very funny, Dagywn," G said, "We just happened to be in the neighborhood and thought we'd drop in."

"Okay, okay. I'm just not sure how to start. There's a lot to talk about," Dagywn said.

"I'll start," I said. "I don't mean to be rude, but what are you doing here?" I asked, motioning to the surroundings with my hands. "It's not exactly where we expected to find you. In fact, we drove right past it the other day."

"Hiding in plain sight isn't exactly a new strategy," he said, "but let me back up a bit. Have you got some time?"

"All the time you want," I said.

"Well, like I said, 'changes,' there have been lots of changes. Shortly after we — that's me, Ainsworth, Charleston, Doolittle, and Roskoloff — arrived here, we hooked up with the Menehune, which was only natural, considering what we had in common. Little did we know that we'd arrived at a crucial time for the Menehune. They were just beginning to debate the merits of assimilation into the larger culture of Kauai — to come out of the shadows, you might say. They weren't the first Menehune to consider such a thing. Back in the early 1800s, a group of a couple dozen Menehune split off from the main tribe and went to live in the Wainiha Valley with the intent of living openly, if quietly, in the midst of the larger culture of Kauai. I, and two Menehune, were elected to go and visit them to see how things had worked out. Long story short, they figured their choice had been a success. In the seventy-odd years they had been living in the open, there had been several inter-marriages between the Menehunes and the local Kauaiians and the offspring were not only taller, but crossed easily into and out of both cultures. We reported all this back to our Menehune tribe. The Wainiha Valley experiment became a major factor in our ultimate decision."

"Pokee told us that there might be Menehune in Wainiha Valley," Mad said.

"They'd be Menehune many times removed by now. I doubt you could tell them from the local population. How is old Pokee? I haven't seen him in years."

"Cranky," Mad said, "but I don't think that's anything new."

"He's an odd duck, that's for sure," Dagywn said, "but he's as smart as they come. We worked with him a few years ago until it became too dangerous — we can talk about that later. Like I said, lots to discuss." He turned and looked at G and said "So, tell me, G, has our tribe had any similar talk of assimilation?"

"Not really," G said, "but certain recent events are probably going to force our hand. But you know how long it takes us to make any kind of decision. I'm guessing something as big as 'coming out of the shadows,' as you called it, is going to take generations to decide."

"Interesting that you should use that word — 'generations' — because that's what made what happened, happen, for us."

"What do you mean?" Mad asked.

"I take it it's still just the men in our tribe, wherever you are. By the way, where *are* you now?"

"In California. In the Napa Valley on top of Mt. St. Helena. And, yes, it's just the men."

"And you're still the only young one?"

"Don't I know it," G said.

"And is the location on Mt. St. Helena isolated?"

"Yes, I'd say so. There's no one around us, except for one old miner on the other side of the mountain and he's as much of a hermit as we are."

"You see, the Menehune here found themselves in a much different situation. First, there are a lot of children in the tribe and, second, the Menehune lived within a larger community, hidden, yes, but still surrounded by the dominant Uplander culture."

"So?" G asked.

"So, over time, kids being kids, they began to see things, hear things, smell things. Most of us are switching to nighttime sleeping now, but back then, we were still sleeping during the day and up at night. Try as we might, it was impossible to keep the kids from wandering the Uplander neighborhoods at night. They heard music very much different from ours, smelled things like hamburgers and French fries... "

"Hamburgers and French fries?" Chuy asked.

"I'm not kidding. The two easiest portals to pass through to a different culture are food and music — the attraction is immediate, familiar and satisfying. And then there's television. Talk about an attraction! The kids could see the Uplanders watching television through their windows at night. A small screen where there were moving images

The world turns in surprising places.

and stories being told? What's not to like? Even I got hooked: *As the World Turns*, every day at 1:30. Wouldn't miss it."

"The soap opera?" Mad asked, incredulous.

"Yep," Dagywn replied.

"My tutu never misses it. She even has a t.v. at the shave ice stand," Mad said, rolling her eyes.

"My grandmother wouldn't miss it either," I said.

"Well, it's all been part of our assimilation. A few years after the five of us showed up, the tribe took a vote — there are about a hundred of us — and those that wanted to assimilate won. The first order of business was to find a place to live where we could have access to modern conveniences. Someone suggested that we explore the old tracts of plantation housing. Most of them were relatively isolated, their former residents long gone, and they were essentially a ready-made community. When we found this one, there were two old plantation workers still living here. We made them a handsome offer and were able to buy the whole tract, lock, stock and barrel. Forty-six houses, just right for the tribe."

"How long have you been here?" G asked.

"About 20 years."

"Any problems?"

"Not really. But remember, we consciously decided not to have a plan to assimilate. We decided not to make a big deal out of it and just let whatever might happen, happen. We also decided to treat each other as if we weren't different from anyone else. It's been amazing how far the right attitude goes in getting acceptance from other people. I'm not saying it's 100 percent, but most times people see you as you see yourself. So our non-plan has worked pretty well, even for the kids. Surprising because you know kids can be every bit as mean and stupid as most adults."

I've got to admit that it made me feel good to hear Dagywn say what he'd just said. They were my thoughts exactly.

"Speaking of kids, where's Leo?" G asked.

"At school."

"School?!"

"Yeah, that was one of the big discussions we had to have. In the end, the kids who wanted to go to the Uplander school went there. Those who didn't are taught at home. The way we figured it was that the kids who wanted to go to Uplander school were probably the ones most likely to naturally fit in and survive. And the kids who were scared and had doubts were probably better off not having those doubts and fears exploited by nasty little Uplander kids. You know how it is."

"What do the other kids think of Leo?" I asked.

"That he's short. And funny and smart." Dagywn said. "I gotta' say – and this has everything to do with him being so smart – what he's learned from the Uplander school is impressive. If he can find a way to combine it with what his own people can teach him, he should be unstoppable."

"This is like that discussion we had on the sailboat, G," Chuy said, "the one about it being easier to stick with your own kind."

"Yeah," G said, "but I think the point Dagywn is making is that if you only stick with your own kind, you're stuck with them and their ways. Not much chance of learning something new."

"I guess it all boils down to whether or not you want to learn something new or believe what your own kind can teach you is enough," Chuy said.

"Or how good the hamburgers – or tacos, or chop suey, or bouillabaisse – smell and the music sounds," Dagywn replied.

. . .

We continued to talk for awhile and Dagywn explained that he had asked permission from the other members of the tribe to meet alone with us today. "Tomorrow – that is if you can make it tomorrow – I'll be a better host and introduce you around the neighborhood," he said. We assured him that we'd be back and he walked us to Mad's car. We were about to say our goodbyes when G pulled me aside and said "I think I'm going to spend the night. There are things Dagywn and I need to talk about. And I want to get reacquainted with the other guys who jumped ship – especially Sulo Roskoloff – you remember I told you about him being my friend? You understand, don't you?"

"Of course."

"There are questions I need to ask Dagywn and I'm sure there's plenty he wants to know from me. I think it'll make tomorrow's conversation easier. We haven't even gotten to the 'get me out of here' part yet."

"Yeah, I know. Something tells me it's going to be complicated," I said. "See you tomorrow. Good luck."

Sure, I thought it would be complicated, but I had no idea of what we were walking into. Not a clue.

The community hall at the Menehune compound looked about
exactly as you'd expect it to look — just the place for
weddings, dances, and other celebrations.

Chapter XVI

An Uninvited Visitor

July 1 – 2, 1968
Menehune compound
Kauai, Hawaiian Islands

Mad dropped Chuy and I off at the Garden Isle. She said she'd be back the next morning around 9:30 to take us back out to see Dagywn. As we were walking back to our cottage, we noticed Mr. Becker, Tova and JP sitting on JP's front porch.

"Hey, have you seen this?" Mr. Becker said.

"What's that?" I asked.

"Take a look."

Chuy and I went up the steps and saw the newspaper on the table.

"Looks like your friends are famous. Speaking of which, where's G?" Tova asked, holding up the newspaper.

"He's spending the night with Dagywn," I said as Chuy and I looked at the newspaper. Right there, above the fold, was a large photograph of Leo and G standing face-to-face on the beach, with Leo holding his surfboard. The caption under the photo said simply "Never too young."

"Oh, jeez," I said.

"What the... " Chuy said under his breath.

"Who took the picture?" Mr. Becker asked.

"I have absolutely no idea," I said. "Did you see anyone taking photographs, Chuy?"

"Nope."

"Well at least whoever wrote the caption thought they were a couple of 5-year-old kids instead of two teenaged gnomes," I said.

"Still, it was kind of a shock to see," Mr. Becker said.

"Yeah, so much for keeping a low profile," I said.

Chuy and I sat down and told everyone about our conversation with Dagywn. They had a lot of questions because, let's face it, it was a remarkable story.

"Did he say what he wants to do next?" Mr. Becker asked.

"No, we're going back out tomorrow. I'm guessing he'll tell us then," I said.

"Do you have any idea of what he's thinking?" Mr. Becker asked.

"I have absolutely no idea."

"Well, whatever it is, you've got to feel good that you actually found him. You've come a long way, literally," Mr. Becker said.

"Yeah, thanks to you. If you hadn't told us to take the day off, we would never have run into Leo," I said.

"I'd say this calls for a celebration," JP said, standing up, "I'll go to the store and get some steaks."

Later that evening we built a fire on the beach and let it die down to an even bed of glowing coals. JP used the grill from the barbecue and cooked the steaks right there on the beach. They were the best anyone had ever eaten and we all had a good time, although it was a little weird not having Mad or G there. After dinner, we all went inside JP's cottage and Chuy and I taught Mr. Becker, Tova and JP how to play multi-hand solitaire. It was all pretty raucous and competitive, so much so that the first time I looked up at the clock, it was after midnight. Considering how late it was, we finished the night giving JP a rather hushed three cheers for being such a great cook and called it a night.

. . .

Mad showed up the next morning to pick up Chuy and me and, just like yesterday, we were at the Menehune compound by 10 o'clock. Dagywn and G were seated at the same table, like maybe they hadn't moved since we left. It didn't surprise me to see a newspaper on the table in front of them.

There were "good mornings" all around and then Dagywn held up the newspaper and said "I assume you saw this?"

"Oh, yeah," I said.

"I think it's a first," Dagywn said, "I don't think any of us have ever been photographed before."

The word "photographed" triggered a thought of Nigel in my brain, but I decided to file it away until later when I could think about what it meant.

"It'll be interesting to see if anything comes of it," he continued.

"Do you think something will?" Mad asked.

"It's possible that there's some old geezer out there — possibly someone up in Wainiha Valley with Menehune in their family tree — who'll recognize what they're looking at and say something. I don't know. We'll just have to wait and see. Meanwhile, Leo's been busy signing autographs in the neighborhood. He thinks he's a star," Dagywn said, chuckling. "Before we continue talking, I'd like you to meet the folks here. Everyone's gathered in our community hall. Follow me."

We followed Dagywn up the hill to a rectangular building that looked just like what it was — a community hall. We walked through the open doors and were greeted by a sea of friendly faces, smiling at our arrival. There were a couple of tables set up containing coffee, iced tea, and big platters of cookies and sliced breads. Dagywn had said yesterday that there were about 100 of them living in the compound and it appeared everyone had shown up to meet us. The Menehunes had arranged themselves in an informal receiving line in a rough u-shape. We started at the front of the line, shaking hands with each of them, exchanging a few words, working our way along. At the very end of the line, G introduced us to Ainsworth, Charleston, Doolittle, and his good friend, Sulo Roskoloff, all the mates who had jumped ship with Dagywn back in 1879. They, in turn, introduced us to their wives and children. I had no way of knowing if they were looked on as outsiders when they first arrived, but they certainly didn't look that way now. Dagwyn hung back until we had made our way down the line and then introduced us to was his wife, Melea. She bowed slightly as she shook our hands and then said "so you're the ones that are going to take my Dagywn away?"

Dagywn's face fell and he excused himself, whispering in Melea's ear and then, taking her by the arm, they disappeared from sight. He returned a few minutes later, apologizing, and said "Let's go back to the table. Like I said, there's a lot to discuss."

We walked back down the hill to the big koa tree and took our places around the table.

"So now you know how we got here and you've met the members of our community. It's time to talk about me," Dagywn said.

"First, let me say I don't think I did the right thing when I jumped ship all those years ago — and believe me, I've had some time to think about it. But I had been so seasick for so long, I just needed some relief. In hindsight, however, considering my position within the tribe, I should have gutted it out for the last leg of the journey. I can't talk for the others — Ainsworth, Charleston, Doolittle and Roskoloff — but I do know they were just as sick as I was. We were all sick of being sick.

"Secondly, going through the assimilation process with the Menehune has been a thought-provoking process for me and it made me think about our own tribe. In talking with G last night, I know it's King Gob's intention to gather our remaining members from the Åland Islands and reunite everyone on Mt. St. Helena. I'll let Ainsworth, Charleston, Doolittle, and Roskoloff know of the king's intentions and let them decide whether they stay here on Kauai or travel to California. My guess is that they will want to stay here, but like I said, I'll let them decide.

"Thirdly, on a more personal note, you heard for yourselves this morning that my wife, Melea, is not supportive of my decision to return to my tribe. At first I thought she would want to come with me, but she is adamant about holding onto the gains she has made in the assimilation process. In short, she says she's not going back to living in a cave and giving up the modern conveniences of the Uplander world. Plus, her very old mother is still very much alive and she has three sisters. It would be very difficult for her to leave her family and come with me. Ironically, Leo would come with me in an instant and has said so repeatedly. He knows all about California — or says he does. But all of these are my problems; I just thought it was important that you know my situation.

"Fourthly, and this is for your ears only. In addition to feeling an acute responsibility to my tribe, I have also come down with a serious case of 'island fever.'"

"What's that?" Chuy asked, sounding like he was worried that it might be contagious.

"It's a feeling of being trapped on a rock in the middle of the ocean. It doesn't affect everyone, but for me, it's like claustrophobia. I need to get somewhere that isn't surrounded by nothing but water. And the sooner the better. So that's pretty much my story. Do you have any questions?"

"I do," said a disembodied voice.

All of us looked around to see where the voice had come from and saw an old lady just kind of appear out of a cloud of dust and a blast of wind right in front of us. She had long white hair and was wearing a long white, flowing robe. She was followed by a very large white dog that looked like an albino wolf with metallic gold eyes. It was super weird and very scary, but at least she had an attached head, I thought to myself. As soon as she appeared, there was a kind of electricity in the air, like when it's dry and windy and any metal you touch gives you a shock. I looked across to Dagywn who had a grave expression on his face. He stood up and said "Please, will you sit down?"

"No," she answered. "I am in need of water and something to eat. Have you anything to share?"

"Of course. My house is nearby. Please follow me." He gave all of us at the table a quick look that said "stay here," and walked off with the old lady and the dog.

"What the...?" Chuy said.

"I think we've just been busted," Mad said.

"What do you mean?" G asked.

"Let's wait until Dagywn gets back," she said.

After about ten minutes, Dagywn returned by himself.

"Where is she?" I asked.

"She just sort of disappeared after I gave her a glass of water and some cookies. Good thing Melea didn't see her."

"Why?" G asked.

"Because she would have had a coronary, that's why."

"That was Madam Pele, wasn't it?" Mad asked.

"Yes, yes it was. In one of her many disguises. It was her way of letting us know she knows what's going on," Dagywn said.

"She didn't exactly give off a friendly vibe," Chuy said.

"No, she's a suspicious one, always looking for trouble. Usually she asks for a cigarette instead of a glass of water," Dagywn said.

"Maybe she quit," Mad said.

"What's it matter to her what you're doing?" Chuy asked.

"I don't think it's me she's concerned about, it's the others. She's always thought of the Menehune as her pets who need her protection. Most likely she thinks I'm planning on taking some of her Menehune away from the island. She can't stand it when anyone takes anything from her. Most of the time when she thinks she's protecting the Menehune, she causes more harm than good. Everyone lives in fear of her powers which she uses without much thought. It's like we're all her hostages. But I gotta tell you, if you went into any house on this compound, you'd find a small altar devoted to her — candles, flowers, a picture of her likeness — even I have one."

"So why did she show up now?" G asked.

"I imagine as a warning," Dagywn said, "warning me not to take anything she considers hers off the island."

"I thought you said Melea didn't want to go. And surely you could convince Leo not to if it was Madam Pele he'd have to deal with," I said.

"We haven't even had a family meeting yet," Dagywn said, "let alone a meeting of the entire tribe. There wasn't any real need to until you showed up.

No final decisions have been made, by anyone, and none will be until everyone has had their say and voted."

"Sorry," I said.

"No, no. Don't misunderstand me. You showing up was very much hoped for, at least by me. But now... it keeps getting more complicated. If I didn't think it would bring down her wrath, I'd curse you-know-who."

"So what next?" G asked.

"I need a little time to consult with everyone. Can we meet back here the day after tomorrow, same time?"

We all said "sure" and got up to leave.

As we were all walking towards Mad's car, I stopped and asked Dagywn "Just out of curiosity, could any of your powers be used against you-know-who?" It seemed natural that none of us wanted to mention her actual name, like if we did, she'd just pop up again.

"She's a goddess. I'm just a gnome, way down the totem pole, so to speak. She has more power in her little toe than I have in my whole bag of tricks."

"Well, if I see her again, I'm going to kick her in the butt," G said.

"Sorry to be the one to remind you, G, but your legs wouldn't reach her butt," Mad said, "Better come up with another plan."

. . .

August 12, 2012
Grandpa Nick's house
Rutherford, California

The library in Grandpa's house is just off the living room. It's basically a square room with very tall ceilings, tall narrow windows on two sides, one straight ahead and one to the right, and a small marble fireplace on the left. There's a mostly-red Oriental carpet on the floor, Grandpa's huge roll-top desk against one wall, a library table in the middle of the room and a couple of comfortable chairs in front of the fireplace. Hanging in the center of the room, over the library table, is a large, very ornate chandelier. Other than that, it's books, books, books, from side to side and floor to ceiling. A lot of books.

It seems like almost every house has a drawer in the kitchen that holds all the small utensils, like potato peelers, garlic presses, and lemon squeezers. The utensils that rarely get used, like a cherry pitter or a curved grapefruit knife, gradually migrate (on their own) to the back of the drawer. I figured that books that rarely get read might be like that and wind up towards the edges of the bookshelves. I'll grant you that there's not much of a connection between kitchen utensils and books, but I had to start somewhere and my theory seemed as good as any other place to start. Remember, Grandpa said the books weren't really organized.

I started looking where it was easiest: at eye-height on the left side of each bookcase, down to the floor, across the bottom and then back to eye-height on the right side. It didn't take long before I started to feel dizzy from reading titles and moving at the same time. I wondered when the last time anybody had pulled any of these books off the shelves; they all looked like they'd been there a very long time. After I had looked on all four sides of the library, I sat down at Grandpa's desk and rubbed my eyes. When my vision cleared a little, I looked straight up. On the very top shelf above the desk there was a stuffed barn owl that looked like it was staring right down at me, saying "Look at me." So I did.

Even if I stood on top of the desk, I still wouldn't be tall enough to reach the top shelf, plus I didn't think my grandfather would approve of me standing on his desk. Over in the other corner of the room was an old ladder mounted on small brass and rubber wheels. I pushed it across the room with some difficulty and got it as close to the desk as possible and locked the wheels in place. I started up the steps, hoping that the ladder was stronger than it looked. My head was practically scraping the ceiling. After saying hello to the owl, I started scanning the titles on the top shelf. There were a bunch of books on gardening, bee-keeping, several on raising chickens, including one titled *The Call of the Hen*, and then a slim blue book with *Homing Pigeons* stamped on its spine. "Yes!" I said under my breath and reached for it at the same time as a voice from below said "Did you find it?" I nearly lost my footing and looked down to see Grandpa Nick standing in the doorway to the library.

"You scared the you-know-what outta' me!"

"Sorry, I should have let you know I was here."

"Oh jeez, there it is."

"What is?"

I had turned my head around and the *Secret Teachings* book my grandfather had written about in the first journal was right in front of my nose.

"Wow."

"What?"

"You were right about the size of the thing. That's the biggest book I've ever seen."

"Is that up there, too? *The Secret Teachings* book?"

"Yep."

"Well throw the pigeon book down to me and then hand me the *Secret Teachings*. Be careful. It's really heavy."

I tossed the pigeon book down to Grandpa and then went after the *Secret Teachings*. Pulling it from the shelf took some doing. When it was finally free of the shelf, it was so heavy that it slipped right out of my hands and nearly hit Grandpa on the head. After jumping out of the way, he looked up at me and said "Jeez, you'd think we were trying to kill each other."

"Sorry!"

I got back down onto firm ground and Grandpa gave me a hug.

"Well, that was easy," he said sarcastically, shaking his head.

"Very funny. But at least I found it. And the *Secret Teachings* book."

"Why don't you take a look at what you found? I'm late for a meeting. We can talk about this over dinner, okay?"

"Okay by me. See you later."

I took the pigeon book to the kitchen, deciding to leave *Secret Teachings* until later. Doyle was at the big table making himself a sandwich. "Want one? Liverwurst and red onion on sourdough bread."

"Sure. Thanks." Call me weird, but I love liverwurst.

"What was the commotion I heard?" Doyle asked as he was making the sandwich.

"Oh, just Grandpa and me throwing books at each other."

"Really?"

"Pretty close. Accidentally."

"What have you got there?"

"A book on homing pigeons. Did you know we have homing pigeons?"

"Well, yeah. I helped moved the dovecote here a long time ago. And I like watching them fly back and forth every day at the same time. They're like clockwork."

"Whoa. Wait a minute. 'Back and forth, every day at the same time?'"

"Yeah."

"Do you feed them? Grandpa said he doesn't."

"Nope."

"You said they go 'back and forth'. Where do you think they go 'forth' to?"

"Well, most likely somewhere where they get fed. Getting them to go back and forth between two locations on a regular basis means they're getting fed in one spot and making their home in another. That keeps them flying back and forth, like I said."

"Any ideas of who's feeding them?"

"I guess I always assumed it was Prince G."

The liverwurst sandwich stopped midair, halfway to my mouth. "So you think the pigeons are flying from here to Prince G every day because he's feeding them?"

"Sure. Why not? He was the one who always fed them."

Not the same "moon over Mt. St. Helena" mentioned in this chapter, but much more presentable and pleasant to look at.

Chapter XVII

Moon Over Mt. St. Helena

July 3, 1968
Mt. St. Helena
Napa Valley, California

The sun wasn't up and the gnomes were already done implementing the plan. Even though they're known for their ability to excavate mines, tunnels, and caves with miraculous speed, the king's deadline had pushed them to their very limits, especially considering they were working without sleep. By the end of the night they were all exhausted, but pleased with their results.

The king was pacing back and forth near the entrance to the cave, muttering to himself, clearly nervous and excited about what was about to take place. True to his word, the sheriff and two of his deputies arrived at first light and announced themselves outside the entrance to the cave. The king greeted them and ushered them inside where it was just tall enough for them to stand upright.

"Come, come. You must see our handiwork," he said to the officers.

"Hold on just a minute, King. Can you explain what's going on here? All we know is that Nigel Stayne has come back."

"Of course, of course," King Gob said, "but we must hurry. He's likely to be here at any moment. Let's walk and talk at the same time," he said, leading them into the cave. "The long and the short of it is that Nigel showed up yesterday with a mechanical monster that's eating its way into the back side of our cave."

"Mechanical monster?" Sheriff Lyman asked.

"Yes, yes. You know... a mechanical monster. Big, noisy metal thing, bright yellow."

"Okay, I get it," the sheriff said.

"Yesterday they came very close to where we store our treasure, so we moved it to a safe location and laid our trap."

"Trap?"

"Yes, trap. Rather ingenious, if I do say so myself. See for yourself," he said, spreading his hands out in front of him.

"Forgive me, King, but it looks like a wooden ceiling held up with six large posts."

"Well, that's exactly what it is. But don't forget the ropes, the ropes."

"I'm sorry, but I'm still not getting it," the sheriff said.

"Arghh," the king muttered, clearly frustrated. "Right above that wooden ceiling is where the mechanical monster is. We excavated underneath it to the point where there's very little between it and the wooden ceiling. Very little. When the monster roars to life this morning, we'll pull the posts out using the ropes, and we're certain the vibration of the monster will be enough to cause it to cave in, burying the monster alive."

"Interesting," the sheriff said. "I hope it works."

"Now we must go. I'll take you to a spot where we can observe the activities undetected. Whitbeck is getting my donkey cart ready. You will follow me and when we get to the spot, you can do what you will. Oh, this is going to be a right spectacle!" the king said, barely able to contain himself.

The sheriff and his deputies followed Gob out of the cave and down to the corral where they got to witness, firsthand, the first spectacle of the day (of which there would be several), namely Whitbeck loading the king onto the cart. At one point, they all had to look away to keep from laughing out loud. Completely unaware that anything unusual had just taken place, Gob maneuvered himself upright and faced forward on the seat of the cart. Snapping the reins, Jenny took off up the mountain, with Gob saying over his shoulder, "Follow me, gentlemen. The mechanical monster awaits its date with destiny."

Luckily, the sheriff wisely thought to bring the same two deputies who had come with him the year before, so they weren't completely taken aback by the strangeness of everything they were witnessing. Instead of walking next to the cart, Whitbeck decided to hang back with the sheriff and his men, allowing the king to make the most of his role as the leader of the team. The sheriff couldn't help but notice Whitbeck shaking his head and rolling his eyes.

Patches of sunlight had started to appear on the forest floor by the time they'd reached the location where they could observe the goings-on without being seen. Gob motioned to the sheriff to catch up with him.

"Do you see that very large pine tree over there?" he said, pointing across the clearing in the forest.

"Yes."

"That's where Nigel was standing yesterday. My guess is he'll stand in the same location today. Should you position one of your men behind the tree in case Nigel makes a run for it?" the king asked.

"Let me handle this, Gob. We've got it covered." The sheriff conferred with his deputies and they took off, disappearing into the forest.

"Splendid, splendid," the king said quietly, and then started humming a little ditty to himself. Clearly he was enjoying the event even though nothing had happened yet. Ten minutes hadn't gone by when the sheriff motioned to the king and Whitbeck to look on the other side of the clearing. It was Nigel and Chet. Nigel was talking quietly but excitedly, while Chet just nodded his head. Sure enough, Nigel took his position leaning against the tree the king had pointed out to the sheriff. Chet ambled over to the Caterpillar and pulled himself up onto the seat. He leaned over to put the key in the ignition. The king felt time slow down. He was so excited he could barely contain himself. He knew that the instant the gnomes in the cave heard the mechanical monster start, it would be their signal to simultaneously pull the posts out from under the ceiling. Chet turned the ignition and it just made a clicking noise. He turned the key again. Same clicking noise. He pumped on the accelerator pedal and turned the key a third time. The Caterpillar finally rumbled and coughed into life, black smoke billowing from the muffler. Ten seconds later there was another low rumble but this time, not from the Caterpillar. Slowly, the Caterpillar shifted and dropped on one side and then the other. Chet looked around, wide-eyed, not believing what was happening. The Caterpillar stayed where it was for another twenty seconds and then — whoosh! — it all but disappeared into the ground with a huge, ugly crashing noise. Nigel stood transfixed next to the tree, his mouth open, but not making a sound. The king couldn't help but whoop loudly and clap his hands. Chet could be heard, but not seen, swearing a blue streak. The deputies reappeared like magic, one at the newly-formed pit, the other at Nigel's side. The sheriff nodded to Whitbeck and the king, saying "Well done, gentlemen," and walked over to Nigel.

"And so we meet again, Mr. Stayne," the sheriff said, "and always in the most unusual circumstances."

Nigel was dumbstruck. He just stood there with a blank look on his face, muttering what sounded like some pretty foul language.

In the next minute, in an unplanned move, the rest of the gnomes began streaming out of the cave to where the king and Whitbeck stood. At the sight of the buried Caterpillar a spontaneous cheer went up which, naturally, the king thought was for him. He waved to the huddle of gnomes, smiling, mouthing the words "Thank you, thank you." While the gnomes were still cheering, the king

When the caterpillar started to go down, it did so with a terrible thud.

called Whitbeck to his side and whispered something in his ear.

"Really? Are you sure, sir?" Whitbeck said.

"Quite. Now hurry or we'll lose the opportunity."

Whitbeck ran back to the cave and when he returned he appeared to be carrying a couple of sticks and some clothing. (Note to the reader: I learned later from G that the gnomes had a special holiday the day after the Winter Solstice that they called "Uplandia." There wasn't much point to the holiday, save for general revelry, dressing up like Uplanders and walking around on stilts and eating and drinking too much. The king had asked Whitbeck to fetch him some stilts and Uplander clothes that are kept from year to year for the Uplandia festival. What happened next defied the imagination.)

The king made it clear to Whitbeck that he wanted to get up on the stilts and to be dressed in the Uplander clothes. "Ask the men to help you," Gob said. And it did, in fact, take a half dozen of them to perform his request, but not without rolling him around on the ground first with a lot of grunting and groaning on everyone's part, especially when they struggled to dress him and stand him upright, propped against a tree.

"No, no, no," the king yelled. "I want to be facing the tree!"

The gnomes were completely baffled by his request but moved him anyway, with great difficulty. Once he was facing the tree, the king called out to the sheriff "Will you bring the prisoner here?" The sheriff and his men had been watching the commotion with the king and his men with silent confusion. Even though he didn't have a clue what was going on, he followed the king's orders and, holding on to Nigel's elbow, the sheriff brought the "prisoner" closer to the king.

"Sheriff Lyman," the king said, looking over his shoulder, "we wouldn't want our determined visitor to go away empty-handed. Would you please reach into Mr. Stayne's satchel and get his camera? I'd like you to take the photograph he so desperately wanted. Tell me when you're ready."

The sheriff did as he was told and readied the camera.

"Ready," he said, "but what do you want me to photograph?"

"Me, of course. Just give me a second." Nobody who was there that day could figure out how he did it, but the king managed to drop his trousers and expose his bare arse for all to see.

"Now," the king said.

Laughing out loud, the sheriff took several shots of the scene.

Pulling his pants up, the king said "Mr. Stayne, you can tell his lordship, that I call this picture 'Moon Over Mt. St. Helena,' and he can publish it anywhere he pleases. Sheriff Lyman, will you please return the camera to Mr. Stayne? Thank you. And now, Mr. Stayne, you have what you came for and you have no further reason to ever set foot on this mountain again. Although I dare say, given my commanding height, you're going to have a very hard time convincing your employer that I'm a gnome, but that's your problem."

All the gnomes started cheering again, only this time it really *was* for the king. Even Chet, the Caterpillar operator, was clapping and whistling. In the mayhem, nobody noticed Nigel inching backwards until he was removed enough from the crowd to turn around and start running. And he kept running without looking back. He knew that if he were caught he'd be in so much trouble with the local police and the immigration authorities that he might never get out of jail, not to mention incurring the wrath of Lord Higgenbotham, which he didn't want to even think about. The sheriff was mightily embarrassed to have let Nigel escape and vowed to find him. The fact is, however, he never did catch Nigel. Which isn't to say I didn't hear from him again, because I did. But that's another story I'll tell you later.

Mad turned us on to the best Chinese food on Kauai; as good as it
was, I continued to get strange fortunes in the fortune cookies.

Chapter XVIII

An Obscure Legacy

July 3 — 4, 1968
Garden Isle Beach Cottages
Kauai, Hawaiian Islands

The next day there wasn't anything we had to do, so Chuy and Mad went on a picnic. I got the sense they were becoming an item. Or maybe not. Mad wasn't that easy to read. Chuy, on the other hand, was like an open book. Every time we were all together, he couldn't take his eyes off Mad. He was so obvious, it was kind of embarrassing. Mr. Becker, Tova and JP took the Zodiac to explore the Na Pali coast, which left me and G on our own. I didn't mind because I felt like I had to catch up with all the things that had happened over the last few days. We both just lazed around for most of the day, G reading and me sitting on the front porch staring at the ocean, thinking that for all its beauty, Kauai was a strange place. It may have looked like paradise on the surface, but just under that surface there was a lot going on — stuff that was foreign to me and made me uncomfortable. The more I thought about it, the more I realized that the whole last year had been that way. Before I went to Walter's and Ma-D's last summer, I had a fairly normal life — or at least I thought it was. And now I was crossing the ocean with a gnome prince in search of a missing gnome wizard, having dreams of a headless Hawaiian goddess — and then meeting her in person — and watching an old guy light his pipe by snapping his fingers, not to mention everything I experienced on Mt. St. Helena last summer. It was like that feeling I had on the sailboat, when we first went under the Golden Gate Bridge and entered the Pacific Ocean. It was all so big and there was no rope attached to the shore any more. I had entered a new world then and I felt the same way now. One thing was the same though. I wasn't able to control much of anything. And I definitely didn't like it.

After sitting for a long time, I came to the uneasy conclusion that, deep down, there was a part of me that wished everything would go back to normal. A world that was what it appeared to be. A world I was familiar with, one I could understand, where cause-and-effect made sense. But as much as I might have wanted things to be normal again. I realized I had probably already come too far, that maybe my idea of "normal" had already been permanently changed. And let's face it, there are only so many things you can forget.

Arrggh! I didn't like these feelings. Normal. What the heck was normal? A peanut butter and jelly sandwich and a glass of cold milk? Playing dominoes with Clyde at his camp? Reading a book? If I were at home (wherever that was — another uncomfortable thought!) what would I do? If I were at school or at Walter and Ma' D's, I'd get on my bike and ride as fast as I could for as far as I could, until my head was clear. If I were at Grandma's in San Francisco, I'd walk as far as I could, up and down the hills of the city, even though it hurt my damn foot. But I was here, in Kauai, staring at the ocean. "Okay," I thought to myself, "I'll go for a swim and swim as far as can. That seems normal — at least for Kauai."

I swam out into the bay, way past Pokee's house and into the open ocean. When I was as tired as I wanted to be I flipped over and floated on my back. All I could see was blue sky with puffy white clouds and an equally blue ocean with white rippling surf. And me, sandwiched between the two. Beautiful. Rhythmically buoyed up and down on the waves, I let myself zone out completely. It felt good to not think about anything. Eventually a big wave crashed over me which I took as a sign. I flipped over and started doing a slow breaststroke back to shore. I took a hot shower and put on clean clothes and felt better than I did before I'd gone swimming. G was still reading, but had moved to one of the chairs on the front porch. He was so absorbed in his book, *The Lessons of History* by Will and Ariel Durant, he barely noticed I was there. His book wasn't exactly light reading. I knew because I had once tried reading it.

I think I mentioned in the first journal that my friends at school call me a "recreational sleeper." It's true, I can sleep just about anywhere, any time. Considering how quiet it was with no one around, it seemed like a good idea to take a nap. Well, I was wrong about that. Ever since being visited by the headless woman in my dream, I have to admit that I thought about her each night before I went to sleep, hoping she wouldn't appear again. Somehow, taking a nap while it was still light seemed safer, so I didn't even give her a thought as I lay down on the punee.

I woke up in a cold sweat, my heart racing, with G standing over me asking if I was all right.

"You were screaming," he said.

"Oh, man." I said, propping myself on my elbows. "It was just a bad dream. A really bad dream."

"You-know-who again?" G asked.

"Yeah. You-know-who."

"What did she say?"

"It seemed like another warning, but this time she was standing in like the middle of a hurricane, with lightning bolts coming down everywhere and thunder so loud it was shaking everything."

"That was me," G said, "I was shaking you. Trying to get you to wake up."

"Well, that's good to know, I guess."

"What was she warning you about?"

"I don't know. I think maybe she wants us to leave."

Just then there was a friendly "yoo-hoo" on the front porch that sounded like Tova and then a big commotion.

"Oh my gosh, are you all right?"

"I'm not sure."

"What happened?"

G and I went out to the front porch to see what was going on. Apparently Mr. Becker, Tova, and JP had arrived home at the same time as Chuy and Mad. Mad had her arm around Chuy's shoulder and was holding what looked like a bunch of paper napkins over his nose.

"Get inside," Tova said, "Let me take a look at you."

Everybody went inside and Tova told Chuy to lay down on the punee where I had just been.

"Well, you're definitely going to have a shiner and a fat lip, but I don't think your nose is broken. Tim, will you get me some washcloths and a pan of warm water? What happened, Chuy? Did you get in a fight?"

"More like a beating. You tell them, Mad," Chuy said.

"Well, Chuy and I decided to stop in and get shave ice from Queenie. We had just gotten out of the car when Queenie appeared from out of nowhere and started punching Chuy."

"I saw her come from under the counter, straight at me," Chuy said. "She was like a tornado, spinning around like that cartoon character, the Tasmanian Devil, hands, elbows and feet flying in every direction."

"She's got a black belt in Kung fu," Mad said.

"I didn't know what to do," Chuy continued, "so I just held my hands in front of my face, for all the good it did. I hope she has those hands — and feet — registered with the police. She's lethal!"

"Why'd she attack you?" Mr. Becker asked.

Chuy looked at Mad but didn't say anything.

"Probably because we were holding hands," Mad said, sheepishly.

I know it's wrong of me, but I couldn't help laughing, which caused G to laugh. JP had to leave the room. Chuy had been my best friend forever and I'd never want to see him hurt but, man, I would have loved to see that tiny Tutu go all Ninja on him. I had to bite my lip to stop laughing. Like I said, I know it was wrong, but still...

"Well, let me get you cleaned up. You'll be all right, but you're going to look like hell for a few days," Tova said.

"I didn't even get a shave ice," Chuy said.

•   •   •

That night, considering JP had been gone all day, we decided to get Chinese food to go. Mad told us where the best restaurant was and, after taking requests, Mr. Becker went to pick up our dinner. Chuy continued to recuperate from his encounter with Queenie on the punee and I pulled G aside and told him I didn't think we should mention my dream until we talked to Dagywn tomorrow. I don't know why, but somehow I didn't want to talk about it.

Mad was right, the Chinese food was most excellent and we all ate too much. It reminded me of that night we — Grandma Hattie, King Gob, Whitbeck, Wycoff, and G — all had leftover Chinese food in the middle of the night in her kitchen in Rutherford. And even further back to last June when Mr. Becker had taken me and some of my friends out for Chinese food in Santa Cruz just before the end of school. That's when I got the fortune cookie that said "A legacy, however obscure, will soon be yours." I still had it folded up in my wallet. When most people think of legacies, they think of money, or a house that a relative leaves you after they die. So I guess you could say that a ship's log from nearly a hundred years ago, mentioning the presence of stowaways who just happened to be gnomes, was pretty obscure as legacies go. But it was, as it said in the fortune, my legacy and I was right in the middle of it, right now.

After we finished dinner, we passed around a little carton filled with fortune cookies and each took one. Chuy's read his and said he wished he had read it sooner; it said "Keep your eye out for someone special."

"I have absolutely no idea what this means," Mad said, holding her fortune in front of her.

"What does it say?" Chuy asked.

"All of your fingers cannot be of the same length." which made everyone laugh.

I opened mine. I'd never seen a fortune with just one word before.

It simply said "Flee."

Pokee put on an amazing fireworks display just for the fun of it.

Chapter XIX

Dagywn's Retreat

July 5, 1968
Multiple locations
Kauai, Hawaiian Islands

After dinner last night, when it was just getting dark, JP made us all go outside onto the beach and handed us boxes of sparklers in honor of the 4th of July. We did what people usually do with sparklers — pranced around with them and wrote our names in the air. Mad even got four going at one time, two in each hand, and did some of kind of interpretive dance with them. Needless to say, the dance didn't last long.

About the time we had used all the sparklers, we noticed that a couple of dozen people — young, old and in-between — suddenly descend on what we considered to be "our" beach. I couldn't figure out what was going on. Within minutes it became clear. A couple of brilliant Roman candles went off over the ocean from the end of the point, followed by at least ten minutes of the best fireworks show I had ever seen. The finale was nothing short of amazing. When it was all over, I asked Mad what the deal was.

"It's Pokee's gift to the community. Actually no one is supposed to know it's him lighting them off, but a lot of people do."

"He just does it for the heck of it?" I asked.

"Pretty much. But I think he does it as much for himself as for anyone else. Remember, you-know-who is his relative. I think he's doing what comes natural-ly to him as a bred-in-the-bone pyromaniac."

"Well, if he's in competition with her, I'd like to see what she can do. That was incredible."

"Be careful what you ask for," Mad said. "Her reputation as a pyro goes way beyond incredible."

.   .   .

"How did your meetings go?" G asked Dagywn when we were back at the gnome compound the next morning, sitting around the table under the koa tree.

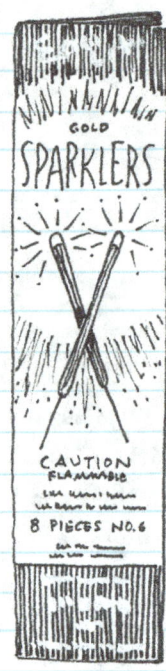

"About as I expected. Nobody wants to leave, except for Leo, of course. Everyone else feels like they're just getting started on a new phase of their lives here and don't want to start over somewhere else. By and large, they're happy with the way things are going."

"What about you?" I asked.

"I need to return to my tribe on Mt. St. Helena. It's my responsibility and I've been gone too long already."

"Do I sense a 'but' coming?" Mad said.

"Unfortunately, yes," Dagywn said, "I'm ready to go, but Melea is dead set against it."

"What are you going to do?" G asked.

"There's only one thing I can do. I hope you can bear with me for a few days. I never thought to ask if there was a date when you had to leave."

"To be safe, Mr. Becker says we have to leave by the 7th of August, so we have some time, but not a lot," I said.

"That shouldn't be a problem. There's a place, known only to me, that I go to when I need to work on problems like these. It's deep in the Na Pali-Kona Forest, completely isolated. I'll leave today and be back on the 9th, next Tuesday. If all goes well, I'll return with a solution to my problem."

"I hope you do, Dagywn, really," I said. "There's one other thing."

"What's that?"

"I was visited by Madam Pele again, in her headless form," I said.

"In person?" Dagywn asked.

"No. In a dream. It seemed like another warning, but this time she was like in the middle of a really violent hurricane, with a lot of thunder and lightning."

"Hmmmm. I hope that doesn't mean she's getting Namaka involved."

"Who's Nāmaka?" I asked.

"Madam Pele has a bunch of brothers and sisters and, if you can believe it, thirteen of the sisters have the same name — Hiiaka. All of them have different powers. Nāmaka is one of her sisters not named Hiiaka. She's the one most likely to cause a hurricane. With a little luck, the solution I come up with won't offend Madam Pele or Nāmaka or any other of her brothers or sisters, and we can avoid them completely."

"That works for me," I said. "The less we have to do with them, the better."

"I'll do my best," Dagywn said.

• • •

I made Mad stop at a tourist shop next to a gas station on the way back to the Garden Isle. I bought a postcard with a painting of Madam Pele on it (I've got to say she's a lot less creepy with a head than she was without one), a few votive candles and two small vases. As soon as we got back to the cottage, I constructed a little shrine to Madam Pele on the kitchen counter, filled the vases with water and plumeria blossoms and lit the candles. If there was a chant I could have sung, I would have. I wasn't taking any chances. Somewhat surprisingly, no one made fun of my shrine. Maybe they were just as scared as I was.

• • •

The next few days, while we waited for Dagywn to return, went by in a kind of blur. G and I took more surfing lessons, Chuy and Mad took every opportunity to be by themselves (and stay out of the way of Queenie), and I got as tan as I'd ever been in my life. When I looked in the mirror, I didn't recognize myself. We played a lot of multi-hand solitaire and dominoes, read a lot, and one day

Better safe than sorry. Whether you believed in Madam Pele or not, most Hawaiians had a shrine to her somewhere in their homes.

Mr. Becker, G, and I even went fishing in the Zodiac. We actually caught some fish, which JP cooked on the beach grill for dinner. If I hadn't felt like Madam Pele was lurking behind every palm tree, it would have been a lot more relaxing. But now that we'd been successful in finding Dagywn, at least the last three days felt like a vacation.

As promised, Dagywn returned the following Tuesday along with the solution to his problem. I'm not sure what any of us thought he would come up with, but it certainly wasn't what he brought with him.

Every time we got together with Dagywn at the Menehune compound, he offered us an incredible assortment of tropical fruit from their trees, including papayas, which I'd never seen growing on a tree before. Pretty exotic.

Chapter XX

Succession

July 9, 1968
Menehune compound
Kauai, Hawaiian Islands

Although we hadn't talked about it with Dagywn, G, Mad, Chuy, and I assumed we'd meet him, like we always did, at 10 o'clock on the Tuesday he was supposed to return. When we got there, Dagywn wasn't at our table, but it was laid out with platters of sliced papaya, mango and pineapple and another platter with what looked like toasted Hawaiian bread. If he wasn't expecting us, someone was expecting someone.

We sat down at the table just as Dagywn appeared, carrying a tray filled with a big pitcher of juice and a bunch of glasses.

"Welcome back," G said.

"Thank you. It's good to be back... I think," Dagywn said, setting the tray on the table. "Help yourself," he said, waving to the platters of fruit, "It's all from our garden."

He sat down and said "I trust everyone is okay," and then noticed Chuy's black eye and bruises. "Whoa, what's the other guy look like?"

"It wasn't a guy," Chuy said.

"It was my tutu, Dagywn. And it's a long story. But Chuy's getting better," Mad said.

"More like a very short story," Chuy said, under his breath.

"I take it you don't want to talk about it," Dagywn said.

"Not really," Mad said.

"Okay, if you guys don't have anything to report, I do."

"Was your retreat a success?" G asked.

"Well, it was a little more than a retreat. And I'm still hoping it will be a success. But let me back up a bit. Things in our tribe are not always as they appear to be. When G spent the night here, he told me he had told you about the role of 'king' not being exactly what most people would think, right?"

"Yes, he told us," I said, Chuy nodding his head in agreement.

"And he told you that it was the women who hold the real power in the tribe, yes?"

"He told us," I said.

"Well, the women have their own hierarchy, and all of them have some role in making sure the tribe runs smoothly. They are in charge of making sure we always have enough money in reserve to cover our needs for at least 100 years and, believe me, they keep a very close watch over it. There is one group that does nothing but genealogical research to determine marriages between the members of the tribe. As you might imagine, with such a limited number of members, we have to be very careful about who marries whom. That was one of the reasons the Menehune welcomed me and the rest of the guys so eagerly when we first arrived. Among other things, each of us were looked on as a fresh set of genes to add to their mix. And then there's another group of women in charge of identifying individuals who have the potential for becoming the tribe's next wizard. Candidates are usually chosen when they are quite young — 8 or 10 years old by your count — and are then subjected to rigorous training to determine their suitability as our 'wizard-in-waiting.' I understand G has also explained to you that each gnome has his or her own unique magical ability, but only one. The new candidate wizard must learn each of those bits of magic from the individual members of the tribe. As you can imagine, it's a lengthy process. The final step in the training is to work with the existing wizard to uncover the candidate's own magic, which is often the longest and most complicated step in the whole process."

"If you're wondering why I'm telling you all this, I'm getting to it. Bear with me. Before leaving our home on the Aland Islands for our exploratory expedition with G's father, a young candidate for our next wizard had already been identified and the training process had begun. Before leaving on my so-called retreat last week, I spoke with Melea about my plan, namely to travel to the Aland Islands and bring the wizard-in-waiting back with me. Then just the two us — I and the wizard-in-waiting — would eventually travel together to Mt. St. Helena where I could finish the training process, providing the tribe with a new wizard and me with the freedom to return to Kauai to reunite with Melea and Leo. Quite frankly, it was the only solution I could come up with that seemed to satisfy everyone's needs and wants."

"What did Melea and Leo say?" G asked.

"Well, naturally, Leo wasn't happy, but he consented. And Melea wasn't all that happy either, but eventually she agreed to agree. So I think we should go forward with our plans for departure, before anyone or anything changes their minds."

"But Dagywn, how long will all that take? Remember we have to leave no later than August 7th." I said.

"What? The final training process?" Dagywn asked.

"No. Going to the Åland Islands, picking up the wizard-in-waiting, and getting back here?"

"Oh, right. No, I've already done that."

"What?" I asked in disbelief. I noticed that both Chuy's and Mad's mouths were hanging open and G was laughing.

"Being a wizard has its benefits, Nick. Folding the space-time continuum is not all that difficult, provided you know how."

I sat there dumbfounded, trying to process what Dagywn had just said. I couldn't wrap my head around it.

"I don't get it." I said.

"Get what?" Dagywn asked.

"The way you travel, if you can call it that."

"Well, it's just what you would call 'science,' science that you don't understand, which is nothing to be particularly embarrassed by."

"But you understand it."

"Yes, and you've forgotten it."

"Yeah, that's what G said, too."

"Would you like to be introduced?" Dagywn asked, effectively changing the subject.

I must not have been the only one a little dazed by what Dagywn had said, because no one said anything. When he looked around the group, looking for a response and not getting one, he said, "I'll take that as a 'yes.' I'll be right back."

In a couple of minutes he reappeared, saying "Lady and gentlemen, this is Aalto. Aalto, this is Prince G, Mad, Chuy, and Nick. Forgive them if they don't say anything right away. I think they're having a bit of a problem believing you were in the Åland Islands yesterday."

"I'm having a bit of a problem with it myself," she said with a smile. "Åland and Kauai may both be islands but, believe me, that's where the similarity ends. Very nice to meet you all."

I think it's safe to say that not one of us, including Mad, expected the wizard-in-waiting to be a young woman. After everything else, I don't know why we were even surprised. Thank goodness for G, who got up from the table and went over to Aalto and shook her hand. The rest of us followed his lead and the mood gradually went back to something like normal. But like I asked myself yesterday, "What's normal?" Maybe it was time to give up trying to have any normal definition of normal. *Maybe it's a new code to live by,* I thought to myself: *Not normal is the new normal.* I just wasn't prepared for how "not normal" it was going to be. Not by a long shot.

In between a few last minute surfing lessons, we used the
Zodiac to ferry supplies from dry land to the Silverado.

Chapter XXI

Letter to the Editor

July 10, 1968
Getting ready to leave
Kauai, Hawaiian Islands

Before we left Dagywn yesterday, the group decided there was no reason to delay departing for San Francisco. I told Dagywn I would get back to him after I talked with Mr. Becker about how long it would take to outfit the *Silverado* for the return trip. Mr. Becker thought we could be ready to depart in four or five days, so we tentatively said we'd leave on July 16th. To tell you the truth, it felt a little anticlimactic. I mean, we'd found Dagywn and everything, but it was much different from what I had expected. The more I thought about it, I think it had something to do with the Menehunes and their desire for assimilation and the changes it had brought about in the way they lived. Everything about King Gob and his men's life on Mt. St. Helena was exotic — Gob's solid gold dining chamber, the fact that the tribe lived in an enormous cave with subterranean jail cells, the giant ball of quicksilver they rolled around on special occasions, their musical instruments and the strange music they played and even the fact that they slept during the day and had their waking hours at night. It was all so foreign to me. I knew Dagywn had extraordinary powers and knew a lot of magic, but he didn't act like he was anyone special. I mean he wore Hawaiian shirts and flip-flops, used a lawnmower to mow his lawn and he watched *As the World Turns* on t.v. during the day, for crying out loud! At this point, as we started making our plans to leave, it all started to seem perfectly ordinary and, I've got to admit, a little disappointing.

As our plans for the return voyage became more concrete, I began to wonder why it was necessary for Dagywn and Aalto to even be on board. I mean, with all his powers, wasn't it possible for Dagywn to simply transport himself and Aalto from Kauai to Mt. St. Helena? I asked Mad to drive me out to see Dagywn so I could ask him in person. We found him at his house, packing for the trip. I just came right out and asked him why, if his last trip aboard a sailboat had been so terrible, what with his seasickness and all, why he didn't just use his powers to transport himself and Aalto directly to Mt. St. Helena? He said he wished he could, but it didn't exactly work that way. For transportation to work, he said, he had to know both ends of the journey. In other words, he couldn't transport himself, let alone anyone else, if he didn't know the specifics of where he was transporting himself to. I asked him what the specifics were and he said it was a little complicated, but it included the magnetic profile of the location: its unique set of vibrations in terms of latitude, longitude, and altitude. Without that information, it would be like he was trying to use a telephone to talk to someone without knowing the their telephone number. "Nice thought, though," he said, "but you're stuck with us."

"It's not that," I said, "I was just thinking that you could avoid all the stuff that made your last trip so bad."

"Well, maybe this trip won't be so rough. And it certainly won't be as long," Dagywn said.

As it turned out, he was right about one thing and very wrong on the other.

. . .

There was one change of plans I hadn't seen coming. Chuy asked Mr. Becker if it was all right if Mad came with us on the return voyage. She had already talked to her father about it and he was okay with her going and told her if it was okay with Mr. Becker, they'd meet and work out the details. Mr. Becker and Dr. Okole met and agreed Mad could sail with us to San Francisco. After that, she was going to visit her mother in San Diego and then fly back to Kauai in time for the new school year. I liked Mad a lot. She was fun to be with and had been a great guide for us while we were in Kauai. The simple fact was, we probably wouldn't have found Dagywn without her help. I just wasn't sure how it was going to be having her and Chuy together all googly-eyed on board the *Silverado*. I mean, as sailboats go it was big, but still there's only so far you can go if you were looking for some privacy. Maybe we could invite Queenie along to act as chaperone. *That would definitely keep the situation under control*, I thought to myself. I quickly dismissed the idea, reminding myself that they were, after all, my friends.

G and I spent the next few days helping JP get the provisions together and ferrying them to the *Silverado* in the Zodiac. We managed to slip in a couple of surfing lessons in between trips to the market and to Nawiliwili Harbor. And I remembered to call Grandma Hattie on Sunday, filling her in on what had happened without going into too much detail. The important thing was for her to

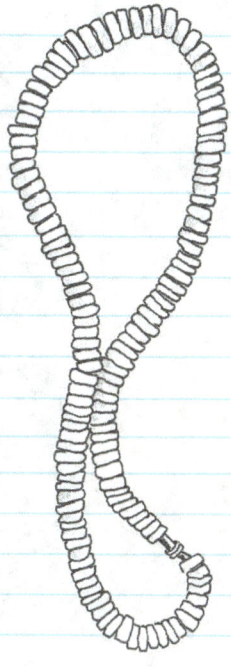

A puka shell necklace.

know that we had what we came for and that we'd be back in San Francisco in two or three weeks. She said she'd keep a candle burning in the window for us so we could find our way home. Chuy and Mad were off on their own most of the time. One day they returned with matching puka shell necklaces. I think that's all I can say about that.

Meanwhile, Dagywn was getting his affairs in order for an extended absence. Melea had insisted on knowing when he was coming back for good. Not a guess, but a firm date. He told her he would return two years exactly from the day they set sail, figuring it would give him enough time to teach Aalto the last of the magic she needed to know as the new wizard. Melea made him swear to it, which he did. Just to be safe, he found himself halting in front of his shrine to Madam Pele several times a day, reciting assurances to her that he wasn't taking any of her beloved Menehune with him, only himself and another member of his own tribe. He had no idea whether Pele heard him or not, but he figured it was worth a try.

The morning before we were supposed to leave, Mad came by our cottage with a copy of *The Garden Island* newspaper.

"My dad gave this to me this morning. He thought you'd want to see it," she said, handing it to me. "Look at the letters to the editor on the next to last page." There, underlined in red, was the following: "Dear Garden Island Newspaper: Re: 'Never too Young' photograph. Fellow Kauaiians, do you have such short memories? Those are Menehune you are looking at — or at least the one on the left is. The one on the right appears to be a gnome from another tribe. Signed, A longtime resident of Wainiha Valley."

"Hmmmm," I said, "just like Dagywn predicted — someone from the Wainiha Valley *did* notice." Chuy read it over my shoulder and passed it to G.

"Does anyone read letters to the editor?" I asked.

"Probably more than you think," Mad said.

She was right. And, as I was to learn later, not only had it been read, but it had been cut out and sent to Nigel Stayne.

Just before we set sail, there was no ignoring what looked suspiciously like a large thunderhead out on the horizon.

Chapter XXII

Stowaway Redux

July 16, 1968
Departing Nawiliwili Harbor, en route to San Francisco
Kauai, Hawaiian Islands

It felt strange and a little sad closing the door to our cottage for the last time. Even though we hadn't stayed all that long, a lot had gone on at the Garden Isle Beach Cottages. A lot of fun, actually. The card games, swimming in the bay, JP's great food, the fireworks display. It was all good – mostly. *Maybe I'd be back some day,* I thought to myself, *this time without a seemingly impossible job to do.* I gathered up my stuff and took one last look at the horseshoe bay and the point where Pokee lived. I took a mental snapshot of the scene, figuring it might be nice to recall it on some dark and rainy day at school next year.

Mr. Becker, Tova and JP had gone ahead of us, earlier in the morning. Kal came back with his cab to pick us up around noon. Chuy, Mad and G were already in the cab, sitting in the back seat. After putting my gear in the trunk, I sat in the front seat and said hi to Kal. I turned around and asked if anyone wanted one last shave ice.

"Ah, if you guys want to, that's fine," Chuy said, "but I think I'll stay in the cab."

"Yeah, Tutu and I already said our goodbyes and I'm not sure I can go through that again. I got a lecture-and-a-half this morning and then another half, just for good measure." Mad said.

G just shrugged his shoulders.

"Okay, I get the picture," I said, "I guess it's straight to the harbor, Kal."

. . .

Dagywn and Aalto were ready to go, too. Melea had wanted to come down to the harbor to see them off, but Dagywn thought that would make it more difficult than necessary and said they should say their goodbyes at home. But when it came time to go, Melea and Leo were nowhere to be found. Dagywn looked around the house and found a letter taped to the mirror in the bathroom. It said that she hated goodbyes and she and Leo had gone for a walk. She told him they both loved him and knew he loved them in return. She wished him safe travels and would be counting the days until he returned. Dagywn was a little surprised. It didn't seem like Melea not to be there, but he was also a little relieved. He had not been looking forward to the possibility of a big scene in front of Aalto. *Well, if that's the way she wanted it, then so be it,* Dagywn thought to himself. Still, it seemed a little strange to him.

Although both he and Aalto could have instantly transported themselves to the harbor, Dagywn thought better of it, especially considering it was broad daylight. He knew Uplanders had difficulty when someone just materialized in front of them, so he had also ordered a cab which was due any minute. He went over and had one last talk to Madam Pele at her shrine in his living room and then he and Aalto went outside to wait for the cab.

.   .   .

Tova was in charge of shuttling people and supplies back and forth from the dock to the *Silverado*. I knew when Dagywn and Aalto were due to arrive, so considering Tova hadn't met either of them before, I went with her to the dock. They arrived just as we did in the Zodiac. I introduced everyone and said "I guess this is it, right? We've done what we came to do and now we're going home." Truth be told, I was saying it more to myself than to anyone else. There was a note of unreality about the moment and I think I thought by saying what we were doing out loud, it would make it more real.

G took charge of Dagywn and Aalto once they got on board and showed them around the sailboat. There was a lot of hustle and bustle going on, above and below deck. I knew Mr. Becker wanted to take advantage of the outgoing tides and was planning on setting sail around 4 o'clock. Everyone, especially the deckhands, were busy making sure we would leave on time. I went to the bow of the *Silverado* and, using my binoculars, looked out at the horizon. I couldn't help but notice what looked like a huge thunderhead not that far away, which seemed odd on what was otherwise a cloudless day. *Tropical weather,* I thought to myself.

JP was busy in the galley, taking advantage of the relatively stable conditions, making a big meatloaf for dinner. As I passed by he looked directly at me and said "And then there's 'The Potato Question.'"

"The what?"

"The Potato Question. It looms large."

"Mashed," I said.

"Good answer," he replied.

"Is there another one?" I asked.

"Lots. Baked. Scalloped. Duchess. Gratin. French-fried. Hash browned. Home-fried. Shoestring. Boiled. Latkes. *Galette de Pommes de Terre*. O'Brien. And on and on. And don't forget the ever popular 'tot,' as in Tater Tot."

Somehow I knew that was going to stick in my brain for a long time: "The Potato Question." I think JP was the one person who could ask that question and have it make sense.

. . .

Four o'clock arrived and Jon, Mike, and Chad raised the sails. As they flapped into position and were tightened in place, our speed increased, the *Silverado* gently rising and falling over the small waves inside the harbor. We rounded the breakwater and were making our way into the open sea when everything happened at once. I was standing amidships, holding onto the main mast for support. I knew the waves would be larger once we left the harbor, but they seemed unusually large. There was a distant rumbling from somewhere. Probably that thunderhead I couldn't help but notice, which sounded ominous. The wind picked up and in an instant, the sky was filled with heavy, dark, low clouds, as if someone had flipped a switch and turned out the lights. I could feel the hair on the back of my neck standing up and a tingling sensation in my hand where it was holding onto the mast. I looked up and the top half of the mast was covered with an eerie, quivering mass of blue light, making a buzzing sound. Jon passed by me, handed me a safety harness and said I'd better put it on or get belowdecks. I put the harness on and he clicked the tether to the jackline. Now, if I got washed over, at least I'd still be attached to the boat.

"What's that?" I said, pointing to the top of the mast.

"Not good," he said. "St. Elmo's fire. Looks like we're in for an electrical storm."

Just as he said it, there was a loud crack of lightning and an almost immediate and even louder clap of thunder I could feel vibrate deep in my chest.

"Do you know where the life vests are?" he asked.

"Yes."

"Grab a bunch and make sure everyone puts one on."

The life jackets were in a big zippered duffel tied down to the foredeck. I

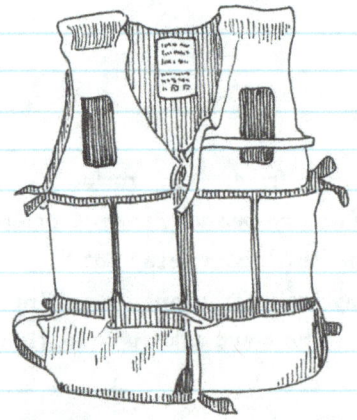

As it turned out, it was a good thing we had extra life jackets on the boat.

managed to untie it and dragged the whole thing to the main hatch and called to Chuy.

"Here," I said, "Make sure everyone puts one on."

"What's going on?" Chuy asked.

"Some kind of a freak storm," I said. "Does everyone have one?" I asked, sticking my head down in the hatch to make sure.

Chuy looked around the cabin and said "Yeah... ah, wait a minute. No."

"Whaddaya' mean?"

"I think you better get down here."

I unclicked the tether to my safety harness and reattached it to the life line so it wouldn't be in anyone's way and went below just in time to see Melea and Leo crawl out from one of the storage spaces under the bunks.

"Oh, jeez," I said.

Dagywn was dumbfounded. He just stood there not able to say anything.

"Aren't you going to say anything?" Melea asked.

"I'm speechless," Dagywn said.

Leo was standing behind his mother, looking down at his shoes.

"I suppose I should start by asking what you're doing here?"

"Aren't you glad to see us?" Melea asked.

"Of course," he said, "I just wasn't expecting it."

"We thought we'd surprise you. Leo and I decided there was no way we could let you leave us for two whole years. What's going on outside? Why is it so bumpy?"

Dagywn looked at me and I said, "Some kind of freak storm."

"Are we going to be okay?" Melea asked.

"I hope so. But I need to get you and Leo life jackets. I'll be right back."

I went back topside and got two more life jackets and wondered how things had gotten completely out of control in just a matter of minutes. It was not a good feeling.

"Here, put them on," I said, handing Melea and Leo the life jackets. Luckily there were a bunch of kids' life jackets that fit them okay. "I'm going back topside to see if there's anything I can do."

"Do you need any help?" Chuy asked.

"I don't think so. You're better off down here."

I ran into Mr. Becker and he said, "This is crazy. I checked the weather just before we left and there was no tropical depression anywhere around here. Help the guys take down the sails, will you?"

The waves were getting larger — ten feet or more. I'd taken enough sailing classes at school to know what was going through Mr. Becker's mind. In heavy seas like this you had a few choices, none of them without dangers. You could position the boat parallel to the waves and run the risk of capsizing the boat if a very large wave hit, basically just rolling the boat over, upside down. Or you could line the boat up perpendicular to the waves, climbing them on the front and sliding down the back side. Again, if there was a really big wave, you could come down the back side of the wave so fast and at such a steep angle that it was possible to pitchpole the boat, so that the front of the boat is buried in water while the stern is being pushed up by the wave behind it, ending up with the vessel standing straight up on its bow, buried in the water. The final option was to turn the boat around and head into the wind. While there were advantages to this, a lot could go wrong and quickly, while making a 180-degree turn in high seas. It was a scary situation and getting worse. But where did this storm come from? We were all about to find out.

By now, the sails were down and stored. I was making my way back to the stern to see if there was anything I could do. As I was passing the main hatch Dagywn's head popped up. He had his right hand over his mouth while pointing to the side of the boat with his left. He had a panicked look in his eyes as I pulled him up and out of the hatch and pushed him toward the lifeline. I sat down behind him, with one leg on each side of his feet, holding onto his belt while he yorked his guts out over the side of the boat. He was wiping his mouth with the back of his hand when a huge voice came out of the clouds. "Dagywn, you lied to me!"

Dagywn looked up and Madam Pele's face appeared in the dark and roiling clouds, all orange and gold with flames licking around the edges of her face.

"I did not," Dagywn shouted back as loudly as he could.

"Then why did you steal two of my Menehune off the island?"

"I didn't. I didn't know they were on board. You have to believe me."

"Why should I believe you when you already lied to me?"

"I told you, I didn't know they were here. They wanted to surprise me."

"I'll surprise you," she said as her hand appeared through the clouds and threw a bolt of lightning that struck right next to the *Silverado*. A huge crash of thunder wracked through the clouds at the same time as the lightning crackled when it hit the water.

"Nāmaka!" Madam Pele yelled and a watery female form arose from the waves: Madam Pele's sister, Nāmaka, goddess of the sea and storms.

"Are we done here yet?" Nāmaka said calmly to Madam Pele.

"Not at all," Madam Pele said.

"I thought you said all you wanted to do was to scare them. I think they're scared, sister."

"They're scared when I say they're scared."

"Pele, you heard what the gnome said. He didn't know the Menehune were on the boat."

"And I'll bring them back. Really I will," Dagywn shouted to Pele.

"Shut up, little man," Pele said.

"You're out of control, sister, you always have been," Nāmaka said.

"You dare to criticize me?"

"I don't think twice about it."

Chuy and Mad had been watching what was going on through the portholes on the side of the forecastle. Chuy turned to Mad. "I think we're in for an epic girl fight."

"Worse!" Mad said, "It's a sister fight. And they don't care who gets hurt in the process. We've got to do something."

"Like what?" Chuy asked. "We're a little out-gunned here, aren't we?"

"Maybe. But Pokee might be able to help. He's the only one who can talk sense to her."

"And how do we talk to Pokee?"

"On that ship-to-shore radio over there. I'm going to try."

Mad went over to the radio and said into the transmitter "Calling Pokee. Calling Pokee. This is Mad Okole aboard the sailboat *Silverado* at KYA472. Calling Pokee. Calling Pokee. Come in, please."

About a minute later, the speaker on the ship-to-shore radio crackled.

"This is Pokee at KHW096. Calling Mad at KYA472. Come in, please."

"Pokee! I can't believe I got you. Listen Pokee, I don't have much time to explain. I'm aboard a sailboat outside of Nawiliwili harbor. Madam Pele is trying to keep us from leaving. She's got her sister Nāmaka here and they've made a terrible storm. Can you do anything to make her stop? Over."

"Madam Pele and Nāmaka? Together? Over."

"Yes, and it looks like they're about to get into it. Can you do something, Pokee? We're in trouble here. Over."

"Maybe, but it's going to take a few minutes. Over."

"Hurry, Pokee! I don't think we've got much time. Oh, and can you call Queenie and tell her to call me at KYA472? Thanks. Over."

"You're amazing, Mad. How'd you know to do that?" Chuy asked.

"Remember I saw his two-way radio when we were at his house? We just lucked out that he was listening."

"Why do you want Queenie to call you?"

"You'll see."

No sooner had she said it than the speaker on the ship-to-shore radio crackled again. "This is Queenie at KS1123 calling Mad at KYA472. Come in, please."

"Tutu. You've got to help us. Over."

"Help you? What are you doing now? Over."

"Tutu, it's a long story. But Madam Pele is trying to stop us from leaving Kauai. She has her sister, Nāmaka, here and we're in a really bad storm. Over."

"What do you want me to do about it? Over."

"I think Madam Pele is somewhere around the harbor, right by you. Will you go and see if you can make her stop? We haven't done anything wrong. She's just crazy. Over."

"She crazy like a fox. But I'll go see her. You want me to go now? Over."

"Yes, tutu. Like right now. We're in a lot of trouble here. Over."

"Queenie to the rescue. Over and out."

"Whaddaya' think Queenie's going to do? I mean, Madam Pele's kind of a rough customer," Chuy said.

"You of all people, Chuy!" Mad said.

"What?"

"Do you think that matters to Queenie?"

As Madam Pele and Nāmaka continued to argue, the waves got bigger. We were still perpendicular to them and our speed slowed each time we climbed up the front of a wave. Once we reached the crest the *Silverado* would hesitate for a moment, start to shudder and make these horrible clicking and cracking noises before sliding down the back side of the wave at tremendous speed, like a completely out-of-control roller coaster ride.

Pele and Nāmaka were now in a full-on fight, screaming, pulling each other's hair, and thrashing around in the clouds in what looked like a death match. The more fiercely they fought, the worse the storm became. All of a sudden there were several loud explosions, right where they were fighting, and a series of super bright flares of light.

Pele and Nāmaka suddenly stopped fighting. "What's going on?" Pele bellowed. No sooner had the words come out of her mouth than three more ear-shattering explosions went off, followed by blinding flashes of light.

Nāmaka started to laugh. "I'll bet it's that pyromaniac relative of yours. He's trying to blow you up."

"He wouldn't dare," Pele said, disappearing from the clouds. "I'll show him."

Queenie watched as Pele pulled her projection from the clouds and reappear out on the end of the public pier. She ran as quickly as she could to reach her. Who knew what Pele was going to do next?

"Off to another fight?" Queenie asked, breathing heavily.

Out of my way, old woman," Pele hissed.

"Not so fast," Queenie said, grabbing Pele by the shoulder. "Was that you and your sister causing all that mischief out there?"

"What if it was?"

"My granddaughter's on that boat and she and all the rest of us are sick and tired of you and your sister making life miserable for us. I've heard lots of rumors about the bad things you've done to each other, but it's time to leave us out of it. Just shut it and move on or Queenie will haunt your goddess bottom from here to eternity." With that, Queenie got in her Kung fu stance and said, "Don't make me hurt you."

"Like you could."

"You want to go a few rounds?" Queenie asked, her hands held up, ready to strike.

"Not now. Maybe later," Madam Pele said dismissively. "I've got to go deal with Pokee."

"Looks like he did a pretty good job of dealing with you," Queenie said, laughing. "You might be losing some of your charm, honey. People are going to catch on that you're nothing but a big bully. I'd start thinking about mending your ways if I were you."

"Nobody talks to me that way!"

"I just did," Queenie said. "It's time for you to go back to whatever volcano you crawled out of." With that, Madam Pele just disappeared. Queenie laughed and punched her fist in the air. "Not bad for an old woman," she said to her-self.

Nāmaka had split the scene right after Pele pulled herself out of the cloud. She had had her fill of Pele too. Within a couple of minutes the dark clouds started to break up, the ocean calmed and it was as if the whole melee never happened. One by one, everyone who was below decks popped up through the hatch and assembled on deck, still with their life jackets on, looking the worse for wear. Dagywn was still a little green around the edges.

"Can anyone explain to me what just happened?" Mr. Becker asked.

"Girl fight." Chuy said.

"Sister fight." Mad said.

"Actually, I think it was my fault," Melea said. "I'm Melea, by the way. We haven't met," she said to Mr. Becker and Tova, extending her hand. "And this is my — our — son." Leo gave a little salute from where he was standing behind his mother. "Leo and I snuck on board today. We couldn't be away from Dagywn for such a long time, so we decided to go with him. He didn't know anything about it. Madam Pele seems to know everything about what we Menehune do and she wanted to punish Dagywn for 'stealing' us away from the island. But like I said, he didn't know we were here. It was all a big mistake."

"Considering we could all be at the bottom of the ocean right now," Mr. Becker said, "I guess things turned out all right. Other than the fact that I'm still shaking."

"Just for the record," Mad said, "I think we owe a thank-you to Pokee and my tutu, Queenie. Pokee was the one who shot the fireworks at Pele and got her to stop fighting and I'm pretty sure my tutu did something to make her give up trying to kill us. I don't know what she did, but I would have loved to see it."

"How'd they know to get involved?" Tova asked.

"I called them on the ship-to-shore radio. They both have two-way radios."

"Then I think we owe you a thank-you too, Mad, along with Nick, Jon, Mike and Chad. You all went up a couple of notches as sailors today. I just hope you never have to experience something like that again," Mr. Becker said.

We all said "hear hear," just as JP appeared on deck, holding a pot.

"I saved the potatoes," he said.

. . .

August 13, 2012
Grandpa Nick's house
Rutherford, California

Doyle's answer, that "it was always Prince G who fed the pigeons," surprised me. I hadn't thought of him as someone who might have information about the story in Grandpa's journals, but I was forgetting that he was there for a lot of it, at least according to what Grandpa had written. Suddenly, I had an idea.

"Do you know anything about homing pigeons?" I asked Doyle.

"A little. My da raised racing pigeons back in Ireland. I used to help him."

From what I had read in *Wikipedia*, I knew that racing pigeons and homing pigeons were basically the same: a homing pigeon returned to its home, usually with a message attached to its leg, and a racing pigeon returned home not with a message, but maybe winning an award for how fast it got there.

"Do you know how to catch one?"

"Sure. It's not that difficult. They're pretty tame."

I stopped for a minute to think things over and decided to take a chance.

"Grandpa found the vial he used back when he was a kid for attaching a message to a pigeon's leg. If I write the message, will you help me tie it, or whatever you do, to the pigeon?"

"I think I can do that."

"And can you not tell Grandpa? If it works, I want it to be a surprise."

Doyle thought for a minute. "I can't see the harm in that. When do you want to do it?"

"Now, if the pigeons are around."

"They should be. They usually leave the dovecote first thing in the morning and return sometime around now."

"Good. I'll go get the vial and the paper. I'll be right back." I ran upstairs to my bedroom, grabbed the vial and the rolling papers and ran back downstairs. I showed the vial to Doyle and pulled a sheet of paper from the packet.

"Haven't seen any of those in a while," Doyle mused when he saw the Zig-Zag packet. "Is that what you use?"

"According to Grandpa. Said it was super-lightweight. He wasn't kidding, was he?" I said, holding up one of the rolling papers, flapping it around. I grabbed a

I had grandpa draw this so you could see what I was talking about – I mean, the fig tree had practically swallowed the dovecote, which is why I had overlooked it for so long.

pencil from the silver cup on the table and hesitated for a minute. I had already decided what I wanted to say; now it was just a matter of making it fit and not tearing the thin paper with the sharp point of the pencil. I took my time and managed to get all the words to fit while keeping the tiny piece of paper intact. I rolled it up tight, stuck it inside the vial and screwed the top of it back on, then handed it to Doyle.

"There. Now what?" I said.

"Let's go out there and see if we can catch a pigeon," Doyle said, smiling.

We walked out to the back of the garden, stooped under the fig branches and looked at the dovecote. Sure enough, the pigeons were there, flitting about, making that cooing noise they seem to make all the time. We both went inside.

Doyle was right: they were very tame. "Here, you hold this," he said, handing me the vial. "I'm going to need both hands." Doyle calmly put his hands around a pigeon that was sitting on a perch right in front of him.

"There," he said, "Now attach the vial to his leg. It doesn't matter which one."

I did as I was told. The little copper tabs on the vial were soft enough to bend around the pigeon's leg. The pigeon didn't seem to mind.

"Is that right?" I asked.

"Looks like it to me. Here, you let him go," he said, handing me the pigeon.

"Are you sure?"

"Yeah. Just be slow and gentle."

I wrapped my hands around the pigeon the same way Doyle had done and walked out of the dovecote. I stood on the lawn, feeling the pigeon's fast heartbeat and a slight quivering in my hands.

"Now?" I asked, looking at Doyle.

"I don't see why not."

And with that I lifted my arms up and threw the pigeon into the air. He fluttered up and flew in a couple of wide circles and then headed north.

"Wow. That was cool."

"Yeah, it was," Doyle said.

"How long will it take him to come back – if he does come back?"

"I have absolutely no idea. Depends on where he's going."

"I thought you said…"

"Listen, Joaquin, it's all conjecture at this point. We'll just have to wait and see."

"How we will know when he comes back?"

"Well, he's not going to ring the front doorbell! You're just going to have to check the dovecote to see if he's there. I don't want you to get your hopes up, but if any of my assumptions are correct, I'm guessing he'll be back in a day or two."

I was excited and disappointed at the same time, and not sure what to do next. It wasn't until tomorrow that I was supposed to meet with Uncle Chuy, so I thanked Doyle for his help and walked over to Grandpa's studio to read in the hammock. Seemed like the only thing I could do right now.

So that's what I did for a few hours and then decided to go for a run. Besides letting the pigeon go, and all that potentially meant one way or the other, Grandpa's story wasn't getting any easier to believe. Pele and her sister Nāmaka and all the stuff they supposedly did, not to mention St. Elmo's fire. It was all too much for me.

While I was on running, I had the thought I should look up some of the weird stuff from Grandpa's journal. It seemed like a good idea to have some facts when I talked to Grandpa about what he wrote. When I got back, I took a shower, changed clothes and started my research by looking up "St. Elmo's Fire" on Wikipedia. It didn't take long for me to figure out that it was real. The entry described it as *"a weather phenomenon in which luminous plasma is created by a corona discharge from a sharp or pointed object in a strong electric field in the atmosphere, such as those generated by thunderstorms or created by a volcanic eruption. Physically, St. Elmo's fire is a bright blue or violet glow, appearing like fire in some circumstances, from tall, sharply-pointed structures such as lightning rods, masts, spires and chimneys, and on aircraft wings or nose cones. St. Elmo's fire can also appear on leaves and grass, and even at the tips of cattle horns. Often accompanying the glow is a distinct hissing or buzzing sound."* I didn't understand all of the description, but enough to know it sounded scientific and real. Chalk one up in the "true column" for Grandpa.

Next I looked up "Pele," or more exactly, "Pele sightings," not expecting much to turn up. Whoa! Pele was all over the web and apparently all over Hawaii. There were so many, it took me awhile to scan all the entries, but Pele was definitely a popular apparition, or whatever she was. For some reason a YouTube video called *"Kimo and What Happened at Makua"* (https://www.youtube.com/watch?v=TYBZ4URXM-Y) caught my eye. It was a three-minute-long interview with an old Hawaiian dude standing at a gas station. It was hard to hear with all the traffic going by but I definitely got what he was talking about. It seemed like a lot of the stories concerning Pele involved drivers picking up an old woman on a road at night and giving her a ride; this one was no different until the very end when the old guy said that the old, robed woman he and his friends gave a ride to did not have a face. That got my attention. Not only that, but the dude's mother made him go see a local spiritualist the next day and she told him that the woman he and his friends gave a ride to was Madam Pele.

I looked away from the computer. No face, no head. An involuntary shudder went through me. This was getting strange again. I didn't know what to think. St. Elmo's Fire was definitely real. Was Madam Pele real too? Another shudder.

"Whassup, Joaquin?" Grandpa practically yelled from the door of the studio.

I jumped straight up off the seat of the computer chair.

"Jeez, Grandpa. You could have warned me." It was the second time in as many days that he'd scared me silly. Maybe I was getting jumpy.

"Sorry. You didn't plotz, did you?"

"Grandpa!"

"Well?"

"No, but you scared the daylights out of me."

"I didn't mean to. Didn't realize you were so touchy."

"Well, I am right now."

"Why?"

"This Pele stuff you wrote about. Have you seen this video on YouTube?"

"I don't spend a lot of time watching videos on YouTube."

"Well, you should watch this." He pulled up a chair and I played it for him. After it was over, he asked me to play it again.

"Hmmmmm," he murmured. "That was interesting."

"Seems like other people have seen her too," I said.

"I think a lot of people have. And a lot of people would prefer not to talk about it. It was a big deal for me when I had that dream. Speaking of having the living daylights scared out of you... it really shook me up."

Grandpa convinced me to turn the computer off and we walked over to the main house. He poured me an iced tea and started pulling stuff out of the refrigerator for dinner.

"What did you do today?" he asked.

Without thinking, I nearly blurted out that I'd sent a pigeon off with a message attached to its leg. I don't think I'd make it as an undercover agent, but at least I caught myself before I said anything.

"Mostly read. And went for a short run. And watched weird videos on YouTube."

"I hear that. What did you read?"

"Your journal."

"Not *The Secret Teachings of All Ages*?"

"I took a quick look, but every sentence has five words in it I don't understand.

"I had the same reaction the first time I tried to read it. Grandma Hattie was sure it would help me understand the gnomes and their powers. All it did was make me afraid of them. As impressive as the book is – just the size of the thing – I'm not sure it adds all that much to your investigation. The illustrations are great, though. Did you take a look at the pigeon book?"

"A little. I'm going to talk to my 4-H counselor and see if I can take it on as a project."

"Good idea."

"Grandpa?"

"Yes."

"I know what you're going to say, but I have to ask you. Did all that stuff you wrote about Pele and her sister really happen?"

"Is it messing with your world view?"

"I don't know what you mean."

"It means, if I say 'Yes, it really did happen,' you wouldn't be able to accept it because it doesn't fit in with your experience of the world."

"I understand now."

"Well I hate to make things difficult but, yes, it did happen the way I wrote it."

"Okay then. It's messing with my world view."

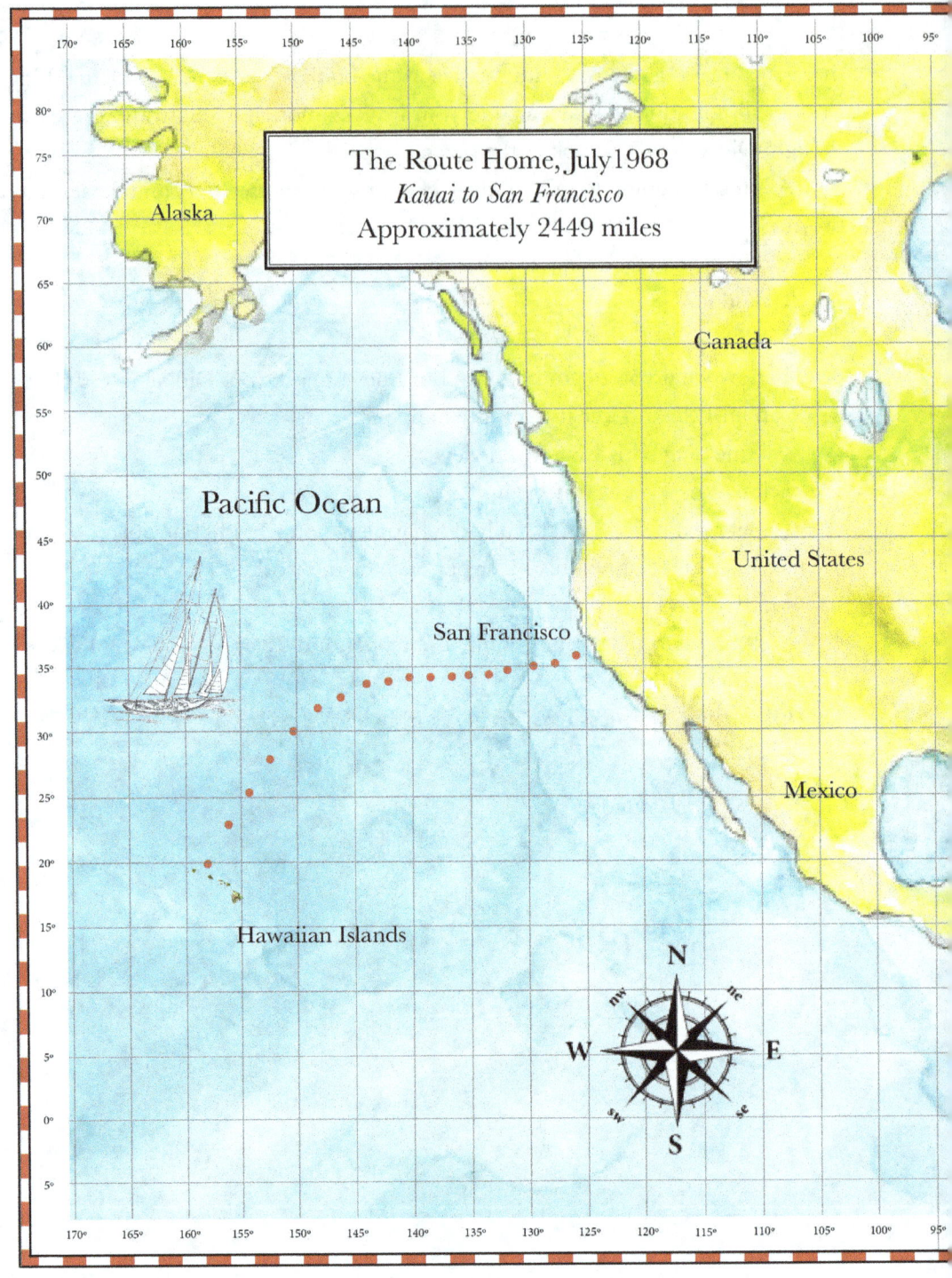

The Route Home, July 1968
Kauai to San Francisco
Approximately 2449 miles

The dotted red line shows our return trip, which took 17 days. Once you get close to California, you approach San Francisco from the north to minimize dealing with the extreme currents and tides associated with a straight-on approach through the Golden Gate.

Chapter XXIII

Calm After the Storm

July 16-August 1, 1968
At sea, en route from Kauai to San Francisco

I think we were all a little shell-shocked after our brush with disaster at the hands of Madam Pele and Nāmaka. It took a few days for all of us to calm down and establish a daily routine aboard the *Silverado*. I think most of us were still thinking that Madam Pele or her sister might suddenly reappear from out of nowhere. Chuy brought it up at dinner one night and Melea assured him it wouldn't happen because Madam Pele's powers didn't reach far from her domain, not very far past the shore of the islands. I don't know how Melea knew that. Maybe she was just making it up to make us feel better. I decided to believe her because, in fact, it did make me feel better.

The return trip to San Francisco was going to take longer than getting to Kauai because instead of sailing in the same direction as the trade winds, we would be sailing against them. I've drawn a picture of our route across the Pacific Ocean on the page to the left. You can see that, from Kauai, we basically headed northeast, which is known as a "starboard tack," which could last as long as a week until we turned and headed in a more easterly direction to reach California. Because of the sheer size of the Pacific, the starboard tack we took is the longest one you can take anywhere in the world. On shore it would be like getting in a car and driving one direction on a straight road for a solid week without stopping.

Because we were sailing straight in the same direction and at the same speed for so many days, the mood aboard the *Silverado* was more relaxed than on our outbound trip. Dagywn was particularly happy because it was so calm he didn't get *mal de mer*, as Tova called it. Jon, Mike and Chad didn't have to be in constant motion tending to the sails. They even got to fish a few times and we had fresh mahi-mahi and ono for dinner more than once. There were even days when it was so calm we could go swimming, certainly nothing I've ever experienced. First, you have to attach yourself to a tether tied to the boat (just in case, you know) and then when you've swum out a way, it's nothing but you and the sea and the sky with the unbroken horizon

It was pretty cool to find all sizes and colors of Japanese fishing floats bobbing around in the middle of the Pacific Ocean.

line every direction you look. It's all unfathomably big, which makes you feel very, very small. And for some strange reason, it made me feel like I was actually on this planet, this orb, that was spinning through space. And getting back on the boat felt like coming home, more than I've ever felt before. Tethered to something, something solid I could stand on, filled with people I knew and felt close to. People who would get me back on board if I somehow became untethered.

It was a comforting feeling.

Another cool thing was finding Japanese fishing floats out in the middle of nowhere. Japanese fishermen use the net-covered glass balls to hold up their fishing nets, just like Pokee's set lines, but these occasionally break free of the nets. Some are as big as basketballs; others about the size of a small cantaloupe. When the seas were calm, you could see them floating from way far away. We found five in all, all different colors and sizes.

Because there was almost no way to screw up, Mr. Becker let me take a few four-hour shifts steering the boat from 4 o'clock in the morning until 8 a.m.. Once I got accustomed to reading the compass and establishing a heading, there was something special about picking out a star in the dark sky above and steering towards it. It was incredibly peaceful and quiet, with just the small waves rhythmically lapping against the *Silverado's* hull. I can't say for certain that I understood what G told us on the trip out about everything in the universe being connected, each with its own unique vibration, but there was something about those times steering the boat by myself, aiming towards a particular star, that made me feel connected to something much, much larger. I mean, I felt like I was connected to the star and that the star was connected to me. Like somehow there was a direct line between us, like being tethered to the boat when I went swimming, but on a much grander, cosmic scale.

I think it was on the third day out that we learned that Melea had a profession: namely, she was the Menehune tribe's official haircutter. I don't know if she got bored or what, suddenly she wanted to cut everyone's hair. She found a pair of scissors in the first aid kit and started walking around the deck, snipping the scissors in the air, yelling "Haircuts, haircuts, who wants a haircut?"

I was up for one, as were Mr. Becker and JP. Instead of a barber chair, we sat on the deck while she stood on top of the main hatch to get her up to the right height. Jon, Mike, and Chad were all letting their hair grow long, what with the Beatles setting a new trend and all that. It looked like Chuy was following that trend too, but I bet his parents would make him get it cut when he got home. G and Dagywn declined as well. I wondered whether it had anything to do with going back to the tribe on Mt. St. Helena, returning to the way they did things there. Tova told Melea "Thanks, but no thanks," saying she was fine with her ponytail. Besides, she said, she had to work on her tan, as she and Mad were having a tanning contest.

At the mention of her name, Melea started yelling for Mad.

"Mad! Where are you? It's time for a new look. A normal one."

Mad poked her head up through the hatch.

"What are you talking about, Melea?"

"Time for a new look. How about a haircut?"

"Oh, I don't think so. Do you know how long it's taken me to grow these things?" she said, holding up her dreads.

"Yeah, probably a long time. All the more reason to do something different. How about we cut them all off?"

"What? And have a shaved head?"

"For a while. It'll grow out."

"You think me having a shaved head is going to make me more 'normal'?"

"You not normal, girl."

"Look who's talking."

"Good one," Melea said, slapping Mad on the back, both of them laughing.

"Sure, why not?" Mad said. "I was getting kind of tired of them anyway."

By this time everyone aboard the *Silverado* was gathered around Melea and Mad, like it was a performance which, I guess, it was. Aalto was there, looking like she was witnessing a murder. Melea started cutting and kept cutting. When she was done, there was a pile of blond dreadlocks on the deck. Aalto couldn't take any more and went below deck.

Melea stood back and looked at Mad's head.

"Uh-oh," she said.

"Uh-oh?" Mad said. "That's not what I wanted to hear you say, Melea."

"I can't cut close enough with these scissors. You look like a leopard."

Mad's head really did look like a leopard with small patches of hair here and there all over her head.

"Like a leopard? Really? Oh jeez, Melea."

"Who's got a razor? And some shaving cream!" Melea asked no one in particular.

"I do," Mr. Becker said.

"Well, go get them. We got an emergency repair situation here."

Mr. Becker returned a couple of minutes later with a razor and a can of shaving cream. Melea proceeded to cover Mad's entire head with the shaving cream. It looked pretty funny but no one dared laugh. Then Melea started working carefully, starting at the back of Mad's neck and shaving to the top of her head. After she was finished, she took a wet towel and wiped off the remaining bits of shaving cream.

"Much better," Melea pronounced.

Tova pronounced it "Very chic, but you'll lose the contest unless you get it tanned like the rest of your body."

"It feels kind of like the way your teeth feel when you get your braces off," Mad said, rubbing her hand over her head. We all followed her belowdecks so she could look in the mirror.

"Cool," she said, when she saw how it looked, "but Tova's right: it is pretty white. My mom's going to have a cow when she sees this. We haven't seen each other in, like, two years."

"Look at it this way, Mad," Chuy said, "She'd probably have an even bigger cow if she saw you with those dreads."

Truth be told, Mad was beautiful whether she was bald or sporting dreads. Like I said, she was one of the most unusual people I've ever met.

・　・　・

One night when I was steering the boat by myself, Dagywn appeared from out of nowhere and sat down next to me. I'd grown to like him and respected the way he thought things through. He wanted to know what was involved in guiding the boat to its destination so I explained it to him and pointed out the star that I was sailing the *Silverado* towards. He seemed impressed.

"I could use a star like that," Dagywn said.

"What do you mean?" I asked.

"Something to latch on to, you know, something to get me squarely to a destination. No going this way and that."

"I'm not following," I said, genuinely confused.

"From the few discussions I've had with G, I think I'm headed towards some confusing times with our tribe. In my gut, I think change is inevitable. We've stayed the same for so long and now things are different and I can't quite figure out exactly why, but I know they are. And I do know that the next steps we take as a group are probably going to be the most important ones we've ever taken."

"Are you talking about assimilating?"

"For the lack of a better word, yes," Dagywn said with a sigh. "The process the Menehune took was different. They had a long history on the island and the Uplander folks still had some knowledge of them. The Menehune had never been forgotten, so I figured for them to slowly reappear wouldn't be all that strange. Our gnome tribe is different. For all intents and purposes, we have been forgotten. For us to reappear, even slowly, would be a big deal. It would shock Uplanders. And, if I'm being honest, I think there'd be a lot of confusion and difficulty for our people, as well. Sometimes I wish things could remain just as they are forever but, like I said, I think change is going to come to us whether we want it or not. Maybe it's already come. It's my job to make the transition as successful as possible, for everyone, including the Uplanders. But I didn't come up here to bore you with our problems. I came to apologize."

"Apologize?" I asked. "For what?"

"I understand G told you about the true nature of our 'king.'"

"Yeah. His father, no less."

"Well, anyone ever elected king of the tribe handles it differently. Gob takes the role seriously and he's done a good job. Over time, some of the elected kings have turned out to be nothing more than lazy sots and disagreeable to boot. But, like I said, Gob has grown into his position rather nicely. I have no complaints."

"If you did have a complaint, would it make any difference?"

"That's what I'm here to tell you. The king of our tribe is our figurehead, as G explained to you. The actual power behind the throne is held by whoever the wizard is at the time."

"So that's you."

"Right. Which is also why I have to get back to my tribe. I realize now that I should never have left the ship in the first place. My duty was to the tribe, not to my ill health. I will say, however, that it was a huge relief to be on solid ground, all those many years ago. But I had no idea Gob would take so long to send someone to rescue us. So long that everything has gotten more complicated — marriages, children, not to mention the whole Menehune assimilation process I found myself in the middle of. Not that any of that matters to you. What does matter to you and me both, is that you're here."

"What do you mean?"

"Well, if I had stayed on Captain Niebaum's ship and gone with the rest of the tribe to California, you *wouldn't* be here."

"How's that?" I said, surprised.

"For two reasons. First of all, there wouldn't have been the need to send a 'rescue' party to come and fetch me and, two, say I had stayed aboard Captain Niebaum's ship and just Ainsworth, Charleston, Doolittle, and Roskoloff jumped ship in Kauai and we wanted to get them back. The simple fact is that I wouldn't have reached out to the Uplanders for help. Gnome tribes are notorious for relying on themselves to solve problems. That Gob struck a genuine friendship with Captain Niebaum, one which passed on to the Captain's heirs — your family — was highly unusual. Had I known about the amulet and Gob's making a commitment to dynastic friendship, I would have found a way to annul it. Furthermore, to have you watched by the crows for all these years does not set well with me. I think it was wrong to involve you to such an extent in finding me and facilitating my return to the tribe. Gob should have found a way to do it himself, with his own men. So I apologize for what I see as asking too much of you. It wouldn't have happened had I been present. I think you've been exposed to things that may make your having a normal Uplander life rather difficult going forward."

"Well, like you said, I'm here now. How it happened doesn't matter all that much to me. And, yeah, I've seen things I never thought possible, but I think I'll have a normal life, whatever 'normal' is. The one thing I think I'll remember the most about all of this is that 'normal' may not exist, or at least that there are as many different kinds of 'normal' as there are stars," I said.

"If that's what you take away from this experience, then I won't feel so guilty," Dagywn said smiling and holding out his hand. We shook hands and Dagywn gave me a quick hug and then went back belowdecks.

"That was a little strange," I thought to myself after Dagywn left. Not so much for what he'd said, but an adult apologizing to a kid struck me as odd. But the more I had gotten to know Dagywn, the more respect I had for him being a decent, thoughtful guy. The more I thought about it, the more I came to think his apology was just Dagywn being Dagywn. It did, however, make me wonder what I'd be doing right now if I hadn't been picked by Gob to do this job for him. Certainly not sailing a sailboat in the middle of the night somewhere in the middle of the vast Pacific Ocean, following a single star in the equally vast heavens above. It occurred to me that instead of Dagywn apologizing to me, I should be thanking him. If he hadn't jumped ship all those years ago, I'd probably be picking prunes with Chuy back in St. Helena just like we did every summer. *What a strange world,* I thought to myself.

· · ·

We continued our starboard tack for a few more days and then changed course to directly due east, headed, more or less, to the middle of the California coast. Almost immediately the roll of the waves changed, the weather got cooler and it seemed like everyone's moods shifted. Everyone got quieter. It was like we were all thinking about the future instead of what was happening now. I think everyone realized that things were about to change — for some, way more than for others.

Everyone started wearing more clothes. Gone were the flip-flops, shorts, and t-shirts, replaced with long pants, hooded sweatshirts, and Keds. Dagywn and G went back to their "layered look," and Dagywn started growing his beard. I wondered which version of these people was the real one: the tropical one, or the one they were transforming into before my eyes. Poor Melea didn't have any warm clothes so she just went around shivering, wrapped up in a blanket. Leo stayed in his shorts and t-shirt and acted like it didn't bother him, but I could tell he was surprised by weather he had never experienced. I wondered if he'd ever been cold before.

When we were about five days from home, Mr. Becker and Jon, Mike and Chad got preoccupied with listening to the weather updates on the radio. Conditions — the weather, winds, and tides — off the coast of California were notoriously difficult year 'round and a real challenge to even the best of sailors. As Mr. Becker put it, it was time for "heads-up sailing." Those last days at sea were grey and windy, with the clouds breaking up only briefly late each afternoon for an hour or so, just about the exact opposite of what we had gotten used to

When the weather starts getting chilly, it's time to put the flip-flops away for another day.

in Kauai. After several tense days, we were all happy to see the craggy peaks of the Farallon Islands off our starboard bow — at least those of us who knew what they meant — namely, that we were only some 30 miles from the St. Francis Yacht Club where we had started some six weeks ago. Had it only been six weeks? It didn't seem possible that so much had happened in what sounded like a very short period of time.

The last leg of our journey — sailing the Gulf of the Farallones and through the Golden Gate — was tricky business, with extremely strong tides and winds that didn't always behave the way they were supposed to. The fog was doing its crazy dance thing in the straits under the bridge, wisps here and there, twisting and turning, urged on by an unseen force. To give us as much control as possible, Mr. Becker had the guys lower all the sails and we motored the final few miles home. It was a little past nine o'clock and just getting dark and extremely foggy by the time we pulled along-side the dock at the yacht club. By the time we were tying up, everyone was standing on deck, looking up at the twinkling skyline of San Francisco, fog trailing the skyscrapers and the last of the seagulls screeching overhead. Nobody said anything. Everyone just stood there looking at the cool cityscape in a hundred shades of grey, awestruck. We certainly weren't in Kauai any more.

"Welcome to San Francisco," I said, thinking somebody had better say something. I'm fairly certain that the fourteen of us on board were all feeling something different at that moment: relief, apprehension, fear, confusion. After all we'd been through, it was only natural to wonder what was going to happen next.

With the excitement and anticipation of returning home, I hadn't given any thought to the practical matters at hand. I talked it over with Mr. Becker and we decided that it made the most sense for everyone, except for me, to stay on board that night. It was still early enough that Doyle would be awake and I could give him a call and have him pick me up. Tomorrow morning we'd figure out our next steps.

I called Hattie's house from a pay phone on the dock and got Doyle after a couple of rings. He was surprised to hear I was at the yacht club and said he'd be right down. I went belowdecks and tossed the few things I had brought with me in my duffle bag and told everyone I'd see them tomorrow, first thing.

As I was about to step onto the gangplank I stopped, leaned down and patted the bulkhead of the *Silverado*, "Thanks for getting us back and forth safely. You did a great job." Yeah, I know. It's strange talking to a boat, but with everything else that had happened since we left, quite frankly, it didn't feel weird at all.

Once we returned home, Grandma went into her "generalissimama" mode, using the library for impromptu meetings and as her command center.

Chapter XXIV

Hattie Takes Charge

Friday, August 2, 1968
Grandma Hattie's house
San Francisco, California

The first day back at Grandma's had started out busy, to put it mildly. I had gone down to the yacht club early in the morning and told everyone to come up to her house. Just as Grandma was coming downstairs, the whole crew from the *Silverado* arrived through her front doors. I must admit that everyone looked a little worse for wear, which shouldn't have been a surprise considering we'd all just spent two weeks crossing the Pacific Ocean on a sailboat. Where there had been just Mr. Becker, Tova, Chuy, JP and G, now there was Dagywn, Melea (still wrapped in her blanket), Leo and Aalto, not to mention Mad with her newly-bald head. As Grandma reached the bottom of the stairs, the first words out of her mouth were, "You attract the most interesting friends, Nick." I introduced her to all the newcomers and she hugged all the people she'd met before, then told everyone to go to the kitchen and get some coffee and whatever else they wanted, which is when Katia completely lost it and ran off upstairs to her room. That left JP to take over the kitchen and see to it that people had what they wanted. Somehow none of it was surprising.

Grandma, who knew Tova spoke perfect German, asked her to go upstairs and try to explain to Katia the presence of not one, but now five gnomes in the house. "We simply can't have Katia freaking out all the time," Grandma told Tova. She returned to the kitchen in about ten minutes and took Grandma to the side and said something privately.

"Oh, Tova darling, you're brilliant! However did you think of it?" Hattie said, hugging her.

"I'm not sure. It just came out without even thinking about it," Tova said, a little taken aback by Hattie's enthusiastic embrace.

"Well, it certainly solves all kinds of problems. Thank you. Thank you."

Apparently Tova had solved the problem by telling Katia that G, Dagywn, Melea, Leo, and Aalto (who she referred to as "our little friends") were part of the troupe of actors who put on the Renaissance Faire each year, which would be opening in a few weeks in nearby San Rafael. Why that explanation did anything whatsoever to calm Katia's fears (and how she even knew about the Renaissance Faire) is beyond me, but it did the trick.

Grandma was now enlisting Tova to go shop for some appropriate clothes for Melea and Leo. Dagywn was wearing what he must have been wearing when he jumped ship back in 1879 which, amazingly, looked in fairly good shape. G had his old clothes from before Grandma had bought him his "makeover" ones, and what Aalto brought with her from the Åland Islands worked fine for San Francisco's bone-chilling summer climate. It was just Melea and Leo who had never had to deal with the cold before. Grandma called for G and told him to give Tova some cash so she could go shopping and yelled at me to wait around because we had more things to discuss. She was like an army officer shouting orders to several different platoons at the same time. It didn't take long for JP to start calling her "generalissimama," which she seemed to enjoy.

After Grandma had finished issuing orders, we retreated to the library and closed the doors. It didn't take long to tell her what had happened on our trip because Grandma was what I call a "speed listener," and only wanted the head-lines of any story. If need be, she'd make up the details at some later date, regardless if they were true or not. It's just the way Grandma was. I wasn't exactly sure why, but I decided to leave out the part about King Gob being a fake king. I figured if he was intended to look like the real king to anyone from the outside, then it was okay for her to keep seeing him as just that from her outsider point of view. The whole situation with the gnomes was already compli-cated enough without deliberately making it more so.

We sat in the two facing chairs in front of the fireplace. Clearly Grandma had an agenda. Without skipping a beat she turned to me and asked "Have you given any thought to what you're going to do with all your friends now that you've completed King Gob's business?"

The question took me by surprise. "Not really. I've been, you know, busy just thinking about getting home."

"I think we ought to have a party. A big one." Grandma Hattie said.

"A party?" This was switching gears fast, even for Grandma. I sat down and said, "Can we back up a little here? What gave you the idea that we should have a party?"

"Well, I just thought we needed to wrap things up. You know, get people back to where they belong. People usually go home after a party. Right? Unless it's a really good one... " Grandma said, getting a look on her face like she was re-membering something from a long time ago.

It didn't take me long to figure out where she was coming from. For as free-wheeling as she often was, there were now eleven extra people in her house and, admittedly, a lot of extra confusion. Although she'd be the last to admit it, it was all probably a bit much for her, so I just blurted out, "Let's do it by the numbers."

"What do you mean?" she asked.

"Well, first off, there's G, Dagywn, Melea, Leo and Aalto. They all need to get to Mt. St. Helena, right?"

"Preferably before Katia figures out they're not part of the Renaissance Faire, yes," Grandma said, catching on to where I was going with my countdown.

"Then there's Chuy and Mad," I said. "Chuy needs to go home to St. Helena and Mad needs to leave to visit her mother in San Diego in a few days."

"Right, if you say so," Grandma said.

"And Mr. Hayes and Diana need to get to Carmel, and JP to Kansas City."

"Correct."

"Chad, Mike and Jon have already gone back home, so that just leaves me."

"Well, you're welcome to stay or go wherever and whenever you want."

"Okay," I said, "so let me work on making arrangements getting everyone where they're supposed to be."

"All right," Grandma said, visibly relieved.

"Do you still want to have a party?"

"Of course I do. I think the successful conclusion of your expedition de-serves one."

"Where do you want to have it? Here, or at Eagle's Nook?"

"Oh, I think we'd better have it at Eagle's Nook. That way we can cut loose, you know? And I think we better have it sooner rather than later. Strike while the iron's hot, I say. Let's have it on Tuesday. That's 8/6/68. Must be some-thing auspicious about that series of numbers."

"Are you sure? That's only a few days away."

"Absolutely."

And that's how one of the most memorable — and yes, auspicious — parties of all time had its beginnings.

. . .

The next morning, I woke up at 5:30, wide awake. I remembered that I'd had weird dreams, but was thankful that at least they weren't about Pele. I decided that it was a good time to finish Grandpa's journal, so I propped myself up with the pillows and started in. I was finished by 8 o'clock and still confused about how I felt about it.

I turned my cell phone on. The screen came to life, telling me it was Tuesday, July 14th, 2012, 8:03 a.m., 67 degrees. The fact that it was Tuesday made me pause. Why? It took a few seconds but I remembered this was the day I was supposed to meet with Uncle Chuy at 1:30. I threw on clothes from the day before and ran downstairs. Grandpa and Doyle were already sitting at the big table in the kitchen, drinking coffee and reading the newspaper. Talk about "old school." Grandpa refused to read the *New York Times* online, even after I told him how many trees had been devoured for his old-fashioned, paper subscription. He said you can't line a canary cage with a computer screen. I reminded him he didn't have a canary. "Yeah, but I'm thinking of getting one," was all he said.

"Morning."

"Morning."

"Hungry?"

"I'll get it," I said, pouring myself a bowl of cereal.

"They're some ripe peaches there on the counter."

"Cool."

I sliced the peaches on top of the cereal. They smelled like summer.

"I finished it."

"Your breakfast?"

"No, your journal."

"Hmmmm. No comment?"

"What happened to the *Silverado*?"

"The mine?"

"No, the sailboat," I said.

"I gave it to the California Maritime Academy. They use it as a training vessel."

"Is it true that Katia really…"

"Whatever you're about to ask, it's all true."

"That sounded like quite the party."

Grandpa and Doyle both put their newspapers down at the same time and said in unison "It was." And then started to laugh.

There were times I felt completely in the dark and this was one of them.

"You know there's a third one," Grandpa said. "You want to read it?"

"A third journal?"

"Yeah."

"I think I have to digest this one first."

"Don't let me rush you. I just thought…"

"No, it's just that I'm still trying to figure out a few things. I think I'll make a list." The list I really needed to make was of the questions I wanted to ask Uncle Chuy. And for whatever reason, I still didn't want to tell Grandpa I was going to see him.

"I'm going to go over and see Darren. We're going to go into town and get some things for school."

"Okay. Be careful on the highway."

"I will, I will. See 'ya."

I did, in fact, ride over to Darren's place, but his mom told me he was at the dentist. I went to Vasconi's and got some supplies for school, then I walked my bike over to La Prima Pizza and ordered a "personal-sized" pepperoni pizza. I was going to eat it there but decided to get it "to go" and eat it at Crane Park, which was basically just across the street from La Prima. The park wasn't all that large, but it was green and shaded by big old elm trees; it was like a little, calm oasis, right next to the almost always busy, noisy Main Street. I sat down on the grass and leaned against one of the trees. I dug into my backpack and fished out one of the spiral notebooks I had bought at Vasconi's and an extra-fine roller ball pen. In between slices of pizza (which was good), I thought about what I wanted to ask Uncle Chuy. I couldn't figure out why I had this negative feeling about going to talk to him. It wasn't anything specific I could put my finger on. One thing was for sure: the Uncle Chuy I knew didn't seem much like the one Grandpa described in his journals. The few times I had met him at family parties or holidays he always seemed quiet and like he wasn't quite there – or didn't want to be. The reason I hadn't thought about talking to him before was that he didn't seem like part of our family. And if Grandpa and he were best friends back in the day, why didn't they ever see each other or hang out together now? The more I thought about it, the more I realized I wouldn't feel comfortable asking him those questions, but maybe he would be able to give me some answers about what was in the journals. I mean like, did they find Dagywn the way Grandpa described? Did Pokee really light his pipe with his fingers? And what about Madam Pele and her sister, Nāmaka: stuff that I found very hard to believe. I was going to write all my questions down, but I felt stupid doing it. It was probably best just to wing it and see what happened.

I looked at my cell phone. It was a few minutes past 1 o'clock. I figured it would take me about twenty minutes or so to get down to Uncle Chuy's house, south of town, on Mee Lane. I threw my trash away, got on my bicycle and headed down Main Street, through town, to where Main Street turns into Highway 29. Mee Lane was about 4 miles south of town, on the east side of the highway. It wasn't paved, just loose gravel and a whole lot of ruts and potholes. There was a green sea of vineyards on both sides of the lane, all the way to the Napa River in the middle of the valley. Uncle Chuy's house was right where the lane makes a sharp turn south. It was a long, cream-colored ranch house with a red tile roof, surrounded by lots of big old walnut trees. I leaned my bike against one of the trees and walked up to the front door which was under a wide, shaded front porch. The shade felt good after the hot ride on the highway. I rang the doorbell and Uncle Chuy answered right away.

"Come in, come in," he said, pushing the screen door open. "You look like you could use something cold to drink. Iced tea?"

"Just water'd be fine. Thanks."

"Let's sit on the back porch. It's cooler back there," he said, motioning with his hand to the glass doors leading to a back porch overlooking the vineyards. "I'll be right back with your water."

I went out to the porch and sat down in one of the chairs there. It was a nice place to sit, cool, like Uncle Chuy said, with a view across a wide lawn, seemingly endless vineyards, and the dusky eastern hills shimmering in the distance.

"Here we go," Uncle Chuy said, handing me a tall glass of ice water. "So what brings you out here? I haven't seen you since when? A couple of Christmases ago?"

"I think that's right."

"Did you come here on your bicycle?"

"Yessir."

"Good for you. Your grandfather and I rode our 10-speeds from one end of this valley to the other when we were your age. I don't think there's a road in this county we didn't explore."

"That's why I'm here," I said.

"To talk about bicycles?"

"No, to talk about Grandpa."

"Is he all right?"

"Oh yeah. He's fine. It's just that he let me read two of his journals about your adventures?"

"Adventures?"

"Yeah, you know, sailing to Kauai and all that, back when you were kids." Somehow I couldn't bring myself to say the word "gnomes."

"Oh, that…" Uncle Chuy said, trailing off.

"It's just that I'm having a hard time believing what he wrote and I thought, since he claimed you were there for a lot of it, you could tell me if it was true or not."

"To tell you the truth, I haven't thought about all that for a long, long time. It was a lifetime ago."

"I know. But did it really happen?"

"I don't know what you're referring to specifically, but a lot of strange things happened that summer."

"It sounded like it. But I mean like Madam Pele and her sister having a fight when you were trying to leave Kauai?"

"Well, I never read his journals but, like I said, a lot of strange things happened."

I was getting frustrated, so I just came right out and asked, "Did you and G and Mad and my grandpa find Dagywn?"

Uncle Chuy was quiet for a minute and then said, "Let me tell you a story, Joaquin. This was a long time ago, several years after that trip to Kauai. A friend and I went to Mexico over summer vacation to go surfing and just to hang out. One day we went to a bullfight in a town near where we were camping. After the bullfight, we were on our way back to our campsite, my friend driving his beat-up truck on a narrow, two-lane road in the middle of nowhere. We were headed south. On our left was a straight-up mountainside that came right down to the edge of the road. On the right, there was a shear drop-off, maybe 60 feet down to a river gorge. In front of us there was nothing but desert as far as the eye could see. I don't think we were going all that fast. The road was dangerous enough as it was without speeding. We started going up a rise, the road twisting towards the left. In an instant, from out of nowhere, there was a huge Pemex gas truck right in front of us, in the middle of the road, doing about ninety. I was in the passenger seat and I know for certain there wasn't enough room on the right for us to avoid crashing into the truck. And we certainly couldn't have swerved to the left. And then it was all over – in an instant – and the truck was gone and we were traveling on a deserted road in the middle of the desert. To this day, neither of us knows what happened. Neither of us has any memory of what we did to avoid the truck. As far as I could tell, both of us should have been dead. But there we were, a couple of guys, driving in the middle of a Mexican desert, both of us shaking like leaves. And we never talked about it after that. It was just too weird. And that's what that trip to Kauai was like for me. I know a bunch of stuff happened, but I'd just as soon not think about it. Sorry to disappoint you, but that's the way it is."

"I understand," I said. Kind of. But I gotta' admit, it was a big disappointment. Maybe because he was being so evasive, I decided to go ahead and ask him. I mean, what the heck, right?

"Are you and Grandpa still friends?"

Uncle Chuy was quiet for a bit and finally said, "After a fashion."

"The way he wrote it in his journals, you guys were like best friends. What happened?"

"Let's just say we had a parting of the ways a while back."

"Can I ask why?"

"It's 'may' not 'can.' Ask your Grandpa."

"I *will* ask him – when I get home. But I'm here now and I'd like to know what you think happened?"

"What *I* think happened?" Uncle Chuy asked, clearly agitated. "I think he went a little crazy."

"Whaddaya' mean?"

"One minute everything was okay and the next it's like he wanted to get in a fight or something."

"When did this happen?" I asked

"After that party at Hattie's, that summer we went to Kauai," he said.

"Did you?"

"What?"

"Get in a fight?"

"No. We'd been friends forever. We never threw any punches. Never. And I wasn't going to start then."

"Then what happened? I don't understand."

"He just started after me, baiting me, saying this and that."

"About what?"

"About me and her."

"Her who?"

"Mad. We were going out then."

"What'd he say?"

"It's like he had it all planned out. Like it was rehearsed. I've thought a lot about that conversation. First, it wasn't a conversation. It was one-sided. Nick said what he wanted to say. And when he was finished, as far as I was concerned, we weren't friends anymore. I just walked away. That was it."

"But what did he say to make you do that?"

"He never came right out and said it, but he might as well have. He basically said I wasn't good enough for Mad, that she was way out of my league. Which maybe she was, but I sure as hell didn't need my so-called best friend telling me that."

He was quiet after that. The only thing I could say was, "I'm sorry, Uncle Chuy."

So that was pretty much the end of that. Not surprisingly, our goodbyes were awkward. I got back on my bike and headed to Eagle's Nook, our conversation looping through my brain as I absentmindedly pedaled. So what was I coming away with? About the only thing I could say I learned was that he did, in fact, go on the trip to Kauai with Grandpa and "a lot of strange things happened." And that their friendship ended on a sour note, seemingly because Grandpa had done some Best-Friend-From-Hell number on him. I was going to have to find out more about that because I believe what my history teacher taught us last year, namely that "there are two sides to every story and then there's the truth," and I hadn't heard the other side of the story yet, let alone the truth.

And all that drama was separate from what I wanted to know, which was very simple: Is this crazy old story in his journals real or not? Uncle Chuy's deliberately vague recollections did absolutely nothing to help me decide one way or the other. Pedaling against the wind, I got to thinking about the other morning when I asked Grandpa if the part about Madam Pele and Nāmaka was true and he asked me if it would upset my "world view" if he said it did. I figured that was what the whole Kauai experience must have been like for Uncle Chuy: It must have upset his world view so much that he just couldn't think about it. Like the Pemex truck that didn't exist anymore. Except it did. And he still thought about it and I could tell he also still thought about his and Grandpa's "parting of the ways," which seemed like holding onto something way too long. I could ask Grandpa about all that but, for today at least, I was done with old people and the whole awkward thing. I remember Grandpa once telling me that "Whenever you're dealing with human beings, sooner or later it's going to get weird." He couldn't havae been more right about that.

Niebaum Lane, where Grandma Hattie had her summer house, went due
west off of Highway 29 in Rutherford in the middle of the Napa Valley.
That's Mt. St. John in the distance. At 2375 feet, it's one of the taller
mountains in the county. The Sonoma Valley is on the other side of it.

Chapter XXV

The Party

Sunday, August 4, 1968
Grandma Hattie's house at Eagle's Nook
Rutherford, California

I admit it. I thought the idea of a big party was crazy. But it looked like I was the only one. When I told the gang, they thought it was a great idea. And, according to Grandma, when King Gob found out, he was practically ecstatic. What do I know? Not that much, apparently.

When Grandma and I had our talk in the library, I said I'd handle getting everyone back to where they were supposed to be. I decided to start with G, Dagywn, Melea, Leo, and Aalto. They were all, understandably, anxious to get to Mt. St. Helena, except for Leo, who seemed reluctant. He actually asked his parents if it would be okay for him to stay in San Francisco. That went over like a lead balloon. Because Dagywn had never been to Mt. St. Helena, he couldn't transport everyone using his special abilities, which meant we had to rely on Doyle. I asked Grandma if it would be okay if he used the limousine to transport them to the mountain and she said "Of course, as long as you're back in time tomorrow morning to take me and Katia up to Eagle's Nook." Doyle assured her he'd be back in time and proceeded to herd the gnomes into the back of the long black car — all but Leo, who wanted to sit in the front seat. We said our goodbyes knowing that we'd see each other again at Grandma Hattie's in Rutherford for the party.

The next morning, Mr. Hayes, Tova, JP, Chuy, Mad, and I jammed into Mr. Hayes's van and took off, followed by Doyle, Grandma, and Katia in the limousine, not to mention Clarence the tortoise, who was in a box in the trunk; Grandma thought he could use some fresh country air. Once we got to the valley, we dropped Chuy and Mad off at his parents' house and then took off for Eagle's Nook, which was only ten minutes away, on the opposite side of Highway 29. Like so many of the lanes in the valley, the one to grandma's house is surrounded on both the left and right by vineyards. Her house is at the end of the lane, nestled up against the base of Mt. St. John, which rises more than

2000 feet behind her place like a big blue, hunched giant watching protectively over the property. Her house is surrounded by ancient oak trees which completely hid it from the road. Because it's so hidden, having it appear suddenly in front of you after the last turn of the driveway comes as a surprise: a pale, three-story Victorian mansion, looking like a gigantic, multi-tiered wedding cake, set in the middle of green lawns and manicured shrubs. Captain Gustav Niebaum and his wife, Susan, built the house in 1883 and, truthfully, I don't think anything has changed much over the many decades since. Mr. Hayes stopped the van in the middle of the driveway before he even reached the house and he and Tova and JP just stared at it without saying anything. "Yeah, I know," I said. "It's quite the place." They looked at me, dumbfounded.

Mr. Hayes parked the van over by the old barn and we walked toward the house, just as Grandma, Katia, and Doyle came out of the back screened-in porch. Grandma was talking fast and pointing this way and that, apparently already giving instructions about how she wanted things laid out for the party.

"You'll find the Chinese lanterns up in the attic, Doyle. They're in the box marked 'Summer Party Stuff.'"

"Okay," Doyle said.

"The bamboo poles to hang them from are in the barn, all bundled together. You'll find them. And the wooden dance floor and the long tables and chairs are out there too. Good thing we've got lots of hands to help," she said, looking at us.

"That's why we're here," Mr. Hayes said, sensing Grandma's need for enthusiastic support. "Let's get to it."

"I like your style, Tim. Cheerful and competent. I could use more of that. Everyone could use more of that," Grandma said.

"'More of that' is right behind me," he said, turning around and looking at me, Tova, and JP.

JP stepped front and center, clicked his heels and saluted Grandma and said, "Permission to speak freely, generalissimama."

"Permission granted," Grandma replied, saluting him back.

I wondered if I was missing something. Was this a party we were planning or an invasion?

"Will you allow Katia and me to be in charge of the food?" he said.

"Of course. As long as she makes her famous Sauerkraut Ham Balls. Have at it." Grandma said with a wave of her hand. "And JP ...".

"Yes ma'am."

"At ease. I'll be in the vicinity for the next several days. You can dispense with the salutes," she said.

"Yes, ma'am!" JP said, automatically saluting her and then starting to laugh.

Katia, who was more or less hiding behind Grandma, looked like she wanted to simultaneously disappear and take advance credit for her Sauerkraut Ham Balls. JP strode over to her and said "We need to talk," and took her by the elbow back into the house. I guess they had a pow-wow and decided who was going to make what: Katia was horrified with JP's suggestion that they limit the food to "heavy pupus" until he explained what it meant, and, more importantly, his suggestions for how they were going to stay out of each other's way.

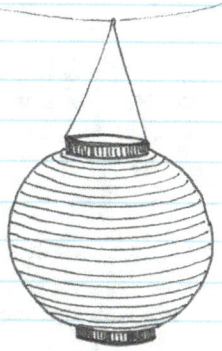

Doyle found the Japanese paper lanterns up in the attic.

From there it was all a blur of activity, which coincided with a heat wave, adding to the intensity of the work. Or as JP, with sweat on his forehead, put it: "This party business involves a whole lot of totin'." We toted stuff from the barn, stuff from the attic, stuff from the grocery store, stuff from seemingly every closet in Grandma's house. We set up the wooden dance floor, ten long rectangular tables, dozens of chairs, tablecloths, napkins, ice chests, bag after bag of groceries from Keller's Grocery and Ernie's Meat Market, candles, cutlery, napkins, vases for flowers and, yes, the paper Chinese lanterns attached to tall bamboo poles all around the perimeter of the lawn. What else? Well, there was the new barbecue from Steve's Hardware for JP, bags of charcoal briquettes, big bags of ice and last, but hardly least, an old Boy Scout tent of mine that, for some reason, Tova wanted put up in a secluded spot in the garden.

As crazy as things were outside, Katia wouldn't even let us in the kitchen, where it looked as if she had every pot and pan and mixing bowl out and in use at the same time. Meanwhile, JP had set up his own outdoor kitchen with three of the big tables, his barbecue, the garden hose for water and a big box fan on the lawn, pointed directly at wherever JP happened to be standing. The tables were piled with big slabs of pork ribs, beef briskets and lots of sausages. Smoke poured out of the charcoal grill, seemingly non-stop, making the whole yard smell like a barbecue joint.

I talked with Grandma about inviting Walter and Ma-D and Chuy's parents to

We went to Steve's Hardware and got a new barbecue smoker for JP.

the party, but we both decided that neither of the couples would be able to accept the gnomes for who they were and decided to just leave well enough alone. If they came, it was almost certain there would be unintended consequences and repercussions, no matter how good our intentions were. I felt bad about it, but it seemed like there was no other choice.

It was two full days of non-stop activity and commotion. Because our two chefs were otherwise engaged, for dinner one night we had pizzas from town and the next night, Grandma's favorite, Chinese food from the Golden Harvest restaurant up the road. By the time Tuesday morning rolled around it definitely looked like we were going to have a party. Everything was set up and ready to go. At the last minute Katia and JP both decided that we needed fresh peach ice cream which meant we had to find the old ice cream maker, which finally turned up on the back porch, still in its original box. Tova and Mr. Hayes volunteered to go out into the orchard and pick the peaches and everyone took turns cranking the machine until ice cream was stiff enough to put in the freezer, but not before everyone took licks off the paddle. If all the food was as good as the ice cream, it was going to be quite the night. After that, it was just a matter of everyone taking showers, getting their party duds on and waiting for the guests to arrive, which was a whole other story — namely, what time does a party start when one half of the guests sleep all day and the other half sleeps at night? Grandma and King Gob finally compromised and decided to get things rolling at twilight. "That has a nice ring to it, don't you think?" Grandma said to me. I wasn't quite sure what time twilight was. JP said he thought it was sometime around "ish-ish-thirty," which sounded about right. Mad and Chuy came early, arriving in one of Chuy's parents' old pick-up trucks, driven by Mad. They were holding hands as they crossed the front lawn, so apparently they were still an "item." The work was done and all of us worker bees were spiffed up. Grandma was wearing a white linen dress with the sapphire brooch King Gob had given to Captain Niebaum, hanging around her neck on a platinum chain. When I commented on it, she said she thought it "was appropriate, given the circumstances." Tova was looking even more exotic than usual, having somehow woven gardenias into her hair so they hung straight down and bobbed around every time she turned her head. I was wearing a clean white shirt and my khaki pants, and most importantly, my lucky straw cowboy hat which, for the first time in a long time, I didn't have to worry about blowing off my head and into the ocean. After so much work, we found ourselves without much to do except stand around in the shade and admire our handiwork until the rest of our guests arrived, which was anyone's guess.

As it turned out, the party started on a high note — literally — at around 8:30. The air was still warm and the sky was just starting to turn an inky blue. High above, the chimney swifts were tumbling through the air like feathered acrobats, catching insects on the fly. The moon had already risen above the eastern hills and there was a faint, light ring around it. The breeze seemed to hold its breath and the crickets clicked and buzzed away in the dry grass bordering the vineyards. Grandma asked me to light the candles in the paper lanterns ringing the lawn. When they were all lit, their light cast a magic glow, transforming the lawn and garden into an otherworldly scene, like something out of a fairy tale. The air itself had an electric expectancy to it, like an audience waiting for a performance to begin which, I guess, is exactly what it was. Everyone was hushed as they drank in the surroundings. Suddenly, quietly, Katia asked, "Do you hear what I do?"

"What?" I asked.

Everyone got quiet and strained to listen.

"That," she said. By then, we all heard it: a high-pitched, trilling sound, possibly from some kind of a horn. Then there was a deep, rumbling beat, followed by staccato taps like a stick hitting something hollow. In combination it gave the impression of an upbeat march. And then, from out of nowhere — between each row of grapevines — the tribe materialized, each with a musical instrument, playing slightly louder with each step forward. They worked their way through the vineyard and assembled, en masse, on the dance floor, playing at full volume, King Gob standing in front of them, directing with his hands. All of us spontaneously started clapping, hooting, hollering and whistling. The party had started... but not before Gob took center stage.

"Ladies and gentlemen, may I have your

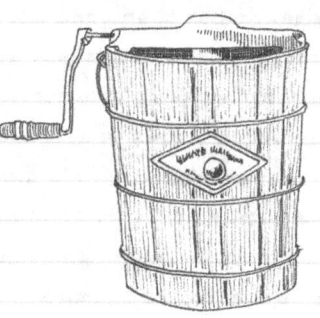

The hand-cranked ice cream freezer — an oldie but a goodie.

attention. We are assembled here tonight to celebrate the successful comple-
tion of a difficult and dangerous mission. Nick and his crew — Tim Hayes, Tova,
Chuy, Mad and my son, G — did a stellar job, just as Hattie and I knew they
would when we planned the expedition a year ago." King Gob already had a goblet
of wine in his hand, which he raised in Grandma's direction on the front porch.
There was no way Grandma and Gob knew we'd be successful a year ago and they
certainly didn't "plan the expedition," but this wasn't the night to quibble over
details. Gob continued, "They richly deserve our thanks for returning Dagywn
to our midst. In recognition of both their individual and collective efforts above
and beyond the call of duty, I hereby bestow upon each and every one of them
the Quicksilver Sphere of Perfection and the title of 'Chevalier' to denote their
elevated standing within our tribe."

Everyone clapped and whistled. King Gob raised his hands to quiet the
crowd. "And now Whitbeck will pin the medals on the recipients. Please come
forward as I call your name."

Mr. Hayes, Tova, Chuy, Mad, G, and I did as we were told and were soon
sporting small glass spheres, about the same circumference as a dime, filled
with quicksilver, pinned to our shirts. I wasn't quite sure what a "chevalier"
was or what I was supposed to do with my new medal, but maybe I was just being
too practical. Maybe it was better to just go along with the magical-mysto-mum-
bo-jumbo of the moment and have some fun. King Gob cleared his throat loudly
and said, "And now I'd like to introduce the man of the hour, along with his wife
and son. Dagywn, will you, Melea, and Leo please come forward?"

Dagywn, Melea, and Leo pushed through the crowd and stood in the middle of
the dance floor. "Please help me welcome our wizard and his family back to the
tribe. He has been gone a long time and has been sorely missed." There was a
hearty round of applause, which seemed to embarrass Dagywn and Melea, but
Leo beamed like a celebrity, nodding left and right to the crowd and mouthing
the words "I love you, I love you."

Having dispensed his awards, titles, and introductions, Gob raised his hands
again and said loudly "And now my friends, let's have a party!" Now that we had
a full complement of gnomes assembled, I wondered whether Katia was still going
to be able to see them as "our little friends" who supposedly worked at the Renaissance Faire. I thought about it for a minute and decided she was a big girl who
could decide on her own how to handle the situation. It was time for me to stop
worrying and to have some fun.

The gnome band assembled to one side of the dance floor, leaving it open to anyone who wanted to dance. Instead of the marching tune they had arrived playing, they started playing something more like dance music. I don't play an instrument but I took a music appreciation class at school and I recognized the 2/4 time as a polka, which the gnomes played enthusiastically. The beat was infectious and in no time everyone was on the dance floor, twirling around, bouncing up and down and laughing whether they knew how to polka or not. The fact that there were few female gnomes didn't seem to make any difference to the gnome men who simply danced with each other. Because Mr. Hayes had a German background and Tova grew up in Switzerland, they were no strangers to polka and it showed. They took to the center of the floor, unabashedly showing off their dance moves which, I've got to say, were impressive. King Gob and Grandma Hattie were doing their best, considering the height difference, but the biggest surprise was JP and Katia spinning around, JP with a beer in one hand and a cigarette in the other. It may have been the first time I'd ever seen Katia laugh. Aalto came over to where I was standing and asked if she could show me how to polka and I said sure, even though I normally avoid dancing because of my gimpy foot. Tonight, I figured, that was going to be the last thing anyone noticed. Aalto stood in front of me and showed me the basic steps. I mirrored her moves and she said I was a fast learner. With that, we were on the dance floor with everyone else, me hunched over a bit but still having a good time.

At one point I saw JP trying to say something in Doyle's ear and then disappearing. A couple of the gnomes — I'm fairly sure it was the Bumm brothers, Boogs and Boodle, rolled a barrel of wine next to the dance floor and set it up there, complete with a small rubber hose with a clamp at the end. As the dancers passed by the barrel, Boodle would unclamp the hose and squirt a shot of wine into their open mouths. The musicians took a break and one of the other gnomes stood on the dance floor and whistled birdcalls, which everyone applauded. JP showed back up with his electric box fan and set it up next to the dance floor with a lawn sprinkler set in front of it. In minutes, there was a cool, fog-like mist of water circulating around the dance floor, much to everyone's pleasure. JP and Katia uncovered the food tables and people moved in a herd to sample the feast they had prepared. Katia's Sauerkraut Ham Balls and JP's barbecued ribs seemed to be the big favorites. After everyone had something to eat, the band started in again, ending the set with a rousing version of *Who Stole the Keeshka*? If you don't know what a "keeshka" is, don't worry, neither did I. Later I found out it's a sausage and, according to the lyrics, "Yasha found the keeshka and he brought it back." I don't have a clue who "Yasha" is, but at least he brought the wiener back, right? Crazy song, but everyone danced to it and even sang along to the simple lyrics.

The music stopped again and Wycoff took to the center of the dance floor all by himself and proceeded to astound everyone with a fire dance that included a lot of spinning, juggling and, most alarmingly, fire breathing. I know I wasn't the only one surprised by the performance because when I looked around everyone's mouths were hanging open. When it was over and all the flames blown out it seemed oddly dark and quiet — that is, until everyone started clapping and whooping. The music immediately started in again, this time playing the *Beer Barrel Polka*, followed by *The Happy Wanderer*, which even I knew the words to from my brief stint in the Boy Scouts:

> I love to go a-wandering,
> Along the mountain track,
> And as I go, I love to sing,
> My knapsack on my back.
> Val-deri,Val-dera,Val-deri,
> Val-dera-ha-ha-ha-ha-ha,
> Val-deri,Val-dera,
> My knapsack on my back.

After the song was over, Tova, somewhat breathlessly, announced that anyone who wanted their fortunes read should follow her to the tent — the one I had set up earlier. Curious as to her fortune-telling abilities, I was the first person in line outside the tent, which was glowing mysteriously from within in its dark corner of the garden.

"You may enter," Tova said in a low voice from inside the tent.

I pulled back the flap and was kind of amazed at the transformation of my old, drab green Boy Scout tent. She had hung all sorts of patterned tablecloths on the sides, covered the dirt floor with an assortment of Oriental rugs, piled up all different sizes of pillows around the perimeter and set up a low table in front of her, covered with an Indian bedspread. There were candles everywhere and Tova was wearing a turban (which I recognized as one of Grandma's shawls) held in place with a large sparkling "jewel" pin.

"I am Madam Pavlova," she announced seriously as I sat down. "I see all and know all. Do you want me to tell all?" All of which sounded convincing, considering her natural Swiss accent.

"Sure," I said, not knowing if I should take the whole thing seriously or not.

She pulled a scarf away and revealed a small crystal ball on the table in front of her, then started motioning with her hands around the globe.

"Surprise," she said.

"Surprise?" I replied.

"Yes, I can see there are some surprises in store for you. You are headed down a special path, reserved for very few. Hmmm... it appears it's a circular path."

"Circular?"

"Yes. The path leads back to this very spot. But like I said, there will be surprises along the way — both externally and internally. It's a long path, one with several important forks in it."

"Do you mean like a path that goes off to the side?"

"Yes. Like everyone else, you will be the product of the choices you make, but I believe you will surprise yourself. The biggest of all will come late in your life. Open your heart and keep it open."

With that, Tova — Madam Pavlova, that is — went silent and then asked "Do you have any questions of me?"

Somehow I wasn't expecting any of this, especially her serious tone. I just stammered "No, I don't think so."

"Go in peace," she said, "and send in the next seeker of truth."

"Thank you, Madam Pavlova," I said, ducking out of the tent, having absolutely no idea what my "fortune" meant. But at least she said it was going to be a long path. Next in line were Chuy and Mad, who wanted to go in together. I wondered how that was going to go. Just then I heard horns trumpeting a fanfare from the dance floor and hurried over to see what was happening. Whitbeck was standing on the porch, addressing everyone on the lawn.

"Are you ready?" he asked the crowd in a loud voice.

Everyone yelled back "Yes!"

"Are you ready for the ride of your life?"

"Yes!"

"A head-spinning, death-defying, cloud-kissing trip to the stars?"

"Yes!!" everyone yelled even louder.

"Then bring them on!"

Mr. Becker and Tova appeared from the vineyards, each holding what looked long leash to which dozens of other leashes were attached. Above their heads I could just make out what looked like a thousand tiny iridescent forms in constant motion. "Hummingbirds," I said out loud. "They brought the flying hummingbird sling!" Later I learned that Mr. Becker and Tova had been pressed into service when it was discovered that the gnomes didn't have the strength or weight to keep the leashed hummingbirds from taking them airborne. No gnome other than the king, that is.

"Who wants to be the first?" Whitbeck called from the porch.

Doyle raised his hand and said "I do." Everyone cheered.

"You're a brave one, sir. Step right over here," Whitbeck said, directing Doyle to where Mr. Becker and Tova were holding the reins to the hummingbirds. "Good thing you're a slim one," Whitbeck said, handing Doyle the sling. "As you may or may not know, there were difficulties in the past getting His Heaviness off the ground but, you sir, I don't think will be a problem. Here, put this behind your fanny and hold onto these tight — and I mean tight," Whitbeck said, "like your life depended on it. Are you ready?"

"I think so," Doyle said, a little reluctantly.

"Off you go then and, if I may suggest sir, don't look down."

Whitbeck whistled and Doyle simply disappeared. He was there one instant and gone the next. Everyone strained their eyes skyward to see if they could see him, but wherever he was, he was long gone. No doubt about it, it was an impressive feat. Even though I had seen G do the same thing last summer, I was still amazed at the sight of hundreds of tethered hummingbirds carrying a human into the sky. There was lots of murmuring and shaking of heads while we waited for Doyle to return. He was gone a long time — at least it felt like a long time. And then, suddenly, he was on the dance floor again with his fanny still in the sling and the hummingbirds all in a holding pattern above him. Whitbeck ran over and got him free and Mr. Becker and Tova took control of the reins. Doyle looked dazed and just stood there, looking up at the hovering hummingbirds. Whitbeck had to guide Doyle off the dance floor to a spot where he could sit down and recuperate. He looked slightly shell-shocked.

"Who's next?" Whitbeck yelled to the crowd.

"Me, me," Katia said loudly, pushing her way through the crowd. "I want to go."

There were a lot of sideways glances and surprised looks; I think I can say that Katia was the last person anyone thought would want to go flinging through space behind a bunch of hummingbirds, but there she was, standing next to Whitbeck, practically jumping up and down with excitement. Whitbeck's eyes were round in disbelief and he said, "Are you sure, Ma'am? No disrespect, but it's not for the faint of heart." Although what I think he actually meant was, "It's not for people who have no interest in having fun." Okay, that was rude, but tonight was the first time I'd ever even heard Katia laugh.

"Oh my heart's plenty strong. Let's go," Katia said, slipping the sling behind her backside.

"Well, don't let me stand in your way," Whitbeck said. "Are you holding on tight?"

"I'm holding on tight," Katia replied.

Whitbeck whistled and everyone heard the first part of a scream and then she was swallowed up by the night sky. She seemed to be gone a long time, longer than Doyle. I'm sure I'm not the only one who wondered if maybe she'd just keep going and not come back. But then from somewhere very high in the air came the sound of more screams and laughter and suddenly Katia was back, standing in front of us, hair going every which way, hiccupping, nose running and laughing at the same time, and somehow missing her blouse but seeming to care not at all.

"That was out-of-sight!" she said to no one in particular.

Mad and Chuy had just come back from Tova's fortune-telling tent when Katia landed. Mad went over, put her arm around her and said, "Why don't we go inside and find you something to wear and you can tell me all about your trip."

"My trip?" Katia said. "My trip was a trip!"

"A blouse-ripping trip apparently," Mad said.

"Ja, you betcha'," Katia said. "Good thing my brassiere was on tight."

"You got that right, Katia," Mad said, laughing, taking her by the elbow up the stairs into the house. Grandma was just coming outside. She took one look at Mad and Katia and said, "Oh my. What did I miss?"

"Katia just took a ride on the hummingbird express," Mad said "and it seems to have blown her blouse right off."

"Are you all right, dear?" Grandma asked Katia.

"Fantastic. Never better," Katia said, eyes sparkling.

"Well, you *could* be a little better if you were fully clothed, but I have a feeling Mad is going to help you with that."

"That I am," Mad said, "Let's go, Katia."

"What got into her?" Grandma asked Mad.

"The heat? The excitement? The wine? All of the above?" Mad answered.

"I'm going for 'all of the above.' You're a dear, Mad. Come by for breakfast tomorrow around lunch time and we'll do a post-mortem."

"You've got it, Mrs. Sinclair."

"Oh, call me Hattie, please."

"Okay, Hattie. See you tomorrow."

I wasn't about to miss the opportunity to give the hummingbird contraption a try so I got in line behind the Bumm brothers to wait my turn. I just assumed that all the gnomes had ridden it before but in talking with Boogs, he claimed that this was going to be his and his brother's first time and they were both very excited. It took a while, but it was finally my turn. Whitbeck got me correctly positioned for takeoff and asked, "Are you ready for the ride of your life?"

"I am," I replied nervously.

Like before, Whitbeck whistled and I was off at a breakneck speed, heading north, up the valley. Farther and higher we went until the entire valley was spread out below me. The cool wind literally whistled in my ears. It was as close to flying as I would probably ever get: just me and the wind and a few lines tying me to the hummingbirds above. It was a dark, vast, star-filled space, seemingly endless and totally awesome. The hummingbirds flew in a wide arc from west to east and headed back downvalley. The moon, with its iridescent ring, was high in the sky now and we were headed straight for it. I looked down and there were a few lights here and there twinkling in the darkness and above me, a trillion million stars, also blinking off and on in the darkness. It was the same, top and bottom, and I was being pulled through it all with a force close to magic. I don't know if it was the wind in my eyes or if I just spontaneously started to cry, but whatever it was, it had a powerful effect on me. And then I was skidding to a stop on the dance floor in familiar surroundings, awestruck and weak in the knees.

"Oh, wow," were the first words out of my mouth. Chuy and Mad were next in line. "Be prepared to have your mind blown," was all I could say. I went over to the porch stairs and sat down. The band was playing again, only softly now, a tune that sounded like a waltz. I looked around the scene and took it all in. It seemed like the party was starting to wind down a little. I looked at my watch: it was 3:35 in the morning. The next thing I knew, Grandma was sitting next to me on the step.

"Some party," she said. "Tova — Madam Pavlova — that is, just told me I was in for some surprises."

"That's what she told me, too," I said.

"I told her my whole life has been a surprise," she said, chuckling.

"Speaking of surprises," I said, "this party's not exactly what I expected."

"What'd you expect? Chamber music? Tea? Cucumber sandwiches with the crusts cut off?"

"Now that you mention it, something like that, I guess. Have you taken a ride with the hummingbirds yet?" I asked.

"No. But I'm thinking about it," Grandma said.

"Well, don't think any more. Let's go," I said, standing up, grabbing her hand. I led her over to Whitbeck and he let her cut in line.

"Hattie, good to see you," he said with a slight bow. "Do you know the drill?" Whitbeck asked.

"Such as it is," she replied. "Put my bottom in the sling and hold on tight. Is that it?"

"Yes, ma'am, that's it. Are you ready?"

"Ready as I'll ever be," she replied.

Whitbeck whistled and Grandma was off. She was an adventurous soul, but I wondered what she'd make of this experience. I didn't think it could be much like anything she'd done before but I was just guessing. Having just done it myself, I was having problems imagining what she was thinking right now. I suppose if you were really scared you could just keep your eyes shut the whole time but, somehow, I didn't think that's what she'd do.

A few minutes later, she was back on the ground. The first word out of her mouth was, "Again."

"Beg your pardon, ma'am?" Whitbeck said.

"Again, please. May I go again?" Grandma asked without even looking at me.

"Ah, of course," Whitbeck said, a little flustered. "Are you sure?"

"Absolutely."

Whitbeck whistled and, once again, she was gone.

"She's an unusual one, your grandmother," Whitbeck said to me.

"You've got that right," I said.

When she finally got back for the second time, Grandma was a little wobbly. Whitbeck and I steadied her and after a minute or so she said she was all right.

"Now that was a surprise!" she said to no one in particular. "Madam Pavlova was right. I just wasn't expecting one so soon. But I guess that's what makes a surprise a surprise, right?"

"Whatever you say, Grandma," I said, walking her towards the house.

"What I say is, I think it's time to go to Bedforshire."

I had no idea what she was talking about. "Bedforshire?" I asked.

"'Bed for sure,' you ninny."

.   .   .

I looked at my watch. It was a little after 10 in the morning and, as far as I could tell, I was the only one up. I made myself a "combo-cup" — coffee with some chocolate in it and a lot of milk. I went outside and sat on the front steps. The sun was streaming in and it was already starting to get warm. I looked around the garden. It looked like a bomb had gone off. There was party stuff every-where. The box fan JP had put next to dance floor was still going, but lying on its side, pointing straight up. One of the stakes had come loose from Tova's fortune-telling tent and it was about to collapse. There were dirty dishes and glasses everywhere and a wine barrel had rolled out into the middle of the dance floor.

As I sat there surveying the damage, I heard a rustling in the bushes next to the steps. A minute later, Clarence the tortoise came plodding out, no doubt sensing there were tasty leftovers in the vicinity. I said "good morning" to him and the next thing I knew the fortune-telling tent started shaking and JP emerged through the front flap just as the whole tent fell over flat on the lawn.

"I've seen the future and I don't know where I am," he said.

"Would it make any difference if I told you?"

"No, not really. What would make a difference is coffee."

"I'll get you some," I said.

"Are we the only ones up?" he asked.

"So far."

"Someone's going to have the taste of chagrin in their mouth and for once, it's not me."

"Who?"

"Little Miss Sauerkraut Ham Ball."

I laughed and said, "I think you may be right."

One by one, last night's partiers started showing up. Chuy was the second, looking like he'd just crawled out from under a rock.

"Oh man..." he said as he walked into the kitchen.

"Where'd you come from?" I asked.

"Mad and I fell asleep on the porch swing. She's still out there. Snoring. Is there coffee?"

"I'm making it now," JP said, already commandeering the kitchen in Katia's absence.

Next through the back screen door were Mr. Hayes and Tova, looking a little rumpled.

"Another country heard from," JP said, eyeballing them.

"Top of the morning," I said, looking at my watch, "if it's still morning. Where'd you land last night?"

"If you're asking where we slept, we were quite comfortable in a couple of chaise longues next to the pool. Even found some beach towels to use as blankets," Mr. Hayes said.

"The stars were awesome," Tova added. "Is there coffee?"

"It's perking as fast as it can," JP said, pointing to the coffee pot on the stove.

Doyle was the next one to come through the back porch door, carrying a box.

"I come bearing gifts," he said, putting the box on the big table. "Breakfast burritos from La Luna."

"Excellent call, Doyle," JP said. Everyone immediately gravitated to the box and started digging out the foil-wrapped burritos.

"And how is everyone?" Doyle asked, with his mouth half-full.

"I'll let you know after the burrito," Chuy said.

"I don't know about everyone else, but I feel like a college athlete," JP said, pouring multiple cups of coffee.

"Yeah, right," Mr. Hayes said, rolling his eyes.

"Is this the party that never ends?" Everyone turned around to see Grandma in a long flowered caftan and matching turban coming toward them.

"You got that right," JP said, handing her a cup of coffee.

"Oh, you read my mind, JP, just like Madam Pavlova last night," she said, lifting her cup in Tova's direction. "Well, that was one for the books, don't you think?"

Considering everyone was chowing down on the burritos, there were lots of nodding heads and muttered responses in the affirmative.

"I'll never look at a hummingbird in the same way again," Grandma said, sitting down at the table. "Where's our party animal?" Grandma asked, looking around the room.

"Who?" I asked.

"Katia."

"Oh, yeah. Who knew, right?" I said.

"Certainly not me. Has she been down yet?"

"No."

"Tova, dear, would you mind going up and checking on her? Say something kind to her in German. Some encouraging words in her mother tongue might help, don't you think?"

"*Ja, das ist eine gut idee,*" Tova said, heading for the back stairs.

"Before I forget, last night King Gob asked me to ask you if you'd go up and see him as soon as possible," Grandma said.

I wondered what *that* was about. I decided I couldn't think about it right then because first things had to come first: namely, how to motivate a bunch of half-dead humans to clean up the mess outside. Grandma, uncharacteristically, went back to bed. I guess Tova's tender words in German didn't do much because we didn't see Katia for the next two days and when she finally made it back downstairs, she didn't say much.

Looking back on it, I think Clarence the tortoise was the liveliest being I saw that morning.

The town of Kelso, Scotland on the River Tweed,
where Nigel Stayne lives.

Chapter XXVI

By the Skin of His Teeth

Sunday, August 4, 1968
Nigel's House, on the River Tweed
Kelso, Scotland

It took everything in Nigel's power — both physically and mentally — to avoid being caught by the cops after the debacle on Mt. St. Helena. He was powered by the singular thought that there was simply no way he was going back to jail. The fact that it wouldn't be his first offense, not to mention that he was traveling internationally under a false passport, would mean a long jail sentence, of that he was certain. He had been in some pretty dicey situations in other parts of the world during his long career as a photojournalist. Everything he had learned about escape, avoiding the enemy and slipping across borders came into play as he half-ran and half-fell down Mt. St. Helena after escaping from Sheriff Lyman's side. He was a bloody, ripped and torn mess by the time he made it to the base of the mountain which, luckily for him, was only a few miles from the Calistoga RV Park where his Airstream trailer was parked. He avoided Highway 29 and all the side streets, opting instead to run, crouched over, between the rows of vineyards, which were seemingly everywhere. Once he got to the RV park he didn't hesitate or look to the right or the left. Pure adrenaline coursed through his veins as he gathered up his passports (both his real one and his fake one), airline tickets and satchel. He ran to the pubic bathrooms that were part of the campground and did the best he could cleaning himself up using wet paper towels. Luckily, there was no one around to witness his desperate efforts.

Now, how to get back to San Francisco and the airport? He considered, for a minute, stealing a car but decided if he got caught, it would only make a bad situation worse. He had seen Greyhound buses on the main street in Calistoga before, so he figured there must be a bus depot somewhere. Once he got into town, he asked the first person he met where the Greyhound bus depot was and was surprised to find out he was basically standing in front of it. He tried to steady his breathing as he approached the ticket counter, trying not to show the panic screaming in his brain. Just as he was about to purchase a one-way ticket to San Francisco, he thought to himself that that's exactly what the sheriff would expect him to do. Instead, he bought a ticket to Clear Lake, which was in the opposite direction, up and over Mt. St. Helena, with no stops except for one in Middletown. The bus would eventually stop in Kelseyville, at the northern end of Clear Lake, where he could catch a different bus to San Francisco. Even though it would add several hours to his trip, it seemed like going north instead of south just might save him from being captured. For all the bad luck he'd had in this whole affair, this time things went in his favor. Three days later he rather miraculously walked through the front door of his cottage in Kelso, Scotland. It took him another two days to stop shaking. No doubt about it, it had been a close call. Close enough to make Nigel decide to call it quits as a photojournalist. It was time to retire.

But to truly retire, Nigel had to figure out a way to get Lord Higgenbotham off his back for good. The first week he was home he thought practically non-stop about his options, which seemed nil to none. From a lifetime of experience, Nigel knew there was no rhyme or reason to a run of good luck or bad, no real cause-and-effect that lead to one or the other. That said, he was more than happy to accept that it appeared his luck had changed. Many years ago, when he first began his career as a photojournalist, Nigel had subscribed to a clipping service — a business that reviewed the world's newspapers and magazines, looking for articles (or photographs) that, in his case, bore Nigel's name as the author or photographer. Once a month, the service would bundle up the clippings and mail them to Nigel, who diligently pasted them into scrapbooks as a record of his career. Last year, almost as an afterthought, he'd instructed the clipping service to look for something else besides his byline, namely the word "gnomes." He figured he needed to know anything and everything about them which, as it turned out, wasn't much. The only article the clipping service had ever sent him was one he'd received several months ago concerning Icelandic gnomes. The article was from the *International Herald Tribune* about how a majority of the current population of Iceland continued to believe in gnomes, fairies, and elves, blaming them for all sorts of things from earthquakes to construction problems in building a new highway — one that apparently threatened to disturb the underground dwelling of a particular band of violent gnomes.

About a week after he had snuck back to his home in Scotland, he'd received a large envelope from the clipping service. He'd opened it rather absentmindedly and it took him a couple of minutes to realize what he was looking at. Inside was a clipping from the *The Garden Island* newspaper, from the Letters to the Editor section. The letter to the editor read as follows: "Dear Garden Island Newspaper, Re: 'Never too Young' photograph. Fellow Kauaiians, do you have such short memories? Those are Menehune you are looking at — or at least the one on the left is. The one on the right appears to be a gnome from another tribe. Signed, Doesn't Anyone Remember? A longtime resident of Wainiha Valley." In addition to the letter there was a small black-and-white photograph of two small kids in swimsuits, standing in the waves, holding surfboards.

"What the...?" Nigel said out loud.

He read the letter again and then sat down to look at the photo more carefully. Slowly it dawned on him what he was looking at. The fact that the photograph had appeared in Kauai's local newspaper meant that it must have something to do with Nick's recent trip there. Nigel checked the date of the clipping and it matched up with when he thought Nick was on the island. Nigel didn't recognize the youngster in the photograph on the left, but the one on the right could have been one of the gnomes he'd seen on Mt. St. Helena the first time he was there — the lack of a long beard made him seem familiar. He re-read the letter. Funny, he thought to himself, how that one little word — "gnome" — had caused the clipping service to send him the article.

Nigel had a thought. Maybe his luck *had* changed. This could be his ticket to freedom from Lord Higgenbotham. He looked at his watch and calculated the local time in Kauai. It was early, but someone should be in the office of *The Garden Island.* He got the number from information and called it. The person he talked to knew the photo and told Nigel that the newspaper had purchased the rights to it from the amateur photographer who took it. Nigel offered an exorbitant amount for all rights to it. The reporter on the other end of the line asked Nigel twice if he'd heard the amount correctly. Nigel assured him he had and the reporter said he would let the publisher of the newspaper know of the offer when he arrived at the office. A week later, the original photograph and its negative arrived in the mail at his cottage and Nigel sat down to compose a letter he had long looked forward to writing.

Lord Higgenbotham,
Enclosed you will find a photograph of not just a gnome but, as a bonus, also a Menehune, representative of a branch of gnomes peculiar to the island of Kauai. I consider my contract with you fulfilled. The only remuneration

I have received since we originally met in June of last year is for the expenses I incurred in my travels related to my business with you. I hereby free you from your obligation of any further payment to me and consider my contract with you terminated. Attached you will find a signed release of all rights to the photograph which you may use in any way you see fit.

Very truly yours,
Nigel Stayne

Three days later there was a knock at his door. A private courier handed Nigel a large cream-colored envelope. Inside was a letter on Lord Higgenbotham's engraved stationery. The handwriting had been done with a fountain pen in a large, unruly script.

Mr Stayne,
You're a twit of the first water, Badger. I don't know why I call you that, because you have none of the characteristics of that determined beast. You have let me down completely. Why you have sent me a photograph of two youngsters in swimsuits is beyond me. Those aren't gnomes! Where are their beards? Their pointy shoes? Their red caps? You make a mockery of me, you nincompoop. I wish I had never met you. Consider our association finished. Forever.

P.S. Of course I'm not going to pay you anything, you idiot. What do you take me for? I didn't get to be as rich as I am by throwing money away on dimwits like you.

Signed,
Lord Higgenbotham

As far as Nigel was concerned, Higgenbotham could insult him all he wanted. Nigel had gotten what he wanted: The words "Consider our association finished. Forever." For the first time since he had returned home, Nigel got a good night's sleep.

Several days later, Nigel was putting his satchel away and realized his camera was still in one of the side pockets. He pulled it out and remembered that last day on Mt. St. Helena when the sheriff had taken a photo of King Gob at the king's request. Curious, Nigel went into his basement darkroom and developed the film. There was only one exposed negative on the roll. Nigel printed it on an 8- by 10-inch sheet of paper and laughed when he saw the results. There, in all his glory, was the king with his bare arse exposed for all the world to see. He thought for a moment that he'd send it to Lord Higgenbotham but decided to let sleeping dogs lie. Nigel ended up pasting the two photographs — the one of the king and the one from Kauai — side-by-side in his last scrapbook. He was about to write a caption for them but decided against it. "Anybody looking at this years from now can make up their own caption," Nigel thought to himself. "Seems appropriate considering it's a story that never was."

Seeing the photograph of the king brought back memories he hadn't thought about since he'd returned home. Visions of the hulking, smoking caterpillar tractor sunk in the dirt came back to him. He had to admit that maybe it hadn't been a great plan after all. "What was I thinking?" he said out loud, shaking his head.

Nigel's day-to-day life gradually returned to normal and he found he was enjoying his retirement, even without the pots of money he had expected to make from Higgenbotham's job. Not having to worry about the proverbial knock on the door in the middle of the night did wonders for his frame of mind. One day while straightening up his living room he ran across Nick's original journal — the one he had stolen from Nick's dorm room.

"Guess I don't need this anymore," he said to himself. And then in a fit of goodwill, he decided to send it back to Nick with a note:

Dear Nick,
As you probably heard from the tribe on Mt. St. Helena, my last venture there was an unmitigated disaster. The gnomes performed quite admirably on their own in foiling my plans. I escaped by the skin of my teeth and now find that I'm quite content in retirement. I am taking this occasion to return your journal in the hopes that you will make better use of it than I did. I didn't get my story, but perhaps you did.
    Yours,
    Nigel Stayne

Nigel re-read the note and hoped it didn't make him sound like a wimp. On second thought, he decided he didn't care one way or the other. After all, he was retired, right?

It took me a while to figure out that the gnome "guest chamber"
had been built for an Uplander — namely me. All things
considered, it was a pretty cool room.

Chapter XXVII

Another Proposition

Sunday, August 4, 1968
Mt. St. Helena
Napa Valley, California

With the clean-up from the party done, Katia finally out of her bedroom, and everyone, I think, back to their respective homes, I had a chance to ride my bike up to Mt. St. Helena and meet with King Gob, as he had requested. Considering it was the middle of the day and the gnomes were all asleep, I wasn't in a hurry. I had plenty of time to stop in and see Clyde, figuring he'd probably be at his lean-to having lunch instead of down in his mine. I was right.

"Well, I'll be. Look who's here," Clyde said, looking up from a plate of what looked like scrambled eggs and some other unidentifiable bits. "I'm 'jes havin' some lunch. Want some?"

"No thanks, Clyde. I already ate," I said.

"What brings you to these parts?"

"I came to see you, Clyde. And I have a meeting with your neighbors up there in the cave."

"Where the hell you been? Thought I'd lost you to the winds of time."

"You almost did. I've been on a quest."

"A quest? That sounds almost important. So how'd this quest of yours go?"

Clyde sat silently while I gave him a shorthand version of the trip to Kauai in search of Dagywn. When I was through, Clyde sat thinking for a minute and then asked, "That doesn't mean they're gonna play even worse tricks on me now that they gots this wizard fellow back, does it?"

"I don't think so, Clyde. He seems like a decent person."

"That's good, cause I was thinkin' of doin' my 'neighbors,' as you call 'em, a good turn."

"What's that?"

"Well, I ain't gunna' live forever, you know. Gots no kids or any other kind of relative. So I thought mebbe' I'd give them midgets my claim here on the mountain. I know they'd take care of it and the donkeys, Sam and Sally, too. But I don't want no hullabaloo about it. I don't even want 'em to know 'till after

269

I'm a goner. Can you help me do that?"

"I'd be happy to, Clyde, if you're sure that's what you want to do."

"Yessir. Made up my mind. Got a lot of time to think up here and I done thought it through. Looks to me like they're settlin' in for the long term. That's what this place needs. Someone with a lot of time on their hands and even more patience. Mebbe they'll have better luck in that mine than I've had."

"Let me talk to my grandma about it. I'll find out what we need to do. Next time I come up I'll let you know."

"Don't wait too long now. Never know when Gabriel's gonna blow his horn and say I crossed the finish line."

"I'll be up again before I go back to school. As far as I can tell, you're not even close to the finish line, Clyde."

"Nah. Still got some mileage left. You go ahead an' run off. I know you gots things to do. Remember. Mum's the word."

"Mum's the word," I said. "I'll remember. See you soon, Clyde," I said, shaking his hand. I pushed down the thought that one day I'd come up on the mountain looking for him and he wouldn't be here. I really liked Clyde.

The trail, such as it was from Clyde's place to the gnome's cave, looked a whole lot different in broad daylight than it did in my memory of that Midsummer's Night more than a year ago. The cicadas screamed their high-pitched buzz as I made the hot climb across the side of the mountain. A slight breeze made the tall oat grass wave all around me and produced a slight moaning sound as it made its way through the tops of the ancient trees. The air smelled dry and dusty, tinged with the sharp odor of pine resin. Even on a bright, white-hot afternoon, the place made me uneasy.

Knowing that I was going to arrive when the gnomes were still asleep, I had sent G a note yesterday, by pigeon, to let him know I was coming. I received a message back saying that I could use the "guest chamber" closest to the underground cell I spent some time in last year. He said that he'd meet me there at 10 o'clock in the evening. I climbed around Jenny and Jack's corral and up the stone steps to the back entrance to the cave. I knew the way to my old underground cell and didn't have any problem finding the guest chamber. G had left the door ajar and pinned a piece of paper to it with my name written on it. It was cozy inside the small, stone-walled room; I say the room was "cozy" and "small," but I finally realized that it may not have been all that big, but it was definitely built with an Uplander in mind — I could stand up easily, the single bed was the same size as the one I slept in at grandpa's and there was a regular-sized fireplace prominent on one wall. There was a tall, narrow slit of a window carved into a wall, with no screen or glass, from which fresh air and shafts of sunlight poured down to the blanket covering the bed. The small table next to the bed had a single lit candle on it, a pitcher full of water, a glass, a pear, and an apple, a hunk of cheese and a small round loaf of bread. On top of the fireplace mantle there was a collection of books and on the other wall, a bunch of hooks for hanging clothes. I scanned the books — which must have been from G's own collection because they were almost all adventure stories — and chose Jules Verne's *Journey to the Center of the Earth*, which I hadn't read. It somehow seemed appropriate given where I was at the moment. I took off my shoes and socks, lay down on the bed, made myself comfortable, and started reading. The next thing I knew, there was knocking at the door and G, Dagywn, and Aalto were standing there smiling. Like I said before, being a recreational sleeper has its benefits.

I tucked my shirt in, ran my hands through my hair and we took off to the dining hall to meet Gob and the rest of the tribe. Along the way I asked him why the so-called "guest room" was the size it was?

"We built it specially for you; I hope you like it," he said.

I certainly appreciated the gnomes' effort but, at the same time, I was a little embarrassed by it. That said, I've got to admit that I liked the idea of having my own "room" inside of Mt. St. Helena to use whenever I felt like it. Talk about a hideout! Surprisingly, for the first time it made me understand the appeal of being invisible to the Uplander world. I had to wonder, if I were a gnome, whether I'd want to assimilate or not? I'm not sure why, but my first reaction was "probably not," which surprised me. We had arrived at the double doors to the dining hall. G put his hand on the handle and looked back at us as if to ask "are you ready?" and pushed the doors open. And there it was, in all its golden, candle-sparkling splendor, just as I remembered it from the last time. As soon as we walked into the hall, all the gnomes (with the exception of King Gob), got out of their chairs and began a round of applause. G and Dagywn both motioned to me, like I was a celebrity or something and the gnomes clapped louder. I was uncomfortable with the attention and thought the best way to end it was to simply take my seat at the table, which I did. The gnomes followed suit and the ovation mercifully came to an end. King Gob was sitting at his place at the head of the long, rectangular table, holding a small transistor radio to his ear. Dagywn walked around to his free ear and said something that caused him to put the radio down and look at me.

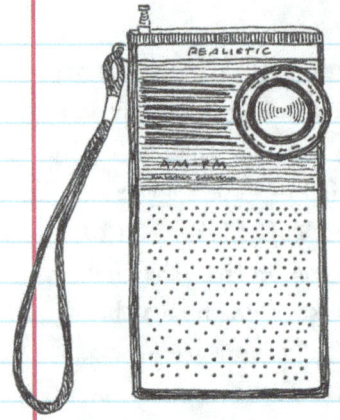

Gob's transistor radio was perfect for holding right next to his ear, all the better to hear his beloved baseball games.

"Dagywn has just informed me that I'm being rude. I apologize. But my boys are playing the Dodgers and it's the bottom of the ninth and Willie Mays just came to bat."

"Your boys?" I asked him.

"Yes, yes, my favorite team, the San Francisco Giants. They're my boys," the king said looking wistfully at the transistor radio sitting on the table.

"Would you like to finish listening to the game before we begin dinner?" I asked him.

"Oh, that would be splendid," he said, quickly picking up the radio and putting it back to his ear. "Talk quietly amongst yourselves," he said, fluttering his hand in the general direction of everyone seated around the table.

"When did this start?" I asked G, who was sitting next to me.

"Remember last year when Doyle drove us to your grandma's in the limousine?" he asked.

"Sure."

"Remember Doyle had the radio on and it was playing classical music?"

"Kind of."

"Well, my father decided then and there he needed a radio. Whitbeck procured one and within a week he discovered baseball, which definitely took precedence over classical music in no time. To say he was a fan would be an understatement," G explained.

"So it appears," I said, thinking Gob's fascination with baseball might just be the first step towards the gnomes assimilating into the broader population. Now *that* was weird. I couldn't have dreamt it up if I'd wanted to.

The king started yelling "We won, we won," punching his arms into the air. It was quite a sight. I noticed that several of the gnomes around the table were rolling their eyes. I guess not all of them shared the king's appreciation for the San Francisco Giants. I noticed Dagywn lifted his knife and more-or-less waved it in the king's direction. Gob noticed and cleared his throat, then addressed the group:

"Ah, yes. That was quite exhilarating. And now to the subject at hand:

dinner! But not before we welcome Nick back to our home with many thanks, again, for his — and his team's — successful efforts in bringing Dagywn back to our tribe. And thanks also for that rip-snorter of a party. As my dear mother used to say, 'As soon as we get over this one, we'll really throw a good one!' Now, let's eat."

Dinner was just like the last time I was there: long, noisy, slightly out of control and tasty. No question about it, the gnomes liked their food and they were good at preparing it. As dinner was finally winding down, Dagywn got up and said something in Gob's ear. Gob clanked a knife against his gold goblet and said:

"Dagywn has reminded me that we are not here tonight to merely sate our hunger and thirst. As you know, we have discussed future plans that once again involve the efforts of our newest chevalier, Nick. At this time I would like to discuss these plans with him. Any and all are welcome to stay for the discussion. Or you may take your leave, as you like."

Whether it was out of deference or true interest in what was about to be said, all the gnomes remained seated.

"All right then," the king continued. "The tribe has come to an agreement that not only do we think that our temporary home here on the side of Mt. St. Helena should become our new permanent residence, but we agree that the time has come for us to be reunited with the members of our tribe we left behind in the Old Country."

"Hear, hear," the gnomes said in unison.

"The question is whether or not Nick is willing to help us with our plans. Nick?"

"Ah, well, I'm afraid you've caught me off guard, your highness. Truthfully, I'd have to give it some thought. May I ask when were you thinking of carrying out this plan?"

"Next summer. Worked out rather well this year, don't you think?" he said, pouring himself more wine. "I have authorized Dagywn to act as my agent in this matter. Any questions you may have as to the details of our plan, feel free to discuss the matter with him. Now, who's up for a game of cards?"

I was taken aback by the abrupt end of Gob's so-called "discussion." I looked at Dagywn and he motioned with his head for me to follow him, which I did. After many stone staircases, up, down, left and right, we finally pushed a big arched door open to the amphitheater. Dagywn lit one of the torches attached to the wall and then lit his clay pipe. We stood in the pool of light cast by the torch, looking out to the empty amphitheater illuminated by the blue light of the moon.

"I'm not trying to be particularly clandestine, but sometimes it's best not to have too many ears listening in. We won't be disturbed out here," Dagywn said, puffing on his pipe.

"I haven't been here since last year. Looks different when there aren't any bonfires or that big ball of quicksilver."

"I'm sure it does look different. If I may say, you look different. Perplexed. You seem surprised at what Gob said in there. Surely you expected something like this," Dagywn said.

"I don't know. It just feels like I haven't really absorbed what we all went through in Kauai and now he's asking me to take on another one of his jobs."

"Job? Is that how this seems to you?"

"Well, they're things he wants done and can't do himself. So, yeah, it does feel like he's asking me to do a job."

"Is it what he's asking you to do, or is it the way he's asking that bothers you?"

I thought for a minute and then said "Maybe that's it. It's like he doesn't get what a big deal it is. We could have all been killed trying to get out of Kauai. Remember?"

"Oh, I remember. And you're right. I'll be the first to admit that being out of touch seems to go hand-in-hand with being king. The rest of the tribe gets it though. They do. G's told them enough that they understand, like you said, that it *was* a big deal. Maybe it's best not to consider the messenger and con-centrate on the message instead."

"The message — that he wants me to gather up the rest of the tribe and help bring them here, right?"

"Right."

"Where are they?"

"The Åland Islands."

"That's right," I said. "G told me about the islands when we were sailing to Kauai. They're between Finland and Sweden, in the Gulf of Bothnia, right?"

"Yes."

"Of course," I said, with more than a hint of sarcasm, "somewhere close by and convenient. And how many are there?"

"Islands or gnomes?"

"Gnomes."

"43. 20 women, 16 men, and seven children."

"43? You've got to be kidding me!"

"And there's the gold," Dagywn said.

"Gold?"

"Yeah. We just brought a little here to get us by while we were scouting. The vast majority of the gold is with them."

"Vast? Like how vast?"

"By last count, 8,869 gold balls, each weighing approximately 16 pounds. And before you try to do the math in your head, that's about 141,904 pounds."

By last count there were 8,869 gold globes that needed transporting from the Aland Islands to California.

"That's crazy, Dagywn. Does Gob even know what he's asking me to do?"

"Probably not. The broad strokes, yes. The details, no."

"I thought gold was supposed to be in bars, not balls."

"Well, it is — for Uplanders. We found it was much easier to roll the gold from one place to another than to carry it, so we formed our gold into globes.

"Well it seems to me this 'project,' or whatever you want to call it, is going to be way complicated."

"No doubt you're right, Nick. I don't mean to add more pressure, but I think you're the only one who can do it. I wish *I* could, but the truth is that it's too big for me and I know next to nothing about the important details of the Uplander world. And when it comes to complicated projects like these, it's been my experience that their success or failure all comes down to those all im-portant "bits." There's a lot at stake here for us — it's the future of our tribe we're talking about."

"I thought you knew everything, Dagywn, including the important bits."

"Not about the Uplander world I don't. Your world changes too fast for me to keep up with. Listen, I'm not saying I won't help — I will — but I have to be in a support position, not the lead."

"Thanks, Dagywn. I think."

"I'll tell Gob you need some time to think it over. We can discuss it when-ever you want to. Don't forget, gnome time is slow time. Sometimes unbeliev-ably slow, so don't fret about it."

"I won't."

"Anything else?"

"How are *you* doing?" I asked.

Dagywn chuckled. "Thanks for asking. No one else has. You could say I'm 'adjusting.'"

"Yeah, I bet. This is a lot different from your life in Kauai. Aalto seems like she's okay."

"She is. And she's a good student. I think that part of my plan is going to work out."

"I couldn't help but notice that Melea and Leo weren't at dinner. Are they okay?"

"Honestly, no. Melea misses her mother and her sisters and our house on Kauai. Living in a cave again and sleeping during the day isn't cutting it. It's hard to go backwards and that's unquestionably how she sees it. And Leo misses everything — school, his Uplander friends, surfing, the weather, television — you name it. My guess is that they'll move back sooner rather than later."

"That's tough," I said.

"It is, but we'll survive. I'm not going to be here forever. Just until Aalto can take over as wizard."

Even with all his powers, Dagywn was just like the rest of us when it came to seeing the future. He couldn't. As the old saying goes, "the best-laid plans of mice and men often go awry." Which they did. And, as I was eventually to learn, sometimes the best-laid plans don't go anywhere at all.

· · ·

August 15, 2012
Grandpa Nick's house
Rutherford, California

I walked into the kitchen at grandpa's house in a funk, something to do with the conversation I'd just had with Uncle Chuy, no doubt. Grandpa was cutting onions on the big butcher block next to the stove.

"What's the haps?" he asked.

"I don't know. Not much," I said and sat down at the table.

"Why so glum?"

I know I wasn't going to tell him about going to see Uncle Chuy, but it all just tumbled out. "I just went to see Uncle Chuy."

"Really?" he said, with interest. But no further questions. He wasn't going to make this easy for me.

"Yeah. I figured since he was there, he'd be able to tell me if what you wrote was real or not."

"And?"

"Like I said, not much. I guess he didn't want to talk about it."

"That must have been frustrating."

"Tell me about it. Hey! Wait a minute," I said, holding onto the thingy on the end of the pull chain that dangled from the stained glass lamp that hung over the kitchen table – the thing I had pulled on a thousand times to turn the light on and off.

"What?"

"Is this the 'sphere of whatever-he-called-it' – the medal King Gob gave you?"

"As a matter of fact it is."

"What's it doing here?"

"I didn't really know what to do with it, so I tied it to the pull chain a long time ago. Better than being in the back of some drawer somewhere. I thought it looked cool."

"It *is* cool. Is that really quicksilver inside of it?"

"As far as I know."

And I know I said I was done with "awkward" for the day, but from out of nowhere I just asked "How come there are a couple of pages missing from the journal?"

Grandpa was quiet for a minute. "Hmmm… I'd forgotten about that.

"Forgotten about what?"

"Forgotten that I'd torn them out."

"Why'd you tear them out?"

"Let's just say it wasn't our best hour."

"You and who?"

"Me and Chuy."

"What'd happened? Uncle Chuy said you didn't get into like an actual fist fight."

"He told you that? What else did he say?"

"Quite a bit, actually. Sounded like he's been holding on to some negative vibes for a few decades."

"It took me a while to figure it out, but I finally did," Grandpa said.

"And?"

"And??"

"What did you figure out?" I asked.

"That my feelings were hurt."

"From what Uncle Chuy told me, sounded like you hurt *his* feelings."

"Well, that's what it's all about, isn't it? Someone hurts your feelings so you hurt theirs. It's an escalating cycle that never seems to stop – unless you become very conscious of your behavior."

"So I take it you weren't conscious of your behavior back then?"

"No. I definitely wasn't. Grandma Hattie told me, too late for it to do me any good, to never meddle in affairs of the heart. Boy, was she right. It's good advice to remember."

"It had to do with Mad, right?"

"Yep. That and other stuff."

"You're as bad as Uncle Chuy."

"What do you mean?"

"You're not really answering my questions. You said you 'figured it out.' What did you figure out?"

"You're not planning on being an attorney, are you?"

"No. Why?" I asked.

"Because you'd be good at it – you know, that 'cross-examination' thing."

"So?"

"So, I figured out that I was jealous of Chuy and Mad. Chuy and I had been best friends for so long and then it was like, just over. It was tough because I really liked both of them, but as soon as they got together, there was no room for me. Now if that's not a 'boo-hoo, poor miserable me' story, I don't what is."

"Well, it *is* kind of a 'boo-hoo' story. Uncle Chuy still seems upset."

"Really? Then I need to talk to him."

"Yeah, I think you do."

"Can we talk about something else?" Grandpa asked.

"I think it's 'may' not 'can,'" I said.

Grandpa looked at me directly, not sure how to react. "When did you get to be such a smart… such a smarty pants?"

"Good teachers," I said.

"Hey, isn't this your day to mow the lawns?

"You're changing the subject, Grandpa."

"An old person's prerogative. You can ask more questions after you're finished."

As it turned out, I was about to have a lot more questions – many Grandpa had no way of answering – all because of what was about to happen.

I went out to the barn and got the lawnmower and tried to start it. It wasn't turning over so I looked in the gas tank and sure enough it was empty. I was just about to go back in the barn and get the gas can when I looked up at the sky and saw the pigeons returning to the dovecote, just like they did every day at about this time. There was one straggler, flying in big loops above the lawn. The next thing I knew, it landed on the grass, just a few feet in front of me, close enough to for me to see it was the one with the copper vial on his leg. I could feel my heart jump a couple of times. I started talking to it very softly and walked over and gently put my hands around it. It felt like the pigeon's heart was jumping, too.

"Grandpa! Now!" I yelled.

Grandpa appeared at the back screen door. "What's wrong?"

"Nothing. Come here."

He walked over to me and asked "What is it?"

"Doyle helped me send this guy off the other day with a message. He's back."

"I'm guessing you want to take the vial off?"

"Yes!"

Grandpa gently took it off and I let the pigeon go, but not before kissing it on his head. "Here," he said, handing me the vial, "It's your message."

My hands were shaking so much that I could barely twist the vial apart. Maybe, I thought, it was just going to be my message coming back to me. But it wasn't.

"Oh wow, oh wow, wow!" I said.

"What is it?" Grandpa asked.

"Here. Read it," I said, handing him the flimsy piece of paper.

"Dear Joaquin: Grandson you say? Time really does fly for your people. Tell your grandfather that it's time for a visit and to bring you with him. There's a plan afoot. Signed, G."

"Well, I'll be," Grandpa said, shaking his head. He looked straight at me and asked "Now do you believe me?"

"Oh wow! I can't believe this just happened."

"You mean you still don't believe it?"

"You know what I mean… I mean I can't believe that it's finally true."

"I guess I'll take that as a 'yes,'" Grandpa said.

The End

And now a sneak peek at the first chapter of *Escape to Silverado*, Part III of The Silverado Journals:

Fill in the Blanks

August 15, 2012
Grandpa Nick's house
Rutherford, California

Once that pigeon came back to Grandpa's with the note from G attached to his leg, G finally became real to me and I had to look in a whole new light at the two journals. I mean, if G was real, I guess the rest of the stuff was real, too, which, I admit, freaked me out a little – especially when I thought about Madam Pele. I'd have to think more about that later (or maybe not), but right now I didn't want to waste any time writing back to G to set up a meeting. I ran into the house to tell Doyle what had happened – that our effort had worked – and he was genuinely surprised. This was exciting.

All three of us – Grandpa, Doyle, and I – sat down at the kitchen table. I already had a very sharp pencil in hand, along with a small sheet of that super thin Zig-Zag rolling paper.

"Now, what should I say?"

"What do you want to say?" Doyle asked.

"It's not so much what I want to say, it's what I want to do… to go up there on Mt. St. Helena and meet those guys, like right now."

"Well that's not going to happen, so…" Grandpa said.

"So I need to set up a meeting."

"Right. And don't forget they reverse night and day, so you're going to have to suggest a nighttime meeting."

"Is that all right?"

"I don't know. Is it all right with you?"

"Sure. I'll meet 'em anytime."

"Okay" Grandpa said, "so just start by suggesting a time. I always found that some time before midnight was good – they have their big meal of the day at midnight and a nap afterwards, so it's either before midnight or well after, which gets pretty late for us night-sleepers."

"I'm going to suggest 10 o'clock."

"When?" Grandpa asked.

"How about tomorrow?"

"No time like the present, eh?"

"Sure, why not?"

"I think the day after tomorrow would be better," he said. "You need to give the pigeons enough time to get back and forth with an answer."

What Grandpa said made sense, even though today was Wednesday and I didn't want to wait that long to meet G. Reluctantly, I wrote a message suggesting we meet on Friday night at 10 o'clock. I carefully rolled the paper up tight and eased it into the vial. All three of us went out to the dovecote and Doyle attached the vial to one of the pigeons (I couldn't tell one from the other so I don't know if it was the same one who brought the message, but I guess that didn't matter. To tell you the truth, I wasn't that sure about anything. This whole thing was just way too exciting.) After he'd attached the vial, Doyle handed the pigeon to me and I gently threw him into the air. Just like before, the pigeon did a couple of big loops and then headed north to Mt. St. Helena.

"Now what?" I asked Grandpa and Doyle.

"Aside from waiting?"

"Yeah, well, I'm not a very good 'waiter.'"

"Come on inside. I've got something you should look at."

We all traipsed back to the kitchen. Grandpa pulled the locker we had taken from the attic a few days ago off the shelf next to the kitchen table. He opened it and took out what looked like another of his journals.

"Here," Grandpa said, pushing it across the table in my direction.

"Really?" I said.

"Why not?" Grandpa asked.

"I don't know. I'm just kind of getting caught up with things."

"You mean you don't feel ready for another adventure yet?"

"Something like that."

"Well, take a look at it anyway." he said.

It felt a little like he was forcing it on me, which was strange.

"Well I'm not going to sit here and read the whole thing right now."

"You might."

With that, I flipped through it, only to discover there wasn't a darn thing in the entire journal.

"What's this?" I asked, confused.

"The third journal," Grandpa said.

"Yeah, I understand, but *blank?* What's the deal?"

"Basically, there was no deal. Nothing happened. I'm guessing the gnomes couldn't make up their minds about how to proceed. Don't forget, their sense of time isn't remotely like ours. It may be normal to them, but I'd definitely say they take the long view."

"So you didn't go to the Åland Islands?"

"Nope. I didn't go anywhere – except back to school and my normal life. My normal *Uplander* life."

"That's weird."

"Yeah," Grandpa said, "I'll be the first to admit I had my reservations about going off on another venture for Gob, but I'd be lying if I said it wasn't a letdown not to hear *anything*, one way or the other. Of course their concept of time is way different from ours, but it still seemed strange that the whole thing just... I don't know... just evaporated. It still feels that way. That message you just received is the first time I've heard from G, or any of the others, in 44 years."

"That's crazy."

"It *is*, actually. What would be really crazy is if they finally decided they wanted me to go to the Åland Islands now. G said in his note that there was 'a plan afoot.' I had my reservations back then, but I've got completely different ones now. I'm too old for this stuff."

"That's why you've got me," I said, not knowing even remotely what I was talking about or what plan was afoot. Or just how quickly one's whole world can change completely.

Afterword

As I mentioned in the preface to this book, this story contains many things that are, indeed, real or that actually happened, some of them quite strange. In the first book of The Silverado Journals, *The Silverado Trail,* I related in the Afterword how I, my ex-wife and our one-year-old daughter, were on a family vacation in Kauai in May of 1980. Our daughter had just started teething, was not napping and very grumpy. So grumpy, in fact, we almost packed it in and returned home. Quite accidentally we discovered that as soon as she was put in her car seat in the rental car she would fall asleep and, more importantly, stay asleep as long as the car was in motion. So we devised a schedule, taking turns driving our grumpy daughter around Kauai so she would sleep and allow the other parent a little free time to enjoy the sun and some swimming.

One day, when it was my turn, I found myself driving without any destination in mind, baby asleep in the back seat. Without knowing where I was, I came upon a turnabout with one of those historical markers at the side of the pavement. The historical market explained that what I was looking at below me was the 'Alekoko (Menehune) Fishpond. Basically it looked like a large pond with rock walls. The marker went on to explain that legends said the fishpond was built by the Menehune who passed the rocks hand to hand. They were said to have completed this task in a single night." While I was standing there taking in the sight, the entire story contained in The Silverado Journals – beginning, middle, and end – in great detail, was deposited in my brain. Bang! One minute it was not there and the next, it was, fully formed. And if you're reading this after reading the book, the story you've read is just as it was received by my brain. I'd love to know where it came from but I'm guessing I'll never know.

Garden Isle Beach Cottages

And in case you were wondering, yes, we did stay at the Garden Isle Beach Cottages on that trip in 1980. The small group of cottages had been built shortly after World War II and lovingly looked after by a devoted succession of owners. Over the years, the surrounding garden grew increasingly beautiful, complementing the quaint cottages and their unparalleled location on that wide horseshoe bay. Anyway you looked at it, it was a slice of paradise, that is until it was simply licked off the face of the earth by Hurricane Iwa in November of 1980 – with 100 mile per hour winds and 30-foot seas. In its aftermath, not even the foundations were left. What a privilege it was to have been able to experience it at its most beautiful.

And it was at the Garden Isle Beach Cottages where I, like Nick in this story, had a vivid dream of a headless woman speaking to me. I can say with certainty that I have never been so scared as I was that night. And the next morning I really did sit next to a couple on the beach who told me about the bird droppings from the banyan tree and the headless woman who roamed the halls of the new hotel. After all this time, I still don't know what to make of all that, nor some very convincing stories I heard about the wrath of Madam Pele, including one harrowing tale from my sister. Some things are best left as mysteries.

Fast forward a few years to the Napa Valley where I was working on this story on my 34th birthday, back in 1986. I opened up the *San Francisco Chronicle* and saw this story:

Friday, February 28, 1986   San Francisco Chronicle

27-Inch-Tall Horse Stolen in Sonoma

By Birney Jarvis

Sonoma County sheriff's deputies are searching for a thief who was low enough to snatch a 27-inch-tall horse.

The victim, a year-old black filly named Sweet & Fancy, was apparently snatched from a barn at the Li'l Horse Ranch near Petaluma early Tuesday morning.

"She's such a sweet little horse," lamented Sami Scheuring, who with her veterinarian husband owns a herd of 50 pedigreed miniature horses. "Why, her legs are just the size of broom handles. She's a little doll."

Sweet & Fancy weighs 75 pounds and stands 27 inches tall at the shoulders. Her feet, which were unshod, are 1½ inches in diameter, and she was last seen wearing a red horse blanket.

Mrs. Scheuring speculated that the thieves took Sweet & Fancy because she had just had a haircut and looked especially nice compared with the other tiny horses with their long, shaggy winter coats. The missing horse is valued at $5000.

The Scheurings' dog, Lacey, a miniature poodle, failed to foil the abduction, which apparently happened while the family slept.

The Scheurings' 45-acre ranch is on Old Lakeville Highway near state Highway 37.

Ron Scheuring, who has a small-animals veterinary practice in Mill Valley, said the horse thief did not need a trailer to transport his prey. Miniature horses are easy to pick up and tuck in the back seat of a car, and travel well in dog cages of the type used on airplanes.

The couple used just such transportation to fly one of their herd to Rome last fall for a television appearance, "and he seemed to enjoy it quite a bit," the veterinarian said.

The animals are used as pets and for show purposes. Like all horses, they trace their ancestry back to Eohippus, a small animal that lived 55 million years ago and was 10 to 20 inches tall.

The Scheurings' horses come from a line of miniature horses bred in Argentina 200 years ago. The little beasts were also bred in Europe in the 16th or 17th century as pets for royalty. Later, they hauled coal in mines.

Miniature horses grow as tall as 33 inches at the shoulder. At birth, they weigh as little as 15 pounds. Although they are too small for a person to ride, they are sometimes used in surrey races, Scheuring said. They have a life span of about 30 years.

A $500 reward has been offered for information leading to the return of Sweet & Fancy. Breeders and horse clubs also have been alerted to keep an eye out for her.

"These horses will be watched closely from now on," said Sami Scheuring. "I'm not vindictive at all, I just want Sweet & Fancy back.

By John O'J

Sami Scheuring trained Lady Natasha, half-sister of kidnap victim

To say I was surprised is to put it mildly. I took it as a sign that I might be on the right path, at least one that was rooted in the real world. A few days later, the newspaper reported that the horse had been returned just as mysteriously as it had been stolen. That said, I felt pretty sure I knew where it had been and it's been my pleasure, dear reader, sharing that knowledge with you.

acorts@me.com

Acknowledgements

You'd think the more you write, the better you'd get, and the less you'd need the help of an editor. That may be true for some, but it's certainly not the case for me! I'm very grateful for my knowledgeable and talented friends, Michèle Amendola, Gail Kenna, and Anne Carey. What a masterful job they all did on this manuscript. A mere thank you doesn't cover my appreciation.

Thanks, Mark Lightner, for recalling the sailing adventures of your youth, which certainly had the ring of truth about them. Here's to some smooth sailing, from here to the horizon.

Thank you Gene Lyerla, my source for all things relating to law enforcement and the intricacies of the sheriff's department – not to mention an active contributor to our imaginary and extremely valuable website, www.ONS.com.

And for his perennial friendship and invaluable advice, thank you Alan Freeland, Prince of the City. How great that you were able to read the manuscript for this story during a stay in Kauai. Thanks for all you do so well.

About This Book

The body text of this book is set in Baskerville Regular. The typeface in the journal entries and illustration captions is my own printing, transformed into a digital typeface using Calligraphr (Calligraphr.com). The color illustrations are watercolors with ink accents. The pen-and-ink illustrations within the journal were created with a black Staedtler 0.5 pigment liner. *The Voyage of the Silverado* was designed and composed on a Macintosh, using InDesign software.